ORFAN

ORFAN

A novel
By

Corie Skolnick

MANNEQUIN VANITY PUBLISHING

This is a work of fiction. Names, characters, places, and incidents are products of the author's imagination or are used fictitiously and are not to be construed as real. Any resemblance to actual events, locales, business establishments, organizations, or persons, living or dead, is entirely coincidental.

MANNEQUIN VANITY PUBLISHING is an imprint of
MANNEQUIN VANITY RECORDS, San Diego, CA.

MANNEQUIN VANITY PUBLISHING trade paperback edition (2011):
ISBN 978-0-9831544-1-9

PRINTED IN THE UNITED STATES OF AMERICA

MANNEQUIN VANITY RECORDS is a registered trademark.
Visit MANNEQUIN VANITY PUBLISHING at mannequinvanityrecords.com; facebook.com/mannequinvanityrecords

Audio version published by MANNEQUIN VANITY PUBLISHING, January 1, 2011
ISBN 978-0-9831544-0-2

eBook version published by MANNEQUIN VANITY PUBLISHING, January 1, 2011
ISBN 978-0-9831544-2-6

Cover design by Natalie Hurwitz and Corie Skolnick.
Book design by MANNEQUIN VANITY PUBLISHING.

ACKNOWLEDGEMENTS

I am grateful to Patty Albright who was there from the very beginning, before there was a manuscript to read, only stories to hear. And after, to all those who read the whole enchilada, some more than once, Tommie Hannigan, Ellie Hutner, Dr. Jean Phillips, Joyce Pedersen, Lynne Shaw, Jerry Shaw, Brennis Lucero-Wagner, Lucy Capuano-Brewer, Mike Wurst, Jody Wurst, Joann Wurst, Maria Hillario, Dr. Caroly Pataki, Melanie Nelson, Carol Jernberg-Hubacek, Beverly Moore, Karen Vedder, Mimi Janes, Roger Moss, Tracey Navrides, Robb Navrides, Bridget Sampson, Donna Accardo, Christopher Wagner, Nancy Harrington, Holly Babe, Janet Stone, Dan Wexler, Faith Fogarty, Martin Downey, Mike Hannigan, Brenda Grohman, Paige Gold, Rose Messina, Sherry Sidesinger, Liz Imler, and Lisa Doctor. A special thanks to Wendy Steinmetz and Rob Steinmetz who previewed the entire audio book and said nice things. For love and support in general, I am grateful to the Hurwitz clan, Gregg, Delinah, Rosie and Natalie. For a home away from home in Portland, many thanks to Rollie, Annie, Julia and Jenny White. And certainly, without my family, Paul, Cat, Dan and Jake, there would simply be no book at all.

I am especially grateful to all the members of the adoption triad who came year after year to my classes at California State University, Northridge, to offer their wisdom and their hearts to the students from my very own TPP (The Psychological Aspects of Parenthood). This book was inspired by the stories shared so generously by Karen Vedder, Mimi Janes, Zara Phillips, Alison Larkin, Patrick McMahon, Chris Thomason, Evelyn Robinson-Mansfield, and also, Nancy Verrier, Sheila

Ganz and Marlou Russell. Concerned United Birthparents made these illuminating visits possible. The mission of this international organization is to provide support to all members of the adoption triad, past, present and future.

For Donna, Chris, Brett and Danny, who taught me everything I know about surviving the worst things that life can throw at you. -cs

You mightn't think it, but our Sloppy is a beautiful reader of the newspaper. He do the police in different voices.
(Charles Dickens' OUR MUTUAL FRIEND)

Prologue
January, 1969 – Chicago's South Side

Judy Dumke, R.N.

Sister Michael drove Mary McGinnis over just after midnight in that big old Plymouth station wagon the nuns had. It was cold and snowing some and she parked the car in the employee lot and made Mary walk through the snow in those cheap little plastic sandals the girls all wore when their feet swelled up beyond even their old white canvas gym shoes. Mary, poor thing, had edema so bad she hadn't had real shoes on her feet in a couple of months.

"The St. Anne's Home is not a shoe store," Sister Mike used to say. Jeez-Louise. Shame on those nuns. I'm surprised she didn't tell them, "St. Anne's is not a taxi company," and make them waddle the whole five blocks when their time came.

We used to flip a coin up in maternity on the graveyard shift to see which one of us would get stuck with the girls from the St. Anne's Home for Unwed Mothers. It wasn't so much that you'd have to put up with one of the mean old nuns in the delivery room all night long, although I promise you, that was no picnic in the park. It was mostly that all of us girls hated like the devil to take those babies away from their sobbing mamas. Even the downright nasty ones wept like infants themselves. It was enough to just break your heart sometimes. But, the Sisters of Mercy owned and operated both Holy Redeemer Hospital and St. Anne's, so the nuns, they pretty much called the shots when a St. Anne's girl was delivering.

It was Ricky Titus who wheeled Mary up to Labor, and wasn't that kind of ironic? He was a sweet young man and a good orderly and he was better with the patients than most of the doctors. Anyway, Ricky, he put Mary into a wheelchair and took a little detour over to linen on their way up. He boosted a couple of clean towels for her and I used to imagine how he must have kneeled down on the cold linoleum floor in front of Mary that night and dried each of her frozen feet and wrapped them up so gently in those pirated towels for the elevator ride. Such a nice young man Ricky was. I think he got drafted not long after that. He never did come back to HoRe.

Mary McGinnis was a good kid, too. You could tell. Hardly a peep out of her until she got into transition, and even then she did everything she could to make it easy on us. Dr. Goss said that night that Mary McGinnis would have made an excellent fourth century martyr. He was a strict Catholic so I think he meant it as a compliment. I was just glad that he was the ob on call that night, since he at least was one of the docs who had a heart. He asked me to tie his gown in back when he took a gander through the scrub room window and got his first good look at Mary.

"Wow, she's a looker," he said. I took a second look myself then.

"Yep," I told him. "I'll bet she's a real knock out when she isn't having a baby." I might have got a smile out of him, but I didn't know for sure because his mask was already up. He was usually careful to put his mask up *before* he went in to deliver the St. Anne's girls. It made him look a little like a burglar when he did that.

That anxious young couple from Florida was already sitting down the hall in the father's lounge. Well, sitting part of the time. Pacing up and down, mostly. The both of them. The Home had called them over from the Holiday Inn when Mary's water broke and they were going to take the baby with them as soon as Sister came up from the admitting office with the papers that we would all forge. That's the way it went. All it took was a piece of paper to make Mary McGinnis and whoever it was that had gotten her in trouble to just disappear. Honestly, there's more fuss when you transfer the title on an old used Chevy. Still, every single one of us, even Mary herself I know, at the time, thought of those two people as the best solution to her little "problem." There simply were no other options available, or at least none that were revealed to Mary McGinnis. She was a single nineteen-year-old girl "in trouble". No family stepping forward to help her and like all those St. Anne's kids, she was guilty of mortal sin and well primed for punishment because of it.

"Where are the penguins?" Dr. Goss asked me. I guess it was no secret to anybody that I had no real affection for those old girls. I told him he didn't have to worry, that for sure one of the nuns would be along presently. The Sisters of Mercy had a whole bunch of hard-fast rules when it came to the St. Anne's deliveries. The principal one was, the birth mothers were not to touch their infants. Just in case anybody had any different ideas, without exception, those old nuns removed their big black habits, scrubbed in and gowned just like ten year olds playing dress up. More than attending, they *presided over* the birth of any baby that was going to be relinquished. Because the Sisters of Mercy owned the hospital, everybody, and I mean the entire staff, gave deference to the nuns. Even on matters of medicine at times. The doctors themselves were just so much hired help to the sisters.

"We can't wait," Dr. Goss told me. "Let's get this over with." I know he didn't particularly like to deliver the St. Anne's girls and it made him kind of short tempered, but it went with the territory for all the doctors. From the chief on down to the residents, all Holy Redeemer physicians were on rotation for the St. Anne's cases. But none of them liked it. I think it made them feel like farmers. Dr. Goss was in a hurry for sure that night. Probably anxious to get things handled and get the girl loaded up on drugs, and then get home himself to the suburbs, before he had to watch her get hysterical in recovery. He backed into the delivery room holding his sterile gloved hands high up in the air out in front. It looked for all the world like *he* was the one who was getting robbed.

"Hi, honey," he said to Mary. Even though he was a little short with me that night, he was real gentle with her. I'll give him that much. "I'm Dr. Goss. I'm going to deliver your baby. How are you doing?" He put a gloved hand out and touched her shaking knee and just held it there until she stopped trembling so.

"I'm good," Mary said. She was trying to smile. "I hurt a little bit though."

"I think we can help you with that, sweetheart," he said. "Nurse, who's on anesthesia tonight?"

"Dr. Wagner," I told him.

"Get him over here, stat. Please," he said. Doc Goss was always polite. He always said *please* and *thank-you,* but he expected you to hop to. "Can I just take a little peek down here and see what you've got going on?" he asked Mary. When he lifted up the green drape that was covering her shaking legs, I noticed that the labor nurses had skimped on sox for her and her bare feet were almost blue they were that cold. Somebody, maybe Mary herself, had taken a few precious seconds to try to remove the chipped red polish from her toenails but a bright red residue around each cuticle made her feet look wounded and sore. Just as I was hoping that the doctor wouldn't notice, he started to yell. I almost dropped the phone.

"Holy shit! Nurse!"

I can't tell you how unusual it was for Dr. Goss to use bad language.

"Delivering in six!" I told the station. I got to the delivery table to see that the baby's head was already crowning. I could already see the full mat of thick curly hair plastered against his skull.

"You are a very brave girl, sweetheart," Dr. Goss said. "Looks like somebody's almost delivered himself."

"Is it a boy?" Mary tried to raise up on her elbows. Boy or girl. That was another thing. The nuns didn't want the girls to know.

"I can't tell yet, but since this little baby is so impatient…" Doc Goss winked. "…I'm thinking that yes, it's probably a boy." He never let on too much when he was worried. Mary McGinnis just smiled then. She knew it was a boy. The first thing you noticed about Mary is how pretty her eyes are. And, that night, because they were so bloodshot, her irises were an even more remarkable green.

"I'm going to have to have you push in a minute now, okay?" the doctor told her. He steadied her knee again like he had done before and he looked her right in the eye. "Okay, sweetheart, you breathe just like this..." Doctor Goss sounded like an old tired dog coaching her. "…And while you do that, give me a real big push...that's right…one more…okay…take a little break now." I don't think I said it out loud just then, but I know I was already thinking to myself, *you poor little baby*.

"I need to make a small cut here. Just so you don't tear when the baby's head pushes through." Dr. Goss was always careful to tell the young moms what was coming. Before he could make the incision, Dr. Wagner came in tying his mask up.

"Wow, it's awfully quiet in here, guys," he said. "Everything okay?" Goss shot Wagner a look. He was annoyed that Mary was going to be wide-awake and even though it wasn't really Dr. Wagner's fault, it had to be somebody's fault.

"Too late to get a line in, Doug," he said. He didn't do much to sound any too happy about it either, and we all knew that Sister Mike wasn't going to like it one little bit when she got there. Things went a lot smoother if the girls were doped up as much as possible. For Mary's benefit though, Doc Goss kind of drawled, like it was no real big deal, "I don't think my brave patient is going to need your services tonight, Dr. Wagner…I think she's going to have her baby the natural way. But, why don't you stick around and see?" I swapped places and Wagner peeked under the drape over Dr. Goss's shoulder.

"Let me swab that for you, doctor," he said. He was sounding all business at that point. He reached over and picked up a pair of extended forceps and pulled a sponge soaked in lidocaine from the dish on the prep table. He swabbed Mary's perineum. She tensed a little.

"Is that cold, honey?" Dr. Wagner asked her.

"No," she grunted. "…but I think I have to push again, right now." Mary's breathing changed. You can tell by the sound of a woman's voice when it's time. I moved to the head of the delivery table and took her hands overhead, waiting for Dr. Goss's signal. I could still watch the action in the overhead mirror. Up top is the second best seat in the house.

"Okay, sweetie, go ahead," Dr. Goss coached her. "You're doing really good. That's good," he kept telling her over and over.

I watched in the mirror. He is such a good surgeon. He made a clean incision. Just the slightest pressure of a scalpel and a long clean straight line of blood formed instantly between Mary's vaginal opening and her anus. I mean a perfectly straight line.

"Nice cut, doctor," Dr. Wagner said.

A second later the baby's head and shoulders were entirely delivered. His little arms were still pinned between his ribs and Mary's swollen vulva.

"Holy Jesus..." The anesthesiologist raised his head up and shook it. It was a comical reaction but it wasn't funny. I looked in the mirror again before I exchanged a significant look with Dr. Goss. Even his eyes had taken on some worry then.

"Dr. Wagner, please!" His impatience with Dr. Wagner was obvious.

"Is it a boy?" Mary asked again. *Does she even know...?* I thought. At the time, it seemed strange to me, that she should care so much whether or not her baby was a boy or girl, when in fact, within the same hour, she was planning to make a present of the child to total strangers. That's how little I knew.

"Not sure yet, honey," Goss said. "Can you give me another big push?" I could feel her getting ready to exhale. Then I could feel her jaw clench and her head nod for the final push and I held her hands over her head and she made my hands go numb she squeezed back so hard.

"Go on, sweetie," I told her. "Make this one count!" It was right then I saw this large dark presence fill up the window in the scrub room. From where I was at the head of the delivery table I could see that Sister Mike was scowling and still wearing her big black habit. She could see right away that it was much too late for her to change into scrubs for the delivery.

"Uh oh...we got company." I said it as softly as I could. I was just trying to give the docs a heads-up. Both of them took a second to glance up over their shoulders. I can tell you, that old nun did not look one bit pleased that Mary McGinnis had commenced giving birth without her.

"This can't be good," Dr. Wagner whispered. The anesthesiologist raised his eyebrows back toward the nun and nodded his head down toward the baby that was still half delivered between Mary's legs. The ob squinted hard and ignored him.

"I need one more really big push, sweetheart," he told Mary. Then seconds later, "Alright, here's my big boy!" The baby slipped into his hands.

"You were right sweetheart, it's a boy!" Dr. Goss remembered too late to try to keep the joy out of his voice. He rotated the baby onto his palm and quickly and expertly aspirated the fluids from his throat. More than I ever had before I appreciated the fact that Doc Goss was not an obstetrician who, like the other old timers, liked to hold infants up by their heels and spank their first distressed breaths out of them.

"Come on Baby Boy, let me hear your pipes," he coaxed the baby. It seemed forever, those few seconds before Mary's baby took a breath. You know, I'm not proud of this, but I almost hoped the baby was stillborn. I know it's awful, but I've always thought that that might have been easier for Mary in the long run.

None of us had moved so much as a muscle yet when finally the baby gave up a soft little cry. It sounded almost like a hiccup. "Oh, a gentleman, huh? Not a wailer." Goss was smiling and I squeezed in between the two doctors with a sterile receiving blanket. It seemed that Dr. Wagner stepped back only one single careful step, like he was shielding the baby from Sister Michael's view for a just few more seconds. I could practically feel her fuming back there in the scrub room and I knew we were all going to get an earful later when it was all over. I stayed in place holding Mary's baby while Dr. Goss cut the cord and attended to the placenta. I want to say that there was something different about Mary's baby. I mean besides the obvious. The best part of my job is getting to hold a brand new human being. A brand new human life. We're a sentimental bunch and I never met a single nurse who wouldn't tell you that she felt the same awe each and every time. But, there was something about Mary's baby…I don't know…something *spectacular*. It just made things that much sadder.

I took the child to the warming table to get an APGAR on him. Sister Michael was waiting for her first peek. I think I hesitated. Maybe it was only a fraction of a second. But, when I finally pulled the blanket away the old nun's mean eyes popped out and her mouth opened so wide I could see her bridgework. She looked just like a character in one of those old silent movies. She was keeling back on her heels, one arm treading the air for purchase and her other hand grabbing hold of that enormous silver crucifix she always wore. When she caught her balance her eyes were still glued to the ceiling and her lips were moving fiercely. It looked like she was searching for something up there. I thought maybe she was praying, but when she leaned forward again her eyes bulged against the glass with such menace I covered the baby back up. If it was God she was talking to, she was giving it to Him good. Her face was beet red. Her lips were a mean gash. She gave me a vicious look for a second and then looked one last time down at Mary's illegitimate baby like she was hoping something might have changed. Then she just spun around and stalked out of the scrub room. Her habit looked like some kind of big morbid black sail billowing out behind her. Later, we would find that she had marked the clean, waxed linoleum in there with long black scuffmarks. Traces.

I just stood there, stunned.

"How's that APGAR coming, nurse?" The doctor's question got me moving again.

I don't know how much Mary saw but she was crying pretty steady by then. Dr. Wagner inserted a belated IV in her hand – something the nun would never have allowed *after* the delivery. Always looking to save the hospital a few bucks any way they could. Dr. Goss finished delivering the placenta and started to suture the episiotomy he had made in Mary's perineum.

"You do good work," Dr. Wagner said. It was a sincere compliment. Dr. Goss was carefully repairing Mary's vaginal opening with stitches worthy of a good plastic surgeon, another thing the Sisters of Mercy wouldn't have been too keen on. Mary's legs were still shaking, but she didn't complain once. When Dr. Goss finished the sutures he covered her legs up with a clean drape leaving her feet in the stirrups. Mary pulled herself up to her elbows and peered at him over the green tent he had made.

"Can I see my baby?" She whispered it, but we all heard. We had all been dreading the question but at the same time we had probably known all along that it was coming. All three of us looked up for one second at the empty window before Dr. Goss said anything.

"Are you sure you want to?" he asked her.

"I do." She had big fat tears in her eyes and I knew what he was going to do. "I know I'm not supposed to." Mary admitted. "They told me it makes it harder. I just want one minute with him. Please!" she begged.

Goss nodded to me. I wrapped the baby up loosely and carried him back to the delivery table. The second best part of my job is that moment when a mother takes her infant into her arms for the first time. By now I've seen it a few thousand times and it still chokes me up. Dr. Wagner took a second to slip a small pillow under Mary's head. I really liked Wagner just then.

The girl held her baby so carefully. She smiled at us through her tears just like every other brand new mother does. Then she looked down and watched her baby practice on his own face all the feelings he was surely going to experience in the future, some, of course, much more than others. He tried them all on. His tiny features puckered and grimaced and smiled. Then something occurred that is so rare. I'll bet I haven't seen it more than a half dozen times in all my years in delivery at Holy Redeemer. That little baby opened his eyes wide as anything and looked his mother directly into hers. It was almost like he knew he wasn't ever going to see her again.

"Hi, honey," she said so softly. It was such a personal moment, I felt embarrassed to be there. She stroked his little dark cheek with one pale finger. Dr. Goss tugged on my gown and pulled Dr. Wagner's sleeve. We all stepped back into a little knot near the door. For those precious few minutes, it felt like all three of us were together guarding Mary and her baby from outside intruders, and trying at the same time to give them as much privacy as the room would allow us to give them. Each of us braced for what was to come. We were all St. Anne's delivery veterans and we knew what was in store on the rare occasion when a St. Anne's girl didn't get sedated in time. After I don't know how long, but it seemed like a while, with Mary just silently holding tightly onto that baby, touching him with such tenderness…she finally talked again. It came out in a desperate whisper. "I'm your mommy, but I can't take care of you. Someone else is going to do that for me." We could all see her body heaving. Nobody moved. "I don't want you to think I don't love you or want you. I love you very much." A sob came out of her beautiful mouth; it looked just tragic. It sounded even worse. I looked at Dr. Goss. His own tears were staining his mask. The girl kept trying to reassure her baby of how loved he was. "And, your daddy would have loved you, too," she told him. I didn't yet know enough to know better, so I couldn't help at the time but doubt the truth of what she had said to her son. I expect that we all did. She just looked up then suddenly where we were all standing.

"Okay," she said. Her voice sounded all of a sudden flat. Eerie. Not even human anymore. Those beautiful green eyes looked dull and unfocused then, like someone had flipped a switch that turned something off inside of her. "You can take him now," she said.

The very last thing in the world that I wanted to do at that moment I promise you was be the one to step forward and take that child out of his mother's arms, but one of the doctors, I don't know which one, put a firm hand to my back and pushed me toward the delivery table. I started to gather the baby up with the same damp blanket I had been all along wringing in my hands. Mary looked directly into my eyes when I touched her child and I had to look away. With surprising strength, she reached out and grabbed at my wrist.

"Please," she said. It sounded like she was choking. "Are the people nice?"

"Yes," I flat out lied. "They are very nice." I hadn't spoken to them. They looked okay. When they weren't pacing they were just kind of huddled against each other in the waiting room. They both looked old enough to have maybe tried like hell to have their own kid for at least a decade or so. They looked nervous. Were they nice? I hoped so. I suddenly hoped that they were.

"Please," Mary whispered. "Tell them that I love my baby very much and I loved his father. It isn't what they think. It isn't what *you* think." She leaned dangerously off the table and tried to touch the baby's face one last time. That touch seemed unbelievably tender; her finger was just trembling. I pushed a lock of her hair behind her ear while I stood there holding her son. I was taking her son away from her.

"I'll tell them, honey," I promised her. I remember wiping her wet cheek with the corner of the baby's receiving blanket and then, God forgive me, I pulled him away. You could almost hear something between them tear. By the time I had the baby on the table under the window again, trying to get a diaper on him, she was screaming. Her voice was something then. High pitched and keening. I've never heard anything remotely like it either before or since.

"Tell them his name is James!" she was shrieking. "His daddy was James! His daddy was James!" Dr. Goss was trying to hold her. She was wild. Thrashing.

Wagner put some tranqs into her IV to calm her down. Goss was talking to her while he pinned her heaving shoulders back. He was desperate to console her.

"Okay sweetheart, everything is going to be okay for your baby…for little James...Dr. Wagner?" He signaled for even more Valium if it was possible. I don't know if his mercy was really for Mary or if it was for us, but Dr. Wagner adjusted the dose. He must have been generous. Finally she stopped thrashing around. Her head rolled against the pillow and the delivery room got stone quiet again, like it does sometimes after we lose a baby.

Even with all of that going on, Mary McGinnis' baby was not really agitated, but, he was much more alert than the average newborn, as if he knew…

"Poor little guy." It just slipped out. I didn't usually say those things out loud. "Poor little guy." I kept saying it. I couldn't seem to stop myself. I didn't know of course what was actually in store for him. I just couldn't seem to stop myself.

We all leapt a mile in the air when the pediatric resident bolted through the door.

"Gentlemen," he said, ignoring the fact, like all the docs did, that I was no man. "I understand we've got a little scandal brewing."

"That was fast." Dr. Wagner shook his head.

"Ah ha!" The resident pointed with a silly expression across the room at the newborn culprit, but then he paused at the table where Mary McGinnis lay practically comatose. The pediatrician stopped and touched Dr. Wagner's shoulder briefly as he passed by. He whispered something. I think he was letting him know that he approved of heavily sedating the young birth mothers. The ones who were relinquishing their babies.

"What are his APGARs, nurse?" He was one of those residents who never bothered to find out our names. His job was simply to clear the baby medically before the child was allowed to leave the hospital, and he made no bones about the fact that he just wanted to get in there and get his job done and get out.

"He was ten at one minute – ten at five." Perfect scores. I stepped back so the doctor could do his job. I could tell by the way the pediatrician examined him that he too thought the baby was a remarkable looking infant. What had so offended Sister Michael, and what would clearly be a potential adoption snafu, was that the baby's skin, though flawless, was several shades darker than Kraft caramels, and his full halo of downy blonde hair was already as nappy as a slave's.

"He's sure a healthy little guy and a good lookin' little bugger," the pediatrician pronounced. "But, no doubt about it, he is a very, very big Black surprise to the very, very *white* young couple from *fuck-ing Flo-ri-da* who are out there sitting in your waiting room." He turned back and peered meaningfully over his mask, one by one making eye contact with each of us as if we were personally responsible for the switcheroo about to be perpetrated on the poor unsuspecting people out in the father's lounge.

"So, how did you hear about our Mary's little surprise?" Dr. Goss wanted to know.

"Are you kidding?" The young pediatrician told him, "Everybody on the floor heard about it. Sister Mike called her buddies at the home from the nurse's station. Let's just say, it was not what you would call a *discrete* conversation, although it *was* a brief and a very loud one."

It was me—I mean that I was the first who thought to ask.

"Did the baby's new parents hear what Sister said?" The pediatrician blinked at me stupidly. It took him a whole minute to seem to comprehend my meaning.

"I don't know how they couldn't have heard it," he finally concluded. He cocked his head. "Yeah, of course they heard. They were sitting right there. I think they heard her up on five." His head jerked toward the fifth floor above us. No one spoke again for a long minute. We all just looked at each other as if waiting for someone else to do something.

"They *know*? And, they didn't leave? Are you sure?" The three doctors looked at me. "Well?" I said and waited. "Who's going to introduce them to their son?"

Don't you know that not one of those doctors stepped forward or even bothered to try to give me an excuse? Oh, I was so mad then.

I elbowed the resident out of the way, a little roughly I suppose, but he moved over. "Poor little guy…two strikes already…you poor little guy…" I talked to Mary's baby while I dressed him. Things I never should have said. I wrapped him up just like a parcel. The whole process took me less than a minute. Then I turned back to those three silly doctors who were all still just staring.

"Finish the paperwork," I barked. I wasn't usually sassy with the doctors, but it felt good to put them in their place that night. I gave them each what I hoped they would see was a scornful look before I marched out of the room. I've always imagined that they probably stood around like mutes staring at the floor for a while after I left. It must have been a powerfully shameful silence in that poor unconscious girl's presence.

I didn't consider myself a Catholic anymore by then or even much of a believer if it comes down to it. Still, with every step I took that night, holding that beautiful little baby in my arms, I was praying mightily that the people from Florida would still be waiting for me outside.

Book one –The Book of Death

Let the dead bury their own dead.
- Jesus (*Luke 9:59-62*)

Chapter 1

The young doctor from the VA clinic made the phone call himself. His voice was sympathetic. Carter Deane's diagnosis was hopeless.

"You have extraordinarily low motility."

Carter was a pilot not a doctor, but even so, he knew it wasn't good.

"Your guys just aren't making the distance," the doctor said sympathetically. "Crappy swimmers. Too tired to make it up stream." Carter *had* done some fishing. He thought it best to get a second opinion before going off half-cocked so to speak and telling his wife that he could not make babies. Then he got a third opinion and a fourth. Two, three, and four were all private physicians with expensive looking offices in Miami. The last one was not an unkind man at all, but, by the time he found himself consulting on Carter Deane's sad case, he had already diagnosed a startling number of these mysteriously damaged young Nam vets, and it was frankly beginning to unnerve him. He had long since grown weary of reporting what was excruciatingly painful news. He especially hated it when the patients insisted on bringing their hopeful little wives to their appointment. It made him irrationally furious at Carter that

Susie Deane was even sitting in his office and he did not look at her once when he gave Carter his results.

"Stop trying." He met Carter's unwavering gaze directly. "You have *zero* motility." The clinician heard what he knew to be the unmistakable sound of tears falling from a woman's eyes. His face abruptly turned crimson and his voice was unnecessarily mean. "Zero," he repeated when Carter only blinked and Susie Deane started to cry in earnest. He made a circle with his fingers and said again, "Zee-row. Zip. Nada. Zilch. Why don't you get a nice dog?" In an instant Carter's right hook made sudden contact with the doctor's beaky nose and seconds later he had pulled Susie through the door. The man felt for the break he knew he had suffered and he was oddly not altogether unhappy about it. Neither was he surprised or upset when the Deanes did not pay his bill a month later.

Ultimately, the Deanes took the doctor's advice. They stopped trying to have a child of their own. Eventually they sought out information about adoption from Carter's cousin, an Episcopal minister who played basketball on an ecumenical team up in Chicago. As it happened, the team's forward was a Jesuit priest, a man who was short for the position, but speedy and sneaky and therefore the high scorer in the league. If Father Kevin Moore had only been ten inches taller he might have gone pro, but instead he took his vows and taught sociology downtown at Loyola. As a university professor it proved expedient for him to maintain connections with the St. Anne's Home for unwed mothers on the south side. An almost unbelievable number of co-eds, particularly the ones at the Catholic schools, were ironically hell-bent on avoiding damnation by denying themselves and their partners the sinful use of birth control.

At the time that Carter Deane's faulty sperm had been confirmed in 1968, all of the major U.S. religions were trafficking to some degree in the unwanted baby business. As it was a good five years before the U.S. Supreme Court decided on Roe V. Wade, there was no shortage of supply; the Catholics were industry leaders. Carter's Episcopalian cousin put the Deanes in touch with his Jesuit teammate, Father Kevin.

The young priest was ahead of his time in embracing the New Age. He was a big believer in synchronicity. The convenient notion of being in the right place at just the right time was a conviction that no doubt appealed to a shooter and perhaps even helped his scoring average. Likewise, when it came to his attention that his point guard's cousin was shooting blanks on the very same cold fall day that one of his best students confessed her illegitimate pregnancy, well, Father Kevin Moore felt the certain and holy hand of God at work through his own carnal being. He in turn put Carter and Susie Deane in touch with the nuns at the St. Anne's Home. The Sisters of Mercy would broker the deal between Carter and Susie Deane, and a desperate illegitimately pregnant young Mary McGinnis.

It was wicked cold on the January day that the Deanes flew for the second time on Eastern Airlines employee passes to adopt Mary's newborn baby in Chicago. The nuns had demanded at their first meeting only that Carter agree to raise the baby Catholic and that Susie agree to give up her stewardess job immediately. Carter had crossed his fingers and thought to himself, *one out of two.* A novice from St. Anne's summoned them to the hospital from the Holiday Inn on Cicero Avenue when Mary's water broke.

The baby's new parents were given less than fifteen minutes to decide on the name for their son. A name, that once it was chosen would be immediately typed onto his contrived birth certificate by a weary graveyard hospital clerk and, well…that would be that. The document would name Susie and Carter Deane as the newborn's rightful parents. As far as the state of Illinois was concerned, Mary McGinnis, and the mysterious boy she identified only as "James" who had gotten her into trouble, would both just disappear. Vanish. They would both be as good as gone.

The delivery nurse appeared still sporting a surgical mask. She planted the well-wrapped infant into Susie Deane's arms with a detectable though ambiguous attitude. Susie looked at her baby's face for the first time and instead of manifesting the nurse's anticipated reaction she smiled and kissed his dark cheek.

"You have a son," the nurse said severely. Her voice was partially muffled but Carter thought he heard something challenging nonetheless. Once she had relinquished the child to Susie the nurse retreated a single wary step. She pulled her scrub cap and surgical mask off tiredly and stood boldly examining Carter for a good long minute. Nothing at all she might have expected occurred. Carter hovered behind his ecstatic wife, circling his long arms around her and around his son protectively. He wasn't a man who particularly liked surprises, and this one was certainly a doozy, but he only looked over Susie's shoulder into the baby's perfect tiny dark face and smiled. A single teardrop rolled down the brand new father's flushed cheek and launched itself from his chin onto his son's receiving blanket. Carter would have sworn that the baby felt it and smiled up at him. His own grin widened and he looked up at the nurse. She grunted then and glanced backwards before she whispered to them both.

"His mother would like you to name him James." It was then that Carter flinched.

"Our last name is *Deane,*" he told the nurse apologetically. He looked again at his new son. "He would be *James Deane."* Carter and Susie had already agreed to eliminate any names for their son that might be suggestive of dead movie stars or has-been country western singers whose careers had progressed into the marketing of breakfast meats.

"It isn't something you *have* to do," the nurse said curtly. The tone of her voice told a different story however. Susie Deane's gaze was still riveted on the perfect oval of the baby's face. She was marveling at him in much the same way that Mary McGinnis had only moments earlier – before the doctors had generously sedated the hysterical young mother into oblivion to halt her piteous weeping.

Carter was thinking ahead and already worrying about all the ways that certain types of kids can make life hell for other children on the playgrounds of the world for just the dumbest shit. Being a grown up did not automatically grant immunity from that kind of common cruelty either he knew.

"Look, I hate to rush you," the nurse said. "But the paperwork has to be completed before you can leave the hospital. We have to fill out his birth certificate. Now." The woman kept her voice low and she looked around in a manner conveying to Carter that she felt that some kind of illicit transaction was occurring. "Give it some thought. I'll be right back." She patted Susie Deane's arm, the one that was cradling the new infant. If Carter detected urgency in the nurse's desire to expedite the Deanes' departure, it only mirrored his own. As overjoyed as he was to finally be a father, a significant part of him just could not believe how easy it was proving to take somebody's baby away. He was going to walk out of that hospital and someone else's child was going to go with him and a part of Carter felt not only guilty about it, but also very nearly physically ill. That was the part of him that would worry every single day, once he returned home, that on some horrible fateful date in the future he would have to pay. Perhaps some stranger would come knocking at their door to reclaim his son and simply take him back. Carter Deane couldn't get his little family out of Chicago fast enough.

"Oh, Carter," Susie pleaded, her blue eyes wide and irresistible. "That's the least little thing we can do. This girl is giving us her *child.*" Under certain kinds of pressure, Carter Deane was a decisive if somewhat resentful person.

"Okay," he agreed reluctantly. "James Deane it is." He took his second good long look at the baby as if he could divine the child's inborn character strength. He sighed. "Well, at least she didn't screw some guy named Booker T." It was the only unkind thing he ever said concerning Jimmy Deane's heritage.

If the young parents had wanted to learn fast, once they returned home to South Florida, who exactly their real friends were, it turned out that they could have undertaken no quicker tutorial than the adoption of a half black baby. Their lessons began quite immediately on the plane heading home. They got to the airport late, arriving at the gate just barely in time to board. In fact, had they not been airline employees, the hatch on the southbound jet would have already been closed to them, but the crew was expecting the new parents and eager to meet their new son. Colorful celebratory balloons had been affixed haphazardly to every possible surface in the forward galley by the first-class stews and a hand-lettered banner proclaimed: "Welcome Baby Deane, Susie and Captain Carter!"

"Le' me see! Le' me see!" The stews squealed. Susie cradled her son and let one of them peel back the blanket.

"Oh, my god!" the wide-eyed girl gasped. A Florida native like Susie, she withdrew her hands and covered her mouth. "Oh, honey," she said mournfully. She looked over at Susie in the same way that people look at mothers of the deformed. "What are you *thinkin'?"* Susie abruptly turned her back on her friend without responding. She pulled her baby close and marched defiantly down the aisle. Until that very moment, she had *not* been thinking. She kept her face squarely focused on the darkness outside the jet's thick window and was glad that Jimmy slept for the duration of the flight. Over northern Georgia, the stews tried to salvage things by dropping off a split of real French champagne and two flutes, but Susie refused to drink even one sip.

"Honey, you're going to have to get a thicker skin," Carter advised, but as the first few days passed back home in Hollywood, it was Carter who assumed a bona fide chip on his shoulder. Susie's strategy was simple; she pretty much stuck to the house. But Carter, every chance he got, and always against Susie's rendered judgment, would load baby Jimmy up in his carriage and take him out walking in the neighborhood. It was almost as if he was looking for somebody to give him some trouble. He didn't have long to wait before he got some in the person of his neighbor, Gillis Wainwright.

Gillis was a good ole' boy. Behind his back Carter referred to him as a Florida cracker, and that he was, for at least a half dozen solid generations back. As a neighbor, he was fine though. He kept mostly to himself and he always tipped his hat, if he had one on when he saw Susie, and he had, on more than one occasion, offered Carter a friendly cold one. It was Coronas when he'd lost money at the track and Heinekens when he was on a winning streak.

By appearances Gillis made his living out of his garage as a mechanic. Harley Davidson motorcycles mostly, though if things were slow or if his gambling losses were proven imprudent, he would fix the golf carts from the country club and even a Cushman scooter in a real pinch. Gillis hated the Jap bikes and flat out refused to work on them, a decision that restricted his steady clientele to an impressive radius of Hell's Angels and guys like Carter who rode their Harleys for purposes other than primary transportation. These were the guys that Gillis called *rec riders*. He always told them that it was short for recreation, although, had he been able to spell, the mechanic's real meaning would have seen the word spelled differently.

"Hey, there, neighbor, what ya' got there?" Gillis wiped his hands on the red grease rag at his hip and watched Carter make a sudden deliberate turn up the driveway. The mechanic stepped out of his garage, bent low and peered in at the sleeping baby. He backed out with a genuinely perplexed look on his face. "Well, Carter," he asked without a trace of guile, "How come your kid looks like a coon?" Gillis Wainwright didn't see Carter's right hook coming and he picked himself up off the greasy garage floor apologizing before Jimmy Deane's daddy could land a second punch.

Both neighbors learned something of tremendous value that day. Gillis Wainwright, quite literally got a crash course in race relations, and Carter Deane figured out that it helped no one at all to troll the neighborhood in search of insult. The mechanic made sincere amends and offered to tune Carter's bike for free, and the two men shared a conciliatory beer standing over Jimmy Deane's carriage. After that first afternoon, Carter and the baby stopped by Gillis Wainwright's garage once a week at the very least to talk Harleys and, if Carter wasn't flying later, to share a beer.

Almost a year after Carter had nailed Gillis flat and a couple of long silent hours after he and Susie had had another episode of their only recurring argument, Carter lifted Jimmy into his spiffy new umbrella stroller and informed his pouting wife that he was going to take the toddler over to the neighbor's garage to show off their new wheels.

"Whatever, Carter," Susie said sourly. She turned the page in the novel she was reading and blew her son a kiss.

Gillis could see immediately that Carter was coming up his driveway with a purpose.

"New wheels, my little man," Gillis said. "Nice!" He bent low and held his oil-stained hand out for Jimmy Deane's tiny hand slap.

"Gillis," Carter sighed sitting on a stack of old tires. "My wife is trying to turn me into a pussy." Gillis chewed on the inside of his cheek and nodded. *Well, yeah, that's what women do.* He waited in silence for Carter to continue while he drained his Heineken dry. Then he set the emerald bottle down on a relatively unstained portion of the cement floor where baby Jimmy could lob his red plush spider at it.

Carter rose to pull two more bottles from the cooler. Gillis silently bent to retrieve Jimmy's spider and right the fallen bottle a dozen times before Carter finally sighed again.

"Now, just for the sake of conversation, Gillis…how much do you think you could get me for my bike?"

Chapter 2

In 1966 Susie Breaux had unknowingly subdued the heart of the handsome new pilot, Carter Deane, while she was counting miniature booze bottles in the forward galley on a bumpy Eastern flight to Detroit out of Fort Lauderdale. Carter had taken a moment to study the way that Susie's uniform hugged her bending torso, and the sincerity with which she addressed the tiny liquor containers and he fell instantly in love. He proposed marriage two weeks later. Elizabeth Breaux begged off from attending her only daughter's very small wedding ceremony claiming illness. Elizabeth had in fact, dramatically waved a perfumed handkerchief under her nose to dismiss the Protestant stench she imagined and she told her associates in the Rosary Society that her excuse was not a prevarication in the slightest because it just made her positively sick that her daughter was marrying an Episcopalian.

In addition to being a Protestant, Carter was a northerner and an only child. His parents were both dead, a fact that had caused Susie to tell him without any meanness intended, *some people have all the luck.*

Back in Tampa, Elizabeth lodged her objections to Susie's marriage long and loud to anyone who would listen. Ultimately, she informed Susie that the Deanes should not expect Elizabeth to ever make the five-hour drive down from Tampa to visit them in their home, or as she put it, to *set foot in their Hollywood den of iniquity*, which was really a disappointingly mundane little south Florida bungalow, as dens of iniquity go. Elizabeth was true to her word on the matter and never once visited. Regarding her own hospitality, Elizabeth granted, Susie and the Episcopalian could, if they felt they must, partake in a sojourn north, but only once a year, and only upon the occasion of Thanksgiving. They never should expect any tendered invitation to come to Tampa for the many religious holidays that Elizabeth Breaux held sacred.

As it turned out, that first isolated miserable Thanksgiving dinner, several years before Jimmy's adoption, had been beyond sufficient for Carter, in spite of the efforts of Susie's highly entertaining and seriously profane younger brother who had done his best to liven things up. As far as Carter could see, other than his wife, Danny Breaux, Susie's only sibling, was the singular redeeming character within the Breaux clan, her father being a dour mute whose pickup truck sported both a full gun rack in its cab and a confederate flag flying proudly from its antennae.

Perhaps not altogether surprisingly, considering Danny Breaux's upbringing, he up and enlisted in the Marine Corps right out of high school. He was already on base out in California when Jimmy's adoption came through so uncle and nephew were never to be acquainted. Nevertheless, Danny phoned his sister from Camp Pendleton to congratulate the new parents and then once again during the week before he was shipped overseas he called his sister and her husband one more time and promised to teach his nephew how to whistle through his fingers – Danny's singular notable talent – upon his return from Southeast Asia.

Since Susie's nuptials had not been performed "in the Church" Elizabeth considered her daughter to be living in sin.

Communications between mother and daughter had always been tense. They grew bitter after Susie's marriage to Carter. Susie's announcement that the Deanes had adopted a baby from up north was simply beyond the pale. Elizabeth expressed no desire to ever meet her grandson. Instead, she referred to him as *some harlot's bastard.* Neither party had mentioned the baby's existence again in any one of the paltry perfunctory phone calls they had shared. Although Susie wasn't *really* keeping Jimmy's skin color a secret from her family, she was not altogether unhappy about their common ignorance of it either. It certainly didn't kill her that her parents were uninterested in meeting her son. Fittingly perhaps, it would be Danny Breaux, and in particular his most outrageous if unwitting stunt, that would at last introduce Elizabeth and Joe Bob Breaux to Jimmy Deane.

St. Benedict's was packed to capacity for Danny Breaux's funeral. A hog for attention of any kind, Danny himself would have enjoyed the service had he been able to attend it in a whole and sentient state. The Deanes arrived slightly tardy. The whole of the congregation was already seated by the time they climbed the wide stone steps. Susie almost passed by a lone weeping girl who was hanging near the rear door and who was known by everyone in St. Ben's parish to have administered countless blowjobs to the deceased in the back seat of Elizabeth's old Chevy Nova. Susie paused and touched the girl's shoulder gently. The girl startled under Susie's hand.

"My brother really liked you," Susie whispered when the girl's tear streaked face showed recognition. Had Danny Breaux really liked this homely, skinny girl with bad teeth? He had certainly liked the fellatio, so what do you say to people under circumstances like these anyway? The girl sniffed. It took her another moment to find her voice.

"Oh," she said wiping her nose on the back of her hand. Then her eyes grew wide as she took in the colored baby in

Susie's arms. She pointed a bony finger with a seriously bitten nail at Jimmy. "Is *that* Danny's nephew?" Susie, by way of answering her, turned around and handed the baby over to Carter. Danny Breaux's felatist smiled broadly in a flagrant display of her poor dental hygiene. Quickly calculating the scandal at hand, she reached around Susie and touched Jimmy's little blue bootie.

"Oh, Danny would have *loved* him!" The girl sniffled and swallowed her snot. "Your mama told me I was not welcome here." She explained her reluctance to go inside the church. "You know," the girl squinted. "Your brother told me once that you were the only one in his whole family that he could stand."

Susie shrugged.

"Thank you," she said softly. The girl pursed her lips and nodded once before she smiled her ugly smile again. Then she shook her head and turned to leave. She hesitated.

"Oh, and I don't think it's true what they're sayin'…" It seemed as if those would be her final words. The girl's head was bobbing significantly as she skipped down St. Benedict's long stairs and hit the ground. Just as the organ dirge started up inside, her voice rang out like the first lines of a tragic hymn. "Danny did *not* want to die! I should know!" Susie watched the girl's retreat for a minute before she turned back to Carter and the baby.

"At least he's out of here," Susie shrugged. Carter patted his wife's back and pushed her gently through St. Ben's door. Susie craned her neck. Her parents had saved a single seat in the front pew.

"Go on," Carter told her. "We're fine." He shifted baby Jimmy in his arms and stepped aside to stand at the back of the hot church. Susie walked forward alone down the center aisle and was well aware of the hush that fell over the congregation as she passed.

"Susan," Elizabeth said loudly staring straight ahead. "Is it not enough that your brother has brought such shame on me? You have to show up late to his funeral?" The congregation in the front ten pews heard every word.

"Sorry, Mama." Susie leaned in close. "It was a long, hot drive and we had to stop to feed and change the baby."

"You brought *him*?" Elizabeth's disapproval of adoption in general, and her grandson's adoption in particular, oozed across the unpadded wooden bench like a stink. The *spawn of sin* was how she commonly referred to babies conceived out of wedlock. And God, she believed, was obviously punishing barren couples. While their transgressions were at times more difficult to divine by Elizabeth, the all-knowing Lord was surely not so easily deceived. They were sinners, every single one of them. According to Elizabeth Breaux, it was sheer blasphemy for the wicked to do an end run around His wishes and get themselves somebody else's child to raise up. She had suggested in very specific terms that the Deanes' unholy union had not known the blessing of children because of Carter's religious background. Elizabeth was certain of this, never mind whatever other terrible sins her daughter had accrued with that Protestant husband of hers. *Episcopalian,* when Elizabeth said it, was synonymous with Devil worshipping voodoo. She did not think it necessary to otherwise explain the proliferation of the general flock of Episcopalians, certainly not in decline, even in Tampa.

Susie gave her father a perfunctory kiss on the cheek and he grunted, not unpleasantly. She took her seat next to Elizabeth and turned to get a fix on Carter in the rear, as if he was her lodestar and she needed to locate him to carry on. Neither of her parents expressed enough curiosity in their grandson to turn around for their first peek. Carter gave Susie a thumbs-up and made Jimmy's little baby hand wave to her. In his father's arms Jimmy arched his back and told him,

"Ma…ma…" One or two parishioners had followed Susie's line of sight to the rear of the church where the handsome young man was standing holding onto the black baby. A rapid contagion of elbowed ribcages, jerking heads, craned necks and stunned facial expressions spread throughout St. Benedict's congregation like a sudden seated contagion of St. Vitus Dance. Ninety percent of the parish knew therefore, before Elizabeth Breaux did, that her adopted grandchild was a pickaninny.

A sudden hush fell at the appearance of two priests in full RC regalia appearing at the rear door of the church. As they advanced down the center aisle, the organ switched over to a somber processional. Two altar boys led the way. One of them, a pale faced skinny child, struggled to carry a gold painted crucifix nearly half his own size, upon which a diapered Jesus had been glued more securely than the original. Little splotches of toenail-red appeared in all the appropriate places on the Lord's scantily clad body. The other youngster swung a pot of smoking incense at the end of a foot long chain, perhaps performing his job a little too enthusiastically and drawing an actual swat from the younger of the priests as they reached the front row of pews.

Father Boyle, St. Benedict's senior pastor, stopped momentarily in front of the bereaved family. He smiled down at Susie who he remembered in a vague way from her own Holy Communion and Catechism classes. They had a brief, whispered exchange in the middle of which Elizabeth's voice rang out indignantly over the organ dirge.

"He's a Protestant!" This time, everyone but the very hard of hearing heard her.

"Yes, Elizabeth," the elegant priest's voice rose too. "But, he *is* a *Christian.*" He smiled then in an unmistakably condescending way and gave Susie a quick affectionate pat on the shoulder. It was possible, (if you were watching as most were), to see Elizabeth bristle.

To be fair, who could hold Elizabeth Breaux accountable entirely for her bizarre behavior that day? The ignominious way that her son had died, for starters, was just going to be for absolute certain, one holy hell of a cross to bear in Saint Benedict's parish. By the time her son's remains, (really just his feet inside his combat boots) had arrived stateside in the traditional flag draped common coffin, nearly everybody in town had heard some version of the story. It was a story that had been vehemently denied by the U.S. military, of course. (And also by the young girl who had sucked his cock so avidly before his enlistment, and who probably knew better than the Marines, or at least had less to hide.) Danny Breaux, in the most austere version of his suicide, had run pall-mall into a rice paddy wearing nothing more than a red bandana and his nearly new Marine Corps issue boots. He had, some said, been higher than a kite on that really excellent Thai stick that was coming into Viet Nam through Cambodia by then.

Elizabeth's hopes that the Marine Corps would have made a decent man out of her only son vanished amongst her curses upon his soul for only making a laughing stock of her instead. The town's enjoyment of the family's scandal was at least exaggerated or probably even manufactured. Everywhere in town Elizabeth imagined people snickering when they saw her, especially the very few Lutherans with whom she had a passing acquaintance.

Still, at his services, Danny Breaux's mother sat regally in the front pew, probably praying earnestly for the strength to go on. She prayed directly to the Holy Virgin of course, a woman who surely knew a little bit about the extremes that a son could go to to embarrass his mother. Before the mother of God had a chance to heed Elizabeth's prayers however, the brief service was over. With a scant amount of her usual zeal, Elizabeth rose out of her seat and was marching down the aisle of St. Ben's, holding her well-coifed head admirably high under the circumstances. Who then should fall right into her line of sight, holding his own son tightly and apparently without a single ounce of compunction? And, dead center in the middle of *her* community, no less? It was none other than the pesky Episcopalian who was her son-in-law, at least by Florida statute. She glared at the *colored* baby in his arms. It took her less than one second to put two and two together and only one more to turn her wrath full volume on Susie. The first sounds were the shrieks of a highly agitated rain forest creature and then, as if she were speaking in tongues, a dozen frothy inarticulate syllables dribbled out of Elizabeth's mouth before she collapsed stiffly right there in the center aisle at the back of St. Benedicts.

Susie Breaux-Deane was enough of a Southern girl to feel that potluck meals trump even a possible cerebral vascular episode, so after she saw to it that her daddy got Elizabeth into an ambulance, she proceeded with the congregation over to the cemetery where Danny got his (some felt undue) twenty-one gun salute. From there she led the mourners back over to the house to make sure that they were properly fed. The unlikely triumvirate of Marine Corps wives, the Rosary Society of Tampa, and Mr. Breaux's cronies from the Brotherhood of the Son's of Robert E. Lee, all converged in curious shifts out on the porch where Carter was rocking Jimmy. It seemed apparent that every single one of them wanted to see up close the nigra baby that had felled his grandmamma.

Out in the kitchen, Susie was overseeing the distribution of dessert with the clucking assistance of a half dozen of the Marine Corps wives when a wild-eyed Elizabeth returned in a taxi cab ninety seconds ahead of Joe Bob's pick up. Uncharacteristically disheveled and red faced, and without as much as a simple glance, Elizabeth blasted past the retinue around Carter and Jimmy on the porch. She headed directly into the kitchen and growled like a wounded bear in the worst kind of demonic possession before she snuck up behind her daughter and gave her a meaningful shove. Consequently, Susie involuntarily defaced the butter cream frosting on the cake that was immediately before her.

"Cursed be Canaan!" Elizabeth growled. Susie turned around wiping frosting from the knife blade with a slow thumb.

"Mama? Beg pardon?" Six young military wives froze, a dozen individually perfect squares of heavily frosted yellow sheet cake poised in their hands for uncertain delivery.

"Cursed be Canaan! The lowest of slaves will he *be* to his brothers!" Elizabeth's voice was guttural, her message obscure to everyone in the room. Susie abruptly stabbed the cake at its center and reached behind her back to untie her apron.

"Mama!" She stared her mother down with unbelievable equanimity. "Slavery was abolished a long, long time ago."

"Blessed be the *Lord*, the *God* of Shem!" Elizabeth bleated back. ""May *Canaan* be the *slave* of Shem! May God extend the territory of *Japeth*, may *Japeth* live in the tents of Shem and may Canaan *be* his slave!" Elizabeth's cheeks were tomato red. She abruptly punctuated her sermon by grabbing hold of a superfluous casserole of baked beans from the stovetop and, like Moses himself throwing down the original tablets of stone, she flung the hot dish against the kitchen wall. Susie slowly wiped butter cream from her hands on a dishtowel and stepped over the steaming beans.

"Oh, screw Japeth, Mama!" she said. Then she stuffed the dirty dishtowel into her mother's blistering hands.

"Time to go," she said sweetly to the other young women. "Sorry about the mess and all. Bye, Mama." Elizabeth clutched the towel to her bosom, lifted her eyes toward heaven and took up howling the chorus of the Battle Hymn of the Republic as loud as she could while Susie and Carter gathered up their things. Baby Jimmy was howling pretty good too as his parents performed the customary quick inventory of personal effects common to all traveling parents of small children. In the future, it would be possible to note, at least by God, that this single moment was perhaps the only time ever that Jimmy Deane came even close to being on the same page with his grandma.

Susie Deane had no further contact with her parents until old Joe Bob Breaux up and died less than six months later. His fatal accident occurred in the fog when an oil tanker fishtailed into his pick up on the parkway and launched him over the dividing wall and directly into the silver Playmate on the grill plate of an oncoming semi.

"Your father is dead, Susan," Elizabeth announced without preamble into the phone at three a.m. "You can come to the funeral if you want, but you may not bring that Protestant or that nigger baby into this house!" She hung up before Susie could even say, thank you, no thank you. Carter was on a layover in New York so Susie had kept Jimmy sleeping next to her in their big bed.

"Your grandpa died today, Jimmy," she told him. "Now you will never know your Breaux kin." It was an idle remark in lieu of any heartfelt sorrow, but it was surely Joe Bob's sudden death that got Susie to thinking almost daily about how dangerous Carter's Harley really was.

Chapter 3

Jimmy Deane

There's a few things you have to know about the man who was the only daddy I ever really had. First of all, Carter Deane was not Southern. Neither did he possess a whole lot of patience for Southern ways, or, to be more specific, for certain Southern people, and I know for a fact, he did not want any son of his to grow up to be a dumb red-necked cracker even though I was never going to qualify on purely biological grounds. He lived down south only because he loved my mom – she always said *fiercely*. "*Your papa loved me fiercely!*" And, he loved a few other things fiercely, too. One of them was flying jets. My daddy did two tours of duty in Viet Nam, and more than a thousand times he landed fighter planes on aircraft carriers in the South China seas, lots of times in bad storms, and he was never afraid. He had his share of weather once he started flying for Eastern Airlines, too, what with all those bad, tail-end-of-hurricane storms that hit the coastal cities. But after Nam, he said that landing on solid ground in any kind of storm instead of on a bouncing ship was a piece of cake. Even my mom, who knew bad weather at thirty-thousand-feet from her days as a stew, she never worried too much about Carter's flying. It was the Harley that caused her to worry. She called it Daddy's *time machine*, as in: *it's-only-a-matter-of-time-before-you-get-yourself-killed-on-that-thing*. It was the only real bone of contention, as he called it, between them. But, that Harley was the only thing besides my mom and flying jets that he was just wild crazy about. And, playing the drums. I almost forgot. My dad just loved to play the drums. And, I believe that he loved me also.

Right from the get-go my pops took to being a daddy, Mama said. He started out right away having long, long talks with me, him doing all the talking naturally. Male bonding, he said it was, or *man-to-man talking*. He pulled a commuter route out of Miami to New York for a few months that meant he had to leave at what he called "the butt-crack of dawn."(My daddy had a colorful way of speaking for a Northerner.) So, anyway, he'd come in and have a little talk with me before he left for work when Susie was still fast asleep in their bed. Sometimes he'd bring all his clothes in and get dressed in my room just telling me stupid stuff like, "This is a tie, JD. Ties suck and nobody likes wearing them, but some things you just have to do if you want to get ahead or if the occasion demands." Then he would stand over my bed and demonstrate the Windsor knot. It didn't matter to him whether I was awake and listening or sound asleep.

Sometimes the talks were about more important things, like the one we had that very first winter night that they brought me home from Chicago. Mama remembered that I was pretty much a mess and not making things easy for them. Carter wrapped me up tight she said and took me out to the rocking chair that had been waiting for me on the little wooden porch of the house they expected me to feel at home in. I can't tell you of course how terrified I was that night, changing hands so many times and none were the ones that I wanted, the only ones that would have made me feel right. But, Mama said that Carter

Deane did his very best and I have to hand it to him here, he did try to give me something I could hold on to, something that would sustain me.

"JD," he said, "I'm not going to bullshit you. You've got a tough row to hoe, little buddy. I know you'd rather be back there in your mother's arms and I don't know what to tell you about her. I know she was pretty. The doc who signed your walking papers told me that she was a knockout and a real nice girl. Catholic, like your new mom used to be, so I guess that she just had some problems in the area of birth control the way some Catholic girls do." Carter stopped rocking for a minute and looked hard into my crying face. "You and I," he said, "will have a few more talks about that subject when you are old enough." That's when he first used the term "man-to-man". I'm pretty sure, of course, that I didn't know what on earth he meant by that, but I must have liked the sound of it or how he held me and talked about our future together because Mama told me I calmed right down after that part.

He went on to tell me how he and Susie had tried and tried to have a baby of their own, but maybe he'd been exposed to that agent orange that we know now was also the agent of misery in a lot of people's lives. It sure was in theirs because after they found out they couldn't make a baby, it just broke Susie's heart in two.

"The truth is, JD, if your new mom and I had had a baby of our own, I never would have asked my cousin about adopting a baby up north at all." He sighed then and sat back. That cannot have been an easy thing to admit.

Because I wasn't crying anymore Carter unwrapped my blanket and laid me out across his lap and made a really careful inventory of all my parts, something neither he nor Susie had thought to do before closing the deal the night before. It was quite a moment I'll tell you, me and him sitting out on the porch, the January night so unseasonably warm it made Chicago seem a million freezing miles away. And the moon was coming up in the east the way it does in Florida at that time of year, like a big old orange slice covered in sugar that might just roll right up our street and bump into our house. I'm not saying that I stopped missing my birth mother. I don't think I will ever stop missing the girl we only ever really knew as a name. (Even Mary McGinnis herself couldn't fix that now.) But, I do think that I was very grateful to have Carter and Susie both try so hard to make me feel at home. To make me feel wanted.

Pops leaned back after he had counted every finger and every toe and he even sneaked the quickest peak down inside my diaper. "Wow!" he breathed, his big strong hands lifting me up to his face. "You are a magnificent specimen, now aren't you?" Then he pushed my T-shirt up with his nose and he gave me my first raspberry. If you've never felt your fathers lips like that… Well, I can tell you, it's really something.

"Isn't that funny," he asked me, "how one person's good fortune often seems to come directly from somebody else's heartache?" I think that Carter was talking about Mary McGinnis and her heartache when he said that, but truthfully, I was already trying hard to move on.

One-day-old and I was already trying hard to be good enough for somebody to love me.

Chapter 4

Jimmy Deane

I would be willing to bet that I was the only newborn baby in America, maybe even the whole world, who came home to a nursery decorated nearly floor to ceiling with rock band posters. It was like I had rock and roll wallpaper. Our little house had only two bedrooms and before I came along the room that was to become mine was previously what my pops called his music room. In honor of my arrival, my mom had persuaded Carter to move his drum kit out of that room and she sacrificed the small living room to his drums. A crib for me and the other stuff that I would need got moved into Carter's music room to make me feel like part of the family. However, those posters of all the bands he loved that lined the walls were not on the negotiation table for even a minute. "The posters stay," he told Mama. "It is never too early for a man to start learning some culture."

He could have made his living playing drums, he was that good, but his own daddy had asked him one too many times, *"Yes, but Carter, how are you going to pay the bills?"* Maybe that's why, if my dad said it once, he said it a thousand times, "JD, don't let anybody ever tell you that music is not a way to make a living." And usually, when he said that, or something along those lines, I knew that he was going to put me in that little baby swing that was the only other substantial piece of furniture in the living room besides his drum kit. After that he'd put one of his favorite albums on the little stereo they had and he would accompany the band for as long as I seemed happy. As I recall, my contentment almost always lasted a good long time, especially if his selection fell along the lines of the Beatles who were my early favorites and whose poster commanded the place of honor, in view on the back of my bedroom door.

"Ringo is a vastly under-rated musician." My dad often lectured. "Drummers in general get a lot of shit and you'll have to get used to that." Then he would put a drumstick up to his lips. "Shhhh! Don't tell your mama I said the 'S' word." There were certain things girls just wouldn't understand and certain vocabulary that was only meant for those man-to-man talks. My daddy took for granted that I would follow in his footsteps and be a drummer, too.

"Sooner or later some wise guy lead is going to ask you if you know the definition of a drummer. And, then he'll piss all over himself telling you that a drummer is just a guy who likes to hang out with musicians." (Piss was another word that my mom would not like.) "You look them right in the eye, JD," he advised me, "and you tell them that you can always tell if there's a guitar player knocking at the door 'cause they never know when to come in." It wasn't that my pops disliked all guitar players, but I'm pretty sure that he was of the opinion, that in general, they were sort of weird. I have to say, in my limited experience, he was absolutely right about that.

Carter Deane was a musician to the core, though, and I never heard him say a bad word about anybody else's playing. He told me that folks who did so were just weenies, pure and simple, and he was no weenie. He had a fondness for anybody who played anything, *anybody who's got the balls to play,* he'd say, but he had a particular fondness for drummers.

When it came to other people besides musicians, a lot of them were just idiots, according to Carter. Most were not worth your time, but sometimes, the really good ones came in unlikely disguises. One like such was Gillis Wainwright who lived on our street and seemed sometimes like a yokel, but Pops said deep down Gillis was somebody you could trust.

When it came to girls, my pops said, there was a vast difference between a girl and a woman and you wanted a woman when the time came, (and that was way down the road for me) but when it did, I should pick one just like my mom, because she was the best woman either of us would ever know.

One more thing. My pops firmly believed that the only real motorcycles were Harleys, and every man should own at least one before he died. On that, he and Gillis Wainwright were in absolute agreement.

"Hey Buddy!" My dad was up before daylight even though he wasn't flying anywhere that day, and he came into my room with his motorcycle boots in one hand and a brand new rolled-up poster in the other. I was already awake and I pulled myself up and stared at him over the crib rail. He sat down on the rocking chair and put his chin in his hand. He didn't rock. After a while he sighed, not sad, just resigned. "Your mama is turning me into a pussy," he whispered. His words were pretty harsh but there wasn't any rancor in his voice. It was altogether something else instead, like maybe what a man's voice sounds like when he's about to do something he really doesn't want to do but he goes ahead and does it for somebody he loves. Anyways, that's what I think now. After a little bit, Pops put his boots on and stepped over to the Beatles.

"Sorry, Ringo," he said and pulled the tacks out of the four corners. He rolled the Beatles up carefully and swapped the rubber band from the new poster and dropped the old one underneath my crib. "I'll find a better place for the Beatles later," he said to me. Instead, a three-foot picture of a nice looking young man wearing a red jacket went up where the Beatles had been. The man had a cigarette dangling from one hand, but otherwise he didn't seem to be doing much of anything special in that picture except for looking good. "Baby boy, this here is your namesake, James Dean. No relation and no extra 'e'." Pops put the first tack in the upper corner. "He's not in a band. Actually, he's dead like your grandpas and your crazy Uncle Dan." Daddy bent over and peeked through the crack in the doorway and looked across the hall, I suppose because my mom would definitely not have approved of the content of this part. He put an index finger to his lips and then let the same finger circle his ear several times. "I'll tell you more about your Uncle Dan later… when you're older and when your mom's not around."

Dawn was breaking outside my window so brightly you could almost hear it. The sun slanted in and lit up James Dean's face and I have to say, he looked a little bit mean but also like he might have been one of those rare people my dad had told me about that underneath the roughness was somebody you could count on. It also looked to me like just before they had taken that picture he had had something he wanted to say and whatever it was you could tell it was going to be of some importance.

Papa put the last two tacks in and stepped back for one final look.

"Okay, little man, I'm going for my last ride now and then I'm gonna take my bike over to Gillis Wainwright and see if he can sell it for me. When I get back, I'll tell you all about James Dean and why the Beatles give way to him and him alone."

When he got to the door Pops turned around like he'd forgotten something.

Every night when Carter was home and my parents stood over my crib together and watched me get drowsy and fall asleep, it was always my mom who would reach in and put her hand on my back. "Just making sure he's still breathing," she'd tell Carter. And, she always whispered, "*love you*" before she left too.

When Carter left me he never came back to make sure I was still breathing, but that morning he did touch the place on his chest where I know he could feel his heart beating. "Okay, then," he told me. "I'll see you later, son." He pulled the door closed just far enough so that I could see James Dean's face but leaving it open enough for Susie to hear me in case I got lonely, and then he went out through the kitchen to go and take his last ride.

Chapter 5

Gillis Wainwright watched from his open garage with some interest when a somber-looking black sedan pulled up in front of the neighbor's house and delivered a package. The Deanes were the only people on the street who were at all neighborly, and the truth was, Gillis had missed them when a week or so had come and gone and Carter hadn't brought his strange little baby over in his stroller for the customary neighborly beer the two men had begun to share on a more or less regular basis. Another day or two passed and still no Carter and baby. For no really good reason he could think of, and more than a little self-consciously, Gillis decided he should check on them.

Susie answered the door in her bathrobe with the whimpering baby on her hip. Her blonde hair hung in dirty strings; it looked as though it had been uncombed and unwashed for many days. The baby didn't look any too good either and one or the other of them just flat out stank. Gillis assumed it was the child.

"Hey, Mizz Deane." Gillis touched the brim of his grease stained John Deere cap and gave a polite little bow. "I ain't seen Carter all week. He ain't sick, is he?"

"No, Carter's not sick, Gillis." Susie's voice was low, her pupils dilated. She paused, took a breath and let it out fast.

"Carter's dead." Jimmy Deane dropped his head down into the crook of his mother's neck, took fistfuls of her dirty hair in his chubby baby hands and started to wail.

"Beg pardon, Ma'am?" Gillis said over the screaming toddler, turning his good ear toward them. Susie pushed the screen door open and stepped back to allow Gillis into the house. Halfway down the short hallway to the bedroom she turned around to see him hovering tentatively just inside the darkened living room.

"Well, come on," she said and disappeared into the bedroom. The window shades in the front room were drawn closed and Gillis gave himself a moment to let his eyes adjust. He surveyed the room. Carter's drums dominated the space facing a baby swing that hung from the hallway doorframe. Otherwise, the room was devoid of furniture. The whole house reeked of dirty diapers. Gillis removed his cap and tried to smooth his thinning hair down flat before he ventured down the hallway after Susie. When he moved forward he wasn't sure what it was he was expecting. He'd never even been inside the Deanes' house before. He felt too big for his surroundings. Even his slow movements were stirring the thick air.

"Ma'am?" he said. He stepped a tentative work boot inside the small bedroom.

Susie was trying to console the crying baby.

"Shhh, now. Shhhhh. It's okay, JD honey." She pointed to where the box containing Carter's ashes was perched up high on the single shelf inside the opened closet. Gillis stepped forward warily. He had to tilt his head sideways and squint to read the typed card that had been stapled to the box's flap.

Deane, Carter S.: d.o.b. 02/28/42
Cremation ordered 07/18/70

McKinnley Mortuary and
Crematorium
Hollywood, Florida

Released to n.o.k.: Deane, Susan
Rose

Gillis blinked a dozen times, shook his head as if such action could aid his comprehension. Then he backed away from the closet, turned abruptly and without a single word he let himself out the back door. Susie climbed into bed with baby Jimmy and rubbed his back until he finally stopped crying and fell asleep.

Late, the following morning when Susie was trying to coax Cheerios into the baby's disinterested mouth, she heard footsteps on the old wooden front porch. A heavy figure shifted around behind the closed door for a minute or two and then took off rapidly down the steps. Susie waited a minute, listening to a car engine start up. When the car had driven off she gathered her dirty robe around her middle and opened the door cautiously. Her tentative fear of the stranger was the first feeling to surface after more than a week of numbing grief. She opened the door wider and saw that whoever it was that had been up on the porch had positioned – no, arranged – a half dozen paper grocery sacks very carefully in front of the screened door. Each sack was full to the brim or overflowing. She made six trips from the porch to the small Formica kitchen table, all the while talking in a reassuring way to Jimmy in between. The baby silently watched her from his perch in the high chair. When the tabletop was full, Susie went to the sink and moved the curtains back from the window so that she could look next door. Faint sounds of activity came from Gillis Wainwright's garage but from this angle she could not see into the opened door. Weary from the effort involved in hauling all the bags inside, and half starved, Susie slumped onto a chair and stared at the tabletop. The baby watched her slightest move, ready to burst into anxious tears if she left the room again. At long last she rose and addressed the first bag. Surprisingly, Gillis Wainwright had had the good sense to provide the Deane widow and orphan with a package of disposable diapers.

"These must be for you, JD." Susie pulled them out and let them drop to the floor. "Oh, dear lord," she whispered reaching into the sack with both hands. With some difficulty, she wrestled free a frozen turkey that had to be a twenty-five pounder at the very least.

"I guess this is for me." Susie settled the turkey onto her chair. A slender wire secured a tag, which recorded several price reductions and the turkey's prior history of rejection.

"Oh, dear lord," Susie repeated. The baby watched her without moving a muscle, not so much listless as he was anxious, attuned to his mother's every move, every breath. She hovered over the neighbor's odd gift of poultry for several whole minutes, her brow furrowed.

"Okay, buddy," Susie gave the frozen carcass a pat before turning to her child. "I guess we're gonna cook us a turkey tomorrow." The toddler allowed her to remove him from his high chair and lower him to the floor. He stepped tentatively forward and stood alongside the headless turkey's chair. He peered over the seat at the newcomer for a good long time before he reached out a cautious hand to touch the frozen wrapper.

"Turkey is cold," he said as clear as day, and looked up as if for confirmation of his pronouncement. "Where's his head?" Jimmy asked, having seen at least one picture of a turkey in his Little Golden Books. Susie Deane had virtually no contact with other families, and she did not know enough about child development to marvel at her son. He had been speaking in whole small sentences since before he could walk and she took his linguistic abilities pretty much for granted.

"Yes, baby, the turkey's very cold," she agreed absently. She pulled the window curtain back again but saw no sign of Gillis Wainwright. It took a while to store the other items that Gillis had purchased to keep the Deanes from starving while they grieved. When she was finished with the task, she again drew her kitchen curtains back. The garage next door was quiet.

Susie filled her bathtub pouring half a bottle of baby wash into the warm water. She removed the baby's diaper and dirty T-shirt and put him into the sudsy water and then she stripped down herself and climbed in too. She gave them both a vigorous shampoo and just soaked until the water grew tepid and all the bubbles were gone. After their bath, Susie carefully cleaned the tub, washing it three times, the last with dishwashing soap. She retrieved the frozen Butterball and let cold water run over it in the bathtub until it was completely covered. Then she went into the kitchen and made a meal for herself from the staples Gillis Wainwright had provided: corn nuts, beef jerky and pork rinds.

"You're gonna be okay, baby," she whispered to Jimmy Deane that night while their floating turkey defrosted in the bathtub. "I don't know why your other mama and daddy didn't keep you, and I don't know why Carter had to go and get himself killed on that damn motorcycle, but you're gonna be okay. I will see to that." She ran her hand over the downy soft fluff of his hair and kissed his forehead. He reached out a tiny hand and held it to her cheek and waited to fall asleep himself until Susie had finally drifted off.

Chapter 6

One month after Carter's accidental death, as if God had decided to provide ambient cues for Susie Deane's personal hell, the Florida temperatures soared to the hottest on record. It was the kind of heat that had the geriatric set fearful of setting foot on the sidewalks, in case some enterprising youngster had slimed the cement in an attempt to see if eggs would fry on it. The humidity, which in South Florida was almost always a burden, was also setting records. On the most miserable day of the current calendar year the highway department finally contacted Susie Deane regarding the disposition of her husband's motorcycle, or, more precisely, what remained of it. Susie had barely left her house in the intervening time, and when she had, it was really only to procure groceries and diapers. She had not given the wrecked motorcycle a single thought until the state demanded that it either be surrendered or picked up. Either way she already owed a hefty bill for the transportation and storage of the tangled wreckage, with more charges promised. The rapidly accruing storage fee alone would not have been enough to force her down to the impound lot to handle the matter in the blistering heat though. She wanted to see with her own eyes, and maybe even touch, the mangled mess of murderous machinery.

The damned air conditioning had gone out in her car, something Carter would have handled, had he been alive, so it was absolutely out of the question to take the baby with her. The child would have simply broiled in the back seat.

Susie waited for signs of life to come from Gillis Wainwright's garage and then she packed up JD, his Cookie Monster Sippy cup and a spare diaper and wheeled him next door. She parked his stroller in the opened doorway of Gillis's garage and told the toddler to be good and watch his reluctant babysitter hammer dents out of a wheel rim. Susie promised a wary Gillis that she would return in under an hour.

The perverse distortion of the slick machine that once had been Carter's Harley Davidson motorcycle had been tossed askew onto a flatbed truck and dumped off at a contract wreckage yard in a seedy neighborhood in Miami. It was a location that was far enough inland to be of no objection to the genteel Miami populace who liked to be spared the sight of life's more unsightly needs, and in a part of town that Susie Deane had certainly never had prior occasion to visit. She parked outside the chain link fence, left her windows rolled down, but locked her doors anyway. As she made her way along the fence line a skinny Doberman Pincher roused himself from underneath the building and unconvincingly threatened Susie's trespass. As soon as he reached the limits of his chain link tether the dusty dog displayed his teeth half-heartedly at her and returned promptly to the shade in a manner suggesting that he was too hot to be anything but bored with his own performance. The office was a prefab modular affair that was mounted on cinder construction blocks. The trailer's dirty and dented exterior gave it the air of hurricane debris. The interior was worse. Nothing critical however could be said of the air conditioning, which was cranked so high that within a minute Susie felt her wedding ring grow loose on her ring finger. A young colored man was ahead of her attempting to negotiate the recovery of his Toyota. On the business side of the counter stood a hugely muscled man who did not seem friendly. Susie hung back near the door so as to let the young man finish his transaction. From there she could frankly examine the appearances of the two men without seeming to do so.

The counter man wore a threadbare and grease stained T-shirt in stark contrast to the young black man's blinding culinary whites. Of the two, the state contractor's physical impression suggested an ironically much more *colorful* history. His large head was shaved bald, one earring piercing his left earlobe and a multitude of tattoos of no visible relationship to each other were inked on every unclothed inch of skin. A large stylized swastika was featured prominently on the inside of his right forearm, and a distinct KKK had been lettered unambiguously on the same wrist. It was easy to imagine that half of his lived years had been spent on a work farm either a few miles from where they stood, or somewhere up in Georgia if his crimes had warranted enough imagination to necessitate inter-state flight.

"I gotta get my car, brother." Susie overheard the young man plead sympathetically at the tail end of his story. "I gotta get to both a' my jobs tonight."

"Yeah, an' I gotta have my three hun'd dollars, *brother. Cash, brother.* I been burned by too many niggahs and they bouncin' checks." The boy looked sideways at Susie, embarrassed.

"Look, I got two. That's all I can give you today. But, I swear, you give me my car and I'll bring the rest back to you by Friday. *An' then some*. You only had it just the one night! Come on, man!"

"Get the fuck outta heah," the bald man snorted. He waved the young black man aside sharply and looked to the door where Susie was pretending to study the stenciled name of the towing company on the door.

"Girlie, you need somethin'?" He summoned her with exaggerated annoyance.

"Yes, sir. Someone called about my husband's motorcycle." She edged over. The young man nodded to her politely and moved aside.

"Your old man the dead guy?" the man with the swastika asked. Susie nodded.

"What's the name ag'in?" From a spike hammered into the wall he yanked a metal ring upon which claim tickets had been impaled in a circle.

"Deane," Susie said. "Carter Deane." The man rummaged through his circle.

"Fo' hun'd," he said flatly.

"Four hundred dollars?" Susie's eyes widened and she swallowed the lump that grew instantly in her throat.

"You gonna take it t'day?"

"I was hoping that I could arrange to have it taken somewhere…maybe later today," Susie told him.

"D'livery is anothah hun'd."

She hesitated, aware of the young black man watching.

"Can I write a check for it?" she asked.

"Yeah, *y'all* can write a check." He gave the Toyota owner a significant look. "Go 'head. Make it out to Sammy's Towing." Susie opened her purse slowly and removed her checkbook. She set it down on the filthy counter and started to write out the check. Before she signed her name she looked up.

"Excuse me, sir?"

"Yeah? What?" The tattooed man returned to the counter.

"Well, sir," Susie said. "I was just wondering why this young man's car requires three hundred dollars for just one night and my husband's motorcycle has been here for over a month now…and…" Susie glanced at the young black man who was slowly shaking his head. "Well, does that seem fair to you?" She closed her checkbook.

"What?" The man's huge bald head swiveled from Susie to the young Toyota owner and back again. "What?" he repeated. Susie opened her checkbook. She wrote quickly, signed her check and tore it carefully out.

"Here," she said handing the check over. "It's five hundred dollars. One hundred for this young man's Toyota, and four hundred for my husband's motorcycle. I'll have someone come by this afternoon to pick it up." The bald man's face reddened. He took the check in his hands as if it was contaminated. He exhaled long and angry. Susie could see his nose hairs vibrate and feel the heat of his breath. He hesitated a few more long seconds and then flipped the check angrily into a drawer. His big head swiveled again back and forth between Susie and the boy who was laying down his two hundred dollars in small denominations. The bigger man grabbed the boy's money and spat on the floor.

"No latah than two o'clock," he barked at Susie. "You show up latah than that, it's another hun'd or I scrap it." He shook his filthy hand in her face.

"Absolutely," Susie smiled at the boy. "Give him his keys now," she said. The bald man hesitated. His eyes squinted into mean slits and he snorted. He could not remember the last time a woman had tried to tell him what to do. Without paying for it.

"Fuckin' seen everything now," he muttered loud enough to be heard. Then he turned his back to them to find the boy's keys. The boy smiled broadly at Susie.

"I wanna pay you back, Ma'am," he whispered to her. "I wanna pay you back with some interest!"

"Just watch where you park from now on," Susie said in a low voice. "And do somethin' nice for your own mama today."

“I will. Thanks, lady. I will. You’re a really nice lady. God bless you, ma’am.”

“Well, that ain’t gonna happen,” she told him firmly, but when he cocked his head for an explanation she merely waved his curiosity away and put her checkbook into her purse. She followed the kid out into the heat. The glass door wheezed closed behind them on the sound of a sinister snicker from inside.

“Niggah lovah,” the bald man growled in an ugly voice. Susie peered back almost involuntarily through the dirty glass. The bald man’s face gaped back with hostility and he made an obscene gesture using both hands. He started to move out from behind the counter. Susie had to force herself not to run to her car. She wouldn’t give him the satisfaction in case he was still watching her. She drove all the way from the junkyard straight into Gillis Wainwright’s driveway checking all the while in her rear view mirror.

Meanwhile, in Susie’s absence, Gillis had run afoul of a dirty diaper, and being unable to negotiate the little adhesive strips on an uncooperative toddler, he had opted to let Jimmy Deane run naked through the weary little sprinkler on his weedy front lawn while he supervised from his front porch steps. Susie’s hands were still shaking on the steering wheel when she registered that for the first time since Carter’s death, her son was laughing.

“I’m sorry, Mizz Deane,” Gillis shook his head. “He shat.”

“I see that.” Susie bit her lips to keep from smiling. “I guess I’m the one who should be sorry. That was more than you bargained for.”

“Them little undiepants is a lot more complicated than you’d think.”

“Well, no harm. It sure looks like he’s enjoyin’ your sprinkler,” Susie said. Gillis beamed. They watched Susie’s naked son run in and out of the wiggling stream of hose water in silence.

"Hey, Gillis, you got any need for Carter's old bike? It's a wreck you know, but, well, I paid the storage and I just hate to let that awful man down at the impound lot have it. Maybe it's worth somethin' in parts. You'd have to go get it though. He said it has to be picked up by two o'clock." Gillis was superstitious about Harleys that had been involved in fatalities, but he was loath to say no to Carter's widow on any account. He bit his bottom lip and nodded as if contemplating his busy afternoon schedule. When he didn't agree instantly, Susie pressed on, poking at her sandal with a nervous finger.

"That man down there? He called me a…" Susie lowered her voice. "He said I was a nigger lover." Gillis turned, a look of authentic perplexity on his face.

"How'd he know that, ma'am?" He asked.

'Know what?" Susie said.

"Knowed you was a nigger lover…I mean…" Gillis meant no harm, but Susie was stunned by the ease with which the phrase rolled off his tongue. He repeated his logic. "I had JD here with me. How could he know you was a nigger lover?"

Susie explained about the young man and his wreck of a Toyota.

"Honest to god, Gillis, I was scared to death that good 'ole boy was gonna follow me home," she admitted.

"Where's it at?" Gillis stood abruptly.

"Sammy's Tow and Store. It's over on…"

"I know where Sammy is," Gillis interrupted. "I'll be back later Ma'am. Go on ahead and use the sprinkler as long as you like. Seems like JD ain't in no hurry to get home." There was unmistakable pride in Gillis's voice. In spite of the diaper failure he'd been an adequate babysitter.

Gillis Lee Wainwright fixed Harley Davidson motorcycles for a living. Augmented by an occasional pot deal for a few close friends and a little luck at the tracks, (the dogs in Sarasota and ponies at Hialeah) it was a good living, all things considered. Among the knowledgeable, Gillis was something of a mechanical genius. Thus said, he was well acquainted with nearly every Hell's Angel within four hundred miles of Miami Beach. Many more than a few of them owed him a favor or two. Several from that category, who were more or less local and who also had a little idle time on their hands of an afternoon, were all too happy to meet Gillis over at Sammy's wreckage yard. Nobody in Gillis Wainwright's circle it seemed was terrifically fond of Sammy.

Gillis knocked on Susie Deane's front door just as she was getting ready to put the baby down for the night. In spite of the day's insufferable heat, she had kept her doors and even her windows locked all day. Gillis fluttered a small piece of paper at the end of his outstretched arm in the door's tiny window. Susie opened up and let Gillis slip his arm around the flimsy screen door. He handed over the five hundred dollar check she had written earlier that day. Susie's face fell.

"Oh, Gillis, he wouldn't give you Carter's bike?" She sounded truly forlorn.

"Oh, no, Ma'am. I got Carter's bike, though you were right. It ain't exactly a bike no more." Gillis bit his bottom lip before a sincerely jovial smile took over his mouth. "I persuaded Mr. Koonz…kinda funny name for Sammy, don't you think?" Gillis tugged at the brim of his cap. "…Anyhow, I told him how it wasn't right how he'd hurt your feelin's earlier today and as a token of his *great remorse…*" (You could tell someone, perhaps one of the more erudite bikers, had provided Gillis with the phrase.) "…he decided that it just warn't right for him to keep your check. He'd a come hisself to apologize but he had a little accident today and he won't be able to drive for a while. He said for me to tell you how awful sorry he is for his *fo paw."* Gillis enunciated the French words carefully then smiled proudly and backed down Susie's steps. "You need anything, Mizz Deane, I'm right over there." Gillis threw an imaginary pitch into his backyard. "You kin unlock your doors and open up your windows now."

"Thank you, Gillis," Susie breathed, and then just to clear the air between them and let him know that there were no hard feelings for his previous *faux pas,* she pushed her screen door wide and stepped onto her porch.

"You're a nigger lover, Mr. Wainwright!" she called softly out into the hot night. But, Gillis's good ear was to the street and he was already almost home so Susie didn't know if he had heard.

Chapter 7

At least twice a week Susie took the baby to the public library, and on her way home, she would almost always wheel baby James into Gillis's garage if his door happened to be open.

"Hey, Gillis." Susie's greeting never deviated.

"Hey, Mizz Deane." Gillis always touched whatever grease stained cap he wore. She habitually turned down his pleasant offer of a cold one and he always lifted baby James up out of the stroller to sit him for a few minutes onto whatever Harley relic he was working on. Neither of the adults acknowledged the obvious when he did that, nor for that matter had Susie ever asked Gillis what he'd done with what was left of Carter's bike. Gillis was their only friend and Susie never complained when the baby's little T-shirts sometimes had big greasy handprints on them. It worried her sometimes though that neither she nor her son had a proper friend.

Gillis Wainwright's successful babysitting enterprise with the garden sprinkler in front of his house had inspired Susie one day not long after to make a small detour. Instead of heading directly home after their library visit, she headed a few blocks out of their way where she knew there was a little park that had a cement wading pool for toddlers. A fountain of sorts squirted up in the center and she had seen kids running through it as their mothers mostly sat on the grass in little gossiping clumps. Today, she thought, would be as good a day as any to introduce themselves to the locals. She parked the little umbrella stroller at the base of a rangy palmetto and undid the strap that secured Jimmy across his round toddler belly. The minute his sandals hit the ground he made a dash for the pool.

"Jimmy!" Susie called. "Jimmy Deane, you come back here and take off your shoes." A heavy set woman with ratted bleached hair and large dark glasses in the closest group of three murmured something to the others and then snickered loudly. Susie pretended to ignore her and took off to salvage Jimmy's shoes from the water. She squatted down in front of him at the pool's edge and unbuckled the leather straps.

"Thank you for waiting, baby," she said. "Now, go on in. See how it feels."

"Cold, Mama!" Jimmy Deane stomped his feet into the shallow pool and squealed with delight when the water sprayed up. Susie jumped back to keep her own sandals from getting wet. "Go on!" she urged him. "Go over and see what the other kids are doing." She stood for a minute with a little brown sandal dangling from each index finger. Jimmy wordlessly joined in the group's pointless running. For a minute or two it seemed as if things would go well. Susie watched, smiling to herself. Then in a flash, so fast Susie had no time to react, an older boy, one maybe five or even six, ran directly across the pool and pushed Jimmy down into the water with both hands. By the time Susie got to them, the older boy was standing over Jimmy, his legs spread and with a look on his face that sent a chill up her spine.

"No niggers allowed here!" the child said in a frighteningly matter of fact growl. He bent down and started splashing water in Jimmy's face. Susie stepped between them and lifted the stunned Jimmy out of the water and ran an urgent hand over his head and down his back.

"Hey!" Susie turned to her son's attacker. "What do you think you're doing?" She grabbed his arm.

"Ouch!" the kid yelled and struggled for freedom. "Lemme go!" he shrieked.

"Where's your mama?" She released him and he made a beeline for the fat woman who had apparently seen it all. The woman was struggling to right herself and more than anything else she resembled a clumsy tilted rhinoceros. Susie clutched Jimmy and was upon the woman before she was upright.

"Did you see what your boy did?" Susie demanded. "Did you hear what he said?"

"I saw," the woman huffed. "I heard him." She had an ugly sun-scorched southern face. She drew it into a snarl. "Look around you. You see any niggers here?" In disbelief Susie's face dropped down to the faces of the two women on the blanket. Only one had shame enough to look away. The other one gave her a blank bored stare and flicked a long cigarette ash at Susie's feet.

"Unbelievable!" was all Susie could bring herself to say before stomping off to the Palmetto. Someone had thrown a browning apple core into the stroller. With a shaky hand Susie picked it up and scanned the park, extending the rotting fruit in her wide-open palm. The three women including the fat one were bending over, crumpled in laughter, sheltering their faces from Susie's glare.

"Unbelievable," Susie whispered again and strapped Jimmy into the stroller. As she walked by, she tossed the apple core onto the center of the blanket in the middle of the three women.

"Maybe if you stuck to these…" Susie said, "…you wouldn't be such a fat ass!" She was so mad her ears were buzzing and she never heard Fatso's two friends laughing. By the time the apple core sailed passed her head she had tears streaming down her cheeks and so she was oblivious to that, too.

She wiped her cheeks with the back of her hand.

"Why are you cryin', Mama?" Jimmy twisted back to look up at Susie.

"I'm not cryin', honey," she said. She sniffed and smiled down at him. "Let's just go back to the library where it's nice and cool." Jimmy Deane turned around and put his thumb into his mouth. It was the first time he realized that Susie didn't always tell the truth and it frightened him more than the bully in the pond at the park ever could.

Chapter 8

Sometimes, the options that a person sees for himself are far more important than the options that actually exist for them. This little nut of wisdom, something that Carter Deane taught his young bride early in their relationship, was what she counted on when she contacted the estranged Elizabeth. Susie was banking on the hope that Elizabeth's perceived options had been winnowed down some by her own widowhood.

"Mama?" Susie got right down to the unspeakable brass tacks. "I'm sick. I've got cancer of the breast and it's the bad kind. The fast kind. The doctor says I'm gonna die. Soon."

That was the easy part. Elizabeth had maintained a tense and utter silence for nearly four solid years; she was silent still.

Susie's voice faltered. "You still there, Mama?"

"I am," Elizabeth said, her own voice sounding incongruously serene.

"Well, Mama, I need to ask you a favor. I need for you to come down and take care of Jimmy when I.... *when I go.*" Susie thoughtfully selected a euphemism since she knew her mother favored them when speaking of death. She had prepared for this request for days. Now she sweetened the pot. "Mama, Carter's life insurance paid this house mortgage off. You won't have any rent to pay. There will be enough money from Social

Security for you to see to Jimmy's needs. And, yours, too. Some," she added honestly.

"I'll get back to you," Elizabeth said and hung up the phone. Without the hesitation of a house cat that has spotted a scurrying mouse, Susie's mother dialed the number for St. Benedict's rectory and requested an urgent audience with the senior pastor. She knew the number by heart. Elizabeth was one of those Catholic women who flirted with her priests. Her long standing unrequited romance with Father Boyle was oddly fueled by his consummate lack of ardor in return. She mistook this disinterest as the burden of the unbearable chastity demanded by his frock. Those frocks, coincidentally, she so lovingly tended to in her long-standing capacity as president of the rosary guild of St. Ben's.

"Father Boyle," his secretary informed Elizabeth, "would be in her neighborhood by chance that very afternoon. Would it be possible," the woman asked politely, "for him to drop by Mrs. Breaux's house?" This was an even better outcome of her request than Elizabeth could possibly have hoped for. Father Boyle's only previous house calls had been following the deaths of her son and husband when each time the good Father had paid her a condolence visit. These events some four years earlier and a scant six months apart still shone like jewels as the brightest moments of the last half of Elizabeth's life. Second only perhaps to the secret groping by her own mother's favorite priest that she had allowed as a young girl after Catechism class. Elizabeth pounced like a heartless feline on the opportunity to solicit a little pastoral comfort that Susie's impending death had unexpectedly provided for her. An appointment was arranged for two-ish.

With her dress exchanged for something affording just a little cleavage and a secondary coat of make-up applied, Elizabeth sat in her parlor, breathless in anticipation of Father Boyle's arrival. At the very last moment she hurriedly retrieved a lace-trimmed handkerchief from the top drawer of her bedroom bureau. She gave it a generous spray of Chantilly perfume and practiced clutching it sympathetically while she waited. It wasn't difficult for Elizabeth to summon wheezy emotion when the priest finally showed up.

"Now, now." Father Boyle sat next to her and patted her heaving shoulder. "What can be so terrible?"

"Oh, Father, it *is* terrible. Just awful. I don't know what I've done that God has turned his back on me. Three times, now!" A fleeting image rose up in Father Boyle's memory. It was of Elizabeth's confession, years earlier, of having succumbed – her word – to her husband's carnal demands, once, (dear God, *once*!) in the eighteen years after their son had been born, without the specific intent to *produce.* The memory of Elizabeth's righteously prim confession caused the priest to grimace.

"Indeed, Elizabeth, these are difficult mysteries to fathom," he said, trying with some difficulty to quell the rising revulsion he felt for his sanctimonious parishioner. "Dear," he said trying to camouflage his true reaction, "you know you can call me George when other *parishioners* are not around." No dummy, George Boyle knew upon which side his bread was buttered and how a little implied intimacy went a sometimes very long way with certain of his female flock, and in particular the aging widows.

"Oh, George," Elizabeth wept and leaned into him, his enjoinder having the desired affect. He put his arm around her and flattened her sprayed hair to check his wristwatch; he had a tee time at four.

"My baby, my poor daughter..." Elizabeth had to gulp for air. "She's dying, George!" To her own surprise, actual tears were stimulated and Elizabeth could only hope that they would not streak her foundation.

"Tell me again, dear, where is your daughter living now?" It wasn't ideal that he could recollect nothing about this alienated daughter, not even her name. He knew that omission played havoc with a parishioner's conviction that they were somehow *important* to him. It was bothersome when he forgot the minutia of their lives.

"She's still down in Hollywood." Elizabeth delicately touched her lace-trimmed, perfumed hankie to her reddened nostrils. Father George waited. "What should I do, George? She's asked me to move there to raise her...*son*." Elizabeth choked a little on the word, giving Father George the opening he needed. He decided that it would be an appropriate time for the two of them to fortify themselves with a little drink.

"Do you have a little sherry in the house, dear?" If he was lucky, where there was sherry there could possibly also be some Scotch.

"In the kitchen," Elizabeth sniffed. "First cupboard on the left." Father George poured a thimbleful of sherry into a glass for Elizabeth and took a generous dose of her cheap Scotch for himself.

"Fortification," he told Elizabeth, sitting back down next to her on the sofa. "God's precious gift for the hard times." He slugged back half his drink and then shifted so that he could take her free hand in his.

"Now, then," he asked. "Where is the child's father?"

"Susie's husband was killed many years ago in an accident. She's a widow…*too*." Elizabeth Breaux batted her eyes and managed to say this with a straight face as if she had been in constant mutually supportive communication with her daughter.

"There's no one else who could take the child? No other family?" Elizabeth shook her head and twisted the damp handkerchief in her lap.

"There is no one," she said. The priest hesitated while he seemed to ponder her dilemma very seriously.

"Well, then, you must go," Father Boyle finally told her. "It would be your Christian duty, Elizabeth." Elizabeth's eyes grew wide. She had not counted on this turn of events. She had rather hoped that Father George would advise her otherwise and even absolve her. Instructing her to go was almost beyond her comprehension. She stared at him, her mouth gaping like a landed fish.

"George," she finally spoke. An unpleasant insinuating quality was sneaking into her voice. "The child is not her natural child. He was *adopted.*" Elizabeth's implication was unambiguous; an orphan-child was an abomination. But Elizabeth Breaux was barking up the wrong tree here. Father George himself had been raised in a Catholic orphanage. He had often thought that with his striking good looks and natural charisma he would have been, had he had a different upbringing, at the very least a Fortune 500 CEO, and not a common parish priest stuck in Tampa, serving a congregation of former car dealers and assorted blue hairs fleeing the cold of the north in their retirement.

"The church is very *pro adoption*, Elizabeth," he said, an unmistakable note of sternness in his voice. He dropped her hand in favor of his Scotch.

"But, I would have to leave here," Elizabeth whined. "Leave Tampa. Leave my home!"

"Perhaps you could bring the child here, then," Father Boyle suggested without enthusiasm for his own idea. Elizabeth regarded him with true horror. The only scenario she could imagine as possibly worse than moving to Hollywood to raise Jimmy Deane, was moving him to Tampa and having to endure the ignominy of raising a mulatto child among her peers.

"But," Elizabeth lowered her voice as if in conspiracy. "He's a child of Canaan!" Father George, unfortunately, was not exactly up on his Old Testament the way he perhaps should have been. He stared at her blankly.

"The child is a *Negro!* He isn't White," she hissed.

Father George Boyle was many things. Shallow certainly. Vain also, in a peculiarly asexual way, and even odious to some among his congregation. However, having been reared in a Brooklyn orphanage among children of color, who like himself, had been abandoned to a group of mostly sadistic nuns, one thing he was not, was a bigot. The priest knocked back the remaining Scotch and another very dim memory of the funeral for Susie's brother surfaced. The redintegration process took a moment or two. When the complete recollection surfaced he was quite suddenly and frankly filled with obvious revulsion.

"You must do one thing or the other," he told her standing suddenly and without patience. "Either bring the child to Tampa, or go to Hollywood and raise him there. It is your Christian maternal duty," he repeated.

Elizabeth bawled into her lace handkerchief with newfound authenticity. Father George ignored her and longed to refill his tumbler with Scotch. Even more so he longed to flee Elizabeth's house and head out to the country club where the bar in the clubhouse comped his drinks.

"I'm late now for another appointment," he announced after what he deemed a minimally appropriate amount of time. He leaned forward and straightened the creases in his expensive gabardine slacks. "Is there something else you wanted?"

In a piteous little girl voice, Elizabeth asked for his blessing. Father George complied hastily and then instructed her to pray for God to fill her heart with Catholic charity and mercy. She nodded dumbly and then walked him to the door. Closing it behind him she felt as if her fate had been sealed. She sat back down on the plastic slipcover over her damask sofa and rended the lace from her hankie.

Chapter 9

In almost five years it was unprecedented for Susie Deane to actually knock on Gillis Wainwright's front door. At least he had the cognitive wherewithal to be a trifle embarrassed about the surroundings when he let her inside.

"Mizz Deane?" He greeted her at the door.

"Gillis, can I come inside? I have a favor to ask you." Susie looked pale. And, thin.

"I s'pose," he said, and pushed the screen door open. Susie turned around and told Jimmy Deane to play out in front for a minute or two while she spoke with Gillis. The child obediently rode his little tricycle up and down the front walk letting the trike's front wheel bump hard against Gillis's front porch step on every lap.

"Gillis, I have a really big favor to ask of you," Susie said and sank into the only chair in the living room, an ancient filthy recliner that had been, in its youth, a dated hue described as *burnt orange*. Gillis moved over to the side of his front door and stood where he could keep an eye on Jimmy Deane.

"Sure, Mizz Deane," he said peeking out the tattered front door screen. "Whatever you need."

Susie Deane sighed loudly and held her hand up to her head.

"I need you to take Jimmy… and...." Susie looked up, her face stricken with emotion. "I need you to raise him." Gillis looked back. He looked as much like a curious chimpanzee as anything else.

"Mizz Deane?" he said.

"I'm gonna die, Gillis," Susie said. "I've got six months. At the outside." Susie knew that Gillis was a gambler. "I have no odds Gillis. I'm a goner." Gillis let his body lean hard into the doorframe.

"Ma'am?" he asked.

"Oh, shit, Gillis. I've got cancer. I probably should have done something a while ago. I just...I don't know." Susie's head dropped low on her chest. Gillis watched little dark tear stains appear on her denim shorts. The only sound came from the little tricycle outside bumping up against the bottom stair step of Gillis's front porch. He'd never once heard a foul word from his neighbor's mouth. The word shit, more than the remaining content of her little speech, impressed him mightily.

"You ain't got no kin, Mizz Deane?" Gillis finally ventured.

"Just my own mama," Susie said and wiped her eyes with the back of her hand.

"Hold on," Gillis said and disappeared. He returned and handed Susie a roll of toilet paper. She couldn't help but laugh.

"You see, Gillis?" she said. "This is why I want you to take him. You are a kind man. There's a lot he can learn from you." Gillis Wainwright's eyes were wide and glassy. "Plus," Susie added. "I'm afraid of what he could learn from my mama." Silence hung in the air for too long.

"Mizz Deane?" Gillis finally said. "I cain't be no daddy to your boy. Hell, half the time I ain't even here. I don't know nothin' about kids. I ain't never had a daddy of my own. And, barely had a mama if you know what I mean." Again, a protracted silence ensued. “I been in jail, ma’am...twice.” Susie’s head dropped again.

“Okay, Gillis,” Susie said wiping her nose. “It’s alright. I already asked my mama to come. I just thought…” Susie sighed and looked him directly in the eye. “You’ll help, though? I mean, keep an eye out? My mama....she...well, she’ll come. She’ll see this as her duty. But, she ain’t gonna love him.” Susie rose and walked over to the door and looked out at the little boy driving his tricycle up and down Gillis Wainwright’s front walk. She turned and touched Gillis’s hand.

“Gillis, my boy is half black in a town which has not been friendly to us. He’s gonna need some help.”

“What do you need me to do, ma’am?”

“Well, for starters, will you take Carter’s drums over here? I don’t think my mama can be trusted with them, you know?”

“Sure,” Gillis said.

“And, when he grows a bit…can you let Jimmy play them over here? My mother would never allow that.” Susie cocked her head to the side.

“You did know that Carter loved the drums?” The recollection of Carter, alive and healthy and wailing on his drums put a wan smile back on Susie’s face.

“Yes ma’am. And, Harleys.” Gillis bit his lip. He looked at the floor. “We mostly talked about Harleys, me and him.” It was barely a whisper and meant as an excuse or an apology.

“Well, tell him about his daddy, will you?” Susie asked. Gillis nodded.

“And sometimes, tell him about me, too.” Her voice dropped down. “I’m tired, now, Gillis. I can’t thank you enough. Pretty soon I’ll have my mama come. You let her know that you’re keepin’ a look out. Maybe that will help.”

Susie Deane walked down the narrow cracked walkway leading from Gillis Wainwright’s porch to the street with

Jimmy Deane trailing her on his trike. When she reached the street she turned and lifted her hand.

“Thank you,” she mouthed soundlessly.

“Uh huh,” Gillis grunted.

Two days later Gillis interrupted the tune up on a vintage Indian and showered and dressed in clean Khaki pants and a brand new, spotlessly white, Fruit of the Loom T-shirt. He drove his Harley over to the public library and went in and got himself a borrowing card. It was easier than he’d ever thought possible.

Chapter 10

Susie's preparations for death were practical. She no longer believed in a merciful God and therefore wasted no effort in prayer. Instead she made a list of the things she wanted to do before she died and she set about accomplishing each task with the kind of urgency only a dying mother can muster. Every item on her list pertained to the five year old child she would leave behind. She tried to anticipate what he would need most in her absence and to provide it as best she could, if only from the grave. She made a valiant effort to continue with most of the rituals they had established after Carter's death.

Each night, before her own strength gave out, she played one side of a carefully selected record album for him, sometimes singing along. She tenderly tucked him into bed and sat with him until he was sleeping soundly. Some nights she talked to him, trying to tell him things that she thought he should know, things about Carter and everything she could remember about every day of his young life up until then. Some nights she was too overwhelmed even to speak. On those nights she only hummed certain songs over and over and stroked the fine fluff around his head while she gave in to her deep regret and fell asleep next to him.

Carter's drums were moved over to Gillis Wainwright's house next door and a thrift store couch and coffee table replaced them. Carter's beloved stereo components were put low to the floor in Jimmy's bedroom. Right away Gillis gamely set the drum kit up as best he could in his unused small second bedroom amidst the considerable debris one might expect someone like Gillis to accumulate in his spare room.

Susie herself moved the record albums that she and Carter had conjointly collected, relocating them from cinder block and board shelves in the living room into Jimmy's bedroom. Sometimes only able to carry two or three at a time she arranged them in milk crates on the floor of his small closet in the order of Carter's favor as best she could remember. The newer ones, the ones she had added to the collection after Carter died, were separated from the others so that when Jimmy played them he would have a sense of each parent distinct from the other. She expected that the distinction would be available to him only viscerally but she didn't care. She knew that the music he inherited from them might be the only way he remembered them and how much they had loved him. She played the musicians whose bands were featured on the posters on every possible inch of wall in Jimmy's room and told him stories about the concerts she and Carter had seen. She spent several nights on all the Jimmies she could think of: Jimi Hendrix, Jim Morrison, James Taylor, Jimmy Page… She told him stories too about the great James Dean who was the greatest actor who ever lived and Carter's favorite.

"And just like you, darlin'," she told the wide-eyed boy. "James Deane's mama and daddy named him after a very famous person."

"Who, Mama?" Jimmy wanted to know everything.

"His mama loved the famous poet, Lord Byron, so she named her little boy, James Byron Dean." Jimmy Deane nodded.

“Was he a drummer, Mama?” Jimmy asked. Susie smiled.

“No, sweetheart, but they say that he loved music very much.” Jimmy listened to Susie each night and he never asked the single question she was dreading. She never wanted to have to tell him that James Dean died in much the same way Carter had.

Elizabeth called Susie and informed her tersely that she was prepared to perform her Catholic duty though she was not at all pleased to do so. She asked no questions and made no statements at all about Jimmy save for a demand that Susie please exhaust all possible alternatives for his care before Elizabeth was forced to give up her life to do it.

“No alternatives,” Susie told her holding back her own sobs. Then the child should be informed that he was to call her only Elizabeth and he should not be told that he was in any real way related to her by blood. She would need no more than a few days notice and Susie should therefore make do without her until the very last possible minute.

After Susie stocked the small dresser and closet with new pants and shirts, (some a little big for him to grow into) and let him pick out a small backpack for the start of kindergarten in September, Susie’s one remaining task was to explain to him what was about to happen and indeed what already had happened to his other three parents.

On the single hottest evening she could ever remember she let him select a record and he picked *James Taylor-sweet baby james.* His selection made her smile and then cry. She watched him carefully lift the dust cover and felt proud that he could, at age five, put the album on the turntable without scratching it. She gave him one final lesson in using the too-big headphones for...for *after*. When Elizabeth was there.

They snuggled under the sheet in his twin bed listening to James Taylor, both of them cold in spite of the temperature outside. When the album was finished Susie heard the deep and even breathing that told her Jimmy had fallen asleep next to her. She sighed deeply but lacked the strength even to cry.

"I'm so sorry, little guy," she whispered. "I cannot stay with you. I wish I could." She had a much bigger speech prepared but since he had fallen asleep she decided to postpone it for just one more night. Not awake, but not quite sleeping either, she was roused around two in severe pain. Worse than any she had felt before. And, she was hot. She had never in her life felt such heat in her body. She slipped from Jimmy reluctantly and made her way to the telephone. Elizabeth answered on the first ring as if she'd been waiting up for the call.

"Yes?" she answered sounding alert.

"It's time. Come, Mama." Susie barely had the strength to speak.

"Can you wait two days? I have some things to tend to here."

"I'll wait," Susie told her and hung up the phone. Elizabeth arrived by taxi two days later and made herself a bed on the living room sofa. Jimmy Deane was over at Gillis Wainwright's place being watched over until the end, Susie's last request of him.

"I'll send my mother to fetch him when it's time," she told Gillis without even attempting to smile.

"Just...just keep an eye out for him, please, Gillis?" Gillis nodded and turned his head.

He held Jimmy Deane's small hand on the way over to his house and then later, when he'd seen the taxi deposit Susie's mother on the sidewalk out front, he put the boy in his truck and drove downtown in search of the right kind of store to buy some drumsticks.

Chapter 11

Jimmy Deane

I watched from Gillis Wainwright's front porch when the men came in the big black car. It was the biggest car I ever saw. I knew that they were coming for my mama and I knew what dead meant. I also knew that what it was they were moving on that table with the wheels was not really my mom, but I did not know where she was or if I would ever see her again. Somehow it was sadder for me when the big truck from Mattress World showed up a while later and I watched two different men carry a brand new mattress in the front door and minutes later bring the old mattress out. The way they threw that old mattress in the back of their truck…well, it was just sad is all.

Gillis walked me back to my house after he heated up some Spaghetti Os. He told me several times, "I want to make sure you know that I am right next door here, JD. Right next door." He had a little tussle with my grandma. Something about *services*. When he left our house and stomped off home he forgot to say goodbye and he looked so mad I didn't know if I would ever see him again, but, sure enough, two days later when my grandma took me to the cemetery, there he was.

I hardly recognized Gillis on account of he was wearing a suit and a tie, his suit looking kind of old and a little small, like maybe he'd borrowed it or had it left over from some other funeral a long time ago. The tie made me think about my dad and what he used to tell me about ties being something men had to do at certain times whether they liked them or not. I guess funerals would be one of those times.

My grandma did not say hello to Gillis, nor did she speak much to the preacher who had come to read some things from a little black book that had long skinny ribbons holding places in it, I guess to mark where the important things to say were. Gillis did not say hello either but a few minutes into the preacher's talking I heard him start to mutter under his breath. I don't know why, but I started to get real afraid just then. The preacher didn't look too happy either and then he got what I would call downright *fitful* when Gillis grabbed the shovel that the cemetery men had stuck into the pile of dirt nearby. They had already put the wooden box with my mama inside down into the ground and Gillis just started shoveling dirt into the hole like he was going crazy. The preacher touched his arm, gently I think, but Gillis just shook him off.

"Mother fucker!" he said real loud, though I don't believe that he meant it personal to the young preacher who was only trying to help.

"Son," he said and he was tugging once again on the too-short sleeve of Gillis's suit. It seemed funny even to me that the preacher was calling Gillis "son" when he looked to be about half Gillis's own age, and when he finally got Gillis's attention Gillis looked wild. I was afraid of what might happen then. But, nothing truly bad did. Gillis spat on the ground, dropped the shovel next to the hole and shook the preacher's hand off.

"Padre?" Gillis was talking to the preacher. "If you try to tell me that God works in mysterious ways, I will lay you out," Gillis said. "And, ma'am?" he turned to Grandma who hardly flinched but I noticed that she was workin' her rosary pretty good. "Ma'am, your Jesus is a mother fucker. Don't you forget that." Grandma didn't even blink, she just kept pullin' on those beads like there was no tomorrow. Then Gillis dropped down on one knee in the fresh dirt in front of me. He didn't even care about getting his pants dirty it seemed. "JD," he said to me. "Your mama is down there in that box. She ain't never comin' home. Your grandma here is gonna take care of you, but, I am right next door. Hear?" He looked up at Grandma who turned away. "You hear?" he told her. "I am right next door." She did not bother to answer him, nor did he wait for a response. He got up quick. Didn't even brush the dirt from his pants leg, just turned around and yanked off his tie as he lurched back toward his truck. It looked to me like he was headed somewhere in a big hurry or I might have asked him could I go along. Just as well, since his truck did not come back home until the next day and even when it did, his garage door, which was almost never shut, stayed closed for two whole days after that.

Book two - Chess

And games of mostly chance

All of life is foreshadowing.
- Steven Kotler, *West of Jesus*

Chapter 12

Jimmy Deane

My grandma was not a talker. That much I can tell you about her. Except for telling me, "eat this here" or "get to bed," I don't think she said anything at all for several days after my mama's funeral. Then out of the clear blue on a Saturday, early in the morning, she came into my room and looked around good. She seemed kind of distressed, like maybe she ate something that did not sit well or maybe she was smelling something that she didn't like the scent of too much. "Boy," she told me. "I'm goin' to mass. Don't get in any trouble while I'm gone." And, out the door she went.

I wasn't hardly out of bed yet, but as soon as she left I took the opportunity to turn on the little black and white television set that she had brought with her which now sat up on my mama and daddy's dresser. Until that one had arrived with her I had not yet seen a television except for the one they had up on the wall in the library, and that one didn't count because it was never on when my mama and I visited. So right there in my grandma's bedroom some old man was hollerin' and talkin' in a way that sounded almost like a song, except for the way he seemed so awful miserable. Furthermore, he seemed to be so all-about-trying-very-hard-to-scare-people that I just could not see the attraction to anything at all he had to say. I climbed up on my mama's big bed, but it didn't feel right and I remembered about the men who came earlier in the week to take away her mattress and I felt like crying so I went back to my own room and put on some records. They made me feel even worse, but somehow better too in a way I cannot say.

I did not hear my grandma return on account of my mom had made me promise that I would use the headphones when I listened to music. I must have forgot to turn off that little television or maybe I mussed grandma's quilt up on the bed. Whatever it was I did, it sure unleashed a fury in my grandma. After her fury was spent, there was lasting damage done to my daddy's records and I still have one tiny little scar up over my right eye that to this day makes my eyebrow on that side look just the tiniest bit short. You wouldn't hardly notice if I didn't point it right out.

I have to admit, and I am not proud, that at one point I had the thought to bite her. I had the opportunity several times and I was surely mad enough. But, I kept remembering what my mama had said: that my grandma would be a hard case, *(that's what she said, a real hard case,)* and that I should not expect her to be either soft or loving, but that she would not hurt me. She told me that the way that she herself had survived as a girl and the best way anyone has of surviving a *hard case* was to be as good as you could be so as not to rile them up at all. So that is why I did not bite her when she was smashing my daddy's albums. I cleaned up the blood from the cut over my eye as best I could since it seemed to make her madder all over again when the bleeding would not stop.

Then, as quick as things had got started, they stopped altogether. It was almost like she was having a spell or something and when the spell was gone she remembered that she had a jelly donut and a cup of coffee that she had got at the

Donut Inn on her way back from the church, and they were still sitting out on the kitchen table, her coffee probably getting cold. I don't know why, but I did not cry. I just waited until she was done with her donut and I did my best to clean up my room, saving even the broken records and hiding them underneath my bed.

In the afternoon she opened up the door to my room again and told me, "Come, boy!" And, I did, even though part of me thought to just say, *no ma'am, thank you, I'll stay right here if you don't mind.* She walked fast for an old lady and I had to run a little bit just to keep up with her. Once we got past the market and then even past the public library, which was the furthest I had ever been with my mama, I started worrying about where it was she might be taking me. Funny to think about it now that I must have been afraid she was going to get rid of me, but when you're a kid, you just don't know some things, so you get afraid for the silliest reasons. Anyways, she walked and walked and I followed right along, like I said, having to run some of the time, and then she went inside a place where there were a lot of cars and lots of people and most of the men were wearing ties and big gold rings on their hands and were right away asking, "How do, Ma'am? What can we do for you, today?" So, it turned out we were at the used car lot that now that I'm older seems pretty close to home, just a block or two beyond the boulevard. What my grandma was doing was purchasing herself a new used car. The one she picked was almost as big as the one that they took my mama away in, but Grandma's was pink and it had big pointy fins on the back that made it look more like a big old boat than a car really. And, of course Grandma's car had a seat in the back instead of a big space for the table on wheels. I must say, that old Cadillac was a comfortable old ride compared to the only other cars I'd ever been in, mama's old Nova and Gillis Wainwright's beat up truck, which was little more than a jalopy, Mama said.

Grandma finished her transaction, made arrangements for the Nova to be picked up at a later date and then ordered me into the back seat of her new car with a warning about what would happen if she caught me playing with those little magic buttons on the doors that opened up the windows. In the interests of not riling her up again I heeded her warning though I had a mighty powerful urge to make those windows go up and down. She did not talk to me nor did she play the radio, though as I recall now, that old Cadillac also had a very fine radio for its day.

We drove for a while and when she finally stopped and parked, she ordered me out of the car and I obeyed, watchful that she was going to get out too, still worrying that she was going to leave me somewhere and never come back. She did get out of the car of course and I noticed two things right off. First, everybody on the street had skin as dark, or darker, than mine. It was a marvel to me since I had never seen another living person with skin so dark. The second thing I noticed, very nearly as obvious, was how nervous it made my grandmother to be where we were. I guess I thought it had something to do with her car at first because of the way she fidgeted with the door lock for several minutes and then went around checking to make sure all four doors were properly locked before she led me down the street. The farther we got away from her new pink car the more nervous she became and whatever it was that was scaring her made her clutch her purse out in front of her as if her life depended on what was inside. She relaxed slightly when we approached and went into a store that had a big fat pole outside turning with big red and white stripes on it. It turned out that this was Sam's Barbershop. A little bell at the top of the door sounded our arrival and though the shop was crowded full, (it was a Saturday, after all) when we walked inside, the noisy room was silenced like a gunshot had been fired. The only sound remaining was the gentle buzzing of the hair clippers.

The chairs along the wall were all occupied with dark skinned men and boys, every single one of them gaping at me and my grandma. The four barbers' chairs in front of the mirrors each had a haircut in progress. After an awkward little moment, the barber nearest the door held his clippers away from his client's head and spoke up.

"Yes, Ma'am?" I don't imagine too many white women had ever wandered into Sam's Barbershop up on Imperial Avenue to ask him for directions but Sam was making no assumptions. Suddenly every patron in the shop turned away from us and seemed to be watching, with enormous concentration, the soundless baseball game on the TV set high in the corner. Grandma turned a hurried eye to the line of men and boys against the wall.

"How long is the wait?" she asked and nodded to me.

"That's good enough, Sam." The neatly trimmed man in Sam's chair swiveled around toward the big mirrors. Sam gave him a nod.

"I'll fit the child right in, Ma'am," Sam told her. He looked over to the men waiting their turn against the wall. "Terrence, what's a matter with you, man? Give this lady your seat." Sam spun his client around, brushed him off with a funny little broom and pulled the green cape away from his shoulders. A young man, not much older than a teen-ager who I supposed was Terrence jumped up out of his seat and gestured to my grandma.

"Ma'am," he said pointing down at his empty seat. Grandma ignored him and remained standing. The boy named Terrence looked down at me. He opened up his hands and pushed his bottom lip out so far I wished I could reach out and touch it. Then he looked back up towards Sam and Sam just raised his shoulders, which I guess meant that Terrence could sit back down to wait for his turn because that's what he did. Even though nobody in Sam's was doing any talking, it still seemed that lots of things were getting said. When Sam's present client departed, the tinkling of the bell over the door seemed too loud. My grandma pushed me toward Sam's chair. Sam touched the top of my head like he was measuring me and then he reached down on the floor and lifted up a little booster seat that he fit onto his big black leather barber chair.

"Well, now." Sam hoisted me up onto the booster and examined the soft cloud of hair that my mom had allowed to get a little out of hand. "What we got goin' on here? You ever been in a barbershop before, son?" I shook my head. "You never had your hair cut?" He turned the chair around so I could see myself in the wall sized mirror.

"My mom usedta," I whispered though my own voice sounded way too loud to me. "But, she ain't coming back," I explained. Sam nodded. He patted my shoulder as if it were perfectly normal for mothers of five-year-old boys to disappear. He glanced in the mirror at my grandma, but she had moved over to the window keeping her back to the whole shop.

"So…your mama been cuttin' your hair?" Sam pumped the chair up to the right height with his foot and made my whole body disappear under the green cape around my neck.

"Well, I can see she been doin' right by you. Yes, sir, she been doin' a fine job. But, comes a time when a man's gotta go to the *Shop*. Ain't that right boys?" The other black men in the barbershop murmured their general assent, all but the one called Terrence, who it seemed had already give up trying to be nice to me and my grandma. Sam clicked a comb against a scissor and paused. He looked at grandma in the mirror. She met his glance for just one second.

"Make it as short as you can," Grandma told him without turning. Sam nodded and exchanged the comb and scissors for his clipper. It took less than a minute and when Sam was finished he touched my shoulder and his eyes met mine. His hand felt warm. He would tell me later, that when he gave me my first haircut he felt like he had just given a lamb its first shearing.

"How much?" My grandmother took a single step toward Sam's chair and opened up her purse.

"Two fifty," Sam said. He reached for a jar of lollipops on the counter under the mirror. She shook her head.

"No thank-you," she said. Her words were polite but her voice sounded hard. She laid two dollar bills and two quarters down on the counter and walked over to the door. Sam took his time brushing the hair away and removing my cape. He lifted me up and out of the chair gently, it seemed a little higher than was necessary, all the while keeping his back to grandma.

"Come, boy." She turned and paused underneath the tinkling bell. "I'll bring him by next week," she told Sam and was outside on the sidewalk before he had even released me.

"Stay out of the sun, boy," Sam whispered. "You can almost pass if'n you keep that nappy head close." I blinked up at him unsure of his meaning.

"Okay," I agreed finally so as not to disappoint him. He opened the door for me and stepped aside. I had to run to catch up to my grandma, now already fifty yards gone down the sidewalk. She paused outside the Vendome liquor store at the corner and waited for me to catch up. Once inside, as fast as she could, she grabbed two big bottles and struggled with them to the counter.

"That be all, Ma'am?" the young clerk asked her politely when she set the bottles down. Grandma nodded. He rang up her sale and she could not get out of the store fast enough. Her hands trembled on the wheel and I touched my head about a million times where my hair had been while we drove home. I did not know exactly why but I knew that what had just occurred had been important.

"What are you staring at?" Grandma put the car into park and turned off the engine. I thought it best not to answer. "Get in the house. Change your clothes. Don't make a mess."

"Okay, Grandma." I was trying hard to be very good. Still she gave me a cold look.

"Don't call me Grandma," she said. "My name is Elizabeth."

"Okay," I said, but I must have forgot before I even got to the front porch.

"Grandma?" I turned and called. Elizabeth stared straight ahead.

"Grandma?" I called still louder. Still she ignored me.

"Elizabeth?" Finally, I got it right. She lowered the power window but never took her eyes off the windshield.

"Is my mama comin' home?" I asked her.

"You heard him," Elizabeth said, I suppose speaking of Gillis and his little speech at the cemetery. She raised the window back up and sat out in the Cadillac for a long, long time.

Chapter 13

Jimmy Deane

That poster that my papa had chosen for me? The one he had put up behind my bedroom door on the day he died? That was the only one to survive the tumult caused by my grandma. It was also the only poster I had with the picture of an actor and not a musician. I think it was not torn to bits like all the others just because my grandma did not see it behind the opened door when she did her damage, and therefore she did not even know that it was there. I don't think it was because she was any fan of James Dean. I saved the pieces of all the others. I don't know why exactly, except maybe I thought that one day, when I was older, I could somehow make them right. Tape them up or something, and maybe, put them all back up. It felt so lonely to look at blank walls that had little bits of tape still stuck all over the place.

I don't really know why she tore the posters all down. I just know that after she had drank half of one of her bottles while she was watching that screechy man on the TV, her mood got progressively worse until she came crashing into my room like a cat on fire. She was screeching just like the man on the TV and hollering and spitting and stumbling around. Once she got it in her head that those posters were a bad thing, "the devil's work" she called them, that was it. She did not stop until every one was torn to pieces on the floor. Every one except James Dean who was hiding behind the door and smoking his cigarette.

"Pick this trash up," she told me and she sounded like she hardly had enough energy to make the words come out. "Then come and eat." Like I said, I hid those torn posters under my bed. By the time I arrived out in the kitchen Elizabeth had prepared a cup of tomato soup but she had made it with water, not milk like my mama would do. I didn't feel at liberty to offer my preferences and anyway she was already back glued to her little TV set in the bedroom with the volume turned up very loud. I didn't feel too much like eating but I ate it anyway and washed and dried my cup the way my mom had taught me. Somehow, doing things the way Mama told me to do them made me miss her just a little bit less.

My grandma had fallen asleep on the bed, still dressed in all her clothes and with the TV set still blaring. I myself went straight to bed and I'm ashamed to say that I was so forlorn I began to cry like I had never cried before. I got up once to check to make sure my door was closed and closed tightly. Just then James Dean looked ridiculously happy to be the only remaining poster in my room, but it seemed to me that he looked guilty too. I think that's what they call survivor guilt, when a person is pretty happy to be all in one piece but maybe they think they shouldn't ought to be on account of some others don't have it so good.

I laid there in my bed for a long time, staring up at James Dean and crying. Mostly I was missing my mama, but I was missing my papa too I guess, and strangely, I was missing my hair most of all. I rubbed my hands against the little bit that was left on my head and felt that something critical, something essential to who I was, had been taken from me by my grandma and left like trash over there on that barbershop floor.

"Hey, little man!" I pushed aside my wet sheet. There was no one in my room, though I was certain I had heard someone.

"Boy!" the same voice called out. "Up here!" I looked straight up to the ceiling. Nothing. "Here...over here!" On the back of my bedroom door, James Dean was clearly waving at me with the hand that was not holding a cigarette. "What's the problem, little man?" he asked out loud. I was afraid to answer. "Don't be a cry baby. She didn't take your mom's records, did she? And, she didn't take me down either. You've still got me." I stared and stared at that poster. "Dry your eyes, Jimmy Deane," James Dean said. "And, go to sleep. The old woman isn't going to find me. You're going to be alright. I'll see to that." I watched that poster for a long, long piece of time, but James Dean stopped waving, and he didn't say anything else either. Finally I just fell asleep and in the morning there was nothing unusual about the poster that I could see in the daylight. I studied on it for quite some time with the bright morning sun coming in my window and the only thing that happened was that I came to the conclusion that James Dean himself was not the happiest person either. He had good hair though, that much I could tell and I guessed then that if I had had hair like that my grandma never would have taken me down to Sam's Barbershop.

Chapter 14

Mrs. Weis, the kindergarten teacher

The first day of school is by far the worst. You've got the parents. At least one shows up for each kid or sometimes both, even more than two if the kid has one of those *blended* families. And the kids are all scared half out of their minds, especially the ones who've never been to school before. Half of them are shrieking and even half the moms are crying. It takes almost a full hour to get the parents out and to get the kids settled down to color or something.

On the first day, I always like to use a technique I learned in teachers college. I get students to draw me a picture of their families. You just learn so much. Right off I get to see which ones have a little something on the ball and which ones are having a hard time just holding a crayon in their hand. That way I kind of know how the year is going to go. You'd be surprised at how many of them are practically catatonic with fear that first day, though. So scared they can barely speak. Those are the ones that worry me. Like, what on earth could have happened to a five year old, for God's sake, to make them so scared? The ones who are just a little freaked out to be away from their moms, well, they usually calm right down when you give them a box of crayons and something to do with themselves. Those are the ones who are all happy, happy, happy by the time they go home. And boy, are they suckers for those little gold stars, too. Yep. Give 'em a little star and you just make their day. But, the ones who sit a little too still and stare, like they are waiting for…well, for something, and probably not something too good…those are the ones that scare me. Because the truth is, most of the time something truly scary *has* happened to them, and they are just never going to get over it, no matter who their kindergarten teacher is.

Not that I think it's my job to fix what's wrong in their lives. No, I got over the notion that I was some kind of savior real quick. They are mine for just one year, and only a few hours a day at that. Then they'll all go on to first grade and maybe have some not-so-good teachers and live in their dysfunctional homes forever, or at least until they can run away, and nothing I can do or not do will really make any difference at all. I know that much. But, sometimes, even after all these years, I still get a kid who just gets to me. Jimmy Deane was one like that.

His grandma showed up with him late that first day though she never did say who she was. She was not holding Jimmy's hand and that's always a tip off. We kindergarten teachers notice little things like that. I told her that school starts at nine and it's always better if the children are brought to school a little earlier than that. She just said, "I know what time school starts. *He* will be here by nine tomorrow." The way she said *he*, well, I knew exactly why she didn't want to bring him when all the other parents would see. Not that they'd have cared that first day. No, they're too wound up in their own little crisis leaving Junior off all by himself at his first day of school to take much notice of the color of one of Junior's classmates. Not that first day. Later is when you hear the comments. Once Junior isn't bawling his brains out anymore they start looking for something to be displeased about and that's when one of them will notice that there's something *wrong.*

Elizabeth Breaux walked out without saying even a "good-bye" to Jimmy Deane, and telling me that she would be in her car on the corner at exactly noon to pick him up. *Could I see to it that he got there, down on the corner*, she wanted to know. I said that I would bring him myself if she came just a little later, so that I could see to the other students first and then close up my classroom. "Thank-you. I appreciate the courtesy," she said. I didn't one bit like the way she said it 'cause it sure sounded to me like she thought I was conspiring to help her out of her unpleasant reality.

I will not lie and tell you here that I had no concerns about having a Black child in my class. I did. I was born and raised in South Florida and even though I went to teachers college up north and I had good friends there of all races and religions, still, the truth is, what I see is a person's color first. I would bet you good money that most folks in the South, if they were telling the truth, would say the same. Like it's bred into us, or something. Well, I'll allow that maybe some folks truly don't. I wish I was one of them, but I am not. And, even though I am a card carrying member of the ACLU and I even marched in some civil rights protests in college, well, when that little boy got left off in my classroom that day…let's just say I had to suppress the immediate wish that he was going to be somebody else's problem. Because I knew beyond a shadow of a doubt, that sooner or later, there was going to be some kind of problem.

Now, here's an interesting thing about your average five year old. It is a rare one, and thank God for this, who is what you might call a true bigot. In fact, it isn't until an older sibling or a parent asks about "*that black kid in your class*" or "*that Puerto Rican kid*" that most of my students even notice that there's anything different about a child of color. Kids are funny like that, so not a single one of them said a thing that first day about Jimmy Deane having dark skin. They just scooted their chairs over to make room for him at the table closest to my desk. I put down another big piece of drawing paper in front of him, and pointed out the pile of crayons at the center of the table, and told Jimmy that we were in the process of drawing a picture of our families. (That's how we teachers talk. With liberal use of the royal *we,* when I assure you it has been at least twenty-five years since I have drawn a picture of any kind unless you count cocktail napkins.)

So, this beautiful little boy just nods once and sits right down to work. I was cruising around the classroom, making my positive and encouraging comments, observing. From the far corner of the room I looked them all over. My little charges. Nineteen seventy-four could be my best crop yet I was thinking to myself. No fights had broken out. There was hardly even any talking going on. Very few of them know each other yet of course and only a handful have the mature social skills to interact with peers in a positive way, like sharing or anything, but, still, they were a pretty well behaved bunch. So, it was pretty quiet and I was grateful for that. When I came around to Jimmy Deane's picture, right off I notice that he's drawing exclusively with a black crayon.

"Hmmmm," I say to him, trying very hard to keep my voice neutral. But, I'm thinking. I guarantee you I was thinking up a storm. He has drawn a pretty decent picture of a little child in the middle of the paper, accurately depicting with little curlicues how curly his hair would be if it grew out a little bit. There was only just that one little person on his paper, and he is busy drawing little squares and rectangles all around the periphery.

"Remember now, everyone, we are drawing pictures of ourselves *and* our families, too." I move on before I say it so that he does not feel that he has failed the assignment already.

And, I keep walking among the tables. “Feel free to use all the crayons, children.” I say this because honestly, some of these kids, like Jimmy Deane, don’t know that they can use color even when the whole jumbo assortment is right in front of them. (I don’t even like to think about what that means.)

I make another lap around the room, answer a few questions, send a pair out to the first potty break. It will be a good enough first day if nobody pees their pants, I think. By the time I get to Jimmy Deane again, the noise level has risen considerably and at least half of them are popping up out of their seats so that they can look at other kids’ pictures. It’s actually kind of cute how interested some of them are already in who’s got a big brother and who’s got no daddy, etc. etc. Jimmy Deane was not one of these. He was still working, in black only, on those little boxes around his margins. The only change he had added to his family portrait stopped me in my tracks. Very carefully he had written across his paper up near the top, “JIMMY DEANE IS A ORFAN”. You know, every once in a while I get a couple of kids who maybe can print their names and read some, but this was highly unusual.

“Honey, did you write this?” My question just popped out, so shocking it was to see this perfect script lettered so, so neatly on this boy’s paper. He just nodded, but in his eyes I could see right away that he was unsure if he was in trouble in some way that I had not yet revealed. Well then, I had to fall all over myself to reassure him that it was a wonderful thing, and not some kind of aberration, to write in full sentences on your first day in kindergarten.

“Oh, Jimmy Deane!” I exclaimed. “How wonderful that you can write! Who taught you how to write like this?” He just shrugged, but it was not because he was too shy to answer. He truly did not know who taught him to write because truthfully, it was technically accurate to say that no one had ever taught him. Or, really, he had taught himself. Anyhow, I made a fuss, and then the kids all came to see, and though none of them could read what it said, it still amazed them that one of their own could actually write words. Jimmy Deane became an instant celebrity, but, as those things go, he also made himself, among some of the kids, an object of envy, and that is never good.

The bold ones took up a chant. "What does it say, teacher?" they all wanted to know. I looked at Jimmy. He looked positively placid and I wasn't even sure that he knew exactly what it was that he had written. I *was* sure I knew who had told him he was an orphan and even though I did not yet know what their relationship was, it made me quite anxious on his behalf.

"Do you know what it means, Jimmy? Do you know what you wrote?" He blinked up at me and nodded and I swear the beauty of that child's face, and those long black eyelashes just damn near took my breath away.

"It means I don't have a mama no more, and I don't have a papa neither," he said solemnly. "I don't have any kin." He quoted the old woman. I was sure of it. And then I told a bold faced lie to my students, breaking one of my own strict rules, but like before, it just popped out of me.

"Oh, just like me, Jimmy Deane!" I lied to him and all the others. "I am an orphan, too!" Then I prattled on and on, like Mr. Rogers for God's sakes, talking all about how families are all different and was there anyone else who had no daddy at home, (at least three others) and did anybody besides Jimmy have no mommy at home? I was desperate that he would have at least one friend, but, of course, kindergarten is a little early, so in my classroom that day, I told a big fat white lie so little Jimmy Deane would not be the only orphan he knew.

I'd like to tell you that this event was something I took in stride, but the truth is, it rattled me. I finished out the day with my heart half broken for this little kid who had no kin. I touched his little head every time I walked by and I smiled to beat the band, my special "teacher's pet" smile, and when the parents showed up to get their kids around noon I told him to wait for me so I could see to he found his ride.

Sure enough the old woman was out in front on the corner as she had said she would be. Sitting behind the wheel of the biggest pink Cadillac ever made, fins so sharp you could cut your hand on them. I brought her Jimmy's picture and while he climbed up into her back seat I forced my face into a smile of sorts.

"I'm so sorry that I did not have the time earlier to make a proper introduction," I said. "I'm Mrs. Weis and I will be Jimmy's teacher for this year." I extended my hand inside the open window and she reached up a cold bony hand and pinched, for exactly one second, the very tips of my fingers. It was a little like shaking hands with a crab claw. She did not speak, but instead made some kind of sound in her throat like she had last night's chicken bone stuck down there. I lifted up Jimmy's picture. "I cannot tell you how extraordinary it is for a child this age to have the ability to write in full sentences." I gave her a moment to take a good long look at his assignment. I don't know what I was expecting. Perhaps the decency of some shame or something. But, all she did was start up the engine on the Cadillac.

"He'll be here tomorrow on time. You needn't walk him out again. He knows now where I'll be." She did not say thank you, good-bye or piss in my hat, and off she drove, little Jimmy in the back, lips sealed tight and those unbelievably beautiful eyes just staring a hole in the seat in front of him.

I have to say that a few weeks later, when Jimmy Deane started acting up a little bit in class, and then a whole year later, when he became a bona fide holy terror in Mrs. Dutch's first grade class, well, I for one was a little relieved and it gave me some hope that he might actually survive.

Chapter 15

Jimmy Deane

The old man's real name was not Odie. The men in the shop called him O.D. because he was *Otis's daddy*. Otis was Sam's best friend but I never knew him to come in to Sam's shop. O.D. turned over time into just Odie. But, his real and true name was Professor Robert Douglas Foster and he was, at one time, a very influential man in the biological sciences over in Alabama at Tuskegee University.

By the time I was a Saturday regular at the shop up on Imperial Avenue, Odie was just some old man who sat in the corner all day long at Sam's listening to the gossip and occasionally playing a game of chess with one of the waiting patrons.

I did not pay much attention to him at first. I was usually in and out of Sam's chair in minutes. Sam never liked to keep my Grandma waiting long, even though she didn't even bother to come inside after the first time. He didn't like the thought of her sitting out back behind the Vendome I guess, on account of what kind of judgments she might be passing about the folks who went in and out.

At first, I thought it was me that Sam couldn't wait to get rid of. The way he'd bump me up in line no matter how many men and boys were sitting against the wall waiting. That was a reasonable assumption I suppose, but it is also true that I'm prone to be sensitive to feelings like that.

Destiny intervened one day. It happened after a couple of month's worth of haircuts when Grandma's car battery died out back of the liquor store while she was waiting for me. Sam had his car parked out there, too, and when he came out to go somewhere we were still sitting and waiting for a tow truck to arrive. Now here is one of those events that you just know were somehow meant to be. Destined to be. And nothing, not even the way my Grandma felt about Black folks could have prevented it. I believe that it was my destiny that day to get a ride home in Sam's Buick, me up front with Sam while Grandma insisted that she ride in the back seat, I think where she could sneak some sips from her pint without us seeing her, or maybe where she could pretend that Sam was her driver and she was a lady of some means. I don't know for sure what she was actually doing, but I do know that after Sam gave us that ride home and when Grandma took me down to the colored part of town the following Saturday, my life was changed in the most significant way for the better.

I arrived at the shop as usual. Sam sent me right back down to the Vendome and told me to tell my grandma that he had too many customers waiting to get to me right away that day. He said to tell her that she could either wait a few hours or she could go on home and leave me to wait my turn. Since he had driven us home the week before, he now knew the way and he could give me a ride home later that afternoon when things at the shop calmed down. She said nothing when I told her. She just started up her car and drove away.

"She gone?" Sam asked when I walked back in. I said yes and the whole barbershop broke into a cheer. It took me a moment to realize that they were cheering because she was gone and *I was not.* An unreasonable happiness flooded my whole being. I must have smiled I think. Then a knocking sound in the corner caused everybody to turn around and look at Odie. He crooked his good finger at me to come on over and I looked up at Sam.

"Go on. Odie ain't gonna bite you," Sam said.

"Odie ain't got no teeth," somebody else said and everybody laughed. Odie smiled too, but only half his mouth moved. His one good eye though was full of laughter as if to say that that was the funniest thing he'd ever heard. I walked on over and stood beside the table. Odie used his good hand and pointed into the seat of the chair across from him. I sat down. The chess pieces were all in place, white ones in front of Odie, black in front of me. Odie's good hand hovered over the smallest white piece. He waited until he was certain I was watching carefully, then he moved it forward two squares.

Sam and the others went back to their own business and continued to cut hair, though I could see in the big mirror that now and then they were all sneaking peeks at me and Odie. Whenever he caught me looking anywhere but at the chessboard Odie's tapping hand would call me right back. Then he'd nod down at the pieces and move another one. At last he had left only five pieces, the big white crown, the two smaller crowns, black and white, and the two horses. He spread his good hand out over the board as if to say, *there, that's what you want to do.* He waited until I nodded up at him and then with his good hand he immediately set about replacing all the pieces back into the rows they had been before he had started to move them. This time though, he put all the white pieces in front of me and he took the black pieces for himself.

He sat staring at the board for a long time. Then he tapped his finger on the table and pointed it at me. I moved the first piece forward two squares exactly as he had. He smiled his half smile and made the second move. I made the third as I recalled it. He made the fourth, and so on. The moves went much faster with me helping him out on every other move. When we were finished and all the moves had been replicated, his little half smile appeared again and he slapped his hand on the top of his leg in an awkward applause. Odie showed me three more chess games that day in the same way, playing first all the moves himself and then watching the second time through to make sure I had memorized every move. It was nearly four o'clock. Almost nobody had left the shop. All of them were watching us. When our last game ended, Odie turned slightly in his chair to pick up his cane and to let me know my lesson was over.

"He everything you thought he would be?" Sam called out. Odie tapped his cane three times and the corner of his mouth turned up and stayed there.

"I thought so," Sam said.

I asked if I could use the bathroom and Sam said sure. While I was inside I heard them talking. It was Terrence who asked.

"So, what you think, Sam? What that ole' white woman doin' with this boy?"

"Don't know and it ain't our business, neither, Terrence," Sam said sharply.

"Well, I think some nigger had hisself a little piece a' white girl and that there is her pickaninny, and then the girl took off and she left her very pissed-off momma to raise the child. That there's what I think," Terrence told them all. A different voice, one that sounded like music called out.

"Once you had black, you ain't never comin' back!"

"Shut up, Lamont," Sam said. "That boy got a tough row to hoe."

" 'Least he smart, man. You see the way he played with Odie? Man alive. He one 'a them boy geniuses or somethin'."

The shop fell stone quiet when I opened the bathroom door.

"Say your good-byes, boy. I'm takin' you home," Sam said and he reached up to retrieve his straw hat from a hook. At the car Sam reached into his pocket and pulled out a lollipop.

"How'd this thing get in here?" he asked. "Can you do me a favor and take this off of my hands. I hate to have these things fallin' outta my pockets everywheres I go. You know what this is for?" I nodded and then I unwrapped it and quickly popped it into my mouth, as much to please him as to impress him with my vast knowledge of lollipops. "Thank-you," he said as if I had done him a large good turn. "Now hop on in. We'll take the scenic route to your house." About halfway home, Sam looked over at me and said, "Hey, you like this here music?" I removed my lollipop.

"I do." I said.

"I could tell," he said. "By the way you was keeping time with your feet there." He smiled. His teeth were huge and his gums were as pink as bubble gum.

"I like this music fine myself," he said. On a break in the music Sam looked over at me. "Sometimes," he told me solemnly, "we got to pay special attention to the fine times so's that the not-so-fine times don't get us down. You know what I'm talkin' about?" I didn't really, but I nodded yes because I did not want to disappoint Sam. When I was done with my lollipop we were suddenly right in front of my house. At the end of our street Gillis Wainwright stepped out of his garage with a polishing rag and a chrome wheel in his hands. He waved the rag at us and Sam let his big hand open at the top of his steering wheel.

"Be cool," Sam advised as I opened up the heavy Buick door. He peered across at my house and shook his head. "I'll see you next Saturday," he said. As he drove past Gillis, Sam raised his hand once more and I saw that Gillis nodded before he went back inside his garage. Sam's Buick rolled smoothly around the corner.

The next week was awful. Long and boring. The only good thing about school and the only thing I liked was going to the library. Sometimes Mrs. Weis would send me over there just because I was driving her crazy. She had tried to get the principal to advance me to the second grade but the principal had shook his head and told her, as if I wasn't standing all ears right in front of them, "Terry, they would eat him alive up there. Just do the best you can."

"He's done all the third grade work, now. He's reading at sixth. He's bored to death in here," she said. "We're going to lose him!" It sounded almost like she might be crying.

"Do the best you can. It's safer," the principal said and walked away. I did not know at the time that she was trying to do me a favor. As I said, it always seemed to me that people were trying to get rid of me and I guess I assumed that about Mrs. Weis, too. I didn't figure out until much later that she was actually trying to help me out.

At the time I thought that the only people who were on my side were the men in the barbershop and I guess that's why everywhere else, especially at school and at home, I was miserable and I tried to make everybody else as miserable as I was if I had half a chance. But, down at Sam's? Down there I was a model citizen.

I spent every Saturday at Sam's playing chess with Odie, listening to the men needle each other in a way that let you know they really cared about one another, and eventually I started sweeping up around the chairs a little bit. At the end of the day, Sam always ran a quick clipper over my head and told me to keep my two-fifty for all the work I had done, and then he drove me home with a lollipop in my mouth.

About the time I started to beat Odie at chess more games than not, he took me back to the little apartment that was behind the barbershop. He showed me his tape deck and a turntable that was very nearly just like my dad's. His music collection was vast and it made the crates of records that I had in the bottom of my closet from my mother and father look plain paltry by comparison. And Odie had him some books, too. Wherever the shelves on every wall of that little room did not hold music, they held books.

When I went into the back we always listened to the albums instead of the tapes because Odie could manage the tapes just fine without any help. With only one arm it was near impossible to put an album on the turntable. I took that chore on as my job and putting on the albums for Odie was a job that I had been born to do. If at first Odie thought it strange that a child of five could manage to take an album out of its cover and put it on the turntable and drop the needle without the slightest mishap or scratch, he did not let on. It always seemed to me, in spite of the fact that he never said one single word, he was telling me that he just expected great things from me. His albums were stored in alphabetical order and once he got seated he would scribble on a piece of paper with his good hand and hold it out to me, and I would find his selection and put it on. Sam must have told Odie that I liked the drums and some days his list would be all about one or another drummer who had played for the greatest jazz bands in America. My favorite by far came to be Mr. Elvin (Ray) Jones.

"Coltrane," Odie would scribble. Then, "Charlie P." Then, "Miles Davis." And if we had the time, "Wardell Gray" and maybe "Charles Mingus." Odie had 'em all and Elvin played with every one of them. Sometimes it looked like Odie was asleep but he never ever was, just dreaming without being asleep. Probably he was dreaming about a time before his first stroke when he might have danced to some of that music with a nice girl or even played the drums himself. It occurred to me once, watching Odie with his eyes closed and his little half a smile on his face, his good hand moving in time, that Sam was right. You had to take the good times and make them really count so that when the bad times hit you, you could still be okay.

My grandma continued to drive me up to Sam's every Saturday, though that was the only nice thing she did for me, if you want to know the truth. I figured out that she went as much to get cheap liquor at the Vendome and to get rid of me for the whole afternoon as anything, but I didn't care. I lived for Saturdays at Sam's. I made the mistake, as most of us do after a while, of forgetting to really focus on my good times, and right when I had started to take those precious Saturdays for granted I had my run in at school with the fourth grader, Billy McCormack.

My second grade teacher did not appreciate what my kindergarten teacher had referred to as my *lively imagination.* Her exasperation with me occurred with amazing regularity and I was a consistent tenant of the bench outside the principal's office. When I asserted to a classmate one particular day that I could remember every single thing that had ever happened to me, clear back to my birth and the day my mother gave me away, the little girl broke down in tears and the teacher sent me packing for the third time in a single week. My referral slip read *Jimmy Deane is talking weird again.* When I arrived at his office, the principal was off attending to a calamity in another classroom, but Billy McCormack, a fourth grader who looked old enough to be in sixth, was sitting on my bench. He was white, and as I said, big, and if only half the rumors about him were true, my fear in his presence was entirely justified. He stared at me for several minutes trying to convince me that he was contemplating my demise before he finally snarled.

"What'd you do, nigger?" Too frightened to speak, I shrugged and he grabbed the referral slip out of my hand. He read it and snorted. "I hear-ed you was weird. What'd you do?" I was friendless and lonely at my school, but I still knew better than to buddy up to Billy McCormack who was every bit as much of an outcast and maybe more. Still, you didn't want to make him mad either since by reputation he wouldn't hesitate to cause personal injury for the slightest offense.

"I told somebody that I could remember my mama givin' me away when I was born," I said. Billy McCormack's face altered into something that made him look almost childlike.

"Your mama gived you away?" he asked. I nodded in the affirmative. "You remember that day?" Billy looked down at the note in his hand. "Hey-ell," he drawled "ain't nothin' weird 'bout that." He dismissed my weirdness by handing my referral slip back. As if he were suddenly anxious to claim the title of weirdest kid in school he leaned toward me. "I 'member every single thing ever happen to me. And, I'll tell you what, nigger boy, I wished my mama'd gived me away. You was lucky." One of the stories about Billy McCormack prominently featured the criminal history of both of his parents, and how at least one of them was doing hard time for what they'd done to their son. I kept my mouth shut another few minutes and Billy, out of boredom, started on a new tack.

"You wanna know how come *I'm* here?" he asked with a happy grin. Before I could decide on a response the principal came back, his face sweaty, his necktie undone, and his shirtsleeves rolled up.

He jerked my referral slip out of my hand and read it. He shook his head and asked me in a real weary voice, "Deane, what is the matter with you?" It seemed like a rhetorical question so I didn't volunteer an answer. He shook his head again and ran his hand through his hair. "Go back to class," he said. "Don't be weird." His advice sounded as if he believed that I had control of such things. Before I could leave the bench, he reached out and took hold of Billy McCormack's neck roughly. He pulled the boy to his feet and steered him toward his office door.

"Deane?" he called after me on his second thought. "You could wind up just like this." Then he pushed Billy through the door, followed him inside and let it close behind them with a frightening bang.

The principal was not an entirely bad guy. He actually reminded me a little bit of my neighbor, Gillis Wainwright, though I'd be hard pressed to tell you exactly why. Somewhere deep inside he had some caring. I just plain could not take it in as much as I needed it. It wasn't like that with Sam and Odie though. I gobbled up anything and everything they offered and still wanted more.

On Friday of that week word had circulated around school that Billy McCormack had got himself taken away for mass murdering the entire fourth grade ecosystem with his bare hands while his class was in the library. Starting with the Uncle Milton's ant farm and working his way through the chain, Billy had systematically destroyed a garter snake, the hamsters, the guinea pig and the bunny. Then he had poisoned the aquarium. I guess the principal had some second thoughts about what he'd said to me about my potential because he sent for me at the end of the day. He more or less apologized and tried to give me some good advice, but, as I said, I could not just then take it in.

Now, I do not mean to be tedious on this subject, but for sure, here is another one of those times I've been talking about when you just know the hand of fate or whatever was hard at work. On Friday afternoon I had made a real show of ignoring the principal and all his good advice about being a decent human being, and then the following Saturday when my grandma dropped me off at the Vendome parking lot, I could tell right away that something was wrong. Maybe it was that all the usual cars I had come to recognize were not there. Maybe it was just a feeling that something wasn't right. I walked down to Sam's slower than normal. Dread, I think, was slowing me down. And sure enough when I got to the shop, the door was locked. Somebody had taped a handwritten sign up on the inside of the door reading,

"CLOSED – DETH IN THE FAMLY."

I knew that Sam had not written the note because of the misspelled words. I peered into the darkness beyond the sign. Nobody at all was in the shop. A panic rose up in me so swiftly that I had to sit down on the pavement in front of the door. I lost my vision and my hearing and a feeling of cold so awful I could not recognize it as such gripped me. I felt for a moment that it was me who was dead. Anyway, I thought I knew in that moment what death felt like. What *deth* felt like.

I don't know how long I sat there in front of Sam's barbershop, but sometime before it got dark outside, a black car pulled up in front. A man dressed in a suit (and even I could tell it was a nice suit) opened the driver's side door and got out heavily, (which seemed kind of strange to me since he was not a heavy man at all). I was still on the ground, so right off I noticed his shoes. Black wing tips, polished so bright they almost looked like patent leather. I looked at his necktie and started to shake.

"Are you JD?" he asked.

"Yes, sir," I told him while I was trying to stand. Except for how nice his clothes were, he looked quite a bit like the men who hung around Sam's on Saturdays.

"Well, come inside," he said. "I have some bad news." Honestly, my first thought was to run. Just run. But when I tried to move I found I couldn't. My arms and legs felt too heavy and I guess that in the end that is what made me follow him inside. He walked straight back to the apartment in the back of the shop and sat down in Odie's chair. Somehow, this shocked me and I wanted to order him up and out of Sam's shop, this stranger who did not belong here.

"My name is Otis Foster," the nicely dressed stranger told me. "I'm Professor Foster's son." I looked for traces of Odie's face in his. "Sam…" Otis Foster's voice broke. "Sam passed away on Thursday evening." Two brimming tears spilled down Otis Foster's cheeks. "Or, was it Wednesday? What day is it?" he asked.

"Saturday," I told him.

"Of course," he said and took his handkerchief out of his breast pocket to wipe his eyes. He rested his head in his hand for a few minutes. I watched transfixed. I had not seen a grown man cry since Gillis Wainwright wept at my mama's grave. Otis blew his nose and looked around at his father's modest little living space.

"How old are you, son?" he asked me.

"Seven, sir," I told him. He nodded.

"So, second grade?"

"Yes, sir."

"I hear you are some chess player."

"Yes, sir." Otis Foster watched my face for what seemed a very long time.

"JD, I am moving Professor Foster to a place where he can be taken care of now…" He paused. "Now that Sam's gone." He looked both sad and troubled. "My father's had another stroke and he needs a lot of care now. I expect that you will miss them both very much." We stared at each other. It was quiet for a long time before he spoke up. "Did you know that Sam and I have been good friends since we were younger than you are?" I shook my head. In all my Saturdays at Sam's it had never occurred to me to inquire about the missing Otis. "He was a second son to my father, and sometimes I think he was a better son than I was." Otis smiled a rueful smile. "I never had children of my own. So, no grandchildren for my father. Do you have any grandparents?" I thought about it.

"No," I said. Otis Foster only nodded.

"Well, son, I know that my father enjoyed your company very much." I shook my head. "He did. And, I know that Sam was very fond of you, too." It sounded to me just then like both Sam and Odie had died even though only Sam had been buried. I guess that is when I started to cry.

"Come here, boy," Otis Foster said and just that easily he took me into his embrace. I went so willingly I marvel at it now, how right it was to sit in the lap of a total stranger and just weep. Here was someone who I had nothing at all in common with except, I suppose, the love of those two other men. While the two of us were there on one of the worst days of my life, among Odie's record albums and eight track tapes and beautiful books and we grieved together, the only thought that I had was pure crazy and didn't make any sense at all: *Hold on to this moment! This is one of those good times!*

Eventually our tears stopped running down our faces and we both just sighed together. We were both plumb exhausted from the grief we had shared. Otis lifted me down off his lap and held my shoulders. The weight of his hands made me think oddly for one second of Billy McCormack who had been taken away from school by policemen. I wondered if Billy knew Sam's trick of savoring the good times for when the bad came, or if he had ever had even a few minutes in the company of someone like Otis Foster. It would have made some difference, I believe.

"Now, JD, I have been given the task of seeing to it that Dr. Foster's things get put where they can be used best. Some, I'm going to send to his old school."

"Tuskegee University," I said.

"That's right," he smiled. "But, he would like for you to pick out some things to keep. Some albums perhaps that will let you remember him and all the good time you spent together."

"No, sir," I said. "I think it would be best if you send his things on to Alabama." Otis Foster gave me a strange look, like he was trying to figure me out, and I didn't want him to press the issue, since I did not want to explain that my grandma could not always be trusted with my belongings.

"Well," he said. "I guess you know best." He looked around the room. "Okay. Let me give you a ride home, anyway. You think you can go another week without a haircut?" I said yes and took a good long look around Odie's apartment myself. I knew that I would not return to Sam's again.

It was dark when Otis Foster's fancy car pulled up in front of our house. Down the block, the lights were on in Gillis Wainwright's garage and Gillis was pulling out on a test ride. He paused and waited, gunning the engine on the straddled Harley several times. It seemed as though he was watching us to see what we were going to do. I hopped out, thanked Otis and waved as he drove off. Gillis pulled out behind the Mercedes and I stood on the curb watching him follow Otis Foster until I couldn't see their taillights anymore. It was a cloudy night; one of those absolutely moonless, starless nights in south Florida, and it never seemed darker to me than it did in those few moments. I had no choice but to go inside where my grandmother was already locked inside her room with the volume on the TV set so loud she never heard the door open and close. I went to my own room and closed the door. I laid down on my bed without removing my clothes.

I had not even known I'd been missing him until James Dean woke me up and asked me, *where had I been so long*?

Chapter 16

Gillis Wainwright

The first time I seen the boy get dropped off in front of his house in that nice new Buick, I figured it somethin' like this: *Good, the boy's finally got hisself a friend, and it's another little colored kid and he been over to the other kid's house, and that's his friend's daddy givin' him a ride home.* But then, after a whole pile of Saturdays I realized that I never see'd another kid. Never. So's then, I started thinkin' somethin' else: *Who is this guy and why is he spendin' so much time with JD?* You know? I become curious-like. I admit I started feelin' the least little bit guilty right around then since I remembered how I had told his mama that I would keep an eye out. Still, I figured I'd mind my own beeswax for the time being.

The kid looked okay. Friendly little bugger. Always sayin', "H*i, sir, how you doin'?"* when he passed by my garage. Then, one Saturday, maybe two years out from his mama's funeral, another guy, this one in a brand new Mercedes Benz, comes pullin' up to the kid's house and drops him off. And again, there ain't no playmate in that car neither. Well, ordinarily my mind don't work in such a way, but, I ain't completely ignorant to what you would call things of a deviant nature. Plus, I had me a little experience of my own when I was about JD's age that I'd just as soon not go into. But, anyways, I figured that if I notice that this here is a good lookin' little kid and nice, too, well…you don't have to hit me over the head with a crescent wrench, you know?

I just happened to be pullin' outta my garage, takin' Austin Weatherly's chopper out to check the brakes I just replaced, and that's when the Benz pulls up and lets JD out. I take note of how dapper the guy behind the wheel is, dressed spiffy, like somebody on the TV, and in one split second a real old terrible thought occurs to me, and I suddenly forget all about minding my own beeswax. I followed his car all the way down to Imperial and he parks the Benz out front of the barbershop down the street from the Vendome Liquor store and goes on inside the shop, even though it is clearly shut up for the night. I pulled Weatherly's bike around and parked it underneath a pole lamp, thinkin' how Austin would kick my ass from here to Georgia if some brother ripped off his chopper from behind the Vendome. But, by then I was on a mission. Ain't was nothin' goin' to stop me then.

I get to the front door of the barbershop and look around. There's a note written up on the door but I cain't read it on account of it's dark and anyways I gotta admit I ain't seein' so good anymore even when it ain't real dark outside.

Hardly anybody comes down to Imperial that time of night except the folks needin' booze and they always park in the back of the Vendome, so it's just me out there peerin' in. I can just barely see that there's a light on in a back room. I tried the door like a damn fool and when it turned I compounded my failure of good sense by walkin' right in. One of them little tinkly bells rung out over the door but nobody was in the dark shop. The dapper guy I guessed was in the back with music turned up pretty good. With some relief I recognized John Coltrane playin' in the back there. Sure enough, *A Love*

Supreme – you just can't miss it. *How bad could this guy be if he's a Coltrane fan*? I thought. I almost turned around and left but next thing was I heard the unmistakable sound of a human bein' cryin'. Any fool could hear that it was a powerful sorrow, too. Well, I thought the least I should do is go back there and ask this guy what the hell's he done that makes him feel so bad he's cryin' like that? You know? And there he sat. His head inside his hands and his face all screwed up and tears just flowin' down his cheeks and onto the album cover on his lap.

I cleared my throat by way of announcin' myself and he nearly jumped out of the chair when he seen me standin' there. I admit I did not look at that moment like I had on my Sunday-go-to-meetin' clothes. That poor bastard nearly lost his load from the looks of him. But, I was maybe only a little bit less scared myself. I tried damned hard to look like a badass and it seemed like at least for the moment he bought that I was.

"There's no money here," he said. "Wait!" He reached inside his suit coat. "I have some money." "Here," he said and laid out his wallet on the small table at his side. "I don't think they keep money in the shop." He held his hands where's I could see them plain.

"I ain't here for money," I told him. "I came to see what you doin' with the boy. With JD."

"JD?" He give me a confused look. I tried to sound as tough as I could.

"You messin' with that boy?" His head cocked up, like he was a dog or somethin' tryin' to make sense of some stupid human command.

"I'm not sure I understand your question," he said.

"Oh, you understand my question alright. Now gimme your answer!" I ordered him.

Somethin' changed just then in his face and even more so in the space in between him and me, 'cause this was not a man who let folks holler at him. That much was pretty clear from that point on.

"Who are YOU?" he asked standing and I'll admit, just then I was not altogether certain that I had done the smartest thing walkin' in on him.

"My name is Gillis Wainwright," I told him in a righteous fashion. "I am the boy's neighbor. His mama told me to look out for him and that is what I aim to do!" His eyes closed sudden like and he touched his necktie.

"Oh, thank God," the man said and shook his head. All the air inside of his lungs leaked out fast like a balloon what's been blowed up but then you don't tie it off. "Take a seat, Mr…Wainwright, did you say?" This was not a man who you said no to. I took a chair. The man removed his suit coat and I could see plain that I had caused him to work up a sweat. He wiped his forehead with a fancy cloth from his pocket.

"The boy…JD...has been coming to this shop every Saturday to play chess with my father. He came today, but as you see, the shop was closed. My father has suffered a second stroke and I'm moving him into nursing care. The boy had no way of knowing. He showed up for his weekly haircut to play chess."

Just then the Coltrane album came to an end and it became awful quiet in the little room.

"Oh," was the smartest thing I could think of to say. I felt a fool. We sat looking at each other for a while until the dapper man moved to the turntable. He removed the Coltrane album and then put it back inside the cover. He put it into my hands.

"Could you keep this for him? Until he's a bit older? My father would like the boy to have it but today he seemed….reluctant to take it home with him. I don't know why, of course."

"I know why," I said, and then I gave him the *what for* all about that grandma of JD's.

"What a tragedy," he said. "A boy like this could be anything. There's no other family that could take him?" I shook my head. I felt guilty again in the way I had back when JD's mama was dyin'. I couldn't speak up to say so, so's I just kept my mouth shut. After a while I told this man the same thing I had told Susie Deane.

"I'll keep an eye out. That's the best I can do from next door."

"Of course," he said. "And, that is why you followed me here. You thought…" We both knew what I had thought. At least we both knew what tree I'd been barkin' up against.

"Well, Mr. Wainwright, JD is lucky to have you. It cannot have been easy to come in here like this." I shook my head. It was not. "I'd like to give the boy a few of these books and some music as well. Would you mind if I had some of it delivered to your house? Could you make it available to him as you see fit?"

"I kin do that," I promised. "Hell, I already got his Daddy's drums and what was left of his Harley. A few more books and records ain't gonna be no bother."

"Excellent. I have to fly back to D.C. tomorrow. Can I have some things brought over in the afternoon?" I agreed and then we parted company. Both of us was glad that I didn't have to kick his ass and that my fears were what he called "completely unfounded".

I drove home on Austin's chopper and felt relief like you cannot believe. But, after I closed up the garage I snuck over to the Deanes' house and took a peek inside the windows. Maybe it ain't right to go lookin' in on people that way, but hell, I had just promised for the second time to keep a eye out for JD. It seemed okay to give a look inside that house to make sure he was alright. The old lady was passed out on her bed in

Susie and Carter's old room. She had a little bitty TV set blastin' away and half a dozen dirty drinkin' glasses up on the dresser top next to it. The house smelled kinda funny from her window. Not like food rottin' or nothin', but still, like somethin' sour and old.

I knew which window was JD's cause they only had two bedrooms same as my house. So's I snuck on up to listen to what he was up to. He did not have no television set, so all was quiet in his room. I was just startin' to take off home when I heard the boy start talkin'. *Now who's he talkin' to*? I thought, and paused to give a second listen. He spoke so soft I couldn't make sense of what he said, but in between I could hear he was cryin' some. I raised my head and peeked in his window, feelin' all the while like one of them twisted peeper-men you hear about and hopin' like hell that nobody would be walkin' by and think I was one.

Poor little kid was just layin' there all alone in his room. Nobody else was in there, but he was still talkin' up a storm. Talkin' to hisself and scareder than hell. I wished I could just holler in that window, "Hey, JD, you are gonna be fine! You are gonna be okay! I will see to that." But, I didn't want to scare the boy, and to tell the god's honest truth, just about then, I didn't think he needed nobody tellin' him no lies.

Chapter 17

Jimmy Deane

I saw two men I knew from Sam's show up on the Sunday after he died in a big white van and carry boxes into Gillis Wainwright's house for a good fifteen minutes. Then, when they were done, Gillis came out with them and the three of them hopped up into the van and drove right up into our yard. All three got out and stood for a while looking at our front door. They had a little talk amongst themselves and then Gillis walked on up to the front porch and knocked on the door.

"Ma'am," he said to my grandma starting out politely and even removing his cap. She just stared at Gillis and then past him to the two Black men out behind him. She squeezed her eyes all beady and reached up and held the screen door closed like Gillis could not just rip the whole thing down one handed if he'd wanted to.

"Ma'am," Gillis said again and gestured to the van behind him. "I was wonderin' if I could interest you in a new TV." Grandma just kept on staring at Gillis like he was speaking in a language she had never heard before. "You see, Ma'am, I won me a brand new television set…it's a color TV…a very nice one. I won it in a contest over at the A&P.

Ain't that right?" Gillis looked back to Tommy and Lamont standing out in the yard. The way both of 'em stood there bobbin' their heads up and down made them look like the marionettes I had seen one time with my mama over at the library. "Well," Gillis explained, "the truth is, Ma'am, right now, I ain't got room in my own livin' room for this here television on account of I got too many Harley parts up in there and I'd just as soon have you and JD here make some use of it…until I can clear some space." Grandma just stared bug-eyed out on the lawn as if the van was a spaceship and Gillis Wainwright's compatriots were alien beings. "It's a color set, Ma'am," he reiterated, as if he were begging.

"I'll come right over and get it if'n it gets in your way at some later date," Gillis told her. She did not say yes, but she did not say no, and so Gillis gave Lamont and Tommy the high sign and they opened up the back of the van and each took an end of a twenty-seven inch console color television set. Once Grandma got her first good look at that mahogany cabinet, she unlocked the hook that kept our front door shut. Lamont and Tommy moved the TV inside, plugged it in opposite Grandma's small sofa and turned it right on.

"Some shows is only in black and white and you got to know which ones those are and which ones you get in color so you don't think your TV is broke. The Rifleman for one is in black and white," he told me. "They play them every day at three o'clock and then one more time at three thirty. Not Saturday and Sunday, though." My grandmother's face was contorted into a mask of emotion that was very difficult to read. Clearly she did not know what to make of Gillis Wainwright's generous offer.

"What about channel twelve?" she asked, her voice all trembly. Lamont turned the TV's dial to channel twelve and stepped back grinning, like he could smell her capitulation. Reverend Lester, the televangelist who dominated the Christian

TV station appeared in glorious and ostentatious crimson vestments. He bore the suntan of a man who spent many hours either on a golf course or maybe poolside with perhaps an alcohol-free libation in his hand. Grandma had never seen Reverend Lester in living color before and to see her looking at him you'd have thought he was God Almighty himself.

"Oh!" she swooned. "Oh, oh!" Her body succumbed to the sofa.

"Well, okay, then!" Gillis smiled at me. "JD, Kung Fu is on tonight at eight o'clock!" he whispered. "You come by this week sometime and let me know how the TV is workin' out for y'all, okay?" I nodded yes, but I was busy wondering where the television set had really come from and why it was that Gillis Wainwright had given it to us.

That same night, when Gillis, Lamont and Tommy were gone and long after Grandma fell asleep in front of the new TV, after I had cleared the dishes and gone to bed myself, James Dean talked to me for a long, long time from his place on the back of my door. He presented at least a half dozen good hypotheses about our neighbor's gift of a television set. I fell asleep before one theory could entirely stick, but just before I drifted off I thought for sure I heard him say, "Ah ha! JD! I know! It was Sam and Odie! That's where it came from. Sam and Odie sent the TV to you."

Chapter 18

Elizabeth was almost always sober in the hours between Saturday morning mass and her first sip of Maker's Mark behind the Vendome Liquor store around noon when she drove the boy up to Imperial Avenue to get his hair cut. True, she had heard that some of the Catholic churches were serving sips of wine at Holy Communion, but she did not approve, and anyway the Hollywood parish was a poor one that would never assume the unnecessary expense of an alcoholic facsimile for the blood of Christ.

Soon after moving to Hollywood from Tampa she had established her own sacrament at the donut shop on her way home from church. Almost always she purchased one chocolate donut and a paper cup of scorched coffee. She had not liked the way the boy watched her eat when she brought her breakfast home – the word *covet* came to mind – so, early on, she had decided that the donut shop was a fine locale for her harmless constitutional. She sat in the corner booth with her back to the shop's other patrons.

By chance, or by fate's design, on the second Saturday following Sam the barber's funeral, Elizabeth had just one bite of donut remaining and a cold swallow of weak coffee in the bottom of her cup, when she heard and recognized a voice that raised hackles on the back of her neck. She did not know the man's name but his voice was distinctive. She listened carefully as he loudly described to his compatriot the details of his previous Saturday afternoon moving a twenty-seven inch color console television set into Elizabeth's living room.

Lamont liked the sharp little boy who came weekly to play chess with Odie. He surely meant the child no harm, but Lamont had a big mouth. He liked to use it, and some even said that he could have done stand up just like Eddie Murphy if he had had the right breaks. Had he known that morning that Elizabeth Breaux was there, sitting in the back of the Donut Inn, and that she was listening to his every word, he would have surely bit his own tongue. He most certainly would have thought better of performing a rather accurate and hilarious imitation of the old white woman's first glimpse of the Reverend Lester in living color.

Elizabeth was still trembling with rage when she pulled the Cadillac onto her street. The boy was waiting on the porch. He could tell by the way she parked the car that something was terribly wrong.

In the afternoon, when she was at least a cupful into her first cocktail, she drove the boy to a new white barbershop. The barber gave them both a look that told them exactly what he thought and then he added a dollar surcharge for cutting Jimmy's *nappy* hair. He did the job in less time than it had taken Sam on even his fastest days, but he had his other customers to think about. To make matters worse, there was a significant mark up on Elizabeth's favorite brands at the new liquor store, which catered to the neighborhood's population of retired northerners. Jimmy Deane's Herculean efforts to *fly low* for the remainder of the day came to naught. By eight, after Elizabeth had passed out in front of the TV set, Jimmy lay in his bed fingering the welts on his thighs from the coat hanger as if they were something precious, and he listened to James Dean make promises that Jimmy knew were very unlikely to be kept. Still, even promises that he knew to be unlikely to be realized were comforting.

Chapter 19

Jimmy Deane

I will admit that when I was a child I had more than just a little tiny bit of confusion about the color of a person's skin. Maybe I still do. It seems awfully important to most folks. White and Black. I knew that my real mama was a White girl. I knew my real father was a Black man. But, that's all I knew about them except that they had not wanted me. I knew that the folks who adopted me, (my mama and my daddy) were both white, and sometimes it made me feel bad when Terrence or some others over at Sam's shop said some things about white people that were not too favorable. Other times, especially if I was feeling angry about one thing or another, I'd agree with what they said about white folks and I didn't feel one bit bad. I knew for certain sure that my grandma did not like it that I was dark skinned, even though when I was a child, she never called me a nigger the way some other white folks had. For one thing, I knew how it pained her to part with the money that she gave me so that Sam would give me a haircut every week. It didn't matter that that money wasn't near what she spent at the Vendome after she dropped me off. Still, no matter what the expense, week in and week out, that two dollars and fifty cents was forthcoming since she could not seem to stand looking at my natural hair. My black hair. And, I know that was how come Sam stopped taking money for my haircuts pretty soon after he started driving me home. He told me that I earned that money for sweeping up and all the help I gave Odie with his records and such. But I knew that he was also being kind to me and that he, on top of that, did not mind being just a little bit unkind to my grandma, since she made no bones at all as to how she felt about Black folks, and especially about the half of me that was Black.

I accumulated a tidy sum of money saving up every week and I kept it in a nice wooden cigar box that Sam gave me. I put it in my dresser drawer and all totaled up on the day that I found out about Sam and Odie from Judge Foster, I had two hundred and five dollars. More cash money than I could truly grasp a hold of back then. I came home that night and went straight to my cigar box. The judge had given me my two dollars and fifty cents – I guess Odie must have told him about that—and I went right inside and counted up my total like I always did on Saturday nights, which came up to two hundred seven dollars and fifty cents. I started thinking that maybe what I could do with all that money was somehow get myself up to Washington, D.C. Even though I was just a stranger to him, and the truth is I only knew him at all for just that one day, it was true that the judge had held me in his lap and we had both cried together, and then he had asked me did I want some of Odie's records and books. I didn't ask him if he wanted a boy like me who knew how to "fly low" – something Sam had tried to teach me. But I wondered for a long while that night if I had, what would he have said?

I didn't know anything about travel. I only ever went to school and to the shop, but I knew that there were Greyhound buses and such, even airplanes if a person had enough money. When I was younger, after my mama died, I used to think a lot about how I could find my real mama and my real daddy. This day was a little bit like that, except the judge was a real person who had shown me some kindness. I had reason to believe that a real person could be found, even if you had to go all the way to Washington D.C. to do it.

Then, without an invitation to do so, James Dean showed up again that same night before I could make my getaway plan. Even though I knew then that I was too old for imaginary friends, I have to say it was a relief to have someone to talk to, even if he was a white man and even if he did not think it was such a great idea to go up to Washington to find Odie's son.

"People go away and some people die, JD," he said to me that night. "You should know that by now. It's nothing personal." I wanted to holler at him, I was so mad, but I guess that I was afraid that my being mad would make him go away, too, so I just kept quiet, except I could not seem to stop crying. He gave me a few minutes to cry some, and then he said some things that I know were meant to make me feel better. They really didn't though.

"Well, what now?" he asked me finally. I thought about it and I could not think of a single thing I wanted to do more than I wanted to be with Sam and my mama and my daddy, too. I told him so. He seemed to think about that for a long while and in fact he was so still I thought that he had gone away, but then he smiled.

"JD, did you know that your daddy was crazy about the Beatles?" It took me a while to give him an answer, but I finally said that I supposed my mama had told me that a few hundred times or more. Plus, I had every Beatles album ever made in the bottom of my closet if you needed proof, even though by then most of them had been busted up by my grandma. "And, did you know," James Dean just kept on talkin', "that when you were just a baby, your daddy came in here in this very room, and he took down his favorite Beatles poster from this very door, and he put me up here instead?" I said, yes, that I knew all of that. "That means that your grandma did not tear up the Beatles when she tore down all your posters! They are probably here—in your room somewhere!" James Dean sounded pretty excited about the possibility and well, I suppose I figured that no matter what I decided to do, whether I would follow Sam and my folks to where they were, or somehow get myself up to Washington to find the judge, it couldn't hurt to locate the Beatles first.

How a person can live in the same space for years and years and not know what else is in that space is one of life's mysteries, for certain. It took me only about fifteen seconds to find that old Beatles poster where my mom had put it all rolled up underneath my bed. Imagine. Something so precious had been right underneath my head and I didn't even know it. I blew off the dust and unrolled the Beatles and put some heavy things on top to make it stay open. I stared at the four Beatles. They had on their uniforms from the Sergeant Pepper's Lonely Hearts Club Album. My favorite one. They looked pretty serious that night.

"Did you know that when John was still just a kid his mama died when she got hit by a car?" James Dean asked.

"Just like my dad?" I asked him.

"Well, maybe she wasn't on a motorcycle," James Dean admitted. "But, still… And, you know that Paul's mama died of the same thing that your mama died of." He let that soak in. "That's probably why Paul and John got to be such good friends." I sat against my bed staring at the Beatles unrolled across my bedroom floor for a long time. James Dean was quiet, too.

"John Lennon said once that if it wasn't for me, there wouldn't have ever been a Beatles." James Dean sounded very proud about that, but I wasn't really sure I knew what John had meant by it. I'm pretty certain that I did not know at the time that James Dean's mama had also died when he was nine years old and what's more what took his mama from him was the same thing that took my mama and Paul's mama too. The cancer. But, sometimes it's hard to remember when you knew a thing.

"Do you talk to John Lennon like you talk to me?" I asked James Dean. James Dean never did tell me if he talked to John Lennon, but I do know now that he was known to be partial to musicians of all kind.

"Before she died, his mama gave him his first guitar, JD." When I failed to comment on that, he reminded me. "Your daddy's drums are over at Gillis Wainwright's house next door." And, that was all he had to say on the subject for a while.

I cried and cried that night and I don't know if I was missing my parents or Sam or Odie, or maybe even Odie's son, who I hardly even knew but somehow had conjured high hopes for in a very short time.

It wasn't too long after Sam died and Gillis brought that big old TV set over that I decided that I wanted to have a look at my daddy's drums.

Chapter 20

Jimmy Deane

My papa's drum kit included four Premier drums: one Bass, a 2000 Metal Snare, a Tuna Can and a floor Tom. He also had a Ludwig Silver Sparkle, which he played in the classic jazz setup: twenty-two inch Bass, thirteen by nine Top, and a sixteen inch Ludwig Supra-Phonic Snare. He had a Ludwig double Bass kit, two twenty-fours with a twelve by eight inch Tom on top and Zildjian fourteen inch Hi-hats. Given how my daddy died, I always thought it was a little ironic that his kit also contained a sixteen inch Crash, and twenty inch Crash Ride, and a twenty inch Riveted Ride. But, whatever. Just a coincidence. Not necessarily a prophecy.

Gillis Wainwright said that my daddy was one hell of a drummer. He could have been a pro. That's what Gillis thought. He told me that he sorely missed the music he sometimes had heard comin' from next door after Papa died. My mama asked Gillis to move the drum kit over to his house when she left me in the care of my grandma. I guess she figured that my grandma could not be entirely trusted and she figured right when you look at the damage done by her to other things left behind by my folks.

Gillis Wainwright set those drums up in his spare room exactly as my papa had used them, and except for a few times when he ran out of space in his garage for spare parts, that room was all mine. It wasn't too long before I moved my turntable and all my record albums over there too, and Gillis Wainwright never once made me feel like having all that stuff at his house was an imposition. No sir. Not that I ever really gave it too much thought. He said, "On the contrary, JD, it is a real and true honor to have your daddy's drums at my house." I believed him and that is how I come to have Gillis Wainwright for my one true friend, not counting of course James Dean, who I have to say could be counted on in the worst of times. The thing about James Dean was, when I didn't need him so much I never even gave him a thought. It did not occur to me to inquire what he did when I didn't need him so much. That is just the beauty of being a child I have come to believe.

Chapter 21

Gillis Wainwright

True to his word, that colored judge from Washington D.C. had two boys bring over a whole load of books and record albums for the kid next door the very next day. I had to figure out how to get JD's nasty ole'grandmamma to take the big color TV set he sent over with the books and all, but I just told her that I won it in a contest at the A&P and that was that. People don't really want to know where free shit comes from anyway.

I was thinkin' all week on how I was gonna give some of them books to the boy when in he strolls to my garage on Friday as if he'd been readin' my mind. I asked how he was enjoyin' the TV set and he says how his grandma don't allow no TV since it is mostly the work of the devil on it. I pointed out that it seemed peculiar that I could see the TV screen plainly from my front porch, and it had looked to me like somebody over there to his house had been watchin' somethin' every single day and night all week long. The kid just gimme a grin then, and I could see that he was a real smart little bugger.

I will say that for a minute I had a half a mind to take the chrome fork offa' Dexter Lemke's hog that was layin' in pieces on the floor of my garage and go on over and put it through that twenty seven inch screen, but then I figured that the kid was right. Whatever kept the old bat off his back was a good thing.

JD watched me work on Dexter's bike for a while that day and pretty soon he was handin' me tools before I even knew which tool I was gonna need. Honest now, if JD hadn't a been such a damn nice kid it would have been spooky how smart he was. But, I got used to it, and used to havin' him hang around after school and on the weekends. Sometimes we'd talk. I'd tell him stories about his mama and his papa, stuff I figured a kid oughta know about their folks. Stuff I'd have liked to know about mine, I guess, if my folks had been at all like Carter and Susie. I told him about the time his daddy laid me out flat on the garage floor for callin' JD a coon.

"Your daddy had a real mean right hook, JD," I told him. "Not just for a college boy neither." Just the memory of that sock to my left jaw made my whole face hurt. But, it made us both laugh a little bit, too, and, man, that was a beautiful thing, because it was so rare when that little boy laughed.

I guess you could say he was a serious sort. And curious? Glory be! That child was the most curious person I will ever meet. He went through those boxes of books the judge give him lickety split and when he was done, he just started readin' 'em all over again. I'll bet he read each one three, four times and when I said, "Hey, what's the point, JD? You already know the stuff in them books. He'd just smile and say somethin' like, "Yeah, well I was only ten the last time I read this. I'll understand more this time."

Me? I never was one much for readin'. Truth is I quit school in the ninth grade and hell, half of them books I kept over at my house for JD I could not get through the first page. That didn't seem to make no never mind to JD, though.

That colored judge had put a chess set in with the records and books he sent over, and JD taught me how to play chess. At first I thought no way was I ever gonna play some fruity tootie game like chess, but, JD would not take no for a answer and by and by I got so's once in a blue moon I could get a game offa him. He told me I was probably a *idiot savant,* which at first hurt my feelin's, but then he said how that meant that I was a kind of a genius and that was probably why I was so good at fixin' bikes and calculatin' the odds at the track and pickin' ponies, too. Well, that didn't sound so bad when he put it that way.

By the time he was big enough to help me hoist a big bike up onto my lift, I thought of him as my best friend and if I had ever had me a son, which I couldn't on account of something my step daddy done when I was sixteen… well, if I coulda? Well, I'd have been proud to be JD's papa. Colored or not.

Now, don't you think for a minute that he was some pansy-assed kid. No sir. Just because he read books written by folks whose names I couldn't even say right, and he loved that game chess, that did not mean he was no sissy. He was cool. As cool as they come. If you needed some proof of that boy's cool all you hadda do was hear him play the drums. He was a drummer extraordinaire. And, he taught hisself, too. All he hadda do was listen to a song one time and he'd just pick up the sticks and play it. Over and over he'd play the song 'til he knowed it perfect.

Acrossed time, together, we listened to all the records his mama and papa had left him, 'ceptin' the broke ones of course, and then we started in on all the ones from the judge. I told him how I'd gone and bought them first drum sticks downtown when the cancer had took his mama, and that I had been hopin' since that day that he would come over and play his daddy's drum kit just like Carter had played them. One thing for sure, you got a neighbor who can play music, you are one lucky man. Well, no offense to Carter Deane, may he rest in peace, but man, JD could blow his daddy out of the water by the time he was in high school.

I ain't no fool, and it had occurred to me that if it hadn't a been for Carter and Susie dyin' like they had, there's no way that little boy woulda been hangin' out with somebody the likes of me. If I'd a been a different kind of man, I suppose I woulda felt some guilt about enjoyin' somebody else's kid so much under them circumstances. I ain't that man though, so mostly, all I was was happy to have the boy's company.

I guess you could say those were the best of times. I had enough work, and when I didn't, I always made due with a little action on the side. Ponies and dogs mostly. Once in a while I turned a pound of grass over for some shit-kicker who had some homegrown he wanted to get rid of. I never smoked it myself no more, and I kept it clear of the kid. He came over every day to play Carter's drums, and if I wasn't pullin' somebody's bike apart in my garage, I'd listen to him for hours upon hours. I ain't never been what you could call a religious person, but when JD would put some Creedence Clearwater up on that old turntable and just have at it on his daddy's kit soundin' more like Soko Richardson than Soko Richardson hisself? Well, when that boy drummed it could make saints out of sinners. I mean you could hear God talkin' when that boy was on. We had us some good times. Real good times.

Somethin' changed over there between him and that grandma of his right around the time he was puttin' on some height. He never said, and I never asked, but all of a sudden he stopped havin' his head buzzed over to the barbershop every single week, and he let his hair grow out into them little piggy tails like ole Bob Marley. About then, he was over at my house damn near every wakin' hour when he wasn't in school. Mostly every single Saturday and on Sundays for sure, when his grandma was gone to church service, we'd go get us some breakfast over at the Lighthouse Café, him and me. I always bought us a lotto ticket each. Just for fun. Never in a million did I think we'd hit it.

I seen it one time somewheres, maybe it was on the TV over at the Lighthouse. Somebody asked a whole pile of lottery winners, if they could, would they go back to the time before they won, if they could have their old lives back? Well, a lot more of them than you'd think said, "*hell yeah!*" They'd give it all back if only they could be the person they was before. Makes you wonder. Makes me wonder sometimes anyway.

Chapter 22

The metal bleachers had been a cost saving decision, and a bad one, for the football stadium behind Hollywood High School. By two o'clock in the afternoon the sun made the seats hot enough to blister the backs of a person's legs if anybody was dumb enough to sit down on them in the middle of July. First hand knowledge was what made the school's band director wince when he noticed the solitary young man on a seat high up in the stands on the fifty-yard line. The boy was hatless and didn't even wear shades. He appeared out of nowhere every day four days running, and he watched the marching band getting their summer kinks out down on the football field until the drum line, the last section to leave, packed up and left for home. Nobody in the band seemed to know him, at least no one ever said anything to him, and he always seemed to just slip away without the benefit of company when practice was over. On the fourth day the band's coach ambled over to the fifty and took two stairs at a time up to the boy's row.

"Hey," the coach said, taking care to keep from touching the metal bench with bare skin.

"Hey," Jimmy responded softly without moving. The coach raised his sunglasses. Close up he detected something skittish, something downright sympathetic about the kid. Again he noted that even in the brutal midday sun, the boy wore neither a cap nor shades. His chin was resting on his hands, his elbows planted on top of his knees. He was staring straight down on the field at the band and his eyes did not blink. His clothing was plain, cheap jeans and a T-shirt, not an ensemble meant to compete with the fierce demands of high school fashion trends. His hair was so short it made the coach think of the time he had contracted head lice and his own father had cruelly shaved him bald because the medicine to cure the infestation was too costly.

"You go here?" the coach asked. Jimmy Deane nodded without smiling.

"Ninth grader?"

"Tenth," Jimmy said and the coach turned to squint down on the field. After a minute of silence Mr. Brown tried again.

"You play?"

Jimmy shrugged. They sat in silence for another few minutes watching the drum major try to get some order to appear out of the chaos on the field below. The coach lowered his sunglasses and put his hands behind his head.

"Drummer, right?" he pursued. Jimmy swiveled without lifting his chin from his hands but did not affirm or deny the coach's guess. The coach grinned broadly and Jimmy Deane raised his eyebrows and shrugged one shoulder.

"Wanna know how I know?"

Jimmy gave the coach a quizzical look.

"You've been here watching them all week. You don't leave when the rest of the band leaves the field. You stay and watch the drum line. Which means…unless you've got a girl on the line…?" The shake of the boy's head conveyed more than simple no, more of a no-way. "…So, that means that you're a drummer." Jimmy nodded as if it somehow pained him to admit as much to a stranger. A kind of rhythm had been established in the conversation and the coach obeyed its structure. After the requisite rest in between his questions he offered another. "You any good?" Jimmy shrugged again. Another teacher might have perceived this quiet young man as bordering on insolent, but Brown recognized the complete lack of entitlement to speak, even when spoken to, that the boy seemed to exhibit.

"You ought to try out," Mr. Brown said, trying to sound casual. "It's a hell of a lot of work though." He reached his big hands overhead then as if pulling himself up by invisible handles in the cloudless sky. He rose to his feet. Without saying good-bye he loped down the bleachers to the field. When his feet touched the grass he turned briefly. The boy's eyes had followed him down to the field. The coach lifted his head and nodded. Jimmy Deane slowly removed one hand from his face and opened his palm wide. The coach smiled and shook his head before moving out onto the field. The next time he looked up, the boy was gone.

The tryouts for the Hollywood High School marching band were held in the school auditorium two weeks before school began in September, and just before the group departed en masse for Band camp, officially, an annual week of band practice at a remote lake camp up in Georgia that was sponsored by the Booster club, and was meant to provide cohesion and camaraderie to the only Hollywood High School extracurricular that brought glory home to the community in any meaningful way. In reality, it was the general hijinks of the group that were the real tradition, and these often became legendary. Band camp cemented the players to each other as band-mates. Mr. Brown and the other chaperones turned a blind eye to all but the most outrageous behavior. It never hurt to have the goods on a few of the wild ones, he thought.

The auditorium buzzed with excitement all day long, each section commanding the stage for discrete portions of the day. The section leaders drew straws to determine the order. The annual tryouts for the school's famous marching band attracted a crowd from the community that the athletic teams envied. Mr. Brown let the band operate democratically, with each section voting only on the results applicable to their own section. It was mandatory that every member numerically rated every student who auditioned for a spot, and then each member voted a simple yea or nay on the aspirant's general desirability. In this way the band had veto power, even if a student was a magnificent musician but an asshole who was unlikely to fit in, either among his section peers or within the band as a whole entity. Occasionally, Mr. Brown would call a section in to defend themselves when they blackballed someone with great talent, but for the most part he let them build their own band. It was a strategy that had brought home ten years worth of state championships and two trips to the national competition under a coach from Mississippi whose own education had been earned with music scholarships and hard menial labor.

The Hollywood High School drum line knew that they would hear from the faculty director the very second that tryouts were over. They had unanimously ranked Jimmy Deane with outstanding scores for musicality, and even if they hadn't, the response of the audience had been unprecedented. No one among them could remember a standing ovation for an audition. But every drum line member, and even the two girls, had voted *nay* to extend Jimmy an invitation to join the band. Instead they had listed six drummers whose performances were inferior, but whom they all agreed, was someone who would fit in.

"Coach, I know why you're mad." Reynauld Harper was the section leader for the drum line and second only to the drum major in the band's strict hierarchy.

"I'm not mad," Coach Brown said frowning.

"Well, you *look* mad," one of the other kids said. The boy immediately received what the kids called the coach's stink eye and he sat back in his chair.

"Okay, then. Why am I mad?"

"It's 'cause of that *octoroon* dude," Reynauld said. The other kids snickered.

"What you mean, octoroon, Reynauld?" One of the only two girls on the line asked. "You mean that boy that's high yellow? That's what my granny call it. I think he's cute." The boys gave her looks that constituted a half dozen variations on censure, and she shrugged and lowered her head.

"Well, look, you guys," the coach warned, "If this is about he isn't black enough for the drum line, well…."

"No, it ain't cause he's white," Reynauld explained while the others, all of them black skinned, nodded encouragement. The coach felt the unanimous vibe, Shondra's appreciation for Jimmy Deane's looks notwithstanding.

"It's 'cause the dude is weird!" Reynauld blurted. Again the kids pretended to hide laughter.

"What do you mean he's weird? Is it because of his hair?" Again the kids snickered behind their hands.

"Okay, Coach." Elray Jones, Reynauld's first cousin, stepped in. "The dude be weird like this. He was in my AP History class last year, right?" Coach Brown smiled.

"Well, Elray, let me point out to you that you were also in AP History, if you're trying to say that being smart makes somebody weird," he said.

"No it ain't just that he's smart. Hell, coach, you know half the dudes in horns are like band nerds. They's all smart. Some of them are white dudes, too. No baldies, though." The boys cracked up but the girls glared at their meanness. When Elray got control of his laughter he tried to continue. "Coach, this dude is like beyond just plain smart. This dude was a *freshman* in AP History. You dig? There was only a couple

Juniors in that class. Me bein' one." Elray grinned and puffed out his chest. "And, anyway, this dude knows more than the teacher does. The teacher half the time was checkin' on shit with the octoroon dude before she say it was okay to put it in our notes." The others giggled, this time not even trying to hide the fact.

"Bald white Boy talked in AP History, Cuz? I had the dude in my AP English class and he never said one word the whole year." Reynauld held out his hands as if that were absolute proof of their thesis. Elray slapped five and the cousins' fists met in mid air.

"Mr. Brown?" The only other girl on the line besides Shondra, a girl who was high yellow herself and also probably a band nerd, but so pretty she got a pass, leaned forward. "I think it wouldn't be good for him to be in the band. I think he's too good for us." The boys hooted and made a commotion of waving arms and gestures. "No, really," the pretty girl said. "You all heard him. Is any one of us as good on the drums as that kid? Are any of you as pure a *drummer* as he is?" The boys looked glum. "Wouldn't he be better off like in the jazz ensemble or something, Mr. B? Those guys are all brainy. Plus, they're better musicians than we are, too." The coach scratched his face. The boys looked as if they had been beaten, but Reynauld spoke up.

"Hey, yeah, Coach, tell him he gonna play over there with all them pimply dudes." Elray fell to his knees gasping for mercy.

"Alright you guys, settle down," Coach Brown said sternly."What about what *he* wants? Obviously, he wants to play on the line or he wouldn't have tried out," he told them. The room was silent. "Also, how am I going to tell somebody that even though they got a standing ovation at the tryouts, the line doesn't think they're good enough?" Every one of them stared down at the floor. "I'm sorry. I know I usually let you guys do the voting, but this time I'm going to step in. Talk about weird. Everyone in town saw him play. I'm more than a little bit afraid of having to defend against a charge of racism." The kids looked up. They were a very small minority in a predominantly white school. The only turf on campus that they were in command of was the athletic field, and this turf the band shared jealously with the football team. Not one of them could comprehend their own prejudice when confronted with it. "I'm going to put him on the list over your veto."

The boys all looked at Shondra.

"What? I just said he was cute. I didn't say I wanted to marry him," she pouted.

Chapter 23

The results of the marching band tryouts were posted outside the auditorium one week prior to the band's departure to camp. A large cardboard box held packets for each new recruit on a folding table underneath the posts. Jimmy Deane pulled the packet with his name on it from the box and retreated to his customary viewing seat up in the bleachers to examine the contents. His hands were sweating.

The first page was a legal-looking document from the school demanding parental signatures for the release of liability should anything unpleasant occur during the week away. The Booster Club sponsored band camp so that the expenses for every single band member were subsidized, a very good thing for most of the drum line, and certainly for Jimmy. The community fathers however did not want to be held responsible if someone's youthful musical exuberance caused bodily harm to someone else, or even if someone just wound up pregnant as had happened at a rival school. (The marching band world was small and everyone knew that the girl's parents had successfully won a settlement against her school for eighteen years of their grandchild's subsequent support.)

Permission was not an obstacle for Jimmy Deane as he so rarely saw or spoke to his grandmother; he doubted that she would even miss him. He decided in advance in his excitement that he might even sign the form himself if the need be. Another three pages were stapled at the top and detailed the instructions (what to bring, what not to bring) to the camp. Jimmy Deane owned not a single one of the expensive inadvisable electronic items on the list, so he would experience no hardship whatsoever in leaving them at home for a week. He determined that he could make due with his scant wardrobe to comply with the list of clothing items he would need, and Gillis might help him out with the necessary toiletries. His excitement drenched his T-shirt and he needed to wipe his forehead repeatedly with a bare hand to keep from soaking the documents in his lap.

The final sheet of paper was the only potential deal breaker. It detailed the manner in which the band members should acquire, and be fitted for, the elaborate formal uniforms that were the pride of the school, if not the whole town of Hollywood. It also explained the payment options. The expense was an exorbitant three hundred and twenty-five dollars, a monumental and possibly prohibitive sum. Jimmy Deane dried his hands on his jeans and replaced the papers carefully inside the large manila envelope. On the slow walk home he calculated that his cigar box holdings hadn't been touched in all the years since Sam's death, and together with the forty or fifty dollars he had earned working for his neighbor, he had at least two hundred and sixty seven dollars. It would not be an easy thing for him to do, but he decided that he would ask Gillis Wainwright to lend him the additional money.

His grandmother did not look up from the television when Jimmy walked into the house. He nodded respectfully but said nothing as well and proceeded into his own room, carefully closing the door. He gave James Dean's faded picture a nervous smile before he turned to kneel at the closet's door. Feeling for the cigar box behind the old milk crate that still held Carter

Deane's smashed records, his hand touched the closet's floor. The box was not there. Jimmy sat back on his haunches and paused. He tried to remember if he had moved the box himself, perhaps hiding it one day when his grandmother had seemed particularly agitated and then forgetting exactly where he might have put it. He reached up on the shelf overhead. There was nothing there except for a few old T-shirts and an empty shoebox. Desperately Jimmy tore the top off the shoebox and touched the emptiness inside. He sank onto his bed and wiped his forehead. His pulse was pounding in his ears. The only remaining possible hiding place was under the bed. He paused for a full minute before he slid to the floor and looked underneath. Relief spread through his body in a cold wave as he dragged the box forward. The tiny metal latch had rusted. He hesitated as if he knew before he opened the box that he would find it empty.

Elizabeth ignored the fact that Jimmy had re-entered the living room. She turned only when he extended the opened box in his outstretched hands. Rivulets of tears were streaming down Jimmy's face and staining his T-shirt front but he didn't speak. He only stood there weeping and holding Sam's box. He knew that she would not give the money back.

"You're a thief," she said without a trace of irony. "You're a thief and a liar." Jimmy regarded the old woman and recalled his mother's words. "My mother is a hard case," Susie had told him. "She won't love you, but she won't hurt you." Jimmy closed the box and carried it back to his bedroom.

Late that night, he put the empty cigar box and the marching band recruitment packet in the garbage can beside the house. He slept fitfully, but in his unrest he convinced himself that it was a good thing that he didn't have to ask Gillis for a loan or try to fit in with the kids from the marching band. In the morning he went to the public library where the librarians had known him as a baby and where they still talked about Susie as if her death had occurred ten days before and not ten years before. Jimmy Deane assessed correctly that time passed differently for people who did so much reading and who virtually lived among books. One of the librarians in particular, who liked Jimmy Deane for his courtly manners and his shy handsome smile, often saved book donations or magazine collections that she thought he might like. It was no accident, Jimmy decided, that immediately upon his arrival she crooked a finger at him and handed over a small stack of old Rolling Stone magazines. On the very top of the small stack the long dead Bob Marley was in a wide joyous stance holding his guitar and singing towards heaven.

"I thought you might like these," the librarian whispered. "Somebody donated them, but we don't keep periodicals this old." Within an hour, Jimmy Deane was something of an authority on the great Reggae star. He noted with interest that Bob Marley had been half black and half white and had suffered racial prejudice from both groups. Furthermore, Bob's oldest son Ziggy, was not only the same age that Jimmy was himself, but Ziggy Marley was also a drummer. In another outstanding coincidence Jimmy read, the boy had lost his famous father to *cancer*.

"Money can't buy life," the article said, was the very last piece of usable advice Bob Marley had given to his young son. Jimmy studied Ziggy's picture for a long time. He wondered about the Marleys and whether or not they had believed in destiny. On his way out, Jimmy Deane stopped to thank the librarian sincerely.

On Saturday, when Elizabeth looked for him to take him into town for a haircut, he was nowhere to be found.

Chapter 24

Gillis Wainwright

It was the craziest damned day. Craziest day for sure of my whole life. It started out strange and just got stranger and crazier ‘til it was over. I was just headin’ out on a test ride. I figured I’d kill two birdies. Check out Howard’s new clutch and spin on over to the donut shop while I was at it. I was lockin’ up when a little blue car, rental from the looks of it—out of state plates—and a real nice lookin’ woman drivin’ – pulls up in front of JD’s house. I give her the once over. Don’t hurt nobody to look at ‘em. Then I hollered over, “Ain’t nobody home, ma’am.” She was a real pretty woman. That much I do remember. I rode up over the grass in between our two places. She got better lookin’ the closer I got. I wasn’t sure she had heard so I repeated myself and she looked like I had just give her the worst news of her life. “The old lady’s over to the church…goes every day. JD’s at school ‘til around three maybe four o’clock.”

“JD?” she says kind of choked up or somethin’. “Is that for… James Deane?” Well, I ain’t heard JD’s entire name said whole like that since he was just a little kid. It made me laugh.

"Yes'm," I told her. "Just like that old dead movie star." She smiled too. "Ridiculous, isn't it?" she asks me, only I ain't certain I know what she means so I didn't give the lady no answer. I just kept a big smile on my stupid face.

"And, Carter? And, Susan? His parents? Will they be home later?"

"Ma'am?" Well, right about then I was wishin' I hadn't a ever come over, even if she was the prettiest woman I think I ever had saw up close. It seemed pretty clear that nobody'd ever seen fit to tell this woman that Carter and Mizz Deane were goners. The both of 'em. I supposed I was gonna have to give her some bad news, no way around it, and you never can tell how folks is gonna respond to that. But, I went ahead and did tell her about Carter and then Mizz Deane. Nothin' else to do. I left out the part about Mizz Deane's mama being such a god-awful bitch. The pretty woman didn't cry or nothin' though she did not look in the least bit happy about the news even though you can't hardly call somethin' news what's happened so long ago, can you? That's when she pulled the little blue bag from her pocket. Tiniest little bag I ever seen. A little blue bag. A real uncommon blue. I could see it was special. At first it seemed like she was just gonna stand there and stare at it but then she asked me, could I see to that the bag got delivered to JD. I said sure, I could and would, and I put the itty bitty blue bag inside my pants pocket, patted it so she'd know it was safe, and then she just took off. Got in that little Hertz vehicle and drove away without sayin' one more thing. I went back inside my own house and put that little blue bag in my top drawer near my underpants where I used to keep my stash, just so's it would be safe. Then I went ahead and headed on down to check my lotto numbers at the donut shop since I am a little superstitious about such things. I always *buy* my tickets at the Lighthouse, *check* 'em at the Donut Inn. Sometimes the other way around, but I prefer to buy them at the Lighthouse because I feel luckier there. So, anyway, the guy at the donut shop, he looks at me real funny for a minute, then he calls up the State Lottery people in Tallahassee or wherever they are and before I know it, I'm barricaded in my living room and I got a lawyer comin' over to *represent me.* Things just plain got totally out of hand after that.

About a hour before JD normally got out of school and come over, there's a couple a dozen news vans out front and the neighbors is gatherin' to see what's up and then a police car come over to see what's the fuss. I half felt like I'd done something wrong and all I could think was if JD got there I could tell him about my good fortune, and it would seem *good* instead of what it was feelin' and by then it was feelin' just weird and a little bit scary, too. Funny, how that seemed to work.

Every once in a while somebody from the TV stations would come up on the porch and knock for a interview, but, I just hollered at 'em to get the hell offa' my porch or I'd sic the dogs on 'em. Didn't matter that I don't have no dogs, they just took off back to the street where they all sat talkin' amongst themselves I guess, and waitin' for me to come out and tell 'em all how it feels to win eighty some million dollars. *Holy shit*, I kept thinkin' *eighty million dollars!*

At long last I seen JD walkin' up the street and he of course sees the circus out front and he gets this real worried look on his face and started runnin'. Maybe he was remembering the time he had to come bail me outta jail when I got into it in a bar one night when some asshole called me a nigger lover. Well, I give that good ole' boy better than he give me, but they throwed us both in the pokey to cool off. I never told JD what spurned the fight. He don't need to hear that shit.

So's he jumps up on the porch and knocks real hard on the door, lookin' back at the reporters who are all hollerin' "Hey, are you Mr. Wainwright's boy? Can we talk to you?

Could you give us an interview, son?" And, all like that. I opened up the door just wide enough to yank him inside.

"Holy Shit! JD," I tell him and he squints and looks me up and down lookin' for some hurt places, and he says, "Gillis, what's wrong? What did you do? Are you okay?"

Well, now. It's tellin' ain't it? That poor boy just automatically leaps to a bad conclusion and I can't say I could blame him. I ain't exactly the most upright of citizens. But, I made me a vow right that second that Jimmy Deane was never gonna have no reason to worry about his good friend Gillis Wainwright ever again.

"No, JD," I say. "I'm fine." We stop then and we both take stock. It was the first time we both noticed that he'd growed taller than me. Soon as he sees I ain't hurt, he turns and looks out the window.

"So, what's going on out there? What are the police doing there?" he asks.

"Crowd control," I tell him with a straight face.

"What?" he says. "Crowd control?" I busted out laughin' then and nearly pissed myself I laughed so hard.

"JD," I says. "I won the lotto, man. I'm a goddamn millionaire!" Jimmy Deane's head starts shakin' and his ole' Bob Marley hairdo is wigglin' and wavin', but he ain't sayin' nothin. I guess I been fantasizin' about the lotto so long he can't quite really grasp the truth of what's happened.

"What?" he says. "What do you mean, Gillis?" And, then we both jumped about a mile in the air 'cause right then, my new attorney from the firm of *Alperstein, Lillian and Groth*, he knocks on the door, and after that our two lives were just never the same. I don't think you can hardly blame me with all that happened that I plumb forgot about that pretty lady. Every time I did remember about that little blue bag, the thought just come into my head and ran right out again before I could tell JD about it.

Chapter 25

Roger Albright's law firm, Alperstein, Lillian and Groth, represented sixty-eight Florida State Lottery winners to date. Gillis Wainwright would become number sixty-nine, a number which tickled Gillis, if not his turgid barrister. The *amount* of his win tickled them both, since it was to date the largest single state lottery win on record. Eighty-six million dollars, which would pay out close to thirty million in very cool cash after taxes, and was potentially worth millions to the Ivy League lawyer in fees and retainers.

"Where are all these people comin' from? What do they all want?" Gillis asked. He peered outside again through at least fifteen years of unaddressed grime on his living room window. The throng in front of his house seemed to grow in direct proportion to his anxiety.

"Mr. Wainwright," the dapper Albright said, "you will have to accommodate to this sort of attention if your future plans include a public life." He looked down and brushed imaginary soil from the lapels of his impeccable suit.

"What do you mean *a public life?*" Gillis stepped back from the window and confronted the much smaller man.

"I *mean*, Mr. Wainwright, that in all probability, if you do not wish to spend the bulk of your future existence looking at small crowds as such in front of your domicile..." Roger Albright gestured to the street. "…you will have to relocate."

"Relocate?" Jimmy Deane spoke up, startling Roger, whose weak and bespectacled eyes were having difficulty adjusting to the dim light. "Gillis has to move? Move where?" There was true alarm in JD's voice.

"Yeah," Gillis asked, "Move where?"

Roger Albright was already on the job protecting Mr. Sixty-Nine from unscrupulous hangers on. He assessed the boy's appearance with a distasteful sweep of his most critical glance. JD's cheap apparel and shoulder length dread locks, combined with a physique that bespoke a youth of hard manual labor, made the lawyer's professional condescension gleam in the dark little living room like the beady eyes of a living thing.

"My most earnest conjecture?" Roger's voice was acid. While he spoke to Gillis his eyes never left JD. "With the acquisition of eighty-six million dollars? Sir... even after taxes...you can go anywhere at all you'd want to."

For the very first time since the media circus had evolved outside, a giant smile spread slowly across Gillis Wainwright's face.

"Holy shit, JD," he clapped Jimmy on the back, "Woooo hooooo! I'm a goddamned millionaire!" Gillis did a little victory dance around his living room while Jimmy Deane, still contemplating the unthinkable news that Gillis would no longer be his neighbor, tried gamely, but unsuccessfully, to give him a big, happy smile. Roger Albright was a litigator who was hell on his opponents during jury selection. He noted that Jimmy looked, quite appropriately, as if he were going to lose his best friend.

"May we proceed, Mr. Wainwright?" Roger Albright laid his briefcase on the sticky card table in the center of the room. He peered over the top of his wire-rimmed glasses at Jimmy.

"May I ask what your exact relationship to Mr. Wainwright is? You are not his son, I presume?"

"Hell, this here's my neighbor! Jimmy Deane!" Gillis said. He clapped JD on the back again. Roger straightened and looked the striking youngster up and down carefully.

"Jimmy Dean?" Roger asked the boy. "Really, now?" He tried to give Jimmy his best intimidating stare.

Jimmy returned the lawyer's stare with remarkable unblinking eyes and a facial expression that was devoid of hostility and positively unreadable. Roger Albright found the need to pull his knotted tie loose and tug at his starched collar before he returned to the business at hand on the wobbly table.

"We can proceed in Mr. Deane's presence, I assume?" Roger peered at Gillis.

"Hell, yeah!" Gillis said. "I ain't got no secrets from JD." Roger pulled a stack of documents for Gillis to sign from his alligator brief case and tried to find the least filthy portion of the table.

"I ain't got no kids. Least none's I know of, if you know what I mean." Gillis elbowed Roger who had to stifle an urge to step away and wipe the cooties from the sleeve of his expensive suit. He offered his newest client a grimace meant to be his interpretation of the conspiratorial smile of a man's man. "I'm pretty sure I'm shootin' blanks," Gillis explained, "since one time, my old man, my mama's third husband, he whipped a ball-peen hammer at my head and missed. He caught me down low pretty good though." Roger Albright gave an involuntary shudder while his left hand dropped to groin level.

"Well, let us hope that you *are* childless. Mr. Wainwright..." he began. Gillis interrupted him.

"Hey, you're my lawyer, now, Rog, so's why don't you just call me Gillis?"

"As you wish...Gillis." Albright exhaled, handed Gillis a pen and pointed where his signature was required. "If you *do* have children, or even if there is a remote possibility that you *could* have sired children, or more importantly, if there are individuals who have reason to believe you did, it is a very high probability that you will hear from them, and you will hear from them very soon. Sooner rather than later, in my experience." Gillis's face was blank. "*Potential heirs*, as it were," Albright said peering over his rimless glasses. Gillis cast a look back over his shoulder in the direction of the window, trying to calculate the possible number of potential heirs who might very likely desire a reunion with their newly endowed Dad.

"One of our clients, Mr. Forty-Six – we refer to all of our lottery clients with numbers rather than names at ALG, for the sake of confidentiality – Mr. Forty-Six, in the two years since his windfall, has accumulated already over two point six million dollars in costs related to his paternity defenses. Not including the laboratory expenses for DNA testing." Roger paused before adding. "Generally speaking, in terms of litigation of this type, DNA testing is considered conclusive, however, it is quite expensive."

"Wow," Gillis said weakly, "Way to go, Mr. Forty-Six!" He stumbled over to and slumped into his ancient, battered and fatally stained Barca Lounger to consider the vast sums he could encounter in paternity defenses.

"Precisely why ALG recommends that you make it as difficult as possible for them to find you," Roger said.

"So, Rog?...." Gillis started to speak, then choked, sucked in air and covered his face in his hands. Roger and Jimmy both were as silent as stone watching Gillis. His unruly eyebrows stayed devilishly erect when he pushed the heel of his palms up over the crown of his head and laced his fingers together on top of it. He didn't look at either of them but seemed instead to be utterly transfixed by the dancing motes in the narrow light beam between the lounger and the front door.

If JD had been offered eighty-six million dollars himself if he could locate another individual in the whole state of Florida who looked less like a millionaire than his dear friend, he doubted he could have found one. The un-cleansable grease and grime that thirty years of motorcycle mechanics had embedded in Gillis's hands and especially under his nails, for the first time, looked to Jimmy Deane only dirty.

Roger and JD continued to watch the mesmerized Gillis stare at the dusty light beam. Too late, Jimmy made a futile wish that the lawyer would fail to notice that the shirt that Gillis had selected that morning had holes, not only where Gillis had dropped burning roaches down the front in a distant past, but also pretty significant ones under both arms. Roger remained the essence of patient indulgence. Gillis was, after all, Mr. Sixty-Nine. At last Gillis lifted his gaze and consulted his brand new attorney.

"Any way I can avoid breakin' Mr. Forty-Six's record?"

"Well, Mr. Wain...Gillis...Alperstein, Lillian and Groth recommends a complete personal identification reassignment. Though it may seem rather extreme, nothing short of that will really help." Gillis automatically responded by dropping his hands into his lap as if his genitalia needed sudden protection, from not only Roger and Alperstein, Lillian and Groth, but also belatedly from his *potential heirs*.

"Are you sayin' I gotta pretend I ain't Gillis Wainwright no more?" He looked sadly back and forth between JD and his lawyer.

"Exactly so," Roger nodded. Why, he wondered (for the sixty-ninth time) did these stupid hicks (and in Florida it was almost always some poor white trash bastard who won the big ones) did they not positively *leap* at the chance to be someone other than who they were?

"What about..." Even in the gloom Roger could see the bottom rims of Gillis's eyes redden. "What about my... friends?" Gillis asked.

"I shall be your liaison with Mr. Deane and anyone else you wish to maintain contact with. I suggest you pack a quick bag, now Mr. Sixty-Nine. I will create a diversion out in front for the media while you slip out the back. The car will pick you up on the easternmost corner of Lark Meadow Terrace and then we shall rendezvous out front. It will take the press a while to realize they've been duped."

Roger turned to Jimmy when Gillis left the room to pack his bag. "For the present, any communication between you and Mr. Wain...Gillis...will have to go through me. Eventually, the press and the curious throngs should abate." He paused and looked closely for some reaction. "They'll go away," he said. "It will let up."

"I know what abate means, Mr. Albright," Jimmy said. The young man spoke without the slightest hint of sarcasm or attitude. His voice sounded both solemn and sad. Roger admired his poise.

"Of course." Roger handed Jimmy Deane his business card.

Gillis reappeared wearing a cleaner, but too-small T-shirt and holding tightly to a hastily packed ancient Nike duffle bag.

"Okay, JD, I got me almost everything I'm gonna need." He patted his duffle. "Anything I forgot, hell, I'll just buy me a new one." He grinned at the boy and then thrust the bag onto his Barca lounger and grabbed him for a long hard hug. Jimmy Deane hugged Gillis back. They both ignored his stifled sob.

"You'll hear from me, kid. Don't you worry." He squeezed Jimmy's shoulders before releasing him. Then Roger Albright headed out the front door to make a statement to the press and answer the neighbors' questions about Florida's newest member of the millionaire's club. Gillis snuck out through the back door and paused when he hit the ground. He turned. JD was on his heels. For a second they froze, their eyes locked. Only Jimmy's dreads bounced gently in the hot breeze.

"Hey, man." Gillis grinned again at Jimmy Deane. "Who'd a' thought that bein' rich would be so hard, huh?" He leaned in for a final high five, "Dude!" he said, his eyes growing moist. "Mr. Sixty fuckin' Nine!" Then, looking like he had just burgled his own house, he slipped through the hole in the back fence and ran the two blocks to Lark Meadow Terrace.

Jimmy Deane went back into the dank kitchen. It was over ninety degrees outside but the little house felt inexplicably cold. Out front on the sidewalk Roger Albright bought time for Gillis's getaway. Jimmy relieved the refrigerator of a cold Corona and used Gillis's talking beer opener. He slipped it into his jeans' rear pocket and wandered back into the living room to watch from behind the broken blinds in the dirty window as Roger tried to convince the press and the small throng of neighbors that Mr. Wainwright had already evacuated the premises, eluding them from the only other exit. They had missed their opportunity to see the neighborhood's new millionaire. The anchorwoman from channel four looked up at the house doubtfully. Jimmy withdrew from the window. He drained his beer and set the empty bottle on the table before opening another.

He heard a clamor from the street when Roger Albright's limousine pulled up in the front to reconnoiter, a slumping Gillis hiding successfully in the back seat. The limo vanished down the street but it took a full hour before the media circus in the front of the house finally surrendered and pulled up stakes. The neighbors milled around for another little bit discussing what each of them would do with over eighty million dollars. Eventually they wandered reluctantly back to their own homes, almost everyone stealing backward envious glances until they no longer could do so.

JD paced between the living room and the kitchen, sitting down on Gillis's Barca lounger and taking a sharp poke from the bottle opener at each pass. A neat row of empty Corona bottles was growing across the Formica tabletop in the kitchen. Two beers was JD's limit under Gillis Wainwright's tutelage, but, *what the hell?* he told himself. Gillis Wainwright was not around, was he?

By sunset Jimmy was standing unsteadily in Gillis's spare room where he had played his father's drums nearly every day since he had been in the fourth grade. He could not bring himself to pick up his sticks. Instead he backed out and opened the door to Gillis's bedroom. He stepped inside. The room was remarkably clean, the bed neatly made. Jimmy Deane felt like a felon as he examined the belongings that his only good friend had left behind. He touched everything once. It made him wonder for the first time, what had become of his parents' things? They must have also left behind personal traces. Clothing. Jewelry. Remnants of their lives. What had his grandmother done with these things? What would become of the items he was holding now? How could Gillis just walk away leaving his whole life behind, as if nothing mattered at all, except his future and what his new life would become?

Fresh tears sprang into his eyes and Jimmy opened up the closet urgently, hoping that perhaps a clue would be there that might explain to him how it was that he could be as easily discarded as the dirty and old shoes that lay on the floor at his feet. He ran his hands down the mostly ancient garments hanging from cheap wire hangers. He knelt in front of the tangle on the floor of old shoes, un-wearable belts, ugly hats and mismatched stretched out sox.

He almost missed it. The box was all the way at the back. He pulled it forth with an entitlement that he himself would marvel at once he sobered up. The box was an old cardboard carton once having held a dozen bottles of California wine. Where Gillis might have obtained such a box would be just one of the mysteries he left behind, since Jimmy Deane had known him only to drink beer and almost always only Coronas. The box was unsealed but the top flaps had been closed. Jimmy hesitated a single self-conscious second before pulling them up. The box was almost full to the top. Jimmy stared for a moment before picking up one of the worn drumsticks. Someone, obviously Gillis, had written along the stick in a shaky hand. "Jimmy Deane, the greatest drummer who ever lived. 1987." He pulled more than fifty worn and splintered sticks from the box, each one "engraved" with Jimmy's name and the date the stick had been retired. Gillis, it appeared, had saved every drumstick Jimmy Deane had ever used. Underneath the collection of worn drumsticks, a second, smaller box, which had been entrusted to Gillis by Susie Deane before she died, contained Carter Deane's ashes. Jimmy set the box aside and wiped tears away with one of Gillis's old sox. He leaned against the closet's doorframe and tried but failed to form a coherent thought. He put the box holding his father's ashes back into the wine carton and then gently lay each drumstick on top. He folded the flaps and moved the box to the center of the bedroom floor. He stood and opened the top drawer of Gillis's dresser. *In for a penny*... he told himself and rifled the contents. At the very front, as if it had been recently placed there, a small embossed gift bag of an uncommon blue had been stowed in between Gillis's BVDs. Jimmy shook the contents of the bag into his hand and a silver chain slipped through his fingers. A small silver medal bearing the imprint of St. Cecilia lay in his palm. A prayer card bearing her image floated to the floor. Jimmy picked up the card. "ST. CECILIA, HOLY PATRON OF MUSICIANS" was printed on the back of the card. Jimmy looked on the bag. On its back, in wavering black marker, his initials appeared. "***JD***".

What the...? Gillis Wainwright was no Catholic and was unquestionably the most profane individual Jimmy Deane knew. He looked once again inside Gillis's underwear drawer. A sappy graduation card featuring a huge foaming beer and urging the graduate to celebrate mightily betrayed Gillis Wainwright's knowledge that Jimmy Deane's graduation from high school was imminent. Jimmy was shocked. He sat down on Gillis's bed. He cried for a long time clutching the icon of St. Cecilia before he slipped it over his head. He moved her over his shoulder and felt her slip safely down his spine before he stumbled to the bathroom to vomit. He rinsed his mouth out with Gillis Wainwright's abandoned Listerine and returned to his own house leaving the empty blue bag on the dresser top. Elizabeth Breaux was waiting when he climbed the two back door steps.

Book three – Sailing Away

What was important, perhaps, was not that the beggar was drunk and reeling, but that he was mounted on his horse, and, however unsteadily, was going somewhere.

- Thomas Wolfe (*You Can't Go Home Again*)

Chapter 26

Gillis sat uncomfortably on the edge of the limousine's plush rear seat and clutched his Nike duffle bag on his lap as if his very life were inside. When Roger Albright offered him a cold Corona from the limo's refrigerator, Gillis accepted it and curled his free arm a little tighter around his bag. He asked if it was possible to get a slice of lime, hoping to pull Roger's leg a little. The immediate production of a fresh lime made Gillis sit back and take a very long swallow. Clearly from now on, no request would be unthinkable.

He watched the freeway exits for Hallandale, Pinewood Park and North Miami slip past in tinted silence while Roger examined the necessary legal documents that would allow him to represent Mr. Sixty-Nine in all his various financial dealings. The driver made a long slow left onto Collins Avenue and Gillis sat forward to admire the exterior of the Fontainebleau Hotel. Roger Albright took note.

"Would you like to stay at the Fontainebleau, tonight, Mr. Wai...Gillis?" Roger used the French pronunciation, but Gillis knew which hotel Roger was talking about.

"Can I?" Gillis's face was filled with wonder and awe. Roger smiled. Mr. Sixty-Nine's remarkable naiveté was already beginning to grow on him.

"Pull in here, David," he told the driver.

"You know, Rog," Gillis said in a childlike voice, "I told myself a million times that if I ever won big, I'd come down here and stay a week at the Fountain Blue." His eyes filled with tears.

"And, so you have, and so you shall." Roger smiled up at the newly designed entrance to the Miami landmark. "She's a stately old girl and they've just completed the renovations. I think she'll do for this week." Roger checked Gillis into the hotel under a false name and arranged for unlimited credit underwritten by the firm.

"One more thing," he said scrutinizing his new client. In the hotel guest shop he selected several pairs of expensive slacks and a number of Hawaiian print shirts. The lawyer coaxed Gillis into tasseled loafers made of soft leather and convinced him to abandon his ancient duffle bag in the shop's dressing room.

"How do I look?" Gillis asked presenting himself for inspection like a teenaged boy trying on his high school prom tux. Indeed the new clothes made an amazing improvement.

"Splendid," Roger said honestly. "But, we'll have one more stop." When Gillis Wainwright stepped into the hotel bar, after two hours in the resort's spa, he could have easily passed for one of the four hundred well-heeled investment types who were convention guests at the newly refurbished Fontainebleau Resort. Roger circled Gillis and frankly admired the effects of the massage, facial, mani-pedi and hair styling. He took the opportunity to give Gillis a short primer on tipping before they adjourned to happy hour amongst the back slapping brokers. An hour soak had done little to bleach his fingernails of the tell tale signs of manual labor, but otherwise, Gillis looked right at home.

Under Roger's encouraging aegis Gillis tipped the hostess for a window table overlooking the new pool and when

Roger Albright did not join him in sitting, he rose again nervously.

"Rog, you ain't gonna stay? You goin' somewheres?" he whispered.

"I've got a previous engagement," Roger admitted. "I'll send David back with the car if you'd like."
Gillis considered his optional destinations.

"I can't go home, can I?"

"Not recommended." Roger shook his head. "Not tonight anyway. Maybe in a few weeks, though."

"Weeks?" Gillis echoed sadly. He was the first of Alperstein, Lillian and Groth's sixty-nine lottery winners to have not a single soul to share in the celebration of his good fortune, unless you counted his next door neighbor, the mulatto boy. Roger wished belatedly that he had suggested the boy come along. Perhaps, in time, he thought.

"Why not have dinner in the hotel restaurant tonight, and tomorrow morning, as early as you'd like, I'll send David to fetch you over to the office. We'll make a plan for your personal identification reassignment period tomorrow. Perhaps tonight you can begin thinking of things you'd like to do…places you'd like to go…people you'd like to meet." Gillis raised his eyes at the suggestion and Roger recognized a complete and utter lack of imagination in the assignment.

"Sure thing," Gillis said solemnly. "I'll be over bright and early."

"David knows the way." Roger handed Gillis another business card and left for his date in South Beach. For about five minutes Gillis watched the late-day swimmers gather up their pool things and leave for showers and, no doubt, festive dinners somewhere with family or friends. He felt a stab of loneliness and belatedly realized that he did not even know what the telephone number was that rang in the Deane's kitchen that could have connected him to JD.

He wandered out to the new four-story grand lobby taking his Corona with him. He circled the enormous room absently making an inventory of the enormous palms and the squat but elaborate potted ferns.

A man who appeared to be around Gillis's age, though dressed more conservatively than Gillis or any of the other hotel guests in dark blue slacks and a starched white shirt, looked up-each time Gillis passed where he was sitting, a slowly progressing game of solitaire before him on a table stashed next to one of the massive palms. On his third pass by the man's table, out of abject loneliness, Gillis stopped to make an idle conversational gambit.

"'Bout how much one of these damn trees cost, ya' figure?"

"I know exactly how much one of these trees costs," the man said looking up into the broad graceful branches. Gillis looked at the man's unremarkable but pleasant face.

"Exactly?" he asked.

"Two thousand, four hundred and sixty-seven dollars. Full grown." The man reported the figure with the air of an accountant. Gillis whistled. He scanned the lobby.

"Hay-ell!" he said. "That there's fifty thousand dollars! In trees!" Gillis stepped back to appreciate the closest tree better.

"Forty-nine thousand three hundred and forty dollars exactly." The man playing solitaire smiled when Gillis looked down. He picked up his deck of cards and started shuffling. "Are you a bridge man?" he asked.

"No, sir," Gillis smiled back. "I'm what you might call a chess man though, if you think we can find us a board somewheres."

Chapter 27

Gillis Wainwright

My new buddy, Warren, who I met at the Fountain Blue Hotel the same day I won me the lotto, he says the same thing JD says. That I'm some kind of a *idiot savant.* I gotta admit that I don't too much like the sound of it, but, Warren says the same thing JD told me. It ain't a bad thing to be one. It just means that when it comes to some things, like numbers and Harleys, I'm a whole lot smarter than almost anybody. Warren says he ain't never lost, hardly ever, to nobody at chess before, and he ain't seen nobody take to that game of bridge the way I did. Never mind the way I took to the damned stock market.

He let me hang out with him up in his big conference room in the mornin's while the market was open and by the second day I was makin' so damn many good trades he said I was gonna attract them boys from the SEC if I wasn't careful. Then him and me played bridge half a day every day with two other fellas he knows, and then we played us some chess by ourselves for a few hours after we ate us some supper. I told him he saved my ass, I was gonna be so lonesome that week, and Warren, he just laughed and said it was me what saved his ass from dyin' of boredom amongst them snooty broker types. Blow-hards is what Warren calls 'em.

But, them card fellas was okay. Turned out one of 'em was sellin' his boat and he took me and Warren out for a little spin out of the harbor at Lauderdale, and damn if I didn't buy the sucker right then and there. Ain't but fifteen or twenty men in the whole country who'd have call for a boat like this one Warren said on account of it comes so tricked out with all kinds of gadgets what let me trade stocks when I'm out fishin' in the middle of the ocean. Computers and such right on board. Warren called her a *hell of a neat little investment*, plus she come with a little bitty helio copter that lands right up on top, and takes two people, so's I can send it over to pick folks up in Miami and bring 'em out to the boat whenever I want. Even if I'm way the hell out chasin' bonito when they're runnin'.

I guess I was thinkin' mostly of flyin' JD over at first, but then I got to listenin' to Warren and the boat fella and that other guy who Warren says is a *solid fourth* but whose name I can't remember, and they was all talkin' about their boys and how they's all away in college and havin' the time of their young lives. At least that's what their daddies is sayin'. Anyhow, I got to thinkin' that I never gave one minute's thought to what JD ought to be doin' at his age. And, him so book smart and all. Well, Jesus H. Christ, I said to myself finally, I sure am a selfish bastard. So's I got a hold of Roger and fixed things up so's I could talk to the principal over to the school and he was a decent sort a' guy. Broke a whole bunch of rules he said, but damn, if there was ever a kid who called for some rule breakin', JD was the one, he said.

I still ain't talked to JD directly, and I sure as hell don't know if I done the right things for him, but Warren says that's the hard part of raisin' kids up. So, I asked him if that's the part of me what's an idiot and he says, "Gillis, you're no idiot. You're just a father." And, soon's he says that I start blubberin' like a damned baby and I asked him how come I'm bawlin' and Warren says, "Because you're letting go, Gillis, and that's what good fathers do when the right time comes. They let their boys go." Then he give me a big old bear hug and off he took hisself to get back to Omaha or some such place where he lives, but he gave me his private number there and said he'd like it very much if we could stay in touch. So, I aim to do just that, 'cause he was just about the smartest man I ever talked to in my whole life, and not just about the stock market neither.

Chapter 28

Jimmy Deane was unaccustomed to having to answer to his grandmother for his whereabouts. He had come and gone from the house since the tenth grade without so much as an interested question, and she, in turn, had provided nothing to him in the way of information about her own dull life. Neither had she prepared a meal, or sewn a button on a shirt, or in fact been present for a single parents' night on his behalf at his school. He did not expect her to attend his graduation in the coming week. Their confrontation the night that Jimmy Deane stumbled home from Gillis's house confirmed absolutely his negative expectation.

"Where have you been?" Her voice was shrill and slurred reminding Jimmy that he was not the only one who had been drinking excessively that evening. He looked down. Her bloodshot gaze locked on his. The contact was startling in its rarity. Jimmy's eyes narrowed meaningfully at the petty little gnome of a woman in front of him. Quite suddenly, he no longer felt sad or anything remotely akin to sadness.

"What did you do with my parents' belongings?" he demanded deliberately. Elizabeth stood mute. Except for the ridiculous style of his hair, the boy had never once been openly insubordinate. She stood her ground, her mean lips pursed into a tight little asshole, her jowls quivering. Abruptly, her whole body shaking, she turned her back on him and left the room. He heard the lock turn on her door.

Jimmy Deane retreated into his own room and knelt beside his bed. He retrieved the garbage that he had stowed there like maimed but treasured relics of his childhood. It had been a very long time since he had last felt the need to visit his shabby shrine of broken record albums and torn posters. For over an hour in silence he knelt on the bedroom floor and pieced together the broken bits of Carter's records all around him like so many jigsaw puzzles. The dust made him sneeze until he pulled his T-shirt off and used it to wipe each piece as clean as licorice before he fitted it into its whole. A deep feeling of inebriated satisfaction accompanied the completion of each black and shiny disk. Stepping carefully around them he went to the kitchen to look for tape. In another hour he had repaired a dozen posters. He tacked them crookedly up on his walls and put the remaining pieces into a much smaller jagged pile. When he knelt to shove them back under the bed the intact Beatles poster that Carter Deane had removed from Jimmy's bedroom door on the day he died rolled forward. It fell into Jimmy's hand as if Carter himself was sending it to him from somewhere in the hereafter. Jimmy unrolled the Fab Four onto the floor and leaned over them. A voice from overhead broke the silence.

"You know what John Lennon said about me?" The voice was clear and real. Jimmy blinked up at the back of his bedroom door. The alcohol had blurred his vision and time had faded the colors on the old poster, but James Dean looked just the same as he had the day Carter had tacked him up. The room spun slightly and Jimmy waited with the patience of a drunk, but James did not speak again until Jimmy turned back to the Beatles on the floor in front of him.

"He said that if it wasn't for me, there never would have been a Beatles." Jimmy looked up again but James Dean was unmoving. Jimmy stared at the poster for a very long time before he removed the tacks from its corners and let it drop to the floor. Then he unrolled the Beatles and put them where James Dean had been. He found a rubber band, secured James Dean into a narrow tube and put him under the bed with the garbage. Then he lay down on top of his spread and tried to sleep.

Elizabeth's door remained closed when Jimmy left for school early the next morning. He passed by Gillis's house on the way home, and he would have liked nothing better than working out on the drums, but he could not bring himself to go inside the empty house. His hand reached for St. Cecilia as he walked by. He was sure that Gillis would call him, but the weekend came and went and no call came. Jimmy stayed in his room and read library books. His turntable and earphones were next door so he could not drown the silence out with music.

Elizabeth left early for mass each morning without acknowledging Jimmy's presence. The remainder of each day was spent by each one avoiding the other.

The following week was the last week of high school for Jimmy Deane. In the middle of his seventh period class on the day before he was to graduate, a hall monitor came with a pass from Mr. Weis's office. "Take your stuff," the teacher said. "You aren't coming back." He handed Jimmy the summons. "Have a nice life, James Deane."

Jimmy rapped on Mr. Weis's door when the secretary gave him the go-ahead.

"Come in," Weis yelled. Another man stood when Jimmy entered. He handed Jimmy Deane a business card with one hand and then extended the other for a quick strong shake. The stranger wore a suit that by comparison made the principal look like a man who might work at Sears as a large appliances salesman. The stranger's bearing caused the principal's office, once a seat of authority, to seem like the shabby, impotent chamber that it was to everyone who had already matriculated.

"This is Lawrence Drummond, Jimmy," Gary Weis said. Jimmy looked at the card in his hand.

"Larry." The stranger smiled and gestured to the other empty chair. "Please, sit down." Jimmy looked at the principal. Weis nodded.

"I'm a partner from Roger Albright's office," Larry Drummond explained. "I have what I think will be very good news for you." The lawyer, who spoke with a slight trace of British accent, had a nice, sincere smile and he was obviously ready to get right down to business. Like Roger Albright, Larry seemed short on tolerance for needless chitchat.

"Your friend, Mr. Wainwright, has made arrangements on your behalf for a scholarship of sorts. A certain amount of his windfall to be set aside for your use." Jimmy blinked mutely. "A trust fund, naming Alperstein, Lillian and Groth as trustees, was established this morning with you as the sole beneficiary." Jimmy looked to Mr. Weis for a reaction; the principal smiled. Lawrence cleared his throat. "Upon your graduation from high school…which, as I understand is tomorrow...is that right?" Jimmy nodded. "Well, then, tomorrow you will become the beneficiary of a trust fund containing ten million dollars." Jimmy blinked. His mouth opened but it took several tries before his mouth could issue words.

"Ten…million...dollars?" He swallowed. His voice came out in a whisper. "Gillis gave me ten million dollars?"

Jimmy's right hand searched for St. Cecilia through the thin cotton of his T-shirt.

"That's exactly right, son." Larry Drummond smiled a professional smile and Gary Weis beamed widely, as if he were the responsible benefactor himself.

"Holy shit!" Jimmy blurted, "Oh, sorry, Mr. Weis."

Weis laughed merrily.

"No, I think, 'holy shit' pretty much covers the situation nicely," the principal said. The two older men grinned at each other.

"This is from Mr. Wainwright." Larry Drummond reached into the leather attaché next to his chair. He handed Jimmy a document.

Dear JD

What a trip huh? I am still not really use to the idea that I got a lot of cash. I mean I got a fuck load of cash! Xcuse my French. But, no matter how hard I try I figur I'll never spend all this doe - so I want you to have a little of it yourself. I already quit playing the dogs and the poneys cuz I figer how much luck can one bastard have - huh?

I like this guy Larry. You can trust him. I'm even geting sort of use to Roger. But he is even bossyer than my ex Loretta. hahaha. I call him "Mom" and he gets so pist! hahaha Anyway now I am a man of leeshure – and I got me some new soots to prove it!

I was thinking that maybe you can go to colige now. Roger says that colige costs a bundle but this doe should help. ☺

I bought me a new boat. It even has a tiny little heliocopter witch I can send over to Lauderdale to pick you up to visit me as soon as you get your colige vacashens.

Sinseerly your frend,
Gillis (Your former nayber,)

ps Larry's going to give you one more little present from me for your graduation which as you know - I never give you no presents before. I hope this makes up for all thos birthdays that I didnt get you nothing. hahaha Don't worry. You bin shifting Harleys since you was little. This won't be no diffrint.

Jimmy let the hand gripping Gillis's note drop into his lap. He looked from Weis to Drummond wide-eyed. Before anyone could say anything more a quick knock on the principal's door preceded the entrance of another school employee. Mr. Ward, the track coach and driver's education teacher strode directly up to Mr. Weis's desk.

"We're all set, boss," he said to Weis. He handed the principal a set of car keys.

"Do you know Mr. Ward, Jim?" Bob Ward didn't give JD a chance to answer.

"Yeah, I know Deane...had him in tenth grade...he coulda been a hell of miler if he'd wanted to." The principal leaned forward and dangled the keys in front of Jimmy's face.

"I'd like you to go out with Mr. Ward for an hour or two, Jim. Then Mr. Drummond will take you over to the DMV." Both Ward and Weis were smiling like idiots.

"The DMV?" JD asked dumbly.

"Mr. Wainwright told us that you don't yet have a driver's license...is that correct?" Drummond asked. Jimmy Deane had been testing bikes for Gillis, taking loops around the block since he was tall enough to shift the gears, and when necessary, Gillis even let Jimmy drive his truck, but it had not occurred to either of them to procure formal documentation from Florida's Department of Motor Vehicles. Jimmy slowly shook his head in the negative as he looked from Drummond to Weis and then to Ward. The principal and track coach were still grinning, their heads bobbing like dashboard hula girls. Jimmy Deane looked like a shock victim. This obsequious constant head nodding he realized, was how people treated the very rich or the very important, and in a lightening bolt, he, Jimmy Deane, had unmistakably become both.

JD followed Bob Ward out the restricted exit where the teacher's parking lot sat behind the low-slung administration building. Weis followed behind Drummond so close he was almost tripping on the lawyer's heels. A black Lincoln Towncar was double parked behind the principal's reserved space. Gary Weis took note that his blue Toyota looked like a different species next to the sleek black sedan. Parked right behind the Towncar, a silver Porsche gleamed in the sun. Stunning polished rims sparkled inside tires so new and black they all had to squint to look at the wheels.

"Let's take her for a spin." Mr. Ward walked over, opened up the passenger door of the sports car and got in. He inhaled deeply and sighed. "I *love* that smell!" JD had not moved. "What are you waiting for, kid?"

The three adults looked at the stunned young man and waited. He finally took what seemed like a normal breath.

"Okay, Mr. Ward," Jimmy said at last in his best imitation of Gillis himself. "Let's see what this baby sounds like." Then he slipped into the driver's seat, buckled his seatbelt and started the engine. "Ahhhh....She purrs like a contented woman." Jimmy quoted Gillis after a successful tune up, and the two teachers laughed. He stroked the fine leather of the steering wheel.

"Attaboy!" Ward responded rubbing his hands together. "Let's hit the street!"

In the Department of Motor Vehicles parking lot, two hours later, Larry Drummond leaned in and brushed an imaginary speck of dust off the roof of the Porsche. He gave the "one minute" signal to the limo driver waiting behind them.

"Okay, Jimmy, mission accomplished." He handed Jimmy another business card. "Can you take it from here, alone?" Drummond meant the Porsche, of course; Jimmy Deane was thinking about the rest of his life. He nodded in the affirmative, but he had his doubts on both counts. The lawyer gave Jimmy's shoulder a paternal pat and then he walked back to the limo and got into the back seat with a weary sigh.

"Is he a nice kid?" the driver asked as they pulled away from the DMV.

"Yes, actually, he seems quite nice," Larry said.

"Good. Every once in a while you want something nice to happen to nice people."

Jimmy Deane sat in the parking lot for almost ten minutes before he could bring himself to start his new car and drive back to Gillis's garage.

Elizabeth was standing at the sink in the stifling kitchen wearing her church clothes when Jimmy Deane returned to his house. She started in. Her voice was shrill and her cheeks were flushed red in a way that even the heat could not account for.

"Where have you been?" Jimmy stared at her, genuinely at a loss for words. They hadn't spoken one civil word to each other in almost a week, since the day that Gillis had won the lotto.

"I asked you where you've been!" The old woman trembled with rage. "I am not going to countenance your insolence one minute longer!"

"Grandma…"

"Don't you call me that!" she shrieked. "Don't you EVER call me that again! I am NOT your grandmother! You are NO kin to me! I am leaving here tonight to give you one day to pack your belongings and leave my house...only because it is the Christian thing to do. When I return on Saturday, I expect you to be gone. And I mean gone for good!"

A car horn honked outside on the street and Jimmy peered through the screen to see an orange taxi. A gaudy sign for the Hialeah racetrack sat on top of the cab reminding Jimmy suddenly of Gillis and stabbing his heart with grief. Elizabeth grunted as she bent over to pick up the same ancient suitcase that had moved her belongings from Tampa. Jimmy bent forward to help.

"Don't you touch that!" she screamed at him and swatted his hands furiously. "Get away from me!"

Jimmy opened his palms and backed away with the air of one who is humoring a mental patient. Elizabeth struggled half way through the front door and turned suddenly. Her face was contorted with hatred.

"Only Father Boyle knows the truth about my burden," she screamed at a public volume. "He knows that I have kept my promises. But, my duty is done, now. Do you hear me? I have KEPT MY PROMISES! I sacrificed my whole life to keep my promise to my daughter, God rest her immortal soul, to raise you up and to give you everything that she could not. But, have you been grateful? Not for one second! Sneaking over every chance you got to that maniac's house! Drinking beer! Giving me not one small ounce of the respect I deserved!" Almost as an after thought her hand flew up toward his head and waggled in a disrespectful circle. "That hair!"

"Wow," Jimmy heard himself say.

"Shut UP!" she screeched again. Her eyes were glowing red. She seemed possessed. "I promised Susan that I would never call you a nigger!" she yelled, "but, you ARE a nigger! YOU ARE NOTHING BUT A GOD DAMNED NIGGER!" Her dress caught in the door as she dragged her case through. Jimmy stepped forward and released the dress. He stood transfixed in the doorway as she struggled down the short walk to her waiting cab with the case banging against her chubby legs. He raised his fingers to his lips and whistled to summon the driver. A young Cuban hopped up out of the car and rushed to the old woman's aid. The young cabby easily took her suitcase in one hand and then put his other arm out to steady her before assisting her into the back of the cab. He threw her suitcase into his trunk and before he slammed it closed he turned to shrug up at the house. His amused smile was blinding white against the dark coffee color of his skin. Jimmy Deane raised a hand and the cab driver shrugged and waved again before he drove Elizabeth away.

Jimmy Deane knew before he looked that the broken records would be gone from the floor beneath his bed in his room and the posters would also be removed. This time she had taken everything. There was nothing left. Nothing, except for Sergeant Pepper's Lonely Hearts Club Band behind the door.

Chapter 29

JD sat down on the worn couch directly in front of the console TV set that had been providing entertainment for his grandmother for over a decade. He in fact sat in the exact spot customarily occupied by the old lady and breathed in the unpleasant mixture of dust and her stale *Chantilly*. He knew logic dictated that he should have been relieved to be rid of her, but for reasons unfathomable, he felt only frightened and alone. His grandmother's remote control device was the only object on the wobbly little coffee table. He depressed the power button. The color screen produced a sudden shocking twenty-seven inch close up of the aging televangelist, Reverend Lester.

"Jesus loves *you!"* screamed the TV preacher. The elderly man's pale blue suit jacket made the peach tinge of his make up look a little too rosy. His complexion had the unmistakable plasticity of more than a few face-lifts, and the toupee sitting on top of his head would have been too blonde and too thick even if it had been properly placed.

"But, do *you* love the Lord?" The preacher's inquiry was not a question; it was an indictment. "He knows that you have sinned!" Elizabeth Breaux's favorite TV preacher drew out his words so that they were comprised of two syllables where only one was due. "*He no-ohs that yoo-oo have sin-duh!"*

"Amen," Jimmy said. He raised the remote and changed the channel.

A clever montage of early Beatles footage had been spliced together over Sgt. Pepper's Lonely Hearts Club on MTV. "*Just in case the surviving Beatles didn't have enough money,*" the caustic MTV dj said. For several hours JD watched the hectic videos on the music channel without moving even the hand that held the remote until he fell asleep in front of the screen. His body was slumped over heavily, when hungry and thirsty, he opened his eyes around one a.m. He didn't lift his head but peered out from his crooked view. The blue light from the television screen illuminated a pair of boots propped up on the corner of the coffee table. The owner's ankles were crossed, his toes were pointing up. JD shifted to a sitting position. The booted young man held what seemed to be a bottle of Corona in one hand and a lit cigarette in the other. On the television screen a Van Halen video flared up on MTV and revealed the blood red color of the young man's jacket. Jimmy deliberately squeezed his eyes tightly closed. When he opened them again the young man was gone, but JD would have sworn that the smell of cigarette smoke lingered.

He tapped the remote power to off and went in search of something to eat. He found a bruised banana in the kitchen and slowly ate half of it looking through the small window at Gillis's deserted house next door. On his way to his bedroom he paused at his grandmother's empty room. By rule, he had not been inside the room in all the years since his mother had died. A full moon bounced light into the only window and caused the room and all of its contents to glow with an eerie silvery patina. His grandma's bed was neatly made. The room smelled of old age and old booze. In the craziest of ways he oddly missed the old woman. He backed out very slowly and slipped inside the confines of his own room shutting the door tightly. For a brief instant he leaned his forehead against his Sergeant Pepper's

Lonely Hearts Club band poster. Then he collapsed heavily onto his bed and closed his eyes and threw a tired arm across his face. He startled only slightly at the nearby voice, as if it hardly surprised him.

"I still love the Beatles," James Dean announced as a matter of fact.

The combination of a feeling that seemed close to panic but also contained pleasure made Jimmy Deane pull himself up on his elbows.

"You want to know what John Lennon said about me?" James Dean spoke as if it were the most natural thing in the world for him to be sitting in Jimmy Deane's bedroom in the predawn hours; as if he furthermore had no intention of acknowledging that he was surely nothing more than an ancient figment of Jimmy's imagination. Jimmy Deane tried to banish the unsolicited hallucination again by squeezing his eyes closed tightly. Before he dared to open them he clutched his temples. One at a time he let his lids slip open. Rather than disappearing, James Dean was sitting comfortably now underneath Jimmy's bedroom window in a ragged caned rocking chair that Jimmy had recently filched off the neighbor's curb on trash day. The young movie star's ankles were crossed as before and he rested his boots up on the corner of the twin bed in the posture of the welcomed. Jimmy could see the familiar face better in the moonlight that was streaming into the small window. A cigarette glowed red in his right hand. He took a long draw from the Corona he held in his left and seemed to be staring up at the Beatles fondly.

"Well?" James Dean prompted. Jimmy blinked rapidly, his heart beating fast. At what point did imaginary friends from childhood become the people of adult psychosis? It was one thing to passively hallucinate. It was quite another to *commune* with a hallucination. It seemed to him that if he responded, as he once had in childhood, that he was committing himself to something. It was not a commitment he was at all sure about making. *Who could be hurt*? he asked himself. But, he was *so* very alone. He told himself that it was just for this one night, just until he could figure out what to do, maybe until he heard from Gillis. He allowed himself a tentative response.

"Lennon said that if it wasn't for you…" Jimmy's voice was barely more than a whisper. Cautious. "…there never would have been a Beatles."

James Dean raised his Corona in a genial toast and grinned broadly.

"Good memory, kid." He took another sip. "So, Grandma really blew her cork this time, huh? Kicked you out? You gonna leave today?" Jimmy Deane sat up and folded his ratty pillow in half behind his head against the headboard.

"I…" When he started to explain to James Dean how utterly lost and afraid he felt a surprising storm of feelings crushed him. He couldn't speak. JD had the cognitive wherewithal to know that most reasonable people would consider such emotions absurd for an individual who had ten million dollars at their disposal, not to mention a brand new Porsche parked in the nearby garage. With the uncanny prescience of a gifted mind reader, James leaned forward.

"Remember what Bob Marley said…*money can't buy life*…or happiness, I would add. I should know." Jimmy Deane's whole body slumped down into his sagging old mattress and he draped a limp arm over his eyes. He tried and failed to hold back tears and did not speak for a long time. James Dean sat politely at the foot of Jimmy's bed taking sips of his beer and otherwise not moving. He said nothing more until Jimmy Deane's body was perfectly still.

"You ever figure out what Lennon meant?" James Dean asked at last. Jimmy Deane let his arm fall down over his chest and his right hand dropped over his heart space as if he were taking an exhausted pledge.

"Lennon's dead, you know," JD said by way of an answer. "He's been dead since 1980."

"So I've heard," James Dean grinned back before inhaling deeply. He blew perfect smoke rings in silence for several long minutes in the general direction of the Beatles. Jimmy watched the smoke rise past their hirsute faces to his ceiling.

"Those things will kill you," he told James Dean with a mean little smile. James dropped his cigarette into his almost empty beer bottle. They both listened to it hiss. "Yeah, I've heard that, too," he said. He set the corrupted empty bottle on the floor and stood. He was surprisingly tall. At least as tall as Jimmy Deane.

"I see right through you, JD," James Dean said. "You go around pretending you're tough…"

"Whoa!" JD interrupted

"I go nowhere. I pretend nothing." Jimmy Deane sounded weary rather than contentious, but his voice was raised.

"You got any friends? Any family?" James Dean asked. Jimmy hesitated. His only friend was gone, Jimmy knew not where, getting *his identity reassigned.* The last deplorable vestige of family, (if indeed she could even be considered in those terms) had just thrown him out of his own house. Kicked him out. He knew, he did, that he should not really be unhappy about this, much less surprised. A normal person in his position would be delighted and probably would already be speeding away as fast as they possibly could in any direction in their new Porsche. But, Jimmy Deane was not normal. He was burdened by a poisonous shyness that no amount of rational thought could counter, a feeling that somehow he lacked some essential information or some important quality that everyone else had. Without it, without such elementary knowledge, he was consigned to orbit around this tiny house and the tiny life he had lived in it forever. He could never leave. He would have to beg Elizabeth to let him stay.

He gave a quick glance up at the poster on the back of his bedroom door. James Dean looked up also. The room was stone quiet except for the birds just starting to chirp outside.

"Okay, you're right. I have no family. I have no friends. No one seems to.... everyone...leaves," he choked. A new cascade of fat teardrops rolled down his face. He looked at James Dean. "Why?" he whispered feeling nothing more than shame. "Why?"

James Dean looked out the window again.

"Oh. Well. Isn't that what we all want to know?" he asked. His shoulders under the red jacket shrugged elaborately, and somehow, another cigarette was burning in his right hand.

Chapter 30

Jimmy Deane woke for the second time on the morning of his high school graduation. The small ancient alarm clock on his dresser confirmed what the blazing sun streaming through his bedroom window suggested; it was already past two p.m. When, by sheer habit, he made his bed, it was with equal parts dread and excitement that he realized in all likelihood he would never again sleep in this bedroom. He headed for the kitchen.

"You missed your graduation, I think." Jimmy stopped in his tracks and turned back slowly to face James Dean, who, for the first time in the broad light of day, was sitting as he had been the night before, as natural as could be, his booted feet propped up on the living room coffee table, the remote control device in his careless hand. James Dean smiled affably up at Jimmy. He tapped an imaginary watch on his wrist.

"Oh, shit," Jimmy Deane responded. He stood stock still, frozen and blinking like a proverbial deer in headlights. James Dean turned back to the KISS video on MTV.

"I miss Pete Criss," he said sighing. And then, as if he couldn't bear to watch the replacement in drummers Pete's band mates had made some years earlier, he pointed the remote at the TV and changed the channel to the financial station. A pretty blonde woman was talking about commodities while stock prices appeared with little up and down arrows in two streaming ribbons at her bosom on the bottom of the screen. James Dean looked over his shoulder calmly.

"You don't have much time, man, if you're gonna get outta here before *Grandma* gets back." Jimmy Deane ignored the visage of the dead movie star and turned his back. In the kitchen he looked about for something that might qualify as breakfast finding only the uneaten part of the previous evening's rotten banana. The ripe fruit's smell was nearly overwhelming. Jimmy took a seat at the old Formica table and tapped the palm of his hand against his temple. Apparitions summoned by dire emotional straits during the wee hours were one thing. And, a thing that JD was not unfamiliar with at all. Wasn't a dead movie star in your living room at high noon worrisome?

"Oh, and your buddy Gillis called earlier," James yelled over the TV into the kitchen.

Jimmy found his legs and then his voice. "You spoke to Gillis?" he ventured. James Dean smiled broadly as if he were gratified that Jimmy had finally deigned to speak to him.

"You were sleeping. I didn't want to wake you." James returned to MTV with a flick of the remote. "Oh, hey, check this out...Metallica's got a new bass player..."

"You talked to Gillis?" Jimmy repeated stepping forward to install himself in front of the TV.

"Sure." James leaned over to see beyond Jimmy and played a little air guitar.

"Who did he think you were?"

"I told him who I was," James Dean said leaning around to catch the end of Metallica. Jimmy moved to block his view yet again.

"You told him you were *James Dean*?"

James smiled, gave up on the TV, and shrugged.

"It was a terrible connection," he said.

"What did he say?" Jimmy stepped toward James and reached out for the remote. James handed it over without objecting. "Well?"

"He said he bought a boat. He was in fact calling ship-to-shore."

"And?"

"I think technically it would be called a yacht, given the dimensions, but…you know Gillis." James Dean threw up his hands as if to say, *what are you going do*?

"That's all?"

"He said he's been doing some investing...*where the real gambling is done in this country*, I think is how he put it."

"Investing?"

"Stock market. He thinks technology is hot. He's putting a ton of money into two companies that he thinks are going to be huge in, uh, something called *compact disc technology*...yeah, that's it." James smiled making little quote marks in the air where a moment previously he'd been playing excellent bass licks. He seemed inordinately pleased to have remembered the unfamiliar vernacular of the upcoming technological advances in the music industry.

"I gotta go," Jimmy Deane told him.

Hurrying, he went back to the bathroom and stripped off his boxers and jumped into the shower. Letting the hottest possible water pound down his back he tried to take stock of all that had transpired since ...when?...was it just since yesterday? The prior twenty-four hours had certainly contained enough of the absolutely incredible to give even the most sensible person reason to doubt what was real and what was not. He considered the implications impugning his sanity, trying to look at each event with objectivity. It did appear that James Dean, *his namesake*, was right that minute garnering stock tips from the color console in his living room. He turned the hot to cold and stood another couple minutes. Toweling off quickly he was surprised to find that he had actually begun to worry that his hallucination would be a fleeting one. His relief was obvious when James Dean was still trolling the cable stations.

"You comin'?" Jimmy made an effort to sound casual, to camouflage his relief. He was dressed in his best clean jeans and a pressed white long-sleeved shirt. He paused at the front door. James Dean looked up, muting the TV yet again.

"Where you goin'?" he asked.

"School. I'm going to get my diploma," Jimmy told him.

"You takin' the Porsche?" Jimmy nodded, denying to himself that a shred of pleasure had accompanied the thought

"Nah," James Dean leaned back in the sofa. "I'm gonna catch Oprah in another twenty minutes. I'll be here when you get back."

"Good," was JD's terse response, but he locked eyes with James Dean. They nodded silently as if more had been exchanged.

"Take it slow!" James Dean advised as Jimmy ran out the door.

The Porsche was in Gillis's garage, the keys still in the ignition. *Okay*, Jimmy told himself, *that* part of yesterday was real. As he pulled the Porsche out onto the street and headed over to the high school he imagined what Gillis would have to say if he could describe to him what his previous day had been like. Without a shred of doubt, JD concluded that had Gillis Wainwright himself not been Jimmy Deane's benefactor, he would have pronounced the acquisition of ten million dollars and a brand new Porsche much more fantastical than a mere visitation in one's living room by a dead fifties movie star. Jimmy checked the clock on the dash, hoping that the principal was still in his office. He had a feeling that whatever he decided to do, it would be a good thing to have his high school diploma.

He gunned the Porsche and passed the slow moving VW up ahead.

Chapter 31

The principal, Mr. Weis

I hardly slept the night before graduation. It isn't every day a lowly high school principal gets to hand over the keys to a brand new 944 Turbo Porsche to one of his students. Hell, I've never even seen one of them close up before and all I could think afterwards was, I *should have taken the damn thing around the block at least once before I gave it to the kid.*

It was a crazy day, just insane. It's always a little wild around here the week of graduation. The seniors are as squirrelly as all get out and making my life generally miserable. I'm still trying to lock down the faculty for summer school. A few kids have always come up short of units and are begging for diplomas, first trying to bribe me, and then doing everything but threatening my life. It's your basic academic nightmare, but I had things under control.

And, then, in the middle of the day, my secretary gets me on the walkie-talkie and tells me there's an emergency I have to take care of regarding one of our *Black* students. That's what she said. She never in a million years would have said, "We have an emergency with one of our *White* students." So, anyway, I get back to my office with fantasies of god-knows-what kind of mayhem and instead there is a very nicely dressed youngish guy with a very expensive leather brief case waiting to see me from some law office. The guy seems affable enough during introductions, and why not? He was sent over on a very happy mission. He points out my window to the brand new Porsche sitting behind a Lincoln Towncar right next to my Toyota, and he tells me that one, Jimmy Deane, has been given not only the car, but also ten million dollars by that yahoo who won the biggest lottery in the history of Florida. Of course I had heard about it. It was on both the national and local news night and day all week long. The poor bastard had disappeared under a veil of secrecy, apparently so he could escape the absolutely unremitting hounding by the press. America loves the lucky. What I did not know was that our very own Jimmy Deane was the yahoo's next-door neighbor, and he had apparently been sort of an ad hoc son to this yokel. I knew this kid's story. My wife had him in kindergarten. The kid's parents died when he was practically a baby and this guy, the lotto winner, sort of took him under his wing. The lawyer put him on the phone with me.

As a graduation present, Mr. Lotto is giving the kid the Porsche, but since he never got a driver's license he wants us to rush him through driver's ed and facilitate the whole transition. Could I help, he wants to know? It's a damn funny thing. You think you know yourself. You tell yourself as a school administrator you treat all your students equally. But, I'll tell you. When it comes to ass kissing, nothing makes it happen on such a grand scale as the instant inheritance of millions of dollars. You should have seen us all scurry around. I guess that's what kept me up all night. I was wishing I could do it all over again and look a little less like a silly old sycophant and maybe have a bit more grace myself. And, maybe take that Porsche around the block. That too, but that didn't happen either.

On the whole, though, I was really glad that finally this poor kid had a piece of good fortune befall him. He's had nothing but shit rain down on him since he was born according to my wife. We've watched his progress, Terry and I, and sometimes, we even spoke of doing something meaningful for the poor kid. Behind the scenes, you know? But, hell, with the needs of twenty-four hundred other students…plus three of our own? Well, it never happened. I just never made it happen.

I talked to him once in a while though. I let him know I had my eye on him in a good way. To tell the truth, the kid had a lot more on the ball than any other kid I ever met. He was a real loner though. I never once saw him hanging out with another kid. Whenever I saw him around campus I'd try to start up a conversation. Terry told me that he was a real reader so I'd ask him what he was reading. It became a sort of a joke between us and it was always an education for me. What kind of kid reads fucking *Ivanhoe* for pleasure, though? I myself was more comfortable when he told me he was into Hemingway for a while. One day I made the mistake of asking him what he thought about Hemingway.

"Well, sir," the kid told me, *"his treatment of the black man is disappointing. The disparaging way he writes about the blues? He certainly doesn't share the sentiment that the Negro is the essence of man's nobility."*

"Really?" I asked him. It would shock you how illiterate the average public high school principal is. But, anyway, that was my shtick with him. Every time I saw him, I'd say, "Hey, kid, what ya' reading?" It was Malraux. Emerson. Melville. I mean really. You know anybody who read, I mean *really* read *Moby Dick in the Ass*? And then Richard Wright and Langston Hughes. Hell. I'd never even heard of Langston Hughes. And, who's got the time to keep up? He must have known from the blank look on my face that I had never heard of Langston Hughes. He looked so disappointed and kind of embarrassed for me. I was the one who should have been embarrassed. And not just because the kid had it all over me intellectually. I never told anybody this, not even Terry, but when he was a sophomore, he had tried out for the school band. He not only made it, the band coach told me that JD was actually in a league of his own on the drums. He didn't have the bucks to pony up for the uniform though. I've done it myself for more than one kid. Somehow, I just let Jimmy Deane slip through the cracks. Could be why I fell all over myself to help this lawyer.

I sent for the kid out of his seventh period class. He had no idea what was about to happen to him, and when he showed up in my office he looked scared to death. He's a good kid. Always has been a good kid. It can't have been easy either being neither white nor black *here*. A few of our staff here were really bothered by his dread locks, too. You can't accuse us of being an enlightened bunch. No wonder his best friend was the next-door neighbor, who, I gathered from the lawyer, was a real character. We practically had to force JD to take the car. I had Bob Ward take him out for a few hours and then the lawyer took him over to the DMV.

He didn't show up for the graduation ceremony the next day and I can't say I expected him. Hell, if somebody had given *me* ten million bucks and a new Porsche, I doubt I would have shown up. But, he did come after everyone else was gone. I was just about ready to leave myself. I had actually been sitting at my desk looking at his diploma, getting set to mail it to him when I saw the Porsche pull into the faculty lot out of the corner of my eye. I knocked on the window and waved him over to the door. It was a little awkward to try and make some casual conversation after all that had happened.

"What are you reading now, Jim," I asked him.

"Ralph Ellison," he said.

"No, shit?" I said and at least he cracked a smile. But, clearly small talk was not going to be easy between us, now that he was a millionaire and I was just his wrinkled old principal.

"So, I guess you came for this?" I handed him the big manila envelope I had just addressed to his house. Inside was his diploma, a big gold seal in one corner reading *Summa Cum Laude*.

"Nobody even came close to your gpa," I told him. "You could have been the valedictorian if you'd had any extra-curriculars." There was a second. No more than an instant. We were both remembering the whole band episode, I suppose. He let me off the hook and just smiled and kind of shrugged it off.

"So, what now?" I asked him. He shook his head.

"Dunno," he said. "Maybe Dostoyevsky. Mark Twain. T.S. Elliot." He grinned at me then and I could see he was trying to forgive me by making fun of himself. I put out my hand. Like I said, he was a real nice kid.

"Okay, Jim. Good luck. You need anything, you give me a call, okay?" He shook my hand. It was a good, firm handshake. At the door he turned back.

"Mr. Weis?" he asked.

"Yeah?" I was in no way prepared for what came next. It took him a second, like he wasn't sure I could be trusted.

"Did you ever hear somebody talking to you who isn't really there?" he finally blurted out. I guess I just looked dumbly back. "…Or, see anybody who *can't* be there?"

I felt like Jimmy Deane was giving me one last chance to come through for him and I badly wanted to. So, I was cautious. I thought about it before I asked him, "What kinds of things do these people say to you?"

Jimmy bit down on his lips hard first and then he said – with even more hesitation, "Well, when I was a kid, I used to imagine that my mom and dad came into my room and talked to me – after they died."

"You were young. Younger than five?" I asked. He nodded and was doing that thing with his lips again. "Well," I told him honestly, "I think that's nothing to worry about. I'm pretty sure that's what little kids do when they're…when they're really hurting." Jimmy Deane nodded. He hesitated before turning to go. He tapped his diploma a couple of times on the door.

"Okay," he said.

"Hey, Jim?" I did not want to fail this last chance he had given me. "Is that all? You ever hear anybody else talk to you?" He seemed to consider this question a long time, working that envelope in his hand against the doorknob.

"Well, to tell you the truth, I kind of thought this morning somebody was talking to me." *Oh, shit,* I thought.

"About what? I mean what did they say?" I had to try hard to keep my voice steady.

"Well, he was giving me some stock tips." Jimmy shrugged. It was my turn to bite my lips together and think about this. I really didn't want to blow it.

"Stock tips?" I asked. "You mean he told you what stocks to buy?" Jimmy nodded.

"Hmmmmm…" I was buying time but I must have sounded every bit like the dope I felt like I was. "Well, what did he say you should buy*?"* He must have known how lost I was in that territory. He shrugged.

"He told me to buy something called *compact disk technology.*" He smiled then. What you'd call, if you were anybody but Hemingway, a *vague* smile. And, again he waited very patiently for my response. It took a minute.

"Have you ever heard that term before?" I asked him. "What was it? Compact Disk?"

"No, sir," he said solemnly.

I gave it another full minute, nodding in a way that I hoped made me look like the sage counselor I wanted to be.

When he stopped sawing my doorknob off with his diploma I told him, for better or worse, "I think it's okay, Jimmy. I don't think it's anything to worry about. I think you've been under some stress, and you've had a big shock. I think it's gonna be okay." I tried to look confident in my verdict.

"Okay, thanks, Mr. Weis. For everything. Really." He smiled again then, a smile that lit up the whole room, and I thought, Jesus, if this kid could just get some happiness in his life, he could rule the world with that smile.

"You're welcome, buddy," I told him. "And, congratulations." I watched him drive away. I sat staring at the space where he'd had that goddamn beautiful silver Porsche parked and then I picked up my phone. I dialed my brother in law, who's a big honcho at Merrill Lynch out in L.A.

"Jerry," I said when I finally got through the maze of his underlings. And here's what I asked him: "Do you know anything about something called *compact disk technology?"*

Chapter 32

Gillis had been right in predicting that all the years of shifting temperamental Harleys had given his young apprentice an ease in handling the 944. Jimmy pulled it up in front of the only home he'd ever known and looked at the simple boxy structure with fresh eyes. The house already seemed a little bit foreign to him after the events of the past week. It would be a charitable overstatement to call the house a *bungalow*, though, this is how it would be described by the real estate brokers who were only just beginning to profit obscenely from the vast migration of Northerners and Midwesterners to South Florida.

For certain, the two least tended properties on the street remained Jimmy's house and Gillis's house next door to it, neither of which had been given so much as a new coat of paint in Jimmy's lifetime. All of the other homes had been gentrified to some degree with, at the very least, a bit of ostentatious semi-tropical landscaping. In flamboyant contrast, only two weary, bloomless birds of paradise struggled for life in front of the Deane house, while in roughly the same two spots in Gillis's front yard, two equally drooping hydrangeas withered, giving the two properties the air of demoralized relatives.

A vague stirring of melancholy swept over Jimmy at the sight of Gillis's garage door sagging closed next door. His own house, as he climbed out of his newly acquired and ridiculously extravagant vehicle, looked suddenly like a fine place to be rid of.

The front door was open and Jimmy immediately took in (with greater relief than he expected) the welcome sight of James Dean, as before, sitting in front of the console TV. He looked up with an amused expression. On the screen Oprah reached over compassionately to pat some remotely familiar older movie star's folded hands to explain that a commercial break would interrupt her stream of sympathy concerning the aging actor's latest drug rehab experience.

"You know what? I *knew* this joker was gonna wind up like this." James Dean sat forward and pointed enthusiastically at Oprah's guest, then he relaxed into the mustiness of the old sofa and patted the seat cushion next to him for JD. "You gotta love O," James Dean said with genuine admiration. After the commercial break, and a few more minutes of face time for the old alcoholic, James Dean sat forward again. "I could've *killed* on this show!" He shook his head muting the television and gave Jimmy his full attention.

"So, what's up? Are you a high school graduate?" Jimmy handed James Dean the envelope containing his diploma. James Dean slid it out with exaggerated care and gave a low appreciative whistle. "Highest honors?" Jimmy shrugged. "So. Now what, genius?" James Dean asked. "You got a plan?" Jimmy shook his head.

"Nope. No plan," he said. James Dean handed him back the envelope and Jimmy dropped it onto the coffee table. "I guess I could go to college, now." He bit his bottom lip and sat down heavily next to James Dean. The two of them sat with their feet on the top of the coffee table and, without the benefit of sound, watched the rest of Oprah's interview with the drug addled old movie star. Finally, Oprah stood, smiled benignly at her television audience, clapped her hands and extended her arms as if to hug the whole studio while the credits rolled rapidly upward.

"Listen," James Dean said. "Just a thought here, but when I was your age, I went out to college in California. You ever think about going out west?" Jimmy Deane turned his head ever so slowly and squinted doubtfully at James in a tilted sidelong glance. James Dean wiggled his eyebrows up and down.

"Santa Monica." James Dean said grinning. "Eh? San - ta Mo – ni - ca." He snapped his fingers in between syllables. "What do you say?"

Chapter 33

Roger Albright arranged a turnkey house rental for Jimmy Deane north of Montana Street in the posh section of Santa Monica proper. A cottage really, the house itself was modest in size, relative to some of the other monsters in its neighborhood. But, it was more than enough for a single person, it came with its own housekeeper, and it was close to Santa Monica College, James Dean's alma mater. The final perfection was a large music studio attached to the back of the house.

"Go!" Roger Albright had said when Jimmy came to his offices in Miami and disclosed his plan. "Go west, young man! Have a little fun. Like your namesake. Have you read the bio yet?" Roger peered over his wireless reading glasses.

"Not yet," Jimmy admitted.

"Oh, you *must!*" Roger said fanning himself with a legal pad. "Such a beautiful boy he was! I just adored Jimmy Dean." Roger squeezed his eyes closed and rocked back in his desk chair picturing the young James Dean in *Rebel Without a Cause.* "You know," Roger's chair snapped forward. "He too went to Santa Monica College when he was your age. Did you know that?" Roger sounded wistful. Jimmy Deane did not tell Roger Albright that not only had James Dean told him all about California, but he had given him his cure for hangovers and had recently begun to offer stock tips. "Well, he did. It is such a fabulous idea to go out to the coast for a little while. I adore the coast! Take some college classes. Take the west coast sun." Roger gazed dreamily out his office window down onto Southbeach. "So much better than our puny Florida rays. I just wish I could be there to see the look on their faces when you tell them that *your name* is James Deane!"

"Have you heard from Gillis?" Jimmy interjected.

"Of course, dear boy. Don't you worry about Gillis." Roger waved a hand dismissing any concerns Jimmy could have and then, noticing the boy's worried face, he leaned forward as if in conspiracy and told him gently, "He is, at this very moment, I mean… as we speak… learning the ins and outs of living aboard the most fabulous yacht you've ever laid eyes on. And, already he has discovered…of all things, the stock market!" Roger literally gasped as if nothing could be more surprising. Having reminded himself of the true business at hand and the real reason for JD's visit he plumped the stack of documents on his desk. "And, that is why you must sign these papers that give us permission to negotiate trades on your behalf according to Gillis's desires." Roger uncapped the pen he kept in his breast pocket and laid it across the documents on the table. "It turns out that Mr. Sixty-Nine is not just lucky at games of chance, but he's a very astute investor as well." Jimmy could detect real admiration in Roger's words. "And, never fear, as soon as the lottery frenzy business dies down a bit, he'll be in touch directly with you himself. For now though, you'll want to try to lay low, so those media thugs leave you in some peace. You can count on that school to leak your circumstances sooner rather than later, and the press will hunt you down, too." Roger's hand batted the media away. "Until your trails go cold, Larry and I will be your go-betweens."

Nobody was better at *laying low* than Jimmy Deane. He signed the Power of Attorney and shook Roger's hand. Under cover of darkness he drove the Porsche into Gillis's driveway with his lights dimmed. Next door, his grandmother had returned and was already installed in her customary spot in front of the television, the volume on the *Dallas* season finale audible half way down the block.

James Dean made a sudden appearance, as if from nowhere, while Jimmy moved his belongings into the boot of the Porsche from the small pile he had stashed on the center of Gillis's garage floor earlier.

"Nice wheels," James Dean said running his hand over the roofline. "You have any problems with her under eighty?" Jimmy leaned over the car and looked with significant silence at the actor who shrugged. "No? I guess they've made improvements…"

"You'll see for yourself," Jimmy Deane said and opened up the passenger door. James Dean stepped back; his eyes grew huge.

"Not this time," he said and backed away another step. "I'll make my own way." He seemed to read the doubt on Jimmy Deane's face in the dark. "Don't worry. I'll find you. I found you here, didn't I?" He paused then moved close to slap the rear fender like it was the flank of a racehorse. "But, take it easy, okay? Nice and easy." Jimmy Deane took a deep breath and hoisted the surviving crate of albums onto the passenger seat.

"Just as well," he said. "Now I have room for these." He rolled up his diploma and put it into the glove box and then closed it solidly. A brown paper grocery sack held his meager wardrobe. He stuffed it onto the floor behind Carter's turntable. Carter's ashes were already inside the boot with the wine carton containing JD's venerated drumsticks. When the Porsche was completely packed, Jimmy lowered Gillis's garage door and turned in the dark to face James Dean.

"Okay then," Jimmy gave James Dean a high five and a soul handshake complete with a one armed hug. "See you in Santa Monica. *San...ta...Mo...ni...ca.*" He slipped behind the wheel and turned the ignition. He had no idea how to get to California.

"Just ask people along the way," James advised. "Everybody knows where California is!"

"*San...ta...Mo...ni...ca!*" James Dean sang out as Jimmy backed down Gillis Wainwright's short driveway.

Chapter 34

The Waitress in New Mexico

Harlan threatened to fire me today. Said it was on account of I was *neglecting the customers* at the supper rush, but it wasn't that at all. Harlan was just jealous cause of that fifty-dollar tip I got from that TV star. Or, maybe he's in the movies. I can't tell you which since I ain't been good about names and faces after my head got busted up a little bit by a flyin' beer bottle some time ago over at the Half Way Inn. But, you woulda known him if you'da seen him. One look and anybody could tell he was somebody famous. Real cute. Maybe he was that one from *Miami Vice.* The black one, not Don Johnson, who I also wouldn't throw outta bed for eatin' crackers, if you know what I mean. 'Cept this guy had them little braids in his hair like that music guy from Jamaica. What's his name? Bob Motley. Somethin' like that.

Anyhow, when that silver car of his pulled up in front, everybody in the café rose up and went over to the window like we was all hypnotized. Nobody here'd ever seen nothin' like it. Looked like a silver space ship more than a car. When that young man got out and stretched? Well, lordy! Don't tell nobody, but I've had me a little secret thing for black men ever since Sidney Poitier played that teacher over in England or wherever in *To Sir With Love.* Some people is just so damned good lookin', don't make no difference if they is white or black or green. You know what I mean?

Well, that young man heads for the front door and everybody scurries around to get back in front of their coconut pie so's that they don't all look foolish for gawkin' and I grabbed up the coffee pot and say, "Hi, y'all. Why don't you take a seat right here at the counter? The service is better." (Harlan says I'm nosy but I prefer to call it friendly.) Alice Rae gives me the stink eye since she is workin' the tables. But I don't care. Sometimes you got to be *assertive* in certain situations. And me? I can smell an opportunity to kill some of the god-awful boredom around here a mile comin'.

I could see up close, this young man does look young. A little too young, though I am still in my head calculatin' if he's one you'd have to throw back. I got my lower limits.

"So, honey," I say, "You want some coffee?" And he smiles and says yes. Well, that smile damn near took my breath away. You should have seen it. Lit up the whole damned café. Harlan is stickin' his fat head out from the kitchen, so for his benefit I tell the young man that we got the best coconut cream pie in all of New Mexico.

"Uh, sure," he says, but he does not sound sure about it at all. "Excuse me, did you say *New Mexico?"* Well, it makes perfect sense that he is lost because what the hell would some movie star or such be doin' way out here?

"That's right," I tell him. "You are sittin' practically in the heart of Las Vegas, New Mexico. You lose your way, did ya'?"

"Where are all the casinos?" he asks real cute like. He ain't the first person to make that mistake, but, I thought that he looked a little sharper than that, and surely they are still teaching some kind of Geography in the schools, ain't they?

"Honey," I ask him. "Are you lookin' for Las Vegas, *Nevada*?"

"Oh," he says, the dawn breakin' on that cute face of his. "I wasn't really looking for it. I was just following the signs…"

"You headin' out west?" I asked.

"Yes, ma'am," he says and I think, *hell, yes, too young.*

"California?"

"Yes, ma'am," he says again.

"Well, darlin' you need to get you a map. This here is Las Vegas, *New Mexico*, like I said, and the closest thing we got to a casino is that Dairy Queen over there 'cross the street."

He didn't take but two bites out of his pie and just let his coffee sit and get cold. Harlan come out and give him some directions to get him on his way out to LA and when he left me that Buchanan next to his plate, Harlan argued that half of that tip should oughta be his. 'Course we all ran back up to the windows to watch him drive that space ship car away, and when Alice Ray asked me, "Hey, Sissy, who *was that anyway?"*

I just told 'em all, "Don't you know who that was? That there was the Lone Ranger. High Oh Silver, High Oh!" Even got a laugh outta old Harlan with that one. I thought it would come to me sooner or later, but I still can't say I know who that boy was for sure.

Chapter 35

Neither the housekeeper nor the agent from the real estate office gave a second thought as to how the handsome young man in dreadlocks had the means to own such a car or rent such a house. Rich people and beautiful people were all in a day's work for the working class of Los Angeles.

It did seem a little strange that it took him less than five minutes to move his belongings into the house. Once that task had been accomplished he left immediately and followed the broker's directions to the college. He found parking in a lot adjacent to campus and located the manila envelope with his high school diploma from the glove box.

Just inside the front door of the enormous room designated by signs as the place to register for summer classes, a painter's easel held a large poster instructing students to fill out applications and present them to one of the five clerks who were typing registration information into computer terminals. Jimmy took a course schedule and filled out his application. The large room was crowded and five long lines of registering students stretched nearly out the door. Jimmy got in the "Out of State Transfers ONLY" line.

The woman working under this sign had pursed full lips and knitted brows, giving her face a perpetual scowl. At first glance, it appeared as if she were simultaneously bored and unhappy with her job. Her plump face and bare chubby arms were many shades darker than Jimmy's while her chemically straightened hair had been dyed into an unmoving shield the unfortunate color of an eggplant. Her irises behind unattractive eyeglasses were as black as her pupils. She had good reason it seemed to be unhappy.

"TPP?" She asked abruptly when Jimmy stepped forward.

"I'm sorry," Jimmy Deane looked down at his course schedule and back at the woman.

"You want TPP, don't you?" It was an irritated accusation, not a question. She did not wait for a response but rambled on sarcastically. "Well, today is your lucky day. They just opened another section this morning...I would like to know what goes on over there, anyways...everybody just *gots* to have that class." She made a face that clarified her opinion of the students who desired registration in the popular course known on campus as TPP. She started inputting data on her keyboard. Jimmy Deane cleared his throat. She glanced up.

"I'm sorry. I don't know what TPP is," he admitted sweetly.

"Oh..." She adjusted her glasses and looked him over. "Sorry," the woman said. "I just thought...from the looks of you...I thought you were an *act-TOR*." Her voice dripped sarcasm. This woman's disdain for the arts was unmistakable.

"Nope," Jimmy smiled at her. "Not an actor." His smile raised the temperature of her chilly demeanor by several degrees.

"Please, do not tell me that you're." She paused dramatically and without shame offered Jimmy Deane a limp wrist. ".....a... *dancer.*" (Wrongly, but without a shred of doubt, the girls in registration were united in the opinion that the good-looking males who registered for performing arts classes, and in particular the dance classes, were all gay.)

"Nope," he said. "Not a dancer."

"A musician then?" Her voice had taken on a sudden flirtatious quality. You could tell she at least liked musicians a little bit.

"Well..." It was Jimmy Deane's turn to pause. He seemed genuinely stymied by the question. He had never called himself a musician. He shrugged. "I guess so. Yeah. I guess I *am* a musician." She gave him a look that did not hide her opinion that he was just a little bit odd, too. She leaned her elbow against the counter and stared while she briefly contemplated asking him if he needed a referral to the disabled student center.

"So you *do* want TPP, then...?" She returned to her keyboard.

"TPP?" Jimmy repeated. The woman halted, looked up and slowly and deliberately moved her eyeglasses down on her nose. She peered over them and looked at Jimmy, trying to ascertain whether he was giving her a hard time on purpose.

"Boy, do you see all those students in this line?" Jimmy obediently turned and looked at the line of students building behind him. He faced back to the clerk.

"Yes, ma'am," he told her politely.

"Well, I cannot go to lunch until every one of them has gotten into some summer class or other, and most of them are going to want to get into *this* class, which at this moment is still open. By the time you make up your mind here, that second section is going to be closed. So....once again, and for the very last time…do you or do you not want to register for the ever popular *Psychology of Performance?*" She enunciated each word of her final question the way she did for the foreign born students or as if she herself were a drama major perfecting her elocution. Jimmy Deane blinked rapidly.

"Okay," he said finally.

"Okay... yes? You want TPP?" The homely clerk let her hands hover impatiently over the keyboard again.

"Well," Jimmy said innocently. "I guess so. If you think so. Why not?" The woman shook her head and exhaled an exasperated breath, her typing fingers a blur on the keyboard. She turned and took Jimmy's paperwork. She examined his new Florida diver's license.

"Florida, huh? You know you have to pay out of state tuition?" Jimmy nodded and pulled a stack of hundred dollar bills from his pocket. Her eyes widened. "Is everybody from Florida like you?" she asked over her shoulder. Jimmy was unsure of her meaning but he was certain in his conviction that absolutely *no one* from *anywhere* was like him.

"No ma'am," he answered her honestly. She shook her head again.

"Well," she told him, "I got some people in Alabama, and they's a little bit strange, I guess..." It seemed she was speaking mostly to herself and required nothing in the way of response from Jimmy.

"You ain't a rapper, are you?" she demanded suddenly, her hands stilled for a brief moment.

"No ma'am," Jimmy said.

"That's good!" Her big hairdo moved like a helmet as she shook her head violently. "That is not *my people's* music. That ain't black music. Aretha. That's some black music. B.B.…Mr. Barry White…them Nevil brothers…now we talkin' some soul music. You like Aretha?" Jimmy smiled again and the clerk blushed.

"Well, you are polite anyways," she offered. "Now, is this here your real name?"
She looked at Jimmy's high school diploma and back at him, her brows knitted in doubt.

"Yes, ma'am," he told her.

"Your real given name is *James Deane*?" He nodded. "Oh, lordy, boy, *they* are gonna eat you alive!" She finished typing and faced him squarely with a serious expression.

"Now listen up, Mr. *James Deane*. Summer school classes are accelerated! That means you got to be in class every single day! You can NOT fool around!" She threw his diploma across the counter. "You are in college now!" A small note of concern had snuck into her advice as if she were sternly counseling a retarded nephew. She handed Jimmy a pink three-by-five card. "Take this to your class. The first day is next Thursday." Jimmy Deane opened his mouth to speak. She held up a hand. "Do not ask me why!" She barked. "Your instructor will collect these in the first week. Don't lose it! It's important! Now, go on over there and get your picture taken for your student ID which will also be your library card." She hesitated just a second before adding, "Doctor Pierce is a big shot from UCLA. He just comes over here in the summer time to teach TPP. I hear he don't countenance no fools over here, so don't be actin' a fool in his class, you hear me?"

"Thank you," Jimmy said. He tucked the pink card into the envelope with his diploma.

"Git, now," the clerk whispered, but she gave him a sweet smile that utterly transformed her face.

"James Deane!" As he stepped away she called him back. She leaned across the counter and lowered her voice. "You come back here and see me if'n *they* give you too hard a time, you hear? You kin think of me as your guardian angel." She let her right hand hover over the keyboard of her computer and gave a quick look to either side. "In Registration we got ways of makin' life difficult for certain folks. You understan' me?" Jimmy Deane didn't, but he nodded understanding anyway.

"Thanks," he said again.

The clerk waved him off, slid her glasses back up her nose and looked past him.

"Well, come on down!" she beckoned the next student in line. "Don't just stand there actin' a fool!" She winked once more at Jimmy Deane and gave him one last dismissive wave of her hand.

Jimmy walked around campus until he found the Main Stage building where the Psychology of Performance was to be held. He wanted to see what the auditorium looked like, so he tried the door but the building was locked. His hand was still on the door pull when two men came around the corner of the building carrying large paper coffee cups. They paused when they saw Jimmy Deane. The short Latino man jingled a huge ring of keys.

"Are you the new tech?" he asked Jimmy.

"No, sir." Jimmy backed away from the door. The other man was tall and dark skinned. Like JD, his hair was twisted into dreads long enough to touch his shoulders. For a long moment he studied Jimmy's face with unguarded interest, his brows knitted together, then he caught himself.

"I'm sorry for staring, son," he said in a deeply resonating voice. "I thought for a moment that you were someone I knew." The two men kept on walking but as they rounded the corner the tall dark man with dreadlocks looked back.

"Uncanny..." Jimmy heard him say.

"You're lookin' at yourself, Bob, ten years ago." His companion laughed as they disappeared.

Jimmy gave himself a campus orientation for a while until he located the library and went inside. He took a seat at a computer terminal and typed in "drums". The card catalog returned 17,000 entries.

"Holy shit!" he whispered and looked up when the girl across from him laughed.

"Narrow your search," the girl whispered. Jimmy nodded and typed in "drumming origins nineteenth century". The card catalogue responded with a more manageable nine entries.

"Thanks," Jimmy whispered to the girl and smiled.

"No problem." She withdrew behind her own monitor. He didn't notice the girl blush a deep crimson and fan her face with her hand. Jimmy pulled four books and employed his new library card to check them out.

He drove back home the way he'd come and pulled the car in front of the garage. The door opened instantly and Maria, his new housekeeper, stepped out of the garage as if she'd been waiting there all day for him. She bent low and handed the garage door opener to Jimmy. He had never seen such a device and only looked at it in his hand stupidly. Maria reached in and hit the button. She turned and extended her hand as the garage door closed. She hit the button again. The door rolled back up.

"Eh?' she smiled as if she had produced magic. Then she patted his shoulder in a motherly way and told him, "Is okay, Meester Jaydee. They don't got these in my barrio neither." Maria had decided to like the young *negrito.* "Oh," she told him. "Meester Roger call you. Three times. He says you got to call him back. I got the number next to the telefono en la cocina." Maria stalled a moment, polishing the window frame of the Porsche with the corner of her apron. She lowered her voice.

"Meester Roger, he tell me about your familia." She looked away embarrassed for Jimmy. "Lo siento, nino," Maria stopped rubbing the car and wiped her hands on her apron. "Venga, venga! I make you some tacos." She bustled back into the house through the open garage and Jimmy Deane pulled the Porsche inside.

Forgetting about the time change, he dialed the number Maria had recorded for Alperstein, Lillian and Groth, but the answering machine told him the offices were closed. It was after business hours in Miami and whatever it was Roger had to say would apparently have to wait.

Chapter 36

The attorney, Larry Drummond

Our firm represents now more than seventy Florida State lottery winners. It was a stroke of genius to cultivate this particular area of representation since all of the clients have liquid money and there's hardly ever any litigation besides paternity suits, and those are always pretty entertaining. From our standpoint anyway. Not always the client's, I assure you. These cases are easy money for us. My boss is right about a couple of things. He says that the lords of luck are partial to America's white trash. This I can attest to. Why it is, well, who can say? Unless it's that reasonable minded educated folks, who know a thing or two about statistics, just don't buy lottery tickets.

The other observation that Roger has made is that the easy and effortless acquisition of enormous amounts of money rather niftily cleaves that fortunate populace into two amazingly distinct groups. Which camp a lottery winner belongs to becomes apparent in a surprisingly short period, and you would sometimes be very surprised who goes where.

Watching the transformation has convinced me that it is far better to earn one's living than to win millions of dollars. I'll keep my paltry high six-figure salary any day rather than have to wrestle with the demons that accompany fast wealth. In the worst of cases it just destroys a person's life. We've had too many of those. Watching it up close is an eye opener. For many of them, after the euphoria wears off, the paranoia settles in, and it settles in deep. I think of it as the Howard Hughes syndrome. They think everyone is out to get their money, and there's a lot of truth in that, which is why our firm advises a period of grace. We call it the personal identification reassignment, but I think of it more as a personal identification evolution. It gives them a little time to figure out who they want to be as a newly bestowed filthy rich person as opposed to who they previously were as a ridiculously impoverished bugger. The unfortunate thing for some is that who they evolve into, when taken out of their natural element, is just a monumental arsehole who also happens to have a lot of money.

The other group. And maybe here's the real surprise. Well, they give you hope for humanity. They learn to share. They set up charitable trusts. They give benevolent gifts and they learn how to invest. They just get better all around.

Take our Mr. Sixty-Nine. As I said, I'm not one to wager, but if I were, I would have put my money on Gillis Wainwright becoming one of the world's all time greatest pratts. It wasn't just the yacht, though that kind of self-indulgence is typical of a total and unforgivable arse. It was the way he seemed so *alone*. No family. No friends. I had him spending and gambling away that lotto money in under a year. And every penny of it on himself. I was so wrong.

Roger took him over to finalize the negotiations on the boat and then brought him back to the office. We're all professionals at ALG. We are trained to keep a very professional exterior when dealing with our clients. When he announced that it was his intent to give the next-door neighbor lad, who was an orphan, nearly a third of his payout…well, like I said, my initial assessment was totally incorrect.

Roger didn't want Mr. Sixty-Nine going over to the boy's school. It was too soon for him to be out and about. The press was still sniffing around you see. So, Wainwright asked me to take the kid's graduation present over to him and get the school's driver's ed teacher to run him through the course so he could get his driving documents. I told him it was my pleasure, and do you know? It absolutely was. I don't mean that it was just a pleasure driving that 944 Turbo out of the Porsche establishment and over to the high school. That goes without saying. But, being the lucky chap to tell the kid about his trust fund and watch him drive away in his new Porsche? That was absolutely a pleasure. The boy was a very pleasant person, too. All he seemed to care about was his chum, Wainwright. He asked me about ten times, was he okay? What was he doing? Did he seem happy? It made me really wish I could tell him where Mr. Sixty-Nine was staying so he could just go over there, but Roger would have had my pension for that. The rules about our personal identification reassignment are very strict. The clients have to all but disappear for at least a few months.

I encouraged the kid to take a little trip himself. Do what I would do, I told him. If I was young. Get in that Porsche and drive. Good Lord! The boy had ten thousand dollars in cash in his hand when I left him at the DMV. And ten million in trust. So what does the kid do? He turns around and gives a couple of million to the old lady. Sets it up with our firm before he takes off for California so that she's taken care of. He even sent painters over to paint the house and asked me to arrange for some gardeners to put in some landscaping. He did the Wainwright place next door, too. You would think the old lady would have been grateful, wouldn't you? Not a chance. A sour old bat, she did nothing but complain about the workers, and when she asked me who it was who sent them over, I said, “It was your grandson, Jimmy.”

She looked me right in the eye and said, “I don’t have a grandson.”

I would bet my life that I know which category of the newly wealthy Jimmy Deane’s grandmother will fall into, and that’s a wager I am certain I would not lose.

Chapter 37

JD reached Roger Albright at nine Eastern time.

"Mr. Sixty-Nine is in Bimini," Roger told him cheerily. "I can patch you through." It took several minutes for the ship-to-shore call to get connected.

"JD?" There was a slight crackling on the line, which alternated with a whistle, but it was such a relief to hear Gillis's voice, that Jimmy Deane's eyes filled instantly with tears.

"Gillis!" he shouted. "Gillis! How's it going? Are you okay?"

Gillis yelled back.

"Oh, man, buddy. I am having the time of my life. Wait 'til you see this here boat. Did I tell you I got me a little tiny helio-copter on the top what can take people off the ship and over to shore?" JD tried to imagine Gillis getting air lifted off of his yacht. The ridiculous image made him smile and he wiped his tears away with the back of his hand. "How 'bout you, JD? You like it out there in California?"

"Well, I just got here, but, so far so good." Jimmy Deane had to swallow a lump that had grown in his throat. "Gillis…I don't know how to thank you…I…"

"Ah, hell, kid, no need to thank me," Gillis yelled over the static. "I got so damn much money, now. Oooops, there we go! Just made another half a mil! Yeeehah!" Gillis held the telephone receiver up to the bank of TV monitors in front of him, then retracted his hand. "Hell, what am I doin'? You can't see that! I'm watchin' our investments on the TV from the capt'n's quarters. I tell you, we cannot lose, JD. This here stock market is more fun than the Kentucky Derby! We got to figure out how we're gonna spend all this dough, though, JD. It ain't gonna be easy, I'm tellin' you!" The only two words JD heard clearly were "we" and "we're".

"When?" Jimmy yelled over the whistling on the line. "When can I come see you, Gillis? Come see the boat and your little helicopter?" The crackling on the line got more severe.

"Ain't … *kshhhhhhweeeeeeeuuuuuwww*…..college, JD? Roger told *ksshhhhhhhhhweeeeuuuuuuww* to college out there in L.A. He *kkshhhhhwweeeeeeuuuuuuwww*…..your namesake… *kshhhweeeeeuuuu*. Ain't that right?"

"It's just summer school." JD yelled into the receiver. "Just for something to do. I can skip it. I could come right back!" There was no telling what was getting through on Gillis's end.

"No, sir!" Gillis hollered over the interference. "You're goin' to….ksssshhhheeeeuuuu….. "I'll come to ….ksssshhhheeeeeuwwww… you hear me? I'm comin'! ….kssheeeeeuw." The line went dead. Once he dropped the receiver, Jimmy Deane realized that he had been holding fast to his St. Cecilia but he had forgotten to mention it. He had missed his chance to thank Gillis for the medal.

Roger Albright called back explaining that a storm in the Caribbean had made ship-to-shore communications difficult if not impossible, but that Gillis was safely docked in the harbor at Bimini. There was nothing for Jimmy to worry about.

"I'm sure you'll hear from him again as soon as he gets ashore and can call you from a hotel on the island," Roger reassured JD.

How much time elapsed while JD stood barefoot in the kitchen watching the birds steal water from the pool outside who could say? A thud at the front door announced the arrival of the Times. Feeling like a houseguest who has risen hours earlier than his host, he retrieved the paper from the porch with some stealth and took it back to the guest bedroom. He went through the paper rapidly but neatly so as not to disturb its order until a full-page ad for Drum World in the Calendar section announced his day's purpose. He removed the single sheet and dressed in a hurry.

"Can you tell me how to get to this store?" Jimmy unfolded the newsprint for the waitress at Patrick's on the Coast Highway.

"Oh, yeah, easy," she said. "Just take PCH south here to the incline and go down to Pico on Lincoln. Go east. No sweat."

"Thanks," Jimmy told her

"I love your work," the girl said refilling his coffee cup. It was a good bet that he was an up and coming something, even if she didn't know what. And even if it wasn't so, she found that her little routine insincere compliment usually didn't hurt the tips either way. "Have a nice day!" she yelled after him when he left.

Drum World opened at nine, so Jimmy sat in the strip mall parking lot and made a preliminary list on the margins of the newspaper while he waited.

The manager noticed the new silver Porsche and the handsome young man behind the wheel as he unlocked the grill in front of the windows. Jimmy hopped out. Once inside, the manager threw his keys and lunch bag on the counter and turned.

"What kin I do you for?" One hundred percent salesman now, he rubbed his hands together and hoped the kid had cash.

Jimmy handed over the page of newsprint. His list went around three corners.

"All this?"

"Can you deliver it?"

"Well, I don't have these Zildjain cymbals in stock…but I can get them." He made his eyes into slits. "You need it today?"

"Today would be nice," Jimmy said.

"An extra hundie." The man tried not to look like the greedy little prick he was.

"No problem," Jimmy Deane smiled. "Ring it up. I'll give you the address."

At a stereo shop down the street from the music store, Jimmy purchased a floor model stereo system without the turntable.

"No demand for these anymore," the man said sadly. "Everything's on tape now. Record companies are hardly putting anything at all on vinyl anymore." The man who had been in the stereo business since the fifties made it sound personal.

"Don't worry about it," Jimmy said. "Disks are coming back. Only they'll be smaller." He held up his hands in a six-inch circle.

"You mean like forty-fives?" The man looked doubtful.

"No, like lps. They'll get a whole lp on one side of a recording disk this size."

"You're dreamin'," the man said. He touched the last of his floor model turntables lovingly. "But, maybe I oughta hold on to my turntables, huh?"

"Oh, you won't be playing these disks on a turntable. It will all be digital."

"What?"

Jimmy Deane smiled. The man took a step back and looked Jimmy up and down. "I get it. You work for a record company, huh?" Jimmy shook his head. His dreads bounced and false recognition spread across the salesman's face. "Hey, I know who you are! You're....you're..."

"No, I'm nobody. But, hold on to at least one of your turntables. Like everything that was ever any good, there will always be demand." Not for one second did the salesman buy that this kid was a nobody.

"I get it...flyin' low, huh? Under the radar. Whatever you say, kid," the man told him. Then, while he continued to try to place the boy he helped him load up the stereo components into the Porsche. "Hey, you're that Marley kid, aren't you?" he said smugly when Jimmy closed the boot. Jimmy shook his head. "C'mon, kid, give me an autograph, huh?" The man shoved a crumpled flyer at Jimmy Deane and pulled a ballpoint pen from his breast pocket. "It'll be good for my business." To avoid an argument Jimmy took the pen and signed his name. He walked around the car to the driver's side and opened his door.

"What? James Deane?" the man said. He looked up, first confused and then angry. "James Deane?" he repeated. "Yeah, fuck you, kid," he said sourly and went back into his store.

Even Jimmy Deane had not been so admired and reviled in such a short span of time. LA, he decided, was a lot farther away from Florida than three thousand miles. He took himself to the beach to people watch and spent the whole day smiling boldly at strangers. Most, if not all, smiled back, and a similarly dreadlocked roller-blader called out to Jimmy as he skimmed by, "Love the work, my man!"

Maria was out in front of the house cutting roses when Jimmy pulled into the driveway. He waved and went to say hi before he unloaded the car.

"Hola mijo!" Maria waved the bouquet at him. "Mira las flores! Que bonita, no? Ver-ry beeyootifool!"

"They're great, Maria," Jimmy told her. "Take them home." Maria looked doubtful.

"Siiiii?....Nooooo!...."she said with hope in her eyes. Jimmy's landlord had hogged his roses.

"Si, yes," Jimmy said and laughed. The housekeeper smiled back. It dawned on her that this was the first time the young man's face had worn a smile.

"Okay. Eeeef you say so!"

"I've got some stuff to unload…I'll be just…" Before he could finish his sentence a small child came tearing around the hedge pulling a man of indeterminate age by the hand.

"Maria! Maria!" the little girl squealed.

"Oh Miss Chelsea" Maria dropped low to let the little girl plant a kiss on her cheek. "You are back so soon? I thought you would be gone a very long time." The girl's father wore very dark sunglasses and a Dodgers cap over close-cropped hair. He was clean-shaven and dressed casually in khaki pants and a Hawaiian shirt opened at the throat. He had the deep tan of a man who has a lot of free time.

Maria's voice dropped very low. "Hola, Senor Pablo," she said without looking up. "This is Mr. Jay Dee." Maria introduced the neighbors to Jimmy. "Meester Jay Dee, these are Miss Chelsea and Mr. Pablo from next door. I go put mis flores in agua. Pardoname." Maria hurried through the front door looking over her shoulder with a worried expression. Jimmy bent down to pick up her forgotten gardening sheers.

"Hey." The man stepped forward and extended a hand. "Sorry for the bother. Like Maria said, we live next door, and I think Chelsea's ball went over the back fence and is taking a little swim in your pool. You mind if we get it?"

"Sure, no problem. Let's get it," Jimmy Deane said. He led the way through the two side gates out to the back yard swimming pool.

Chelsea was clinging shyly to her father's leg. She kept her thumb planted firmly in her mouth. Her father hoisted her up to carry her into Jimmy's back yard and then set her down gently next to the pool. He retrieved the floating ball and wiped it off on his pants before he handed it to his daughter. She tucked the ball immediately under one arm and returned her thumb to her mouth. The father continued to dry his hands on his pants as he looked around the yard.

"Maria said that you're renting the house from Hal?" he asked. Jimmy nodded. "He's in Africa?"

"I think so," Jimmy told the man.

"Listen, if you talk to him, tell him I said… thanks…for everything."

JD held his opened hands out.

"You know…. I don't really know Hal," he told the man. "I rented the house through a lawyer friend of his in Florida."

"Oh, sure. Nevermind, then. Well, good luck with the house. Welcome to the neighborhood." He turned to the little girl. She was staring up at Jimmy Deane, her blue eyes huge in her face.

"Where's your mom?" she whispered around her thumb.

"Huh?" Jimmy Deane bent toward her.

"Is your mommy home?" she asked the slightest bit louder. Jimmy looked at the father. The man grimaced. He took a deep breath.

"Chels has been a little curious about moms in general lately," he said.

"My mom went overboard." Chelsea removed her thumb just long enough to speak.

"Overboard?" Jimmy looked at the little girl's father. The man stepped behind his daughter and mimed a hypodermic needle going into his forearm.

"Oh!" Jimmy Deane said. "Overboard!"

"Where's *your* mommy?" Chelsea removed her thumb to ask. Jimmy looked at the man and hesitated before kneeling down to the little girl's level. The child's eyes were the bluest eyes he had ever seen. It almost hurt to meet her frank gaze.

"My mom kind of went overboard, too," JD told her softly. She nodded then soberly and handed her father her ball. She stunned both men when she stepped forward and deliberately put her arms around Jimmy Deane's neck.

"That's okay," she whispered. "Dr. Anita says that sometimes moms do that, but you're going to be okay." She patted Jimmy on the back and then stepped next to her dad again and embraced his leg. She looked up at Jimmy. "I've never touched a black person before," she said matter of factly.

"Chels!" The child's father blanched.

"That's okay," Jimmy smiled. "Kids just say the truth, you know?" Jimmy stood and watched Chelsea's father swallow several times before he nodded gratefully. He dropped the ball and lifted the child up in the air. "Hey, why don't we invite Mr. Jay Dee over for dinner some time?" His mirrored sun glasses turned back to reflect Jimmy Deane's frightened expression. "What do you say? How' about tonight? You doin' anything tonight?" Jimmy Deane had no experience with dinner invitations. He did not know how to respond. He didn't think he would know what to do as a dinner guest. He gestured lamely toward the kitchen.

"Um, I think Maria's already cooked chicken," he demurred. "And… I'm kind of waiting for a delivery." He pointed in the direction of his front door stupidly as if the deliverymen were already on the stoop.

"Ah, tell Maria to take the chicken home to her boys and put a note on the front door. They can come get you next door when they get here." The neighbor waited. His pulse was visible in his temple. He looked at his daughter and set her down again before he raised one hand to lift his sunglasses. His eyes were bloodshot and pleading. "C'mon, man. It's our first night home. We could use the company." His sad smile looked more like a grimace. It clicked that the invitation was more than to make up for Chelsea's remark.

"Okay, sure," Jimmy relented. "What time?"

"Any time! Hey, come over now and you can watch Chelsea take her music lesson."

Chelsea beamed.

"I play the guitar," she said, for the first time entirely removing her thumb.

"No kidding?" Jimmy grinned at her. "Let me just tell Maria about the chicken and get a clean shirt on."

"We'll see ya' when we see ya'." Chelsea's dad looked genuinely pleased. JD walked them to the front of the house approving of the way Chelsea's father held her hand tightly. As they walked to the sidewalk he let Chelsea stop and turn back every few feet to wave. Jimmy stayed put in front of his own front door, waving whenever Chelsea turned around. As the neighbors approached their own house the white van from Drum World pulled up on the street between the two properties. Jimmy saw the neighbor take a long look at the truck's ostentatious logo before he hurriedly stooped to pick his daughter up and carry her quickly into the house next door. It almost appeared as if he was trying to shelter his daughter's face. When she dropped her ball he let it roll across the lawn without retrieving it.

Jimmy rushed down to the street to help the driver unload his drum kit, unaware that the neighbor watched the entire process from behind his lowered shutters. Maria clutched her dishtowel to her chest and bit her lips together when Jimmy announced the neighbor's dinner invitation. He sensed her disapproval but found suddenly that he had no interest in whatever objections she might have. He changed into his best clean T-shirt and cut across the lawn, leaping over the hedgerow. He rang the bell. Chelsea's father opened the door himself, but little more than a crack.

"Hey, look, man," he said installing himself into the narrow opening. He seemed clearly distressed. "I'm sorry about this, but we're going to have to postpone dinner. I've got a thing..." He gestured vaguely with his thumb over his head. "Gotta be down in Hollywood. I forgot all about it. I'm gonna have to eat fast and take off." He watched Jimmy's face fall and bit his bottom lip.

"Sure," Jimmy said and nodded. The older man looked pained.

"Hey, kid? Another time, huh? Soon?" The two men only nodded to each other. JD could hear the neighbor exhale as the door closed solidly behind him.

Maria was backing out of the driveway as Jimmy approached his house. She honked and waved.

"Venga, mijo!" she hollered and waved Jimmy to her car.

"Que paso? You no eat with the Berman's?" Jimmy looked at the neighbor's house.

"The Berman's?" he asked Maria. She looked at the house, too.

"Si, si. Meester Berman. Pobrecito little Chelsea. She lose her mama just like you, mijo. It was in the papers and on the TV. I thought you knew. Mr. Hal, he find Senora Berman on the driveway just two weeks ago. Que triste! Such a beautiful girl. Muy simpatica, pero, loca, no? Las drugas! Que lastima!" Jimmy could understand only half of what Maria was saying, but he knew who Paul Berman was, even if the man next door looked nothing like the famous rocker.

"Go on home, Maria," Jimmy told her. "I'll get something out. Go take the chicken to your boys."

"You okay, Meester Jay Dee? You don look so good."

"I'm fine. I'll see you tomorrow." The housekeeper chattered in rapid fire Spanish as she continued to back up. She put the car into drive and offered a worried wave to Jimmy. Inside he found exactly half of Maria's picked flowers in a vase with fresh water.

He walked through the house turning on lights, then he retraced his steps and turned them all off again. In the kitchen he grabbed a beer from the well-stocked fridge and twisted off the cap. He stepped on the release for the trash compactor. He dropped the cap into the empty plastic liner. A pleasant puff of lemon accompanied the satisfying sound of well-engineered machinery when he pushed the drawer closed. Everything in this house, even the trash, was beautiful and modern. It was the antithesis of his house in Florida. Jimmy opened and closed the trash compactor twice more, inhaling lemon before he took his beer back to the living room with a bag of Fritos. Choosing the man-sized wing back chair from which he could easily watch the Berman's driveway, he took up sentry, nursing his beer. He let his new house grow dark around him. For over three hours he watched. Paul Berman's garage doors never opened. No other cars pulled up in front of the Berman property. The neighbor clearly never left for Hollywood or anywhere else.

Around nine, with an unreasonably heavy heart, JD gave up and went to the back of the house to set up his drum kit in the studio. As he approached the door, raucous rock and roll escaped the soundproofing. JD pushed the door open warily. James Dean was lying on the sofa, one of the toms squeezed between his knees and drumsticks poised in midair. A frenetic Motley Crue video was on the TV screen against the opposite wall.

"You know what the definition of a drummer is?" James Dean yelled over the music. Jimmy shook his head. "A drummer is just a guy who likes to hang out with musicians! Ha!"

Jimmy Deane smiled a half smile, then shook his head and leaned forward. “Is that *eyeliner*?”

Chapter 38

Gillis Wainwright

Who'd a thought? I asked my pilot, how many folks you know can't get into their own helio-copter? He says, more than you would think. Don't worry about it, he says. Take the skiff over. So I did. I ain't got no problem takin' the Zodiac over to Key West. Rog picked me up and we drove up to Miami. He's waitin' to see me off and I get half way down the little hallway to the plane and my knees start shakin' and my heart starts beatin' hard in my chest. I'm sweatin' like a pro football player and I cain't hear my own self think. That little stewardess comes up and she starts talkin' only she sounds like she ain't right there at all but somwheres far away. "Sir? Can I help you, sir? Are you not well?" And, I'm thinkin' hell yes, I am not well. But, I can't say so. I can't even see straight and my insides is jumpin' around and I'm petrified I'm gonna lose my load right there in front of a whole plane full of people. They was real nice though, them folks from the airline. Said it happens *all* the time. Fear of flyin' they said and ain't nothin' to be ashamed of cause lots of folks got it, and you'd be surprised how many really important folks have done the same exact thing as I done. But, the worst part was, I had to call JD up and tell him that I was not gonna be on the flight. Somethin' come up, I said. Somethin' real important and I'll try to get out there as soon as I can. I don't know why I couldn't just tell him that I was afraid to get on the air-o-plane. He'd a understood. Pride, I guess. Didn't want him thinkin' that I was no pussy. I'll come soon, I said. And, at the time, I meant every word. It's just harder than you think.

'Least the market's up. Me and JD we almost doubled what we had when this whole mess started. Just can't lose no money no way, even though lots a' folks has been losin' their shirts the way the market's been lately. Warren and Roger both says it ain't all bad that I couldn't go out to see JD. They both says that kids need a little time to adjust when they go away to college. Seein' as how they both been to college and I ain't, I figure, okay. That's fine. JD can have his little bit o' time in college. I'll stay here and make us some more money and I'll try again in a bit. Maybe this here fear of flyin' is a passin' thing.

Book four - Passion

Those who danced were thought to be quite insane by those who could not hear the music.

- Angela Monet

Chapter 39

JD left for his first day of college in plenty of time to sit impatiently in the coastal highway traffic and still arrive more than early for his class. When he arrived the auditorium was empty except for a cluster of four students who were engaged in animated conversation close to the aisle up near the front. Only the tall boy with longish, sun-bleached hair even glanced up when Jimmy slipped into a seat in the twentieth row. He gave Jimmy a quick look-see.

"Nobody," he told the others. A slender girl of heart stopping beauty in a polka dot mini skirt and strappy tank top leaned against the tall boy's side. Jimmy's heart raced at his first sight of her and he had to actually force his gaze away. An Asian boy who wore his Yankees cap backwards on his head sat on an armrest with his feet up flatly on one of the seats. JD could see his concerned profile perfectly as the boy seemed to listen to the blonde boy and the pretty girl argue with a fourth boy. The fourth boy's face was hidden entirely from JD's view but a pair of drumsticks was visible sticking out of the side pocket of his backpack, which he had slung carelessly over his seatback.

The girl pulled suddenly out from under the tall boy's arm. She opened her mouth and Jimmy strained to hear her words. The texture of her voice was enhanced by the acoustics in the empty auditorium and there was something about the way she moved, with a particular kind of grace or an economy of motion that stirred him. For a self-conscious moment he studied her again. Her hair was so blonde it was nearly white and her skin was so flawlessly pale and creamy it appeared as if she stayed entirely clear of the sun. Even from this distance, Jimmy could see the uncommon icy blue of her eyes and her long black lashes.

"What goes around comes around, Ryan," she told the drummer in a matter of fact manner as if she were instructing him as to the secret of life. The drummer's response sounded bored but it echoed loudly in the empty auditorium.

"Yeah, yeah, Lindsey. Bite me, okay?" Jimmy felt a sudden surge of completely irrational protectiveness. It almost brought him to his feet. *To do what*? The blonde boy, who should have defended Lindsey's honor Jimmy thought, only made a disgusted face and raised his middle finger tiredly. The auditorium doors opened at the back and students gradually started piling inside and filling up the seats. Their argument was over.

The Asian boy swiveled around also extending his upraised middle finger for the drummer's benefit and dropped into a seat in the row directly in front of him. The tall blonde boy wrapped a protective arm around the girl and took his seat next to her in the very front row.

Within minutes every seat in the large auditorium was occupied. More than a dozen students were left standing in the back and a few were even sitting cross-legged on the floor in front of the first row. Jimmy took note that there were very few minority students in the auditorium. The ethnic make-up of the Santa Monica College population, though much larger, was proportionately similar to Jimmy's high school back in Florida. Exquisitely sensitive to unfriendly looks and whispers, he had noticed none of either. He settled into his seat feeling only invisible. Since it was the first day of the summer session and few of the students knew each other, the conversational din was at a minimum. In another week the pre-class noise in the large hall would be deafening and difficult to halt by all but the most revered professors.

At nine exactly the rear stage door opened on the silhouette of a tall, lean man sporting shoulder length dreadlocks. He paused dramatically and let the students begin to quiet down before he walked gracefully to the podium just left of center. In the middle of the stage, a few short feet just to the left of the professor, a single folding chair had been placed behind two microphones, one slightly higher than the other. Besides the professor's podium, these were the only objects on the dark stage. They were the perfect props for The Psychology of Performance. The professor gestured subtly and the tech in the control booth at the rear of the auditorium bathed the professor and the chair behind him in two soft white spotlights from high overhead. Jimmy recognized the man at the podium immediately. *Ah, so that was Pierce.* The public address system buzzed and the professor shuffled the four pages of his attendance roster.

"Good morning." Dr. Pierce's voice was impossibly deep. The amplification from the public address system seemed nearly unnecessary. He looked sympathetically at the students on the floor beneath him.

"If you don't have a seat, stick around. A few rats will leave the ship during the break once they see what's in store for them." A polite smattering of laughter was offered up by the student audience. The professor let the noise level die down to complete silence, hesitating for dramatic effect just the right number of seconds while he looked at his role sheet. Pierce was all about creating dramatic tension in this class.

"Rappaport?" he called into the mic abruptly. "Is Mr. Joel Rappaport here this morning?"

A hesitant student close to the front and near the center, presumably Rappaport, straightened in his seat and raised his hand tentatively.

"Good. Good," Dr. Pierce smiled at Joel Rappaport. With absolutely no preamble he issued a sudden invitation. "Please come up on stage, Mr. Rappaport. Entertain us this morning." The professor took one step back and gestured with a sweeping motion to the empty chair and microphone. The unsuspecting Rappaport cringed under the professor's unwavering stare. The other students shifted in their seats uncomfortably, happy not to be singled out themselves.

"Huh?" Joel Rappaport sat up straight but showed no indication that he intended to accept the professor's tendered invitation to perform. The audience again laughed, but this time there was a note of anxiety in their laughter. Dr. Pierce stepped forward.

"No?" He intensified a quizzical look. With deliberate effort he folded his hands on top of the podium and rose up on the balls of his feet and rocked forward. He cleared his throat. "You *did* register for the Psychology of *Performance*, Mr. Rappaport?" Poor Rappaport could barely nod his assent. "Am I to assume then that your hesitation to take the stage means that you are going to pass up this supremely golden opportunity to perform for us this morning?" Joel Rappaport's nod grew vigorous. "You're going to waste this audience?" Pierce either was, or sounded like he was, incredulous.

"No, sir," Rappaport squeaked. "I mean, yes, sir…I'll pass." The mortified student seemed to shrink. The other students laughed nervously and briefly.

"I see." The professor nodded once and again scanned his role sheets. "Ah," he smiled as if he were amused by something. "Mr. Deane. Is Mr. James Deane with us this morning?"

Professor Pierce scanned the dim auditorium as a general stir in the audience located Jimmy Deane's erect hand some twenty rows back. "Ah, Mr. Deane! We meet again." Pierce paused as if he might change course. Then instead, he asked benignly, "Were you aware, Mr. Deane, that your famous namesake was also a student here at Santa Monica City College back before...." Dr. Pierce grinned. "...Well..." he cleared his throat. "...before *you* were all born certainly. I know that to most of you, everyone hovering the advanced age of thirty seems ancient, but, I can assure you all, that I was not even alive yet when that other James Dean attended here, so I was not *his* professor." More scattered laughter. Clearly Dr. Pierce liked to entertain. "I will however, at the end of this term... I suppose, thanks to you, Mr. Deane... be able to make the legitimate boast to one and all of my colleagues that it was *I* who taught James Deane everything he knows about the Psychology of Performance." Another ripple of polite laughter spread out while people craned their necks to see what the namesake of James Dean looked like. None of the faces seemed particularly hostile. *Was this what the young woman in registration had meant by eating him alive? If so, no sweat, JD thought to himself.* Speculation about how the student named James Deane had already met Dr. Pierce intensified as the class regarded him frankly. The snide boy with the drumsticks turned around in his seat and squinted.

"Check it out," he said loudly. "Bob Marley lives!" His laugher was an unpleasant cackle. No one even breathed in the wake of such an obvious faux pas. En masse the auditorium turned to await Dr. Pierce's reaction.

Pierce ignored the boy's comment and waited instead silently for a full meaningful beat before continuing. He inhaled an impossibly long breath before grasping the podium in both hands.

"A performer, a *true* performer must be *ready*, *willing* and, most of all, *able*, to do just that...to *perform*...at the slightest provocation to do so. If you cannot, or will not, you should stop deceiving yourself immediately." He paused, to let what he considered the first lesson of his most important lecture sink in. The room was impossibly still. He continued. "A *true* performer does *not* play coy. They do not *feign* modesty or humility. It is fine to be humble *after* a performance. *Never* before." Dr. Pierce had a compelling oratory style sounding much like Orson Wells, and he consciously employed it. His reputation was well earned. Even at nine a.m. he could mesmerize his sleepy, summer session audience. The drama students liked to say, that if you were casting God's voice from heaven, you couldn't do better than Dr. Robert Pierce. The teacher scanned the rows and again paused for dramatic effect before fixing Jimmy Deane with the look that had become the department joke: the professor's signature *piercing* look.

"Now, Mr. Deane? How is it that *you* would like to entertain us today?" He beckoned to Jimmy Deane, took one step back and made another sweeping motion toward the chair.

Once again, the boy, Ryan, turned, along with almost everyone else up front, to see what Jimmy would do.

"Ten bucks the black dude's a rapper!" he snickered loudly and secured a reluctant high five from the boy next to him. A tiny buzz of scattered uncomfortable laughter was followed by an even more uncomfortable silence. Half the audience were watching Pierce, waiting for the teacher to rebuke Ryan, while the other half turned back to see if James Deane would take the professor's challenge and rise to the stage.

For a single second, the blonde girl made eye contact and Jimmy was certain that she had smiled at him. Every synapse fired. He hesitated a minute fraction of a second more before rising. He had no plan, and would not later be able to report what had come over him. He only knew one thing. Once he was on his feet and moving, there was nothing that could have stopped him. He passed the first ten rows in three quick strides and the whole of the large auditorium fell immediately into absolute anxious silence.

When Jimmy paused next to Ryan's seat, the air in the auditorium was electrified. Even the professor was holding his breath. He loved real life drama. It was why he was known for his provocative teaching methods. But he wasn't sure it would be a good thing to have inspired a student, especially somehow *this* student, to knock someone's block off on the first day of summer school. Jimmy leaned in front of Ryan and reached over his head into the backpack hanging from his chair seat. He withdrew the drumsticks in a move so fluid more than one witness would say later, when retelling the tale, that the black drummer had called to mind no less a swordsman than Zorro himself.

Undeniably relieved, but eager to be a part of the performance art, Ryan cringed back and made a believable pantomime of fear. Jimmy clicked the sticks together in front of Ryan's face and twirled one over his head before bringing both down on Ryan's desktop. He expertly drummed a few bars of simple beat bringing his face close to Ryan's. Then, straightening slowly, and turning toward the stage, he looked forward while slipping the drumsticks into his jeans pocket. As casually as if he were strolling through campus, he walked down to the front of the room as if nothing at all extraordinary was taking place. The air in the auditorium was electrified.

Students shrugged at each other, but no one said a word out loud as they all watched Jimmy Deane pick up one of the metal trash cans next to the stage stairs and shake it upside down, letting a few pieces of paper trash fall to the floor. He upended the can onto the stage and repeated the process with a second one. Next, he relieved Dr. Pierce's teaching assistants of the folding chairs they were sitting on at the professor's feet. They obliged and then scurried off to the side. He hoisted their chairs up onto the stage, and then vaulted himself up there too. Dr. Pierce gave a second subtle signal to the control booth and the spot surrounding the chair and mike expanded to include Jimmy Deane's props. He spent a moment arranging the TA's chairs and the empty cans while the student audience continued to exchange curious looks and shrugs and now even a few brave whispers. At last, Jimmy leaned in close to the microphone and started to speak.

"Percussion instruments have been used since prehistoric times."

Jimmy Deane's voice was calm and melodic as if he had prepared in advance for this extemporaneous performance and had practiced it many, many times. His soft Florida drawl was barely detectable.

"The earliest drums consisted of fish or reptile skin stretched over hollow tree trunks, and were struck with the hands."

He drummed with his hands to punctuate each sentence using every surface of his makeshift drum kit, and even using the tops of his thighs.

"Somewhat later the skins of wild or domesticated mammals were used to make larger drums which were struck with sticks..." Jimmy pulled Ryan's drumsticks from his back pocket.

Dr. Pierce moved into the shadows and scanned the auditorium. It was the dance majors, he guessed, who were starting to sway to the rhythm in their seats.

*"Frame drums were used by the ancient civilizations of the Middle East about 5,000 years ago. They were later adapted by the ancient Greeks...*Jimmy drummed on the bottom of a

trash can. He kept a constant beat on his thigh as he talked on. His voice had a timbre itself that was drum-like.

"Large kettledrums, long used in the Middle East, were introduced..."

"The bass drum, a large tubular drum, was rare in Europe..." He returned suddenly to tapping a gentle rhythm on his thigh top.

"Timpani became an important part..."

By striking the varying surfaces on the folding chairs, Jimmy created a striking melody of percussion. Dr. Pierce was smiling broadly in the shadows as he watched. Something like pride was kindled and he let himself enjoy it thoroughly. It didn't happen often at Santa Monica that a student of color was bold enough to....to *what???* To be so damned visible!

"An important development in drum manufacturing occurred in..." Jimmy pounded on the chair seats as if they were the highest quality drum skins.

"During the twentieth century..." Jimmy played the makeshift kit for another final minute. When his lecture and drum performance concluded, he rose and bowed modestly. The audience broke into wild applause. When they finally stopped clapping, Jimmy Deane raised his sticks in the air and clicked them together over his head and bowed low, honoring their applause.

At the very instant that he straightened, a second electric hush started to spread throughout the auditorium.

The little blonde from the front row had threaded her way through the students on the floor and she was walking forward to the stage unbidden. She climbed the stairs never taking her eyes off Jimmy Deane. As soon as she reached center stage Jimmy moved the vocal microphone for her. Dr. Pierce signaled the control booth and a second spotlight appeared around her. She looked up. Her voice, distinct and strong wrapped around the sounds of Leonard Cohen's *Hallelujah.* Her rendition of the beautiful song was rich and warm and resonated with a depth that seemed impossible to come from such a petite person. Jimmy knew the song. He knew it well. He used his hands on the upended cans to provide a soft beat. The girl turned and smiled briefly, nodding. The duet somehow sounded as if they had been practicing for months. Professor Pierce was beaming. He was not the only member of the audience that had to shake off the chills. He could not have orchestrated a better first day for TPP if he had stayed up all night plotting to do so.

The duet went on for four full minutes. The girl's a-cappela performance was so pure, many in the audience were moved to tears. A handful of the bolder dancers rose and swayed in front of their seats. The auditorium went crazy when it ended. Students applauded and stomped and jumped to their feet. Loud whistles and shrieks went on for several minutes. Jimmy escorted the little blonde down off the stage gently caressing her elbow. His hand was warm but shaking. He slapped down the borrowed drumsticks on the white boy's desktop as he passed by and winked. Both *performers* were blushing modestly but they faced forward attentively until Dr. Pierce stepped up to the podium and turned his own mic back on. He was beaming behind his own vigorous applause.

"That, my friends, is what is known among performers as *a tough act to follow."* The audience laughed and the professor grinned and said, "Let's take a short break. Be back in your seats by ten, and I will have your syllabi at that time. Mr.

Deane, could I have a word?" It took Jimmy several minutes to burrow through the appreciative crowd. His classmates clapped him on the back and congratulated him. Some just reached out to touch him as he struggled through to the stage.

"That was remarkable." Professor Pierce bent down so that he could touch his fist to Jimmy's, and then he stood and crossed his arms over his chest and smiled broadly. "What's your friend's name?"

Jimmy Deane glanced at the back of the auditorium where the blonde singer was standing again under the protective arm of the tall boy. They were both surrounded by admiring classmates.

"I don't know that girl," Jimmy said. "I think someone said her name was Lindsey." Dr. Pierce looked at him doubtfully.

"You don't know each other? You've never performed together before today?" he asked.

"No, sir," Jimmy said. "I don't know anyone. I just moved here last week."

"Remarkable!" the teacher repeated shaking his head. "Well, no matter." Pierce leaned down to touch Jimmy on the shoulder. "Welcome to The Psychology of Performance, James Deane. It looks like we're going to have an interesting summer."

The teaching assistants were standing back, waiting to speak with the professor. One of them nodded to Jimmy as he passed by. "Dude," the boy said and held his hand aloft for a quick high five. Jimmy smiled shyly and brushed the boy's hand. He heard a whispered "awesome" as he worked his way up the aisle.

Chapter 40

Carly Lindsey

When I was a little kid, as soon as I could write, I started keeping lists that separated everything in my world into good and bad. There was nothing in between. On my good lists, the early ones, I wrote things like flower, duck, mommy, daddy, ball and bow, which was my earliest word for brother. I had a lot on my bad lists. I didn't like naps, peas, duff, (an early word for pillow stuffing, which scared me to death, I don't know why) and sometimes, when they had done something to make me mad, mommy, daddy and bow. If I was mad at someone, they easily slid off my good list over to my bad.

My brother was always much bigger, stronger, smarter and better in every way, which made him a god to me. But, like all gods, that meant that he got way more credit and way more blame than he ever really deserved.

We are twins from different mothers, me and my brother, Mick. When Julia and Tom Lindsey made plans to adopt me, they did not know that Jules was pregnant, which I guess is pretty common when couples *try too hard* to have a baby of their own. I was born on April Fool's Day in 1969 and Micky came one week later. Because there were "complications" I was kept in the hospital for that week in an incubator and the two of us came home together, like real twins. Everybody always wants to know if our parents named us after Carly Simon and Mick Fleetwood. No.

It's true that Jules and Tom have always been fair. It's life that isn't, so where I have always been small for my age and undistinguished in every way compared to Mick, my "little" brother has enough for the both of us of everything that makes a human being outstanding. I learned early though, that some things cannot be shared, no matter how much both parties want to do it.

Everybody loves my brother. If I had a dollar for every time somebody asked him, *"She's* your sister?!" I would never have to work a day in my life. He never tells them that I was adopted, though.

Micky has never seen my defects. And, I know that Jules and Tom have tried not to see them. The problem has always been that *I* can see them.

Even at my worst, a few years ago, when I stopped calling Jules and Tom "Mom" and "Dad" and there was not one single thing on my good list, and all my clothes were black and even my long blonde hair was dyed black, and everybody insisted that I go to a therapist – not because I was sick, they said – only because they wanted me to find out what was making me so unhappy. Even then, Micky still told me everyday that I was the best sister anyone could have. And, I was so mean I just said, "I feel sorry for you." Even though I knew it hurt him, I couldn't stop myself. And, the meaner I got, the nicer Micky got, until I had to admit to my shrink that my lists had boiled down to just two words. *Micky* was good. *Carly* was bad.

You would have thought that that would make me hate my brother, but it didn't. And I suppose it could have made him hate me. But, it didn't. Somehow, (my shrink would probably like some credit here) we all got through the worst of it, and even though I still mostly call Julie, *Jules* and Tom, *Tom*, and when I look at the three of them, I still feel like I am that fourth thing that you circle on the tests that ask you, "Which of these things doesn't belong?" – things are better between us. And, that's how it goes in all families, my shrink says, even the ones that are *real*.

It was Mick who discovered that I could sing. I didn't even know it myself because I hardly talked from twelve on. Who was going to sing? But, Mick got a guitar for Christmas one year and he started writing songs, and first he said that he needed me to do back up, and then he made me learn the bass, and before I knew it, he had me singing lead on some songs, though only in our garage and never in front of anybody else.

He talked me into joining the chorus when I was a junior in high school by insisting that I wouldn't get into college with him if I didn't have some extra curricular activities on my record. Even though I knew I didn't have a prayer of getting into the colleges that were vying for my brother, I don't know why, I just did it. I know he told the teacher to try me out for the chorale lead, since how would she have known? But, that's when I discovered that I felt like someone else whenever I sang in front of people, you know, like those people you hear about who stutter, but when they sing, they sound so great? I heard this voice come out of me, and it didn't even sound like my voice at all, and I actually felt sometimes like I could look down at myself from up above. Other people would say the same thing. "Where is all that *sound* coming from?" How should I know? We put a band together with two of Mick's friends. We were sounding pretty tight before our drummer bailed on us. He knew we were going to break up when Mick left for college in the fall.

Mick is going to go to Berkeley. Pre-med. Full ride. I had no clue what I wanted to do, but I told everyone I was going to go to Santa Monica City College to give myself some time to decide, and really just to get everyone off my case. Jules and Tom agreed to Santa Monica College for me since it's pretty decent for a junior college and anyway I had screwed up so much in high school I wasn't going to get in anywhere else.

Just before graduation, Mick and his friend Kevin heard about this great class at SMC that they said everyone was talking about that we could all take in summer school. The teacher was some guy from UCLA with a bunch of degrees in music and Psychology, and he was also supposedly a famous jazz musician, though jazz was not my thing. They said that the classes had gotten so popular they had to hold them in the auditorium. It was rumored that two of the guys from the Chili Peppers might be in the class, but that turned out to be bullshit.

I was mildly curious, I guess, but really, I just wanted to spend as much time as possible with Mick before he went away. Besides, Jules and Tom told us if we took summer school at Santa Monica, we didn't have to get crappy summer jobs at Rite Aid or something. I think that maybe my brother was just trying to get me acclimated to the place before he left me there alone, which was something he had never done before. Whatever.

That class changed my life.

First off, the UCLA dude turned out to be Dr. Pierce. He came in and scared the hell out of everybody the first thing right off, and then this reggae looking guy, who turned out to be Jimmy Deane, he got up in front of the whole class and did this unbelievable street drum set on chairs and trash cans. There's another guy who does something like it down in Venice every weekend, and he gets a massive crowd, but Jimmy Deane made him look like amateur city. I wasn't the only one who was blown away, but I was the only one who reacted. I watched Jimmy Deane play for less than thirty seconds. I knew what I had to do, even though I felt like I was a totally different person when I did it. Dr. Pierce told us afterward that he had "never seen an impromptu performance like it in his whole tenure." It was funny. I didn't even know what a tenure was, but for the first time in my whole life, I knew what I wanted to do, and I knew what I wanted to be.

Book five – The Mystics

Chapter 41

At nine p.m. Jimmy Deane's doorbell started to ring insistently. He peeked out his security window at the top of the door.

"Hey, kid, long time no see. Ya' got anything goin' on tonight?" JD was so thrown, he couldn't even shake his head. He swung the door open. A nervous Paul Berman shifted his uneasy stance and scratched his ear. It had been more than two weeks since Jimmy Deane had been turned away from the house next door. The very few sightings he had had of the reclusive Bermans in that whole period had all been through the slotted openings of his window blinds, and through the tinted windows of one or another of the Berman's expensive cars as they glided in or out of their garage.

"Come on, then." Without an explanation Paul motioned for Jimmy to follow him to the black limo idling at the curb. When he reached the end of the stone walkway, Paul turned to see that he had left Jimmy paralyzed at his open front door.

"Ya' comin'?" Paul called out. Jimmy held up a "one minute" finger and ran back inside. He shrugged at James Dean who returned the gesture.

"What the hell?" James Dean said. "Why not?"

Jimmy patted his pocket for his keys, pulled the front door closed, and ran toward the limo. The driver knew where he was taking them. They rode down to the Coast Highway and turned north, and after they turned again, inland this time onto Sunset Boulevard, Paul finally offered an awkward ice-breaker.

"So? Dreads, huh?" Paul tugged at an imaginary dread lock on his own head. Jimmy Deane did not respond. "No, I mean it's a good look for you," Paul said. "I like it." Jimmy said nothing. The car covered ground.

"The silent treatment, eh? Okay. Maybe I deserve it." Paul rubbed the tops of his thighs and blew out a hollow breath again. A long moment passed before either spoke.

"No. No you don't," Jimmy said at last. "*Nobody* deserves that."

"Well, I wasn't exactly what you'd call *hospitable* when last we met." Paul gave Jimmy an apologetic shrug.

"Understandable," Jimmy told him. "I mean I understand." The limo swept past several long blocks of impressive homes along Sunset.

Paul Berman cleared his throat. His statement was more of a question.

"So, I guess you didn't know who Chelsea's mother was when I invited you to dinner?"

"I didn't know who *you* were until Maria told me. I saw an article about it in People a couple days later."

"You see the one in Rolling Stone about chick drummers?"

Jimmy nodded. Paul Berman looked out the window. When he spoke his voice choked. "They said they tried to stop it from going into print…after…" Paul paused. "Couldn't do it. It was already out by the time she…you know…" He glanced back at JD. "Weird, huh? Goes to show. One minute you're on the cover of Rolling Stone, and the next…" Paul Berman threw up his hands instead of finishing the thought. "So anyway, I've been trying to live down my infamous reputation. Laying low. I know this is no excuse for my bad manners but, man I freaked when I saw that van pull up from Drum World…" Paul's head swung back and forth twice. Jimmy Deane was quiet. "I didn't want Chels to see them start hauling drums out of the back of that van. You know?" JD nodded but said nothing.

"Yeah, well...I can pick 'em." Paul leaned forward to depress the button that raised the window to close off the driver's seat. "I should have come over a couple weeks ago. I've had my head up my ass. I just wanted to say I'm sorry."

"I understood, Mr. Berman," Jimmy said formally. "Really, it's okay. And….I'm sorry, too. For your loss." His formality caused Paul Berman to hesitate.

"Well, that's not exactly the only reason…" Again Paul tugged his ear nervously. "I also need to ask you something." He paused. "It's about Chelsea. I need your help with her." He glanced forward to make sure the driver could not hear. "I was gonna ask Dr. Anita...her therapist...but, I'm actually a little afraid." Jimmy Deane's head tilted quizzically. Paul Berman blew out a long breath. "I'm worried that she'll think Chelsea's crazy, or that I'm not a good dad, or something." He paused, but obviously did not want to dwell on the thought. He glanced again nervously at the driver and lowered his voice to a barely audible level. "Can we keep this between us?" Jimmy nodded. "After her mom overdosed, there was an investigation. There always is when the cause of death is from an overdose, I guess. But, it was suggested… by more than one person… that maybe I wasn't the most fit parent." He looked pained. "Because of the drugs. You know that my drummer od'd the year before, right?" The tragic overdose of Paul Berman's drummer had been international news for weeks. Jimmy said yes. "Well, two od's in the same house. I thought they were gonna take Chels away from me." Paul's lower lip disappeared.

"Oh," Jimmy said.

"Not a lot of people *know this...*" Paul hesitated, rubbing his cheeks hard before deciding to continue. "My old man was a drummer, too." He locked eyes with Jimmy Deane, his face betraying emotion. "Strictly small time," Paul all but spit. "The dude walked out on me and my mom when I was twelve."

"Twelve," Jimmy repeated softly.

"I never saw him again. Never once heard from him." Paul's voice was so low Jimmy had to lean forward to hear him. He seemed to be staring somewhere beyond Jimmy, his eyes unfocused and glassy. "Sometimes I think I must have done something terrible to a drummer in another life. I got such terrible drummer karma, and every single one of them has been a fuckin' nightmare." His head jerked up suddenly. "Hey, no offense, man," he said. Jimmy Deane offered him a small forgiving smile.

"None taken," he said. He watched Paul Berman fidget. "I don't really understand how I can help you with Chelsea, though."

"It's because of what you said that day. You told Chels that your mother had gone overboard, too. When you were her age. 'S that true? Your mother's dead?" Jimmy's head bobbed once. "Well," Paul continued, "I figured you might know...." He stopped, examining Jimmy's face for any sign of judgment. All he could detect was kindness. And frank interest. "Well, about a week or so after her mom died...after we came back home…actually, it was right after we met you, maybe even the next day. I heard her talkin' to somebody on the staircase. I figured it was Yolanda, the housekeeper, but then I heard the vacuum cleaner running in the studio. So, I go to see who Chels is talking to 'cause there isn't anybody else in the house. She tells me...get this…" He hesitated again and shrugged. "She said she was talkin' to *Jimmy Dean*. At first I thought she meant you, but then she points up to the top of the stairs. Her mom was a real James Dean fan. Did I tell you that? Right before

Nina died, she bought that Andy Warhol painting…the original…and she had it hung at the top of our stairs. You ever see it? Rebel Without a Cause…you know, like the movie?" Paul Berman touched Jimmy's shoulder. "You'll come over some time. You'll see it. It's really something. If you like Warhol." He let a deep sigh escape and rubbed his eyes. "Anyway, Chels? I thought it was a one-time thing. No. She says she talks to him everyday, JD. She says… *he talks back.* I was thinkin' I gotta sell the Warhol or give it to charity or somethin'. What's the shrink gonna make of that?" Berman shook his head sadly. Jimmy waited until Paul looked up, so that he was looking directly into his eyes.

"I'm pretty sure the shrink would tell you that it's normal...under the circumstances." Jimmy had a quick recollection of Mr. Weis, and how reassuring the principal's advice had been.

"Really?" Paul looked doubtful. "Normal to make up shit like *that*?" Jimmy nodded smiling.

"Yeah, when my mom died...I was five…like Chelsea. I talked to Ringo pretty much every day for a long time. Maybe even years."

"Ringo *Starr*?" Paul Berman looked amused. "No shit? *Ringo*?"

"Yeah, my mom had put a Beatles poster up on the back of my door when she died. I think she knew I'd need a friend. My mom was really smart like that." He didn't think Paul Berman would want to hear just then that James Dean was watching Jay Leno back in his next-door neighbor's family room.

Jimmy gave Paul Berman a sincere reassuring smile. "Really," he said. "It'll be okay."

The two sat in companionable silence as Paul Berman tried to believe what Jimmy Deane told him and Beverly Hills rolled past outside the limo's tinted windows.

When they turned onto Doheny heading south, Paul Berman broke the silence.

"I've actually been thinking of putting some players together. Maybe cutting a new album. I needed to make sure Chels was okay first, though." His hands made a nervous pass over his shaved head. "You're sure this imaginary friend thing with Jimmy Dean is normal?"

"Yeah," Jimmy told him. "Don't I seem normal?" A shred of relief passed the older man's face and gave way to a crooked grin.

"Except for the dreads, maybe," he joked.

"Is that so? I suppose *your* generation has room to talk?" Jimmy smiled back and started listing the top hair bands on his fingers. "Ah…let me see…Metallica…Black Sabbath…Iron Maiden…Motley Crue…and let's not forget the ever beautiful… Guns N' Roses. That's some good lookin' hair!" Paul laughed and ran a hand through his own recently shorn locks.

"Okay, okay. Point taken. Do me a favor though, huh? Don't make any cracks about hair when we get to where we're goin'."

The driver made a left on Santa Monica Boulevard and then a quick u-turn to pull the car up directly in front of the Troubador. The valets down at the Palm restaurant and Dan Tana's looked up to see who was disembarking from the limo. Otherwise, the street out front was deserted. The club was closed on Wednesday nights. A bouncer, a huge young man several years older, two inches taller, and a hundred pounds heavier than Jimmy, opened the locked door and admitted them into the vestibule. The bouncer's face was so dark that in the dimness of the interior Jimmy could barely distinguish his features, but a half dozen gold chains illuminated his throat and chest. His voice rumbled.

"Good evening, Mr. Berman. Very nice to see you again, sir. How's Miss Chelsea doin'?"

"She's good, Chris, real good. Wanted to come with me tonight, but she's got school tomorrow. Can't have her club hopping at night no more now that she's got obligations in kindergarten."

"Won't be too long, sir, before she's headlining down here, that's what I think."

"Bite your tongue, son. I'm savin' up for medical school." The bouncer chuckled and ran a hand across his own bald pate as if he had just noticed something new.

"That's a good look for you, Mr. Berman," he said sincerely. Paul winked at Jimmy Deane and hitched a thumb in Jimmy's direction.

"This here is my new neighbor, Chris. JD." The bouncer extended a large strong hand.

"Very nice to meet you, sir," Chris said. He held on to Jimmy's hand just a beat longer than was right.When he released it and spread his own massive paws out, he told Jimmy, as if he were a crystal ball reader. "I'm feelin' success for you." Then he winked. "And, I would tell you otherwise, sir if I thought so." Paul Berman nodded in the bouncer's direction.

"You can take that to the bank, JD. Chris here calls 'em as he sees 'em. Never been wrong yet. Far as I know."

Suddenly and surprisingly Chris grabbed Jimmy by the shoulder with one massive hand and put his other wide open palm over Jimmy Deane's heart and held it there. It was such an odd thing for someone to do, certainly uncharacteristic for a guy who looked like a linebacker for the Rams. Jimmy felt captured, unable to move in the bouncer's grip. The warmth from the big man's hand was so intense it almost burned. Except for formal handshakes, and a recent spate of high fives, Jimmy Deane had not been touched by another human in such an extraordinarily intimate way since Susie Deane's death. He felt his heart flutter wildly.

"You're a drummer, aren't you, sir?" Jimmy gave Paul a sideways glance and Paul grinned back and raised his brows. Chris deliberately retracted both hands slowly leaving his fingers spread wide as if they were sensing something in Jimmy Deane's soul as they pulled away.

"It's in the heartbeat," the big man said nonchalantly. "I can usually tell right away, but some people are harder to read than others. Sometimes I need contact, you know? You keep things pretty close to the vest, don't you sir?" Jimmy nodded, open-mouthed, and Paul smiled broadly.

"This guy's got a gift." Paul patted the big man's bicep. "What can I tell you? Never seen him fail."

"Thank you, Mr. Berman." Chris looked pleased. "You gentlemen have a nice night, hear? I hope I'll see you back soon, Mr. JD." Paul led Jimmy into the Troubador.

"Hey, that was spooky." Jimmy leaned into Paul's ear while the older man scanned the interior of the legendary club.

"You'll see far spookier than guys like Chris if you hang with me," Paul told him. He gestured toward the interior of the club. "You been here yet?" Jimmy shook his head. A dozen or so men, all talking in small groups, were scattered throughout the first floor. At least half of them were musicians that Jimmy recognized from bands he had just ticked off in Paul Berman's limo. No one was up on stage, but music, (no band Jimmy recognized), was playing low over the PA. Another half dozen men were sitting at the bar, and Jimmy could hear laughter and voices from overhead on the second level. At the table farthest from the door, two men, both of them senior to Paul's age, were hunched over what looked like a row of huge dominoes.

"My man!" One of the two lifted a hand toward Paul and JD. The dominoes, upon closer inspection, turned out to be audio cassettes.

"Little John," Paul nodded pulling Jimmy over to the table in his wake. "How's it hangin'? Deetch." Deetch Claymore, the club's manager stood and gave Paul a bear hug.

"Been too fuckin' long, man, how you doin'? You doin' okay?" Paul's presence was obviously enough of an answer for him. Deetch pulled two chairs out and sat back down. "Who's the kid?"

"This is JD. He lives next door." A silence fell at the mention of Paul Berman's next-door neighbor, Jimmy's landlord, who had found the naked corpse of Nina Berman in his driveway. "Not that one," Paul said.

Deetch's mouth made a silent *oh*, and the other man simply nodded relief.

"Hey, Paulie..." Little John stubbed out his cigarette. "Hey, man, I'm sorry about...you know... your troubles." Paul nodded. "How's your little girl? Your girl doin' okay?"

"Yeah, she's cruisin'," Paul nodded. "Better every day." He shot JD a quick grateful glance. "So," he said looking down at the cassettes. "What ya' got on the table? Ya' got anything for me?"

"Crap. Nuttin' good. These are the dark ages of rock, man. Will you listen to this shit?" Deetch pointed up to the empty stage and yelled over to the bartender. "Neily, turn this bullshit up, will you?" The bartender lifted his index finger and nodded yes. Then, recognizing Paul Berman, he gave the thumbs up.

"Hey, Mr. B. Good to see you back," the bartender yelled over the music. "What are you drinkin'?"

"I'm comin' over, Neil," Paul said. He jumped up. "John, you ever think about playing again?" Little John shook his head.

"You don't want some old fuck like me, Paulie. You need to get you some young stuff." The truth was, and everyone at the table except Jimmy Deane knew it, was that musicians were a superstitious bunch and nobody who knew anything wanted to replace Paul Berman's dead drummer. Paul gave the man's shoulder an affectionate squeeze.

"Take care of the kid, here. He's one of your own. I'm gonna make the rounds at the bar." He pointed down at the cassettes in front of Deetch. "Keep an ear out for me, Deetch."

"Will do, Paulie," Deetch said and saluted Paul. Then he and Little John exchanged an awkward glance while Paul went to the bar.

"This is good." The club manager waited a few seconds and then pointed a cassette box in Jimmy's direction. "I could use some advice about your generation. What is up with yous?" He waved his hand over the tapes on the table. "This is just half of this week's haul," Deetch told Jimmy. "You hear this shit?" He waved his cigarette toward the empty stage again as if the band on the PA was performing live. "Tell me, son, would you pay good money to see these assholes?"

Jimmy shrugged. "Exactly," Deetch said. "Every week...more and more demos come in. It gets worse all the time. I hate my job." Little John chuckled.

"The Beatles were rejected by every major label in England until they finally got signed by EMI in 1962," Jimmy told them in a respectful voice. Little John acknowledged the fickleness of the music industry with a curt nod and pursed lips, but Deetch Claymore scowled.

"Are you trying to tell me, wise guy, that the next Beatles might be hiding in this pile of horseshit if only I give them another listen to? Have a drink, kid! Let me tell you what the problem with your generation is. You guys got no roots. Half of yous can't play for shit. Please. Blow me. Four power cords on a Fender your mommy and daddy got you for

Christmas and you think you're makin' rock and roll." He punctuated every few words with an angry stab at the tabletop with his lit cigarette. "You *ain't* paid your dues… and, you got *no respect*…none… for *musicians*… that's right, *musicians*… who have paved the way with decades of hard work for your crappy garage bands… and this post punk whiny bullshit…."

JD looked at Little John who raised his eyebrows, but, except for a twinkle in his eye, did not seem ready to contradict the club owner. "Case in point…" Deetch was clearly just getting warmed up. "Do you have any idea *who* this is?" He pointed the plastic box at Little John. "You even ever heard of Little John Hartman, kid?"

"*The* John Hartmann?"

"You little shit, you goofin' on me?" Deetch pretended to throw a punch. Jimmy looked wide-eyed at John Hartman.

"You started the Doobie Brothers...with Tom Johnston." Both older men registered pleasant surprise, most of all Little John Hartmann. "First album in seventy one…*The Doobie Brothers*. Then one out every year until...*Minute by Minute* in seventy eight." John Hartman gave Jimmy a high five and laughed out loud.

"A lucky guess," Deetch said, but he was grinning.

Chapter 42

While the usual skateboarders tried to kill themselves on the railings outside the Humanities building, Jimmy Deane watched them as he tried to work up enough courage to pay a visit to Dr. Pierce. He checked the time. Twenty minutes left in Pierce's office hours. Now or never. He launched himself gracefully down off the wall and walked quickly up the steps.

As a visiting professor, Pierce utilized a borrowed faculty office from someone in the African-American Studies department who was on a summer sabbatical. The office's odd furnishings and unique décor suited him perfectly.

"Come in," Dr. Pierce called out. When he saw Jimmy's face poke into his office the professor rose and smiled. "I should have known it was you. You make music just knocking on the door!" Dr. Pierce gave Jimmy an old-fashioned soul handshake.

"Sit…take a load off." He gestured to the chair in front of his desk. When he collapsed into the ancient green leather swivel chair behind the desk, the cushion farted softly. The two men grinned at each other, then Professor Pierce looked Jimmy Deane over for a long moment, like a relative who had been abroad during a growth spurt. "You know, I've been expecting you at my office hour."

Jimmy sat up straighter.

"Me, sir?"

The professor smiled kindly.

"Two Chinamen on the moon…you know…" The teacher made the desk chair rock. Jimmy Deane slowly shook his head.

"Chinamen, sir?" he asked.

Dr. Pierce leaned back and made the old chair squeak.

"It's from Social Psychology. Attraction theory specifically. Human beings are attracted to, or have an affinity for, people who they judge to be similar to themselves." Dr. Pierce gesticulated while he talked. "The phenomenon is greatly enhanced if the two similar persons are in a foreign environment or context." Jimmy nodded with a slight smile.

"Ah, two *Chinamen* on the moon…"

"Or," Pierce grinned. "Two brothers in Santa Monica. Two brothers *with* Rastafarian hair dos." He tweaked one of his own dreads and chuckled.

"Does it always work that way?" Jimmy asked.

"Well, let's see. There are over three hundred students in your section of TPP this term. Besides yourself, there are eight black students. Care to guess how many of those eight have already made it a point to come introduce themselves during office hours?"

"All eight?"

"And, if you don't count the ladies, and that one boy with the corn rows, not a one of them shares the second most salient feature that we do…" Pierce tugged again at one of his shoulder length dreadlocks.

"Is hair that important?" Jimmy asked naively

"You mean in general, or in the Black community? Or, specific to this phenomenon?"

"All of it, I guess," Jimmy said.

"How important is it to *you?*" Jimmy hesitated. His lips formed a perfect "O".

"You ever read the Bible?" Pierce asked. Jimmy nodded.

"I did a book report on it in ninth grade." The professor did a double take.

"On the whole thing?" Pierce asked with a smile that said *no way.*

"It was long," Jimmy acknowledged. Pierce chuckled and shook his head.

"Well, do you remember the story of Sampson?"

"Oh." Jimmy touched his own hair. "Yes, sir."

"It's funny how important hair is. It's that way in almost every culture in the world. Most have strict codes about hair length and style. Look at your Native American tribes. Your Sikhs. Even Western culture observes the importance of hair. You're too young…and actually, I am too, but, the Beatles' hair was a signifier of youthful rebellion long before their music was political. Did you know that John Lennon said there never would have even been a Beatles if it wasn't for your namesake?" His question was rhetorical and so the professor didn't wait for a response. He was never happier than when shooting the breeze with a bright student, and there was something about this one, not just his hair, that was compelling. He went on talking about cultural norms, and then James Deane's namesake and his hair and his undeniable and enduring influence on youth culture and music for a long time. For quite a while he didn't seem to notice that Jimmy Deane had stopped talking or even blinking.

"Am I getting boring?" he grinned.

Jimmy shook his head emphatically. "So, was it personal or political for you?" Dr. Pierce asked a little abruptly.

"My hair? You mean the decision to let it grow?" Pierce nodded and his chair squeaked again. "Personal," Jimmy Deane's voice was barely a whisper.

"Me, too," Pierce let his voice drop into an even lower register. The two men held each other's gaze. "Well, let's have that discussion another time, shall we?" Jimmy looked relieved. Pierce backed off just a little to a slightly less personal topic.

"Tell me, Mr. Deane. Have you managed to introduce yourself again to our beautiful chanteuse?" Jimmy blushed red and felt heat rise up from his core.

"Oh, man," Dr. Pierce enjoyed a hearty laugh that brought him forward. He reached out and gave Jimmy a high five. "I don't think I've ever seen a brother blush so deep. You got it bad, my man, you got it real bad!" He laughed and then rocked back impossibly far. He shook his head as if remembering first love not so many years ago. His *personal hair-do* trembled like the points of a jester's cap. Another brief silence passed. The professor interrupted it. "So, is this just a social call you're paying? One Chinaman come to visit another up here on the moon?" Dr. Pierce asked with an impish grin. "Or, is there something I can do for you? Are you enjoying the class?" The professor's chair stopped rocking, but his head moved in an encouraging nod.

"Well sir, I was wondering if you knew something about something…" Jimmy paused and bit down on his lips.

"Well, I guess I do," Dr. Pierce said gently. "I know a few things about a few things. You have something particular in mind?"

"Yes, sir. I um….I saw in the course catalogue that your PhD is in Psychology. You have an MFA in music from NYU, but you're a Psychologist, too."

Pierce squinted, his eyebrows bunched together. It wasn't usually a good thing when a student started off this way, but he couldn't help but be flattered.

"I see you've done your research," he said. "Is my resume that critical to your question?" JD shook his dreads but said nothing. Dr. Pierce waited a second before explaining his complex skill set. "Well, music is my addiction, but I figured out pretty early in the game that for me, music wasn't going to pay the bills steady. My second love is Psychology. I didn't take to clinical work. Just wasn't my thing. But, I truly love both fields, and I guess that I'm a natural born teacher. My parents were both teachers. It's kind of like the family business. Now, I guess you could say I teach to support my music habit." Jimmy nodded and took a deep breath. When he exhaled he bit down hard on his lips. Dr. Pierce leaned toward him just a few inches.

"So," he said. "Did you have a music question or a Psychology question?"

"Sir," Jimmy blurted. "I wondered if you've ever heard of anyone who's sane, not crazy I mean, but they….they hear voices. I mean for real…" Jimmy detected a sudden alarm in his professor's bearing. It was the alarm of a psychologist who hears the hallmark of schizophrenia spoken of, perhaps in regards to a beloved family member. "I've got this friend…"

The professor's chair stopped moving.

"It's actually my neighbor. Her mama died a little while back, and her daddy's concerned that she's been having imaginary discussions on some regularity with…" Jimmy's face betrayed the irony. He shrugged elaborately. "With…James Dean. The actor, sir. Not me."

"Hmmm." Pierce picked up a pen and bit the end. "How old is the child?" he asked.

"She's almost six."

"Any idea how she knows who James Dean…*the actor*…is?" Jimmy told Professor Pierce about the Warhol painting hanging in the foyer of the Berman house, and the mother's fascination with the famous actor before her overdose.

The professor nodded as he absorbed the information. He clicked the ballpoint pen several times.

"Tell your friend not to worry too much. This is the kind of creative coping the human mind is capable of in crisis. It's a coping strategy. Nothing to worry about…" Dr. Pierce watched Jimmy's reaction carefully. "…in a child of this age."

"Oh. Okay. That's what I thought. That's what I told him." Jimmy responded.

Dr. Pierce stood abruptly and pulled two books down from the shelves behind the desk.

"Here. For *your friend.* Dinnowitz's *The Child's Magic Mind*…and take this one, too. It's a general Developmental Psych text. Good stuff. Every parent should read this." He pushed the two books across the desk. Jimmy examined the book covers.

"Now, myself," Dr. Pierce told him with a straight face. "I talk to John Coltrane 'most every night." Jimmy Deane scrutinized his teacher's whole body for any hint of ridicule in his words.

"John Coltrane?" Jimmy repeated.

"Now, don't go telling nobody…" The professor made a face and lowered his voice an octave. "…'Trane's daddy died when he was in the seventh grade…same as me. I was only thirteen when my daddy died. 'Course I didn't know that about 'Trane until after he died himself and I read his obituary in the New York Times. I was a grad student at NYU when 'Trane died. It wasn't long after that… in the middle of the night… one particularly difficult night in the way nights in New York City can get difficult for a boy from Indiana…" Pierce gave Jimmy a meaningful look. "You dig?" he asked. Jimmy nodded. "Well, I woke up and John Coltrane himself was sitting on the edge of my bed." He paused and he and Jimmy Deane both turned to the window where applause was coming out of the open doors of the auditorium across the courtyard as if it had been cued.

Professor Pierce's gaze lingered out the window. His face had an awed, dreamy quality, as if he were back in his tiny New York apartment in Harlem looking into the face of John Coltrane. "…had that soprano sax with him." His hands held an imaginary saxophone. He smiled then and looked meaningfully at Jimmy Deane.

"Been talkin' to 'Trane ever since," he said, and allowed the pen to tumble from his hands onto his desktop. Jimmy let a minute pass while the professor's chair started again to creak under his rocking. "Now, that's between two Chinamen on the moon. I don't want it getting around that I talk to the departed. Lord knows there's enough crazy talk out there 'bout me as it is." He smiled and nodded and they leaned toward each other, their fists bumping over the scattered papers on the professor's desk. Jimmy Deane liked how familiar it felt being with Dr. Pierce. He liked the way the professor's way of talking changed one on one and became something that reminded him of his time in the barbershop with Sam and Odie and the others.

"You tell your friend everything is going to be okay, JD." Dr. Pierce smiled. He looked at his watch and announced that it was time to close up shop.

"I have a lady friend waiting on me." He winked and smiled a mischievous smile. Jimmy was almost home before he realized that the professor had called him JD. He thought about what that could mean for more than two hours, and then he started to wonder what events might have occurred to make Robert Pierce decide to let his hair grow down past his shoulders.

The professor meanwhile was half way across campus on his way to the faculty parking lot before he remembered what the boy had said about his next-door neighbor's Warhol of James Dean. He had assumed from the boy's clothing, that the kid lived pretty close to the poverty line, with no spare money for a trendy or expensive wardrobe. He had him pegged from day one as one of those kids from Watts or maybe Compton who wants out of the ghetto so bad they are willing to endure the discomforts of being a Chinaman on the moon. A kid with prodigious musical talents, but no money in the home for proper drums.

"Ain't no Warhol originals in Watts," the professor whispered to himself. "That is fo' sho!" He shook his dreadlocks vigorously and dumped whatever his concerns about the likable young student were into his car trunk with his brief case. He cranked up the AC and put the soundtrack from Round Midnight into the cassette player. By the time Robert Pierce arrived home Herbie Hancock had successfully forced any worries about JD or anything else from his head.

Chapter 43

Two rainbows arched over opposite ends of the Island of Granada a scant mile off of the Wainwright yacht's starboard bow. Gillis stood at the rail for an hour or more and stared tearfully at one and then the other. The concerned crew elected Henry, the first mate and chopper pilot, to intervene.

"Captain?" The first mate approached tentatively. "Is now a good time?"

"For what?" Gillis sniffled.

"Well, boss, for anything. Is now a good time?" Gillis shook his head but stared at the island in the distance. The sea was calm. The motors were idle. The boat was drifting westward.

"No, Henry, I don't suppose now is a good time for anything." He turned to his first mate. "Funny ain't it? I spent my whole damn life layin' down bets, tryin' like hell to get rich quick. Now, I'm rich. That one thing is for sure. I just don't know what else I am." He winced at the truth. "I think I'm lost, Henry." Henry stepped up to the rail and pointed.

"That's the north shore of Grenada, Skipper. That's the South shore, there. You aren't lost at all. Directions are my specialty. Be right back." Henry disappeared below deck and returned with a large red leather box. He sat down on the deck boards and beckoned to his captain.

"Sit," he ordered. He opened the red box between them. He extracted a silken cloth, some ancient looking bronze coins and a plain pad and pencil. He put the three coins into Gillis Wainwright's wary hand and spread the cloth. He took a well-worn book from inside the box and set it with reverence beside him, giving it a gentle pat.

"Take some time, Cap," he said. "Meditate on your most urgent question." Gillis gave Henry a doubtful look then examined the coins in his hand. He closed his eyes.

"Okay," he said.

"Keep your heart and mind focused on your question, Skipper, and throw the coins onto the cloth." Gillis raised an eyebrow, but complied. Henry looked at the coins where they landed and began urgently scribbling lines onto the pad. He consulted the worn leather bound book and uttered an indecipherable commentary.

"Ummmm. Uh huh. Oh. Oh boy. Oh yeah. Of course." At last, he looked up. "You ready, Cap?"

Gillis nodded though he had no idea what Henry was up to.

"Well," Henry pointed at the scribbled lines. "The image of Difficulty at the Beginning…" He glanced up quickly. "Thus, the superior man brings order out of confusion."

"Me?" Gillis asked. Henry pursed his lips and nodded. He picked up the coins and closed Gillis's right hand over them. "Again," he said. Gillis squeezed his eyes closed and after a few seconds threw the coins. Henry peered down and scribbled another series of lines on the pad.

"The perseverance of a dark man brings good fortune," Henry said.

"Well, hell," Gillis said. "Sure." The process was repeated four more times and after each, Henry consulted the little book.

"Look here," Henry pointed again. "If you are sincere and loyally attached, you are rich in your neighbor." Gillis reached for the coins and nodded patiently in between each of Henry's pronouncements.

"It furthers one to cross the great waters."

"To go on this way brings humiliation. The fetters should be removed."

"It furthers one to consult the great man." Gillis looked up at the cloudless sky for a second and then checked the Rolex on his wrist. He rubbed his chin.

"Henry, if it's five o'clock here, what time is it in Omaha?"

"Nebraska, sir? It must be two o'clock. Maybe three." Gillis jumped to his feet and climbed the ladder to the Captain's lounge. Henry carefully wrapped the I Ching in the silk cloth and replaced the ancient Chinese coins in a small, embroidered pouch. By the time he had stowed the box in his quarters Gillis was finishing his ship-to-shore call.

"You sure about this, Warren?" Gillis yelled loudly across the Caribbean ocean and three time zones. "I'm countin' on your advice." He listened intently. "Uh huh. Sure. Absolutely. Worth a try. Thanks a heap. I'll be in touch." He replaced the phone and turned his back on the black screens of the TV monitors. He squinted into the sun as it started its descent toward the starboard rail.

"What did the great man say, Cap?" Henry asked.

"He said I gotta start givin' this money away to folks who will do somethin' good with it." Gillis and Henry exchanged a look that was at once bemused and certain. Beside the Wainwright yacht, not four hundred yards away, a graceful sloop was gliding silently by under full sail toward the island. Gillis stepped forward and peered at the sailboat and the painted green lettering against her hull.

"What the hell is *Greenpeace*, Henry?" he asked.

Chapter 44

Elizabeth prepared her face as she always did for the morning broadcast of Reverend Lester's sermon, with a fresh coat of powder and a swipe of bluish red lipstick across her thin lips. A neatly wound nylon headscarf had protected her heavily sprayed hairdo from the previous night's sleep, and she carefully unwrapped it and folded it back into her top drawer. She removed the red stationery box containing her most private documents from under her bed and carried it to the couch.

When it had become too much trouble to back the Cadillac out of the driveway for mass at St. Mel's each morning, she had begun to substitute the Reverend Lester's ministries on TV. She had lately begun to think of herself as more of a born again Christian than merely a Catholic, though she would never in one million years allow anyone to submerge her in one of those filthy swimming pools. Well, no one but possibly the Reverend Lester himself, if he were offering.

Recently, the Reverend's new bride, Mary Beth, (a woman clearly at least Elizabeth's age or older, who had obviously had plastic surgery, and wore way too much make up, even for Elizabeth's tastes), had become an annoying dominant presence on the show. Half of the telecast was now devoted to Mary Beth's sofa chats with Christian personalities, as if Mary

Beth were some kind of sanctified Oprah. Elizabeth did not approve. Neither did she quite understand what Reverend Lester saw in Mary Beth, who had terrible taste in clothes, and wore her bleached hair so foofed up she called to mind that country western singer with the enormous bosom who was now in so many movies. Nothing about Mary Beth seemed very Christian to Elizabeth.

Precisely four ounces of warm ginger ale sat on the coffee table as a tonic in case Elizabeth's heartburn acted up. She removed the top of the stationary box and reviewed her most recent correspondence with the Reverend while she waited for his broadcast.

The recent windfall from *Susie's bastard* had allowed Elizabeth Breaux to make the kind of donations that certified her as a GOLD MEMBER in Reverend Lester's congregation. She fingered the gold border at the edge of her certificate and read the letter admitting her into Jesus' flock with GOLD MEMBER status.

My dearest Elizabeth...

An eight by twelve glossy of the Reverend in his most glorious vestments had accompanied the personal letter and her certificate. The portrait had been suitably framed in gold gilt and sat on her night table where she could fall asleep each night looking upon the Reverend's glory. Elizabeth favored the severe horn rimmed glasses that the Rev wore in the picture, as they gave him an undeniable air of intelligence, and though she had long known that he was the most righteous man in the whole world, she knew with the arrival of the photo, that he was quite possibly also the smartest. The second picture featuring the Rev *and* Mary Beth, Elizabeth had discarded, since she felt that it did not do the spiritual leader any real justice, and Mary Beth had scandalously allowed an inch or so of wrinkled cleavage to show at her bosom.

Elizabeth rifled through the remaining contents of the red box. She paused over one letter in particular that had arrived just after Jimmy Deane's departure. The pale blue parchment envelope was addressed in a beautiful cursive hand to Susie and Carter Deane but Elizabeth had opened it immediately without a shred of discomfort. At the time, she had been angry at the person for not knowing that Carter and Susie were dead, and she had assumed that she would just give the letter a quick look, and then throw it away. The substance of the letter however had not been quite so easy to dismiss. She stared at the brief, hand written note and tried now for perhaps the tenth time to decide what to do with it. Her reflections were interrupted when the opening theme song signaled that the Reverend's services were about to begin. Hastily, Elizabeth replaced the various documents into the red box and postponed any decision about the letter one more time.

A typical introduction to the daily show involved the emergence of Reverend Lester, cloaked in full ostentatious regalia, from the overhead fake clouds on the set, holy scripture in hand.

To Elizabeth's dismay however, Mary Beth appeared on the screen. Through extraordinary effort it seemed as though the Reverend Lester's new wife was withholding an undisclosed and unbearable burden of sadness. And, in the case that it wasn't obvious, she told her audience just that. Her newlywed's heart was beyond heavy, and the Rev would need everyone's prayers that week as a serious illness had befallen him. Not to worry, he was in the Lord's care, and with everyone's prayers and an up tick in donations he would surely recover by the taping deadline for the next week's Sabbath sermon.

"The Lord giveth the flu and the Lord taketh away, also," Mary Beth tittered. Her demeanor changed abruptly as she started to introduce her very, very special guest for the portion of the morning's show she called Christian Chat.

If Elizabeth Breaux disliked Mary Beth before that morning, it can be assumed that she could only be said to have come to fatally loathe the Rev's wife in the moments that followed. For another type of woman, Mary Beth's interview might have presented the opportunity for a paradigm shift. An awakening of insight and tolerance perhaps. Not so in spades for Elizabeth Breaux. Instead, she had neither the character, nor as it turned out, the time, to repent of her sins, and truly, truly, come to Jesus.

On screen a swaggering young black man emerged from the green room on the ministry's sound stage and sauntered across the set toward a beaming Mary Beth. He wore the uniform of a Detroit rapper: sports apparel four sizes too large and a baseball cap turned backward. The toes of his enormous basketball sneakers peeked out from under the folds of his drooping pants. The canned TV audience gave him the warmest welcome ever. Mary Beth rose and the young man grasped her outstretched hands and kissed her, (kissed her!) not on the cheek, but full on the lips. MB swooned and dropped weak-kneed to the couch.

Elizabeth struggled through the interview to learn that the young man had been both a pimp and a drug dealer before beginning his career as a hugely successful rap star. Busted on a murder charge, he had learned from his cell-mate (and revealed partner in sodomy) all about Jesus' tender mercies. His story of repentance and salvation brought tears to MB's glistening eyes in several well-timed close up shots.

Elizabeth burped and reached for her ginger ale. As she leaned forward to replace the glass, the slightest vertigo made her sit up suddenly and shake her head, as if one of Florida's myriad flying insects had assaulted her ear. The TV screen blurred. A warm feeling behind her right ear grew rapidly into a sharp pain and then arced up and over her head exploding in her right eye. As her hand went protectively to her afflicted eye, she rose from the couch in a panic. Her visual cortex processed its final image: the Reverend Lester's wife, Mary Beth, in the full body embrace of the handsome young black sinner, who had, only moments earlier, declared that he knew he was bound for salvation's heaven.

Elizabeth was already dead by the time her body toppled back into a remarkably natural pose on the couch. Her left hand landed on top of the resting remote control device and her right hand remained open on her tightly knitted brow, giving her corpse the appearance of someone who was perhaps diligently trying to recall the channel number for Dallas re-runs.

The stationary box had fallen open to the floor distributing in a neat fan at her feet her certificate of membership from the Church of Mysterious Ways, the personal letter signed by the Reverend Lester himself, and a pale blue, sherry-stained letter addressed to Susan and Carter Deane from someone in Chicago.

Chapter 45

Robert Pierce was rarely wrong about anything, but his prediction that his summer school course at Santa Monica College would suffer from student attrition did not come to pass. Instead, word about the remarkable drummer and the amazing singer had swiftly gotten around campus and by the end of the first week an additional two dozen unregistered students were cramming into the auditorium. One of the legitimate students called the Santa Monica city fire marshall and the course crashers were all forced to leave by campus security. It produced a scene, but Pierce framed the whole incident as public performance art and everyone got through it just fine, if you didn't ask the ejected.

Ironically, among the disgruntled, was the young man whose drum sticks had figured so prominently in Jimmy Deane's already legendary performance; the poor lad had failed to follow protocol and could not produce the necessary pink card for class admission. After he was evicted JD usurped his seat, ten rows closer to his blonde vocalist and the tall handsome surfer who seemed to be always at her side. Jimmy was determined to report to Dr. Pierce the next time they chatted that he had indeed summoned the courage to speak with *the beautiful chanteuse.*

Weeks went by however and JD had only managed to eavesdrop intermittently on a few of the couple's conversations. So with only a little over a week left in the term, JD had managed only to confirm that the girl's name was indeed Lindsey. JD kept what he thought was a safe distance while stalking them surreptitiously on campus each day. The surfer and the girl were seemingly each other's constant companions all day, every day until Lindsey finally got into the surfer's BMW and drove west on Pico Boulevard.

On most days, after they were gone, JD went to the library to read books from Dr. Pierce's recommended reading list, if he could concentrate. Once he arrived home himself, and soon after Maria left for the evening, he played his drums over albums in his studio while James Dean badgered him in between about *getting a life*. He spoke twice with Gillis ship-to-shore, but gave up any real hope on his unrealized promised visit. Instead, he planned that when summer school was over he would fly back to Florida and surprise the millionaire mechanic on his boat, wherever in the Caribbean ocean it happened to be. Each short call had been so wrought with static, both electrical and emotional, that JD had forgotten until too late to thank Gillis for St. Cecilia, though he never removed her from around his neck, not even to shower or swim. The touching gift, as uncharacteristic as it was, was probably the only reason that JD did not give up on his quirky friend. It truly meant almost more to him than the ten million dollars that Gillis had gifted him.

As it was at most colleges, by the middle of the term, especially in the summer, torpor fell over the administration, and very few students had call to visit the registrar's office. The clerical staff took license for long hours to simply loaf and gossip around a single desk. When Jimmy Deane approached the counter, one of the annoyed clerks leaned forward, squinted at him and very nearly fell from her perch on her desktop. She touched Monique Libby's shoulder and then pointed behind her. Monique's purple helmet turned around slowly. To say that her face lit up would be an understatement of enormous proportion.

"There he *is!*" she said, revealing inelegantly that James Deane had been the current topic of conversation. The other clerks enviously watched Monique's back as she scurried over to be of help to the gorgeous, now locally famous young drummer.

"I *heard!"* Monique leaned over the counter and held her hand up for a robust high five.

"Heard?" Jimmy responded with a tentative hand.

"About *you!* About TPP! You be the talk of the whole campus, boy!" Monique beamed as proudly as if she was a family member. "You done good, my brother!" The young woman grasped JD's upheld hand in her own chubby one and shook his arm so hard his torso shimmied and his dreadlocks trembled. He glanced at the staring circle of clerks behind Monique and blushed.

The clerk looked over her shoulder and released JD abruptly, turning all business.

"Don't pay them no mind! What you need James Deane? Monique takes care of her own people," she said in a grim tone. JD smiled shyly and she gave him back the smile that transformed her homely scowl into a face of sudden real beauty.

"I was…I …"

"C'mon boy! Speak up! What you need?"

"Well, the girl…the one who did the…"

"You talking 'bout the little singer? That girl they say had the voice of a angel? A *black an-gel,* some said."

"Yeah," JD blushed again. "The singer." Monique's head and hands beckoned.

"Yes?" she said. "That singin' angel….?"

"Well, I'd like to get her phone number." Jimmy looked again at the clerks who were suddenly all occupied with feigning busy-ness. Monique dismissed them with a brusque wave over her shoulder. She straightened her back. She grabbed up a pencil and started to scribble on a piece of paper as she chanted in a mechanical voice.

"I'm sorry, Mr. Deane, but we are bound by the Federal Family Rights and Educational Privacy Act here in administration. What you call your FERPA laws." She spun the paper around. Monique had written in small letters: "*What's her name*?" JD looked up.

"FERPA?" he said, but took the pencil from Monique and scribbled back. *"Lindsey ???"*

Monique shook her head. "That all you got?" she whispered. JD nodded and shrugged an apology. Monique exhaled exasperation.

"This federal law pertains especially to student records," she said loudly, and then leaned forward to whisper, "Stay put!" As she walked away from the counter, she spoke ostentatiously. "I'll get you some information on the law, Mr. Deane, and also on the Buckley amendment of 1976." She hurried toward the back into the records room. One minute later she handed a print out across the counter. It was a Xeroxed copy of the entire wording of the FERPA law of record. JD looked at it dumbly. Monique turned it over to reveal a scribbled note.

"Gym – 30 minutes – out front!"

JD smiled. "Thank you," he said. "Thanks a lot."

"Well, it's my pleasure," Monique smiled back with her stunning smile. "It is my job to protect student records and privacy!"

Promptly, one half hour later, Monique Libby bustled across the campus toward her rendezvous with Jimmy Deane. In her hand a computer-generated print out fluttered like a paper scarf. She waved at JD and indicated that he should follow her inside the gym.

"Nobody thinks twice about a black man hanging around the gym," she explained. "You try sittin' out front of the Chemistry building, somebody gonna come by – and soon – to ask you why is you *loitering?!* But, the black man *owns* the gym!" Jimmy nodded and followed her into the almost empty weight room. Two football players, both of whom confirmed Monique's theory, were horsing around with a barbell at the far end, but otherwise, not another soul was present. Monique spread her printout against the wall and removed a pencil from deep within her stationary hairdo. Five names and addresses appeared in alphabetic order.

"Now, there was five students. Five Lindseys," she said pointing. "This one here is not your girl, since she is a black Puerto Rican girl." Jimmy cocked an eyebrow. Monique peered up at him through her lashes. "On her mama's side. Only 'bout a hundred brothers and sisters here. I know who's who. I like to take care of *my* people." Jimmy patted her shoulder in recognition of her accomplishment. Monique grinned. "Now, these two…looks like Lindsey is they last name. One be Michael. Michael Lindsey. And this other one be Carly. What fool kinda name is Carly? That a white girl name?" JD shrugged. She slashed through the first three names with her pencil. "Anyway, which leaves you these other two. Lindsey Serisawa…sounds Asian to me…and Lindsey Rowan. I think that's your girl. Lindsey Rowan." Monique slashed through Lindsey Serisawa's information and circled Lindsey Rowan's name and address several times. "Here's her address right here. This is my mailing program so it drops the phone numbers." She looked up at Jimmy. "Sorry. You gonna have to do some investigatin'." She folded the printout into a neat small square showing only the name and address of one Lindsey Rowan, 1462 Twenty-Fifth Street, Santa Monica, California. Less than a mile from the college. JD accepted the document from Monique with both hands as if it were a delicately folded origami.

"Thank you," he said sincerely. "How can I thank you? You broke the rules for me."

"Oh, never mind, Mr. James Deane. You just let me know next time you and Missy Lindsey Rowan gonna bring the house down, you hear? I don't wanna miss that the second time around." JD smiled and leaned over to kiss Monique's soft cheek. She grabbed his head in her hands and kissed him full on the lips before she bustled away, her hands flapping at her sides. JD's knees buckled beneath the weight of his first kiss, as strange as it was. He touched his own lips and then stroked St. Cecilia, all the while clutching Lindsey Rowan's address in his sweating palm.

Once he had sufficiently recovered from his encounter with Monique, Jimmy ran to his car on the other side of campus. He drove immediately to Twenty-Fifth Street and parked several houses south of Lindsey Rowan's address. He slumped behind the wheel and waited. Twenty-Fifth Street was a quiet residential avenue with large leafy trees and lots of Spanish architecture. The homes were not as ostentatious as those on JD's block north of Montana, more like the size of the guesthouse on the Berman's property next door to him, but they were still pricey, and he tried to envision *his* Lindsey living in the one at 1462. He had no plan but was not at all uncomfortable sitting three doors down and simply staring up at the window that he thought might be her bedroom. Hours went by. Several neighbors walked past with dogs straining leashes. When a Rottweiler paid a little too much attention, Jimmy started to think that he should either go up and knock or leave to come back fresh the next day. He opted for the next day scenario and drove home.

Maria was gone but a casserole was in the oven with a note. In the studio James Dean was plugged into the headphones.

"What's up?" JD said pointing a fork at the stereo. James Dean leaned forward and unplugged his phones. Bartok, at high volume, filled the room.

"Harnoncourt," James Dean identified the conductor over loud strings.

"Tough stuff," JD said.

"Percussion!" James Dean yelled and replaced his headphones. Jimmy smiled and went back to the kitchen. He picked up the phone and dialed information, asking for a number on Twenty Fifth Street for a Rowan. No luck. He went back into the studio to listen to Bartok. Tomorrow, he promised himself. Tomorrow, he would walk right up to the door at 1462 and…

Chapter 46

A letter from the nurse

*June 20,
1987*

Dear Mr. and Mrs. Deane,

I am so sorry to inform you that Mary McGinnis, the birth mother of your son, James, passed away one week ago by her own hand.

I am writing to you because Mary and I worked together. You might remember me from the night that James was born. (I was the nurse who brought him to you.)

Shortly before Mary passed away, she told me that the boy who was James's father was a young man that she knew from school, James Johnson. (Loyola University is a very good college.) She said that James was a civil rights worker who was killed. I'm not sure when this happened, but, as you might remember, we had our share of troubles here that spring when Dr. King was killed. Your son's father could have been involved in that. Mary said that she had not yet told him about the baby, and she gave her baby away because her family would not help her, and she did not think that this would be a good (safe) place for a mixed race child to grow up. (I can vouch for that opinion. I hope it is different in Florida now, but, here in Chicago, things are still not too good between the blacks and the whites.)

Mary McGinnis was a nice person and a good nurse. She helped to bring many babies into the world and she was always kind and caring to the mothers and the babies.

Eighteen years is a long time and maybe this letter will never find you. Or, maybe you and your son won't be able to find the Johnson family or won't want to. But, it won't be because of me and that is why I am sending you this letter. So that I can sleep at night knowing that I did the right thing.

Yours truly,
Judy Dumke, R.N.
p.s. I always thought that you were real nice people.

Chapter 47

The neighbor three doors down from Lindsey Rowan's house became alarmed when the young man in the silver Porsche parked in front of her own house the second day in a row. He seemed to be innocently watching something down the street, but it occurred to her after the third hour that the car *could* be a stolen one. She called the Santa Monica police. The young officer's tap on the driver's side window startled JD who was deeply involved in a fantasy evaluating the many possible outcomes if he indeed approached Lindsey's door. The cop was polite but insistent. He examined JD's new Florida driver's license and called for a trace on the Porsche. The kid was too polite to be a burglar or a car thief but the officer thought it best that he accompany JD up to Lindsey's front door to confirm his story. Showing up with Santa Monica's finest in tow had not been one of JD's fantasies.

The officer let JD do the knocking. A young female, not JD's Lindsey, and not as pretty by half, answered the door promptly with unmistakable disbelief already plastered across her open-mouthed face.

"You!" she swooned.

"Do you know this man?" the police officer asked stupidly.

"Of course," she said. "He's James Deane!" The cop looked down at JD's license.

"He a friend of yours, Miss?"

"I wish!" the girl said with naked lust. "Are you kidding?" Her enthusiasm threw the cop off.

"According to your neighbor, Miss, Mr. Deane here has been sitting in front of her property for two days in a row. *All afternoon*, Ma'am." The young girl's face ignited in much the same way most women's faces did when confronted with Jimmy Deane. Instead of reflected passion, JD's face looked only miserable. The cop was embarrassed for her. Just as suddenly as her heart had lurched to joy, common sense prevailed.

"Oh," she said sadly. "You don't know me, do you?" JD's head shook no. The girl's enthusiasm instantly flagged. "I'm in your TPP class at SMC," she said sadly.

The young cop was getting confused amidst the girl's acronyms. "I'll bet you're looking for Carly…?" she continued. A miniscule fragment of negative hope clung to her question. Jimmy felt for Monique's computer printout in his pocket, but he knew it would betray her to let anyone know of its existence. He stood silently looking from Lindsey Rowan's disintegrating joy to the cop's amusement.

"Wrong girl?" The cop smiled.

"This isn't the first time," Lindsey Rowan confessed. "She went to high school with me. It's happened before." She sighed but managed a rueful smile. "Stay here. I've got her address in my old directory." While Lindsey Rowan went off to get the other girl's address for JD, the cop offered some advice regarding the pursuit of women.

"Dude," he said rather kindly under the circumstances. "You just can't park on their street and… *wish…you know?"* JD shrugged. "Flowers, man. Real nice flowers." The cop chucked JD on the shoulder. "Works for me every time!"

Lindsey Rowan returned with a sheet of paper which Jimmy examined and then folded to add to his pocket.

"I'm really sorry," Jimmy said to her. "I…"

"Forget it," she said. "Are you kidding? My dad would *kill* me if I brought a drummer with dreadlocks home!" The cop rolled his eyes but JD smiled at her.

"Well, thanks for this." He patted his plump pocket and backed away from the door. "I guess I'll see you tomorrow," he said.

"Yeah, sure," she said. "Hey, do me a favor?" JD turned to face her. "If you do see me tomorrow…" She glanced nervously at the cop who looked away. "Well, would you say *hi* to me? Especially if my friends can see. It would really raise my social currency if they thought…"

"No problem," JD said and smiled again. The girl waved and reluctantly pushed her door closed.

"Hey," the cop asked JD giving him back his license. "What the hell does that mean?"

"I have no idea," Jimmy told him honestly. "But…?" He shrugged.

"Women!" The cop shook his head. "Hey, are you going over to that other girl's house now? I don't want to have to answer a call from *her* neighbor today."

"You won't," Jimmy said.

"Okay. Get a California license. Soon!" The cop looked at JD with mock sternness. "And get some flowers!"

Chapter 48

The seas in the western Caribbean were calm. What sailors call a dead calm. In the middle of a dreamless sleep, the dimmest recollection of a little blue gift bag sitting in his top bureau drawer back in Hollywood, dislodged itself from the deepest recesses of Gillis Wainwright's memory and floated to the surface until it burst like a bubble into his consciousness. How or why the memory surfaced so many weeks later without one whiff of it in between, Gillis had no idea. He woke and sat bolt upright in his bed in the captain's quarters, sweat dripping down his sides onto the Egyptian cotton sheets. He had a very bad feeling about the woman who had given him the undelivered present for JD. Fumbling for his Rolex, he read the time in the light from the full moon. Three a.m. in the West Indies. Calculating the time zone difference he postponed the ship-to-shore call to JD in California that he urgently wanted to make. Another day wouldn't matter either way to JD, but once the image of the blue bag and the beautiful woman who had delivered it invaded his sleep, Gillis found that further slumber was impossible. He stared at the moon shadows on the ceiling of his cabin until an orange sun finally rose up out of the ocean. Gillis dressed and went topside. The sea was blue glass. For the first time since taking over the yacht Gillis Wainwright did not tune in to the international financial news on the bank of television monitors up on the bridge. Instead he deliberated over possible courses of action. He could simply call JD and tell him about the woman and the blue bag and offer to have someone from Roger Albright's office go to the house to retrieve it and bring it to California for him. Alternatively, he could stop being such a pussy and take the little bird over to the mainland and get the bag from his house and hop a flight to California to bring it to JD himself. He could be there to greet him by the time JD got home from his summer school class, if he left immediately. Gillis imagined standing at JD's door in Santa Monica with the tiny blue bag in his hand, a shit-eating grin on his face, and joy in his heart. He could not believe how much he missed his young neighbor. He woke Henry.

"We're goin'!" he told the first mate. "Get the birdie ready."

"Where, Cap?" Henry rubbed sleep from his eyes and sat up. "Where are we going?

"Home!" Gillis said. Henry smiled.

"Give me twenty," he told Gillis.

"Make it ten. I got a flight to catch out of Lauderdale this afternoon."

"Hallelujah!" Henry saluted his captain and reached for his pants. Ten minutes later the helicopter on top of Gillis Wainwright's yacht was in communication with the tower at Fort Lauderdale, and its rotor blades were a blur.

"Take this, Cap," Henry hollered over the whirring helicopter blades and handed his boss a small blue pill. Gillis looked at it closely. A tiny, almost unrecognizable butterfly was imprinted on one side.

"What's this?" Gillis yelled.

"Methylenedioxymethamphetamine," Henry yelled back with an impish grin.

"What's it for?"

"It's for your nerves," Henry loudly reassured his boss.

"*Methyl……?*"

"Methylenedioxymethamphetamine," Henry hollered louder. "MDMA!" Gillis Wainwright looked doubtfully at the little butterfly.

"It's X," Henry screamed.

"X?"

"You'll like it!" Henry assured him at top volume.

"If you say so!" Gillis swallowed his words and the little butterfly.

"You'll like *everything!*" Henry laughed loudly and lifted the little chopper high into the air.

Chapter 49

Once their radio headphones were working properly, and in between declarations of deep affection for his pilot and first mate, Gillis managed to tell Henry the complete details of his previous life right up to the day he won the Florida lottery.

"I ain't no angel, Hank," he said. "But this here's the first time I think I might 'a done somethin' pretty terrible to that poor boy. The damn thing is, it ain't what I done. It's what I didn't do!"

"Look, Cap," Henry consoled Gillis. "Anybody could have forgotten that little blue bag on a day like that." Henry's words were scant consolation. Gillis looked dolefully down where the Caribbean Sea stopped only at the horizon.

"Hey," Henry offered, "I've got a buddy in the tower at Miami International. I'll get them to have someone from your lawyer's office go get it and meet us in Lauderdale. You'll be putting it into the kid's hands this afternoon."

"I love you, man," Gillis said nearly weeping. "Have I told you how much I love you?" Henry suppressed a giggle and pointed down and low at what seemed to be debris floating on the ocean's choppy surface.

"What is it?" Gillis asked. Two ink black torsos were barely visible floating amidst the shattered boards of a splintered raft.

"Haitians from the looks of 'em. Trying to make it to Florida." Henry brought the little helicopter lower for a closer look. Two men, boys really, were clinging to the remains of their homemade craft. They gestured wildly at the helicopter.

"What the hell?" Gillis lifted his sunglasses and peered down.

"Yep," Henry said and circled. "Looks like their craft fell apart. I'll bet they've been here a while. I'll radio Miami Center and see if there's a Coast Guard vessel in the area. They'll pick 'em up. They'll send 'em back, but at least they'll survive."

Gillis looked worried. "How long will it take 'em to get here? Are you sure they'll make it that long?"

"All depends on how tired they are, Cap," Henry said. "Nothin' we can do." He hesitated and then pulled his own life jacket out from under the seat. "Unless you want to drop these down…?" He looked at Gillis for the go ahead.

"And, what if *we* need 'em?" Gillis said, but he was already dislodging the other life jacket from under his own seat.

"Well, then, Cap…they'll have 'em… and we won't." Henry smiled. "I'll go down as low as I can. Try to drop 'em real close. From the looks of those boys, they can't do too much swimming." Gillis shoved the two life jackets out the small door port. They landed almost directly on top of the refugees.

"Here," Henry said. "Give 'em this, too." He handed Gillis the insulated water container. Gillis looked back at Henry with concern. Henry pointed at the hatch. "Might as well, boss. We'll be in Lauderdale in less than an hour. And, if not…how far can *you* swim?" The mate grinned. Gillis made a second drop, and one of the boys in the water grabbed onto the water thermos while the other one waved up, mouthing words that Gillis understood as *thank-you so much, I love you!*

"*I love you, too!*" Gillis mouthed. Henry chuckled and picked up the radio.

"Miami Center, this is Bell helicopter one, five, nine, three four. Come in." The FAA command center in Miami responded.

"This is Miami Center, Bell chopper. Go ahead."

"We're about 86 miles east southeast of Key West, Miami. We just spotted two people on a disabled craft. Individuals are in the water. Repeat. In the water."

Gillis Wainwright leaned toward the pilot. "Two *beautiful indie-vidge-you-alls!*"

"Roger, Bell. Say again," the voice from Miami said. "Did you say, *beautiful* individuals?"

"Roger that," Henry said.

"What's your altitude, Bell?"

"We're moving up to five hundred feet. We just dropped some life jackets and a little water down. Is there a Coast Guard ship anywhere nearby?"

"We're pulling you up on radar now..........there's a cutter about a half hour from your location. What's your fuel situation, Bell?"

"We love you!" Gillis shouted.

"Bell? Say again." Henry put his finger to his lips and made a "shhh" sound.

"We've got one hour to destination. Fuel capacity right around there, center." Henry ran his fingers across his closed mouth and turned a key at the corner of his lips, winking at Gillis. Gillis covered his mouth and nodded. The controller's voice came over the radio.

"Anyway you could stick around 'til the Coast Guard gets there, Bell?"

"That's a negative, Miami. We'll be on fumes as it is to make it to land. Sorry."

It took Miami a few seconds to come back.

"No problem, Bell. They'll get there when they get there. You did your part."

"Roger that, Miami. Say, is Mike Curtis on today?"

"Negative, Bell. Curtis is at Disneyworld with his sister's family from Chicago today."

"I love Disneyworld!" Gillis whispered. Henry "shhhhed" him again.

"Well can you give me a frequency to get a telephone patch? I've got an important call to make for my passenger."

"Use one, two four, point nine, five, Bell. You copy?"

"One, two, four, point nine five?"

"Roger that."

"Thank you, central. We're out."

"We'll give you a holler when we pick up your boys, Bell. And keep east of that weather coming over the keys. Miami central out."

"*Our boys*!" Gillis said and tears formed in his eyes.

"Don't worry, Cap," Henry said. "They'll get picked up now just fine. Let's put that call in to Mr. Albright's office, okay?"

"Okay," Gillis sniffed. "I love Roger, you know that, Henry?" Henry smiled.

"Anybody you don't love right about now, Cap?" Gillis gave the question a full minute.

"Nope," he said. "I love *everybody*!" Henry laughed and placed the call. A worried look fell across his face when he turned toward the Keys.

Larry Drummond volunteered to head over to Gillis Wainwright's place to retrieve the little bag.

"You can swing by, pick up one bag, and listen to the other bag bitch for a few minutes and still make it to the airport in Fort Lauderdale before they land," his secretary said. He would have made it too, with time to spare and even enough left over to have a drink to celebrate Mr. Sixty-Nine's conquest over his *Fear of Flying*. *If only,* the contents had still been in the little blue bag. And, *if only*, the old bag, Elizabeth Breaux, had answered the knock on her front door.

Chapter 50

Larry Drummond, Esq.

Fucking Hell! Pardon my French. It's just that it's the only rational response to that day's events. A calamitous day by anybody's standards. My volunteering to dash over to the Wainwright house to fetch the contents of some little blue bag was not exactly as altruistic as some initially thought. Self-serving it was, if you want the truth. In the weeks prior to Mr. Wainwright's call from the chopper, my secretary had informed me no fewer than two times that Mrs. Breaux had failed to cash two of her grandson's checks. This in itself signaled a very bad turn of things since, concerning the boy, she seemed conscientious only about taking his cash. I *had* put in a few calls to the old bat's house. And, it was nagging that she had answered none of these. But, you see, she was such a disagreeable old person. It was quite easy to avoid her in spite of the hefty retainer our firm collects each month from Mr. Deane's trust.

With a smug I-told-you-so look, my secretary handed me the telephone the second I arrived at the office. I was immensely relieved when Mr. Wainwright needed only one small favor. It would be a pleasure, I assured him.

It was my clever intent to get to Fort Lauderdale International in plenty of time for his flight to Los Angeles, and to be able, as my secretary so poetically pointed out, to provide a positive status report on the old bag at the same time I handed over the little blue one.

I swung by Mr. Sixty-Nine's house first to locate the latter. I considered my inability to find its contents ominous. While you couldn't say there was much in that house to interest a burglar, there didn't seem to be any signs of either forced entry or a robbery. All the junk a junkie might take was still in place. But, the blue bag? Bloody empty. I didn't relish showing up at the airport empty handed because Mr. Wainwright's sole purpose seemed to be to deliver this forgotten item to the Deane boy. He seemed quite agitated about it as a matter of fact. I couldn't call him en-route to further inquire, but I scoured the house looking for anything that might have been so precious. Whatever the contents of the blue bag had been, it seemed that they were no longer on the Wainwright premises.

I will admit that as I walked across the newly installed thick sod lawn in between the two houses, I entertained the notion that the grandmother had stolen the contents of the blue bag. Even though she displayed monumental disinterest in either the neighbor or her own grandson, it seemed like something the wicked old witch would manage: carting off the one meaningful item in that pathetic house, just to prevent her grandson its pleasure. I was in fact mounting a confrontation in my head when I noticed the circulars lying in her driveway. At least two weeks' worth. I knew right away what I would find inside. Let me just say, it's a good thing she didn't have a dog. A dog will get terrifically hungry in two weeks without food.

The front door was unlocked, another bad sign. Even from the porch, the stench was unbearable, so I lingered only long enough to confirm my worst fears and then telephone the coroner and my own office.

I drove to the airport in the heat with my top down to purge the smell, but I'm afraid that I'll never completely get the memory of it out of my head. There was nothing to do but go ahead to the airport to meet Mr. Wainright's chopper and face the music. He was no fool. I did not expect that his heart would exactly break at the news of JD's grandmother's fate. I just wasn't keen on reporting that while she was supposed to be under my watchful eye she had somehow gotten herself quite dead and had been reliably decomposing for several weeks.

This turn of events, plus my failure to recover the requested item from the blue bag was probably what caused me to resort to the frantic entreaties I occupied myself with on the way to Fort Lauderdale International.

I'm not what anyone would call a religious bloke, but, I do, as I'm guessing others do, occasionally send *up* (as good a direction as any) a sort of missive. Like a prayer, I suppose, though it's a rather vague prayer. Destination and recipient absolutely unknown to me. Still, in troubling times, I do have a need to ask for help from the Unknowable out there. I have to say the fact that such help never arrives has not quite squelched the impulse entirely.

So there I was, speeding along Interstate 95, the sun baking down on my unprotected pate and the recent odor of deceased grandmother wafting from my memory when I had the following thoughts in immediate succession. Thought one: Please, get me out of this somehow. Next thought: I conjured images of what events could reasonably occur to get me out of my pickle. The first image involved of course a ghastly auto accident. A fender bender would not be sufficient to buy adequate sympathy, if not outright forgiveness, for my malfeasance. I rejected (for obvious reasons) the accident scenario immediately.

Next thought, because this is how my mind works (I am a lawyer after all): I envisioned a number of equally destructive possibilities that would preserve my own well being, but would prevent Mr. Wainwright from completing *his* itinerary.

Now, I'm most certainly not saying that this is evidence for the Divine. And, I don't believe for an instant that my entreaties had anything at all to do with the way Mr. Wainwright's helicopter and its two occupants came up missing somewhere out over the ocean. But, it *is* why I took it upon myself to fly out to Los Angeles when I could have just as easily phoned the bad news in as they say on both accounts. And, furthermore, I had nothing of value from within any little blue bag to give to Mr. Deane, which had of course been the whole purpose for Mr. Wainwright's sudden trip. So why, you might ask, did I go? Why indeed? Why? Indeed.

Chapter 51

The best flowers available in the little florist shop on Wilshire Boulevard were ivory roses. The long stemmed variety. JD bought two dozen and waited patiently while the clerk put little water capsules on the end of each stem. Very precise directions to Carly Lindsey's address in the Pacific Palisades were provided by the extravagantly tipped deliveryman.

The roses bounced gently on the passenger seat as JD wound his way up the hill. As he had at the other Lindsey's address, JD parked several homes down from the target house. This time he let only a few minutes slip by before he picked up the bouquet and then reached bravely for the handle on his car door. At that exact moment, a familiar BMW slid past and pulled into Lindsey's driveway. No fewer than four surfboards were racked on top of the car. JD's heart sank in an unprecedented way. The surfer honked his horn. JD's whole body sank behind the wheel when Lindsey, the right Lindsey, opened the front door and ran to the surfer's assistance. The boy unloaded several pizza boxes from his back seat onto Lindsey's outstretched arms. He carried another load of parcels himself, presumably more food, and when the tall carved front door slammed behind them, there was simply nothing for JD to do but start up his engine and make a U-turn to head back to Santa Monica.

On his own street a stretch limo idled in front of the Berman's house obscuring at first the unattended rental car behind it. JD took scant notice of both and pulled the Porsche into his own garage taking the flowers inside to give to Maria.

Larry Drummond rose from the couch as JD entered. The attorney was already shaking his head as he removed the roses from Jimmy's hand and passed them to the weeping housekeeper.

Chapter 52

The ticket agent at LAX informed Larry Drummond that the red eye flight from Los Angeles to Miami was only half full.

"You mean half empty," Larry responded seriously. The agent laughed a weak, unprofessional little laugh, assuming that this remark was the product of British humor. The unsmiling lawyer purchased a first class seat and when informed that the airline could not absolutely insure that the seat next to him would be unoccupied, however light the passenger load, he also bought the seat adjoining his. His immediate plans for the cross-continental flight back to Miami involved many tiny bottles of free airline booze and not one sentence of idle chit- chat with an inane stranger.

The flight attendant arrived before takeoff with his first neat Scotch on a small tray and Larry told her with a minimum of grace, "Keep them coming. I've had a very rough day."

"Most people will sleep on this flight, sir," the girl responded in a breathy voice. Larry fixed her with a steel-eyed look, drained his drink, and put his empty glass back down on the center of the tray.

"One can only hope," he said. "Bring me at least three more." The girl immediately brought six miniature bottles and as many tiny bags of nuts and pretzels.

"I don't much like Florida myself," she whispered while Larry piled his stash on top of his brief case in the empty first class seat next to his own. He grunted once, waved the girl away and plugged his headset into the easy listening station. After the first gulp of his second Scotch he slowed his drinking down to a sipping pace and stared at his own reflection in the window.

"Fucking hell," he murmured a little too loudly over the Muzak. The passenger in the row ahead turned around to give Larry a dirty look. The lawyer merely raised his glass crookedly and took another long pull on his scotch. The chastened and home bound Florida blue hair turned back to his own non-alcoholic business with a sound from his nose that Larry fortunately could not hear.

The L.A. trip, a less than twenty-four hour turn around, was providing Larry Drummond with no less than a genuine religious conversion. It could not have been predicted on the day that his boss, Roger Albright, a senior partner and a good person in the firm to be chummy with, had assigned the care and feeding of Jimmy Deane to him. Prior to that assignment, Larry had been a lifelong and devout atheist. In just a little over a month's time, in service to the young mulatto boy, Larry's personal convictions had come to include the undeniable existence of an almighty God. In addition, and without a shadow of a doubt, as his jet cruised eastward, Larry was also nurturing an incipient yet unwavering belief that whatever deity it was that had prevailed over the course of Jimmy Deane's life thus far, not only existed, but was one sadistically mean son of a bitch, to boot. How else to explain the kid's tragic luck? It had become suddenly preferable to Larry Drummond to believe that an omnipotent (if cruel) some*one* controlled the boy's consistent bad fortune, rather than to accept the possibility of sheer random chance striking any one individual quite that often. Good lord! How much calamity could befall a single person? Larry unscrewed the plastic cap on the third Scotch bottle somewhere over Texas. His hands were still shaking from his afternoon meeting with Jimmy Deane. He held them out and watched his fingers tremble.

The decision to fly in person to Los Angeles and to give the boy the trunk load of bad news Larry had brought had been his alone. There was no one else to blame. He had assumed that he would feel noble afterward, but all he felt as he headed back to Miami was hollow and vaguely ill. The latter had certainly been facilitated by the first two pre-boarding Scotches he had had in the airport VIP lounge while waiting for his flight, unaccompanied as they were by anything remotely resembling real food.

The stew's insights about passenger habits on the red eye were realized before Texas turned into Louisiana beneath them. The first class cabin was dark and, except for the howl of the jet engines, completely quiet. Larry Drummond removed his headphones and took the opportunity to review from memory his conversation with Jimmy Deane. It was a litigator's habit to facilitate the learning of possible lessons from one's mistakes.

Had he missed anything? Was there something he could have done differently that would have made a difference?

Larry tried to picture the young man's face as it had lit up at the recognition of his Florida lawyer sitting out of place on Jimmy Deane's own sofa in his rented Santa Monica house. Was it his imagination or had the boy seemed already preoccupied? Distressed even? There had been precious little small talk between them. At the first sight of the lawyer in fact, the boy had seemed to jump to an unpleasant assumption.

"Mr. Drummond! What are you doing here? Is something wrong?"

Larry's response in turn had been a cliché.

"I think you'd better sit down, JD." Rationally, Larry had decided that it was best to rank order the items of bad news that he had borne to the West Coast. He had begun with the least terrible and worked his way up to the last and worst item (by his own estimation) that he had come three thousand miles to deliver.

"I'll start at the beginning. Mr. Wainwright… Gillis… called me a couple days ago and asked me to go to his house to fetch a small blue bag from the upper bureau drawer in his bedroom." JD nodded. "There was something of great importance in the bag, JD. Something that he wanted to give to you. He was en-route from his boat on the chopper when he called."

"Gillis was flying? Are you sure? I didn't think that he…" Larry glossed over Gillis Wainwright's fear of flying with one sentence.

"Nor did I."

He proceeded.

"As I say, it was of great importance to him, and ultimately, he said…..to you. The pilot got the Miami tower to provide a frequency so that he could call us." Jimmy's hand reached up and traced his medal under his T-shirt. "Unfortunately, when I got to the house, the blue bag was empty." Larry shook his head and inhaled a deep breath. "Gillis had intended to bring it to you that very day. He was going to meet me at the airport in Fort Lauderdale and bring it out himself. But…" Larry looked up nervously. "Nothing else seemed amiss at the house, but… apparently, whatever it was that had been in the bag…it had been stolen." The lawyer looked genuinely forlorn about the missing contents. A flood of relief washed over Jimmy Deane. He urgently yanked his St. Cecelia out of the neckline of his shirt.

"No. It wasn't stolen!" he said smiling, and holding the medal out for inspection. "I found it! I took it! I found it the day Gillis left. I knew it was for me because it's St. Cecelia. See? It's got my initials on it!" Larry Drummond let his fingers hold the medal for a brief instant. He confirmed the engraving and nodded recognition. If anything, the lawyer looked even more forlorn. “She’s the patron saint of musicians!” JD informed him.

“Oh!” Larry said in a weak voice. He dropped the necklace and withdrew his hand.

“That’s not all, is it?” JD asked tucking his medal protectively inside his shirt.

“No,” Larry inhaled again and plunged ahead to the second catastrophe.

“After I discovered that the contents of the blue bag had been stolen…well, you see, I thought then that it had been stolen…” Larry drew a quick breath. “Anyway, I went next door to check on Mrs. Breaux.” He grimaced.

“Oh!” Jimmy interrupted the lawyer again, although this time with much less enthusiasm. “It’s Grandma.” Larry Drummond nodded slowly.

“I’m sorry,” he said. “It was very sudden. And, I’m quite sure painless. A stroke.” Larry skipped the part about Elizabeth’s corpse lying in the heat for at least two weeks before discovery, trapped twenty four hours a day around the clock in front of a terrible cable station at annoying volume. He also skipped the details about things involving certain tropical vermin, and especially insects, that happen to a person who comes to that kind of end. Jimmy Deane looked at the floor.

“I don’t know what to say,” he told Larry honestly.

“I’ve actually had an opportunity to get to know your grandmother a bit…in your absence,” Larry said. “She’s not an…”

“She would want to be buried in Tampa, I think,” Jimmy pronounced. “Her other family are all buried there. Can you arrange that?” Larry nodded again, but licked his lips in a way that told JD he was just getting started. They both took a break to breathe hard.

"Oh," Jimmy looked frightened. "That's not all, is it?"

"I'm sorry to have to tell you this," Larry started.

"It's Gillis, isn't it?" Larry winced. JD's face crumpled and his hands rose as if to catch the fragments. "No!" Jimmy cried. Then softly, "No, no, no…" Larry waited until JD's sobs stopped.

"How?" the boy finally asked.

"His chopper went down just east of the Keys. A sudden storm. There was no wreckage. A helicopter like that sinks like a stone. The coast guard told us that Mr. Wainwright had dropped the chopper's life jackets to two Haitian refugees in the water just prior to losing contact with Miami. We don't know exactly what happened." Jimmy Deane's body curled into a fetal position, and he wept into his hands for a long time. Larry Drummond sat motionless, knowing there was even more to come. When the boy's grief had finally achieved a small respite he unfurled his long body and sat erect.

"I don't know what to do," he said simply. "I don't know what to do."

"JD?" Larry Drummond had one final piece of bad news.

"More?" JD looked at him. He shook his head. There was nothing more that could be taken from him.

"I took the liberty…"

Larry Drummond explained how the firm's investigators had swiftly pieced together a scenario that was sure to only provide the boy with more immeasurable grief. But, did he not need to know the truth?

"So, this is what I think happened," Larry said. "Your birth mother flew down to Miami and came to your house on the day that Mr. Wainwright won the lottery. That part was just sheer dumb coincidence. We believe that she gave Mr. Wainwright the blue bag to give to you. We think that because you had also turned eighteen, that she had come to get permission from your adoptive parents to make some kind of reconciliation. That's not uncommon these days for women who gave their babies up for adoption."

"My mother? She came looking for me?" Jimmy's eyes refilled with tears. Larry Drummond braced for the worst of the news, but he did not mince words.

"She took her own life the day after she returned home to Chicago," Larry said. The truth echoed much more harshly than he had intended. "We're not sure why. She didn't leave a note. One of her colleagues believes that it was because…"

"She met my grandmother?" Jimmy looked pale.

"Yes." Larry Drummond's own eyes misted. A long minute of silence passed as the clever attorney fitted the missing puzzle pieces together. "She obviously gave the St. Cecelia medal to Mr. Wainwright to give to you first. He must have forgotten all about it when the lottery business happened. I think he just remembered it two days ago, and that's why…"

Never in his life or career had Larry Drummond felt as though he had been in the presence of true anguish. One look at Jimmy Deane and he had no doubt. He reached out a hand. He shook the boy's arm.

"JD?" he said. "JD?" But, wherever it was the boy had gone, there was no way to summon him back.

Chapter 53

The sight of young Dr. Pierce strolling across the SMC campus, his lean frame erect and graceful, his unconventional hairstyle bouncing rhythmically, always caused a significant number of heads to turn. Such was certainly the case on Thursday morning, when he interrupted The Psychology of Performance an hour into his lecture, and headed purposefully over to the administration building, an unmistakable aura of *something happening* surrounding him.

The professor was not the only one aware of JD's absence from class. *The beautiful chanteuse* had also taken notice that the drummer had been missing. On Monday evening that week, he'd been spotted sitting in a silver Porsche that was parked in front of her neighbor's house. Was it a coincidence that he'd failed to show up to class since that sighting? Carly Lindsey didn't think so.

Dr. Pierce approached Monique Libby's station in the administration office.

"Yes, sir?" she said bustling over. "Can I do something for you, sir?"

"You may," Pierce said, impatiently drumming his fingers on the counter. "One of my students has been missing from class for three days now. I wonder if you can get me his contact information."

"Yes, sir." Monique's back straightened. "Right away, sir. Your student's name?" But the question was unnecessary. She knew before Pierce said JD's name that he was the student in question. "It won't take but a minute, Dr. P," she said and turned to her computer, her fingers already a blur on the keyboard. The professor took the information back to his office.

Fifteen minutes later, Professor Pierce took the auditorium stage again to restart his class. He made a slight joke about the interruption and tried to look unbothered, but his mind was whirring. A Spanish speaking woman had answered the phone number he had been given for James Deane. The agitated woman had repeated several times that the boy was *en casa,* but *no quiere venir,* which Pierce understood to mean, JD wasn't coming to the phone. The address given to him by the administration was in the best section of Santa Monica. Homes that Pierce knew could be worth many millions. *Who was this kid anyway?* And, more importantly to the professor, why had the boy suddenly dropped out of class? For unknown reasons, Dr. Pierce had a bad feeling. Before he could in earnest resume the second portion of the day's lecture, Carly Lindsey approached the bottom of the stage. She looked up and beckoned.

"Dr. Pierce, could I have a minute?"

Pierce turned his microphone off and stepped to the edge of the stage. The auditorium grew pin-drop quiet as the other students strained to hear the whispered conversation in the front. They watched Pierce nod several times. It could be assumed that he was questioning the girl. Her responses were punctuated with the body language of one who seemed in possession of very few answers. At last the instructor gave her a perfunctory, joyless smile and patted her shoulder in dismissal. He gave Carly a moment to take her seat while he gathered his thoughts. He drew himself taller and stepped into the podium's overhead light.

"Where were we?" He picked up the dangling thread of his lecture, pretending that the interruption had been staged. "Ah, yes. Dramatic anticipation. Did you notice just then how potent the *absence* of audible dialogue can be to a scene?" Many of his students nodded in thoughtful assent and scribbled notes. "Silence, as you have seen, can be the most powerful manipulator of an audience…."

Time dragged while Dr. Pierce struggled to conclude his lesson. He checked his watch for the twentieth time.

"No doubt, the more observant of you in the audience have by now detected a subtext to today's lecture. A message provided to you, not by what I've *said* on the stage this morning, but rather, by what I've *done*." He waited a slight moment allowing the audience to form their hypotheses. The darkened auditorium was silent except for a single cough.

"Well…?" A half dozen hands rose politely into the air. Dr. Pierce pointed at each raised hand. In succession each of the six offered their best guess as they dropped their arms.

"There's something going on with you this morning…not here…somewhere else…"

"You had an emergency…"

"Maybe you were sick…you know…you had to…" A few people laughed.

"Whatever it is, you're really thinking about what that is, not what's going on here. You're not really here at all."

Pierce nodded his appreciation. He pointed to the single remaining hand held straight up over Carly Lindsey's head.

"There's someplace else you badly need to be…now!" she said without blinking. Instead of lowering her arm she turned and pointed to the exit at the back of the auditorium. The professor nodded once and leapt off the stage.

"What the hell?" someone said loudly as the auditorium door clicked shut behind Pierce's running back.

He ran directly to the faculty parking lot with Jimmy Deane's address clutched in his sweating hand. A sense of unexplained foreboding hovered around him. His better sense told him that his flare for the dramatic had finally caught up with him, and that the boy would simply be down with a case of the summer flu. On the other hand, his sixth sense about certain things had proven reliable in the past, and though he didn't like to admit it to himself, in a very short time, this kid had become unduly important to him, both as his student and in another role that he would have had trouble explaining. He had admitted to himself after the boy had come to his office hours that something about him had been compelling from the first moment the professor had laid eyes on him at the auditorium door, and it went way beyond all that Chinamen-on-the-moon bullshit. What *was it?* Maybe, he just liked the kid, he told himself. Or, maybe it was what Jose Valles had suggested, the boy reminded him of himself ten years earlier.

The short drive took only minutes. Dr. Pierce rang the bell, anticipating a Spanish-speaking housekeeper, and at least in that regard, he was not disappointed.

"Hello," he said. "I'm Dr. Pierce from Santa Monica City College. I was hoping to…" This dark skinned young man looked nothing like Maria's schema for *doctor*, but in desperation she pulled him across the threshold. Her comprehension of English was superb, but when she was excited or upset, her command of it failed to make the trek from her brain's language center to her tongue.

"Si! Si!" She pushed Pierce through the house. "Tu es el doctor! Venga! Venga! Meester Jaydee he is en la studio. Esta enferma."

"Enferma?" the professor asked. He was not nearly as conversant in Spanish as the housekeeper was in English, but he knew enough Latin to translate badly. “Enferma? Infirm? Sick? Is JD sick?” he asked as Maria pushed him through the house.

“Si! Si!” she shook her head enthusiastically. “Meester Jaydee is muy sick.” At the door to the studio she dropped the professor’s arm and knocked gently.

“Meester Jaydee?” No sound came from behind the door. She knocked again, harder. “Meester Jaydee! Por favor! Abre la puerta! El doctor esta aqui!” She tried the knob, but it failed to turn. She turned a worried look to Dr. Pierce. “Tres dias! El no abre la puerta! No come nada!”

“Three days?” Pierce asked. “You’ve heard nothing for three days?”

“Hablas. Y algunas veces hay musica. Pero, muy, muy triste.” Pierce put his hands on the door and leaned forward.

“He talks? Is someone inside?”

“No! Nadie!” Maria said and wiped a falling tear. “Tengo miedo, Doctor.”

“Right,” he nodded, and then wrapped a short, demanding staccato. “JD?” he called. “JD? It’s Dr. Pierce. JD, can you hear me? Will you open the door, please?” Maria hung her head and covered her face with her apron. She wept for a full minute until a soft click finally made her look up hopefully.

“Vaya!” she whispered backing away. “Y darle ayuda, Doctor!”

Pierce turned the knob slowly and pushed the door open just far enough to step inside. The slightest trace of cigarette smoke hung in the air. The windows were shuttered closed and there was barely enough light inside the darkened room to make out JD’s silhouette less than ten feet away. He seemed small, as if in three days he had shrunk to the size of a boy younger by several years. As Pierce’s eyes adjusted to the dimness he could see that JD was shoeless and clad only in jeans that hung low on his narrow hips. A flash of silver moved against the boy’s hairless chest on a long chain. Pierce stepped forward and craned his neck to identify the sliver medal around the boy's neck. He almost gasped, but instead reached a hand up to the center of his own chest and felt through his shirt where he wore an identical silver St. Cecelia. He traced the edges of the disc with trembling fingers and stared at JD's necklace. Without a word, he reached inside his collar and pulled his own medal out of his shirt. He held it out to Jimmy and then kissed it gently.

"My moms gave me mine," he said very softly. "Who gave you yours?" Robert Pierce did not confide the circumstances of his mother's gift.

What happened next, Robert Pierce had seen only once before, or, more accurately, had *felt* once before. He was in no way prepared for the experience a second time. He had been a graduate student on the psych unit at Bellevue Hospital in New York. A Sudanese refugee, a boy of only thirteen, had been brought to the hospital by his American sponsors, because he was refusing to eat. They described the boy as practically catatonic, and told Pierce that recently they had been informed that his village in Sudan, (one of the very first to do so) had been all but wiped out by government mercenaries. It was presumed that his entire family had been killed. The skinny child looked like a zombie. Pierce had asked that boy just one question. "What happened to your family?" The boy had not so much crumpled as he had shape shifted, his whole body becoming nothing more than the physical manifestation of pure grief. It was not something a doctor saw with his eyes as much as he felt it in every nerve of his own body, the pain of another human's unbearable suffering being conducted sympathetically. No stranger himself to unspeakable loss, Robert Pierce had resonated unwillingly to the Sudanese boy's pain, and now he was doing it again in Jimmy Deane's studio. He had discovered in the intervening years, no Psychological intervention that would be useful in such instances. He knew intuitively that this state was as close to crazy as an otherwise sane person could get. For the second time in his career he responded intuitively by simply waiting in absolute stillness. The experience in New York had rocked Robert Pierce to his core, and the resulting crises had been enough to cause him to detour away from his clinical training and into the safer worlds of academia and music. He had assumed that he had done everything in his power to avoid a similar experience, yet here he was, facing another young black man sinking fast into a world of pain that would be as difficult to survive as quicksand, and with no knowledge that could rescue him.

Time had no meaning for either of them. JD was rocking autistically. His pupils had assumed all but the narrowest ring of green and the effect was chilling. Pierce reached out and with the gentlest of touches put his hand on JD's shoulder. JD simply collapsed into his professor's arms. His body shuddered violently. Pierce held onto him as gently as he could, feeling that his arms around him were the only thing keeping the desperate boy's soul from fleeing. Finally spent, Jimmy Deane raised his head. Robert Pierce looked into the face of sorrow and it took his breath away. No words existed that could console the boy. He waited again without speaking.

When JD finally broke the silence his voice sounded small and hollow. Young and angry. He recounted his mother's two-time betrayal in childish words. He pleaded with her to come back. Then he wailed for another long time. Pierce recognized abandonment first hand. He knew Jimmy's was not recent. The howling sounds the boy made were the sounds of an infant.

"JD," Pierce said gently but firmly. "I want you to try to listen to me. Can you do that?" Jimmy nodded and wiped one cheek with the back of his hand. He stopped rocking and looked as if it required immeasurable concentration to meet Pierce's gaze.

“It only hurts because you really loved her. That’s the price we have to pay when we love somebody and we lose them. It hurts. Plain and simple.”

“I didn’t love my mother. How could I love my mother?” JD asked. “I never knew her. And, now…” Jimmy’s voice failed. When he looked up again his eyes were bright red and brimming with new tears. “Now, she’s made it impossible…to ever… She left me. She left me twice. Gillis left me twice, too.” Dr. Pierce nodded.

“Love is funny like that. The other person doesn’t have to know you love them and they don’t even have to be there. Love is much more unilateral than it is mutual.” This much was true, Pierce believed. The people he had loved most had been dead for twenty years. He knew how to survive this. He wanted more than anything to teach Jimmy Deane how to survive.

“I know that at your age it feels like a tragedy, but, it isn’t. Try to get your head around this. The real tragedy is when you lose someone and you *don’t* hurt. When you feel nothing.” A glimmer of recognition flickered in JD’s eyes. Pierce was encouraged. Elizabeth Breaux’s death provided a near perfect reference for this profound wisdom. JD blinked. His teacher’s words were true. Compared to the pain of losing his mom and Gillis, the news of Elizabeth’s death had almost no impact at all. He had no choice but to accept Pierce’s assertion; it *was* more tragic to lose someone so close and feel nothing.

“Think about it,” the doctor continued. “We’re all going to die. Nobody doesn’t die. I think the Buddhists have it right. Death isn’t a bad thing. Just movin’ on. Movin’ to the next plane of things. But, no doubt about it, when you love someone, you don’t want them movin’ on without you. It hurts. It hurts bad, like now. Like you’re hurtin’ right now. I know. I’ve been there. My own father. Then my brother. I hurt so bad. I thought I might die myself. It hurt so bad…I *wanted* to die.” He took a breath. “Maybe you’re wantin’ that….?”

Jimmy Deane nodded, ashamed of his transparency, ashamed that Dr. Pierce could see how vulnerable he was.

"You gotta believe me though. You gotta tell yourself that you are just payin' the price for having that person in your life. For havin' love in your life. You were waiting all these years for your mom. She must have been so ashamed of giving you up. She couldn't face you. Shame, JD, makes people do desperate things." Pierce kept talking. "The only other way is to *never* know love. That's always an option. If you don't get close to nobody, if you don't love nobody…you don't *ever* have to feel like this. But, then you never get to feel love either." He paused quietly before asking. "What's it gonna be? Which way do you want it?" JD was silent for a long time.

"I don't know," he finally said. His eyes looked worried.

"Well, right now it isn't easy to make that choice. Not when you're hurting this bad. But…"

"No," JD interrupted. "I mean I don't *ever* know what I want." Pierce considered this and considered the solemnity of the boy's words.

"You got a broken *wanter?*" he asked him. JD shrugged. Pierce stared at JD for a long moment. He considered the boy's surroundings. Just materially, it made no sense that he could have so much without wanting anything. Pierce had known people who truly had lost the will to desire. But, in most cases, they were people whose lives were bleak. They wanted nothing and they had nothing.

"What was the last thing you ever wanted?"

JD shook his head. Pierce squinted.

"JD, man," he said. "Look around! This is a beautiful home you got. I'll bet there's a fine car in that garage…?" Jimmy nodded. "Well, hell, son, *somebody* wanted all that." JD shrugged again. James Dean had wanted most of it. And, maybe Gillis too. Gillis had surely wanted things on behalf of JD. Pierce shook his head slowly.

"The drums," Jimmy whispered. It sounded like a confession. "I wanted those drums." Pierce looked at the fine drum kit. There was a long pregnant silence. "And, I wanted Gillis to come visit me, or…" Jimmy's lip quivered. "I wanted him to take me with him." The weight of the admission caused two fresh fat tears to roll down his cheeks.

"Gillis? That was your friend?" JD nodded and covered his face. Pierce watched the boy sob into his hands for a full minute before he reached out and touched his shoulder. When Jimmy flinched under his hand he only leaned toward him and squeezed gently. He knew he had seen but the tip of the boy's iceberg. "You want to tell me this whole story from the beginning?" he asked carefully. JD looked up, nodding almost imperceptibly. Dr. Pierce patted Jimmy's shoulder again. This time Jimmy did not flinch. The professor leaned back for what was to come. He listened to the saddest story he had ever heard, until the sun had long past slipped into the ocean at the west end of Montana Street.

Chapter 54

The sun was only barely above the eastern horizon. Except for one lone rollerblader, and uncountable widely-dispersed seagulls, JD encountered not a single living being on the beach in Santa Monica who was not already in the water or headed for it. Surfers ruled the beach in Santa Monica at dawn. He parked the Porsche in the lot south of the pier among the oddball fleet of surfer's cars and watched with some curiosity. He looked for the BMW but it was not in the lot. Almost all of the surfers were zipped into black neoprene wetsuits because the Pacific stayed cold until late into the summer. Those already in the water drifted on top of their boards in a neatly spaced out pod of at least two dozen.

JD had come to the ocean at daybreak to do as Dr. Pierce had advised: to scream his objections directly into the sea at the way it had gobbled up his best friend. He had not expected an audience of twenty or so surfers to be present to witness such an act of absurdity. Who could have known that surfers were so industrious? JD had a thought. What other simple things about the world did he not know? He removed his shoes and walked south along the shoreline, but as soon as he felt that he had claimed enough linear space to insure some privacy for his tirade, another shaggy haired boy came along to drop his backpack into the sand and begin waxing a board. Not one of them acknowledged JD's presence with as much as a glance in his passing direction. Surfing, it seemed, was a private venture.

It took him over an hour marching southward to reach Venice Beach where a few hundred yards up on the boardwalk people on bicycles in pairs and larger packs were starting to appear traveling rapidly in both directions. JD stood at the shoreline with the waves dousing his bare feet and watched the bikers glide along the boardwalk dressed in garments that made them look like colorful rainforest birds. Even from a distance JD could tell that the bikes they rode were fast and light. A realization struck him like one of the waves. He would be nineteen years old soon, and he had never ridden a bicycle. Neither had he surfed or roller bladed or even tried to. He had never been on a boat, never been on a plane, never skied, or snowboarded, or sky dived, or bungee jumped, or any of these things. He had never been outside the United States, and he didn't even have a passport. He had never seen snow. He had never tasted fine food or good wine. He had never made love. He had only been kissed once, and he had Monique Libby to thank for that. If Monique's kiss had buckled his knees, what would it feel like to be kissed by someone you loved?

JD felt something inside his chest shift and with a sharp inhalation he thought he recognized a feeling that he might describe as wanting. Did he *want* to do these things?

He turned around and jogged north towards the pier. He didn't yell at God, or the ocean, or even Gillis for leaving him, and instead, he got a donut at Ziggie's on the way, and made it to campus in time to get coffee from the machine and take his seat almost within touching distance of the beautiful chanteuse.

Chapter 55

Keeping his promise to Dr. Pierce, JD slid into his seat a minute before the professor took the podium. Jimmy looked pale and a little shaky, but Pierce was enormously relieved that the boy had come. The professor made a quick pistol with his hand and shot JD between the eyes as he winked. He had worked late into the wee hours on a lecture composed specifically for Jimmy to hear.

"I was saving this lecture for the last day, but, I've decided that…for my own reasons…I should talk about this today. The branch of psychology known as existentialism posits a never ending task for the authentic self," he boomed. "Each of us must not only find a way to give meaning to our lives, but we must continue to revise the search for meaning throughout our lifespan."

The professor rubbed his hands together in a manner that suggested he was warming to this subject.

"The second major existential task is the endurance of the *vicissitudes* of life." He grinned happily. "Use that word on your parents, so that they know you're really in college, now," he joked. "The vicissitudes are the ups and downs that randomly occur in every single life. How do we get through the bad times? The downs? Can we learn to use the bad times to give meaning to our good times and indeed our very existence?" He let the question hover. "If I ask you today, most, if not all of you will say that what gives your life meaning is your art. For many of you, that means performance." The students were nodding, each of them certain that the young professor could see directly into their hearts and minds. "Let us speak of the ups and downs of a performer's life in terms of the reviews one has to face as a performer – every single time he or she takes the stage, or steps in front of the camera, or even puts on the clerical collar and rises up in church, or just joins the choir." Professor Pierce smiled down on Carly Lindsey. "When the performance is over, the reviews will always be there, and, as anyone can tell you who has a little experience, they will not always be good. Well, unless you're Mick Jagger." Everybody laughed. Jimmy Deane smiled up at the professor.

"Life," Pierce continued, "and especially a life in performance, is like a long train ride. Sometimes your train pulls into a town and the station is crowded with people there to happily welcome you. Signs and banners in your honor. Everything - including applause. Lots and lots of applause." The students chuckled in all the right places. "But, then, in some towns, *nobody* shows up at all, and in still others, there's an angry mob at the end of your performance, all of them shouting for your head. Or, their money back, at the very least. And, all you can do is do your best and never ever break your part of the performance contract – which you will remember from week one, oh so many weeks ago." More scattered laughter. "And, don't forget about the other passengers, for none of us rides this train alone." The professor dared to look directly at Jimmy as he spoke. "When someone rides on our train, and we become fond of them, and then, for some reason unknown to us, they have to get off at another station, how do we endure the pain and go on? How do we decide to keep on riding the train to our own conclusion? I'll tell you how. It is nothing more than a conscious decision to accept the pain of loss as the inevitable price we must pay for the relationship and the love and joy we experience as part of it. And, there is no way around that pain if you live life authentically and open to the experience that love provides. The only other option," Pierce said quietly, "is to live half a life. Less than half. Never daring to love with your whole heart. And, I challenge you, my dear students, to try to do that and have anything at all of interest to perform. A performer who does not love and does not risk is not worth the price of admission. And, that, my friends is the meaning of the old expression, *the show must go on!*"

The auditorium stayed quiet while the students contemplated this truth. Then slowly a thoughtful applause followed. Pierce smiled and bowed and dismissed them for a break.

"Take fifteen minutes, but come back!" he said meaningfully. "I have much much more existential wisdom!" He grinned again at JD and stepped away from the podium.

Minutes later Jimmy was removing a cup of steaming coffee from the vending machine outside when a hand touched his shoulder. He lifted his cup and turned slowly to find that he was looking into the face of the surfer.

"Dude," the boy said. He lifted his head in a gesture that told JD to follow him. He hurried around the corner of the auditorium and leaned against the wall. JD's stomach clenched. Whatever happened, whatever the boy said or did, JD had it coming. He braced for the worst and stepped around the corner to face the music.

"I need you to do something for me, man." The surfer touched JD's shoulder and peeked around the corner of the building. He pulled his head back quickly. Jimmy Deane was stupefied. He stared back mutely.

"Swap seats with me, man," the boy said in a pleading voice.

"What?" JD asked.

"Swap seats with me. You know. You take my seat and I'll sit in yours." Jimmy waited for something bad to happen, but the boy only went on talking earnestly.

"But, you go first, and then I'll come in after, so it looks like it was your idea." Jimmy shook his head slowly. The boy took one last peek around the corner. When he faced JD again, he looked at him quizzically for a short second.

"You do want to sit next to Carly, don't you?" Uh oh, JD thought. Here it comes. He was prepared for this confrontation, but it could have come on a better day. He only continued to stare stupidly at the surfer's animated face.

"Okay, great. I thought so. One more thing. Don't say anything about this little talk we're having to my sister." The boy put a fraternal hand up to JD's shoulder, as if to underscore his meaning. Jimmy looked down at it but did not shake it off.

"Your sister?" Jimmy repeated.

"C'mon, man! Give me a break here!" The boy patted JD. "My sister's drivin' me fuckin' nuts, man. She's been waiting for you to make a move since day one. If you knew my sister…well…just don't tell her I told you this. She'll kill me. I just figure… we got what? Maybe one more week before the class is over? And Jesus, man, if I wait for you to make your move…you are one patient mother fucker…but, if you don't *do* something, she's going to make the rest of my whole summer miserable." The surfer's face grew serious. "She doesn't have many friends. She's shy. *Really, really shy.*" The surfer dropped his head down an inch. "Do you know what that's like?" It took JD a moment but finally he nodded. "Thought so," the other boy said. "I mean, I guessed you might know." The boy's posture changed slightly. He was revealing too much. "My sister doesn't have many friends. Actually… I'm pretty much her best and only friend." The boy looked embarrassed to be admitting his sister's faults. "I kinda figure though that you been pretty much staring a hole in the back of her head and followin' her around ever since that first day, so…I just figure I'd help things along. You cool with that?" JD blushed and nodded.

"Yeah, okay," he said. "I'm cool with that."

"Good, that's what I thought. You two are made for each other." The surfer patted Jimmy on the back and gave him a little push. "So just go on back in there, and sit next to Carly. I'll pretend that I've got no choice because…Damn!..." He threw his hands up. "That drummer dude took my seat! Got it?"

"Carly? I thought her name was Lindsey."

"Yeah, it is. Carly Lindsey. I'm Mick. Mick Lindsey." Mick Lindsey held his hand out in an awkwardly formal handshake. "What's up?" he said grinning. "We cool now?"

"Yeah," JD said soberly. He walked into the auditorium and slipped into Mick Lindsey's seat without saying a word. Carly Lindsey looked up and her mouth dropped open. Her eyes blinked rapidly. The corners of JD's mouth turned up briefly.

"You're in my brother's seat," she choked.

"Yeah, I know." JD leaned toward her. Up close he was so gorgeous he literally took her breath away. His eyes looked directly into hers before he asked, "So, why haven't you said anything to me since, you know…?" Jimmy looked at the chair and microphones still up on the stage. Carly's eyes followed his and then moved back to look directly back into Jimmy's. Neither of them blinked. Carly swallowed, and then finally, she answered his question with the abrupt honesty of someone who has too little social experience.

"I can't talk to people," she said. "I'm very shy. My shrink says I have rejection sensitivity. I'm adopted." The sentences came out of her mouth like rapid-fire confessions. JD recognized in her strange syntax the same awkwardness that kept him silent most of the time. He started to laugh and her blue eyes grew bright with tears.

"What?" she demanded in a strangled voice. "Why are you laughing?"

"Me too," he said and opened his hand. He reached for Carly's. "All of it. Everything you said. That's me too." His hand closed around hers and they turned forward together to watch the professor take the stage again.

Chapter 56

As drunk as he was when his flight landed in Miami, Larry Drummond had nevertheless formulated a plan. He rushed by taxi to his office and summoned the firm's top investigator.

"Child's play," the detective declared when Larry told him what he wanted. The firm's private investigator was a man who was expert at uncovering the off shore hidden assets of Chicago mobsters when their ex-wives came to Florida to retire or re-marry. A little sleuthing on behalf of an orphan was a piece of cake. He promised Mr. Drummond a forty-eight hour turn around and called from a downtown Chicago pay phone under the wire.

"The nurse is legit. Didn't even know about the kid's money. Says she just wanted to do right by the girl."

"Do you believe her?" Larry Drummond asked. He had seen every variety of worm crawl up from the depths to try to milk money out of the lottery winners, and like his boss, Roger Albright, Larry would be damned if such lowlife scum succeeded on his watch.

"Yeah. She talked a blue streak and didn't ask for nothin'. She even paid for my coffee."

"What's her story?"

"My best guess? I think she feels guilty 'cause it was her that talked the McGinnis woman into trying to find her son. Blames herself for the suicide. You know how broads are."

"Right," Larry agreed. Even for him, "broads" were hard to figure sometimes.

"Did you check on Mary McGinnis?"

"Sure thing." Larry listened as the investigator sifted through his notes. "It looks like you thought…she got pregnant at eighteen, had the baby at nineteen at Holy Redeemer. She never named the father. Looks like she never got over it. She never married. Never even dated so far as I could tell. Lived more like a nun than the damn nuns did. And she was a real looker, too. Here's something interesting. She gave most of her money away. Couple 'a two three orphanages looks like."

Back in Miami, Larry tapped his pencil on the desk. This guy was good. How he had obtained Mary McGinnis's financial records was not something the lawyer wanted explained.

"Any extended family on her side?" he asked.

"None you'd want the kid to know about. They had nothing to do with her after she had the baby and quit Loyola. Looks like she was some sort of genius. On a full scholarship up there. Pre med. Probably supposed to be the family's great white hope, ya' know? When she didn't come through for 'em, they dumped her. Near as I can tell, she hadn't seen or talked to any of them since 1969."

"That's a long time," Larry said. "People change."

"Not these people. Trust me. You don't want your boy lookin' to this group for any long lost relatives."

"You checked them out?"

"Fuckin' A," the investigator said. "You'll pardon my French, counselor. Trust me," he repeated like he meant it. "You wouldn't be doin' the kid no favors there."

"Pardoned," Larry said. "What did you get on the Johnson boy? Was he the father?"

"Looks like." The detective rustled more papers. "James Johnson. Also some kind of whiz kid. Had his choice of schools too. Got involved with a Jesuit priest who took a group of Loyola kids down to the west side to demonstrate when King got shot in '68. Two of 'em, including the Johnson kid, were killed by police fire. You remember the riots?"

"Not much," Larry said. "I was just a kid in the U.K."

"Not our finest hour as a country…that whole goddamn year was shit in Chicago. Sorry, it's my home town and I hate the fuckin' place. I left in 1980 and I ain't looked back once, except on business for the firm, and only when I absolutely have to." Larry heard the man turn a page.

"Mary McGinnis told the nurse that the baby's father died down south. Is there any real evidence that this kid was the baby's father?"

"Yessir. The best kind."

"You can't get DNA from a dead man," Larry said.

"Second best then. I'm standing on the street in front of the political science building at Loyola. That priest? He's still up here teaching."

"Did he remember the kid?"

"Not only did he remember him, he still had a picture of the kid on his wall."

"And?"

"And, you ain't gonna believe it. I'll fax the picture over as soon as I get back to my hotel, but I'll tell you, if I twisted James Johnson's afro into dreadlocks you'd swear to Jesus that it was your boy, James Deane." Larry Drummond's heart was racing.

"Was the priest co-operative? Did you get any information on his family?"

The detective chuckled. “That’s why you pay me, Mr. Drummond. I’ll have the addresses and phone numbers for you in the fax.”

Chapter 57

ALG's investigator had traced James Johnson's mother from Indianapolis to the improbable address on a Venice canal less than five miles from Jimmy Dean's Santa Monica rental. Larry Drummond outlined the dossier over the phone before he faxed the second generation of the photo provided by the Loyola priest to Jimmy at the Kinkos in the Palisades.

"If I didn't know the origins of this photograph, JD, I would almost swear it was you in the picture," the lawyer said. "But, see what you think yourself."

Jimmy took notes as the lawyer laid out James Johnson's brief history over the phone. It seemed extremely likely that Joann Johnson could be Jimmy Deane's paternal grandmother.

"Joann Johnson, born in Fairmount, Indiana. She was an only child of an unmarried woman who worked as a laundress and cook for a wealthy farm family. The farmer paid for Joann to go to a boarding school up near Baltimore since the Indiana public schools were still segregated and there was no school for a black child to attend in Fairmount. Looks like she came home summers though, and helped her mother. Attended college two years and then went to live in New York. Was quite the cabaret singer there. She might have really made a name for herself, but instead, in the winter of forty-nine, she showed up back in Fairmount expecting the boy that we know was James. Your father. She never identified the baby's father and gave him her family name on his birth certificate. She stayed put there until the little boy was five, then she moved him, kind of abruptly…nobody knew why…to Indianapolis, about fifty, maybe sixty miles south. Looks like that farmer put her through college then down there or at least gave her some help with it and she got a teaching job at a music conservatory. Married one of the other teachers there and had two more boys. Her husband died in a car accident and then the oldest son, the one we think was your father, he got killed in Chicago in the riots of sixty-eight. Thirty-nine people died in those riots. Most of them were shot by police. The priest who gave our investigator the picture said that it was very likely that James Johnson was the father of Mary's baby. He told us that they were both students of his and he described their relationship as very, very close." The lawyer took a deep breath. Jimmy Deane had chewed the eraser on his pencil down to a nub.

"How did Joann Johnson get out here, to California?" he asked.

"Looks like the old woman, her mother, has some dementia. They had some family living out there, cousins and what not who offered to help Joann out with her care if she moved out. Then the youngest son got a full scholarship at UCLA, and that sealed the deal. They've been out there ever since. Joann is teaching at the LA Magnet School for Performing Arts in West LA, and her mother still lives with her in Venice. The sons are in the general area, too. You could have a grandmother, a great grandmother, and two uncles, within a couple miles of where you're standing, not to mention a number of extended family members, too." Jimmy Deane was silent on the other end of the line.

"I've got a lot more information here. Details. You want me to send the full report?" Larry offered. "I mean before you decide what to do with it, you might want more details."

"No," JD said. "I don't need any more details."

The faxed photo had lost some clarity, but the original had been good, and there was no mistaking the resemblance. The clerk at Kinkos examined the picture before handing it over.

"Tha' be some nasty old fashen hair you had there, my brothah. I like the dreads mo' bettah." For a white kid the clerk put on a Jamaican accent pretty well. JD looked at him.

"You think that looks like me?" he asked.

"Damn straight!" The boy took a second look. "Could be your evil twin, dude…"

Chapter 58

Two long-necked geese cruised along the foggy canal like escorts while Jimmy Deane checked the crumpled address in his hand against the mailboxes. He found the right house and admired how well kept it was. Near the sidewalk a miniature replica of the two-story dwelling served as its mailbox. The tiny reproduction was mounted atop a four by four in the middle of a thicket of rose bushes, and if someone didn't come soon to thin the flowers, the mailman would have a hard time making deliveries. An emerald manicured lawn rolled from the walkway to a wide wooden porch that spanned the entire width of the house. The gangways between the neighboring homes were unfenced and this gave the neighborhood a friendly air while it appeared as though at least a modicum of horticultural competition prevailed among the residents. The homes were structurally modest but lovely to look at and surrounded by well-cared-for gardens. The slightest breeze moved the old-fashioned swing on the Johnson's porch but the oiled chains made barely a sound. Jimmy Deane looked again at the faxed photo of a young James Johnson, a long arm around a short statured man in a clerical collar who looked boyish enough in spite of his slightly receding hairline. Jimmy resolutely approached the door and knocked once softly. No one answered.

He knocked harder the second time and longer until a voice from the side porch startled him. You could tell by her voice that the woman was a singer.

"Hello? Is there something I can do for you?" JD took a single step back and located the owner of the voice amongst the trellised jasmine at one side of the porch. He had not expected that his grandmother's face would be so instantly familiar and he found it impossible to stop tears from brimming suddenly in his eyes. Joann Johnson's mouth dropped widely open.

"Oh dear God!" she whispered. "Oh, my dear God!" Her hand reached slowly to cover her gaping mouth, and her eyes too were filling with startled tears. As if in trance she stepped lightly onto the porch, her feet barely touching the wood, and she reached both shaking hands up to Jimmy's face. He took a single step back. Joann Johnson's hand fluttered at her throat as she too stepped back, mouth still agape, tears coursing now toward her quivering chin. The oxygen in the whole world had suddenly evaporated. Before she even knew her body was moving, she reached out toward JD again, and embraced him with surprising strength. This time he did not move.

"Oh, my God!" she cried a third time, and then a fourth. "Oh, my dear God!" Her hands felt so soft as they caressed his face that Jimmy started to cry in earnest. He could no more have spoken in that moment than he could have sprouted wings to fly. His father's mother held him at arms length touching his face gently as if reading his features with her fingers. She grasped his wrists and lifted the photo that trembled in Jimmy's hand.

"I knew it!" Jo said. "I knew it! I felt it in my bones. I felt you were out there!" There was something so right in her touch that Jimmy Deane gave himself up completely to his grandmother's embrace. "You look just like your daddy when he was your age!" Her voice was choked with emotion. "It's almost as if…." She shook her head and led him into the house by the hand.

Like the yard outside, the interior of the house was immaculate. The furnishings looked very old, and possibly precious. They made the room seem as if it belonged to another era. An ebony upright piano stood against one wall with a dozen large framed photographs crowded across its top. With JD in her wake Joann stepped to the piano and delicately removed an ornate silver frame. She turned and held out a hand. JD relinquished his photocopy. For a long moment Joann compared the two. She had to bite down hard on her lips to keep from sobbing. When her hands started to shake, she extended both pictures to JD like gifts. He looked from one image to the other and listened to his own heartbeat. He was aware of an old clock ticking somewhere in the room but its percussion seemed to have little to do with time. A soft scraping sound alerted him to movement.

From beyond the piano a dozen feet or so from where he stood with Joann Johnson, a tiny elderly woman emerged from a darkened hallway. The woman's small feet were slippered in tiny black ballet shoes and she shuffled as she walked as if she were afraid to pick her slippers too far up off the ground. She was petite rather than wizened and still pretty. Her hair, a close-cropped silver helmet, seemed to brighten the dark room. The remarkable color of Jimmy's own eyes was just visible in a golden green corona around her huge pupils. She wore a simple denim jumper over a black cotton T-shirt and as she drew toward them from the hallway her smile glowed. She paused a single foot from Jimmy.

"Jamey!" the old woman whispered. "Jamey, you came!" Then, a stunned Jimmy Deane watched Clarice Johnson as she shuffled slowly past him and into the waiting arms of James Dean. Clarice lowered her head onto the chest of the movie star's red jacket and stood in the center of the room swaying to a personal internal rhythm. She allowed James Dean to tenderly embrace her in the way a mother would let herself be held by her son. James Dean's face wore a smile that Jimmy Deane had never seen. His hands were empty. Not even a cigarette. JD's first instinct was to seek out Joann's reaction, but other than a fondness, and something a little sad, he could detect no indication that she too could see the other young man.

"Miss Johnson," James Dean whispered. There was reverence in his voice, a voice that sounded completely new to Jimmy also.

"I knew you'd come back, someday, Jamey!" Clarice whispered to James Dean patting his shoulder affectionately. JD stared, his mouth gaping. He was absolutely paralyzed. Joann stepped forward and touched her mother's arm carefully and deliberately as if fearful that a sudden movement would startle the old woman. It was again clearly apparent that James Dean was not visible to Joann, but James looked longingly at her, and even reached out to almost touch her hair as she reached past him to cup her mother's elbow.

"C'mon, Mama, let's go out onto the porch for some fresh air. You can take some air today, can't you?" Joann ever so gently led her mother out to the porch glider.

"Come along, Jamey," Clarice said reaching back. Following her daughter the old woman pulled James Dean outside, and once settled into the center of the porch swing seat, she immediately slid over to make room for him. Joann smiled an indulgent smile watching her mother pat the place next to her for her imaginary visitor, and then lift her hand, as if it were being held. Joann sighed and touched her mother's cheek gently before she returned to the parlor.

"I'm afraid that Gama sometimes doesn't see the people right in front of her…" She looked back to the swing. "But, she sees some folks who aren't really there. I'm sorry she didn't acknowledge you." Joann's face and voice betrayed a duplicate sadness. JD watched his grandmother look out onto the porch where Clarice Johnson was involved in a spirited discussion with her imaginary friend. He felt a sharp stab of some feeling he could not name. Finally, when she turned her attention back to Jimmy, he simply shrugged with a faint smile that took her breath away. It felt as if the boy was oddly resigned to his great grandmother's condition, and had been for a very long time.

"The human mind is a remarkable thing," he said with gentleness. Joann shook her head slowly in wonder.

"Lord, you sound just like your uncle," she marveled. Out on the porch James Dean was making Clarice Johnson shake with laughter. Jimmy Deane and Joann turned remarkably similar smiles toward each other. Joann touched her brow and sagged down onto the old divan. She pointed to a wing-backed chair.

"I think we need to sit down. I have a million questions. I don't even know your name!"

"It's James," JD said. "Like him." Joann bit down on her bottom lip. Some element in the way he looked at her made her squirm.

"Oh," she cried. "Him?" Was the boy being coy? Surely he meant James Johnson, her son and his father.

"My folks were Carter and Susie Deane," Jimmy continued. "So, my full name is James Deane. With an e." Joann's jaw dropped. A sharp inhalation brought her clasped hands to her mouth. Her eyes grew wide with an emotion that Jimmy Deane could not identify.

"James Dean? That's impossible!" She shook her head again. JD looked out onto the porch where James and Clarice Johnson were having a very nice reunion. He felt his pulse quicken and a sudden warmth that originated in his heart space spread instantly throughout his entire body. When he turned back to face Joann he knew that her gaze had never left his face. Her bottom lip quivered.

"Did you know James Dean?" JD asked pointedly. "My namesake?" There was nothing hostile about the question, but nevertheless Joann allowed a long meaningful silence to hang between them before she answered. Even longer pauses punctuated each sentence of Joann's long kept secret.

"I was the only black child in Fairmount." The clock ticked.

"Jamey always said that he knew what it was like to be black in Fairmount because he was the only orphan." An even longer pause ensued.

"He was the only one who was kind to me." Joann rose to fetch a box of tissues. She took three out in three swift pulls and then handed the box to JD. "And, to my mother." Joann took a deep breath and then blew her nose. She was silent for a time and looked benevolently out onto the porch.

"When I went to New York, Jamey helped me. He knew people." She rose suddenly and pulled a heavy photograph album from a shelf next to the piano. She paged through the photos.

"Here," she turned the album to reveal a black and white picture of a half dozen young people sitting at a table in what appeared to be a night club.

"It's Jerry's in New York on Fifty-Fourth. A hang out for us. There." Joann pointed to a smiling pretty black girl. "That's Eartha Kitt. You know who she is?" JD nodded. "And, that's Jamey." She looked at JD directly, and when he turned to meet her eyes she whispered. "Your grandfather." JD looked away first. James Dean was wearing thick, horn-rimmed glasses in the photo. His arm was draped affectionately across a much-younger Joann's shoulders. "He was very near sighted." Again, Joann's gaze went out to the porch. "Mama always kidded him that it was why he didn't seem to know that we were Black folk." Her mouth worried itself into a weak grin and she sniffled.

Lena Horne and Julie Harris were easy to identify. "Do you recognize them?" Joann asked and Jimmy nodded. "And, that's Dennis Hopper." He recognized Dennis Hopper, and then he stared at James Dean in the center of the picture for a long time. He turned the album around. Joann closed it on her lap as if closing that part of the conversation at least for the moment.

"I guess you had some nice folks though," she said. It was not quite a question.

"My parents…my adopted parents…both died before I was five. My mother's mother raised me. She was white," he said simply. Jimmy felt funny saying that Elizabeth had raised him. Really, it was Gillis Wainwright who had raised him. And, James Dean. "With some help," he added.

"Did you ever meet your mother?" Joann asked

"No. She's…she died recently," he told her honestly. "Before I had the chance."

"Oh," Joann said meaning it sincerely, "I'm so sorry." They sat again in silence for another long moment. "If your father loved her…I'm sure she was…" Joann bit down hard on her lips. After another long pause she spoke with obvious distress.

"I never told your father who his father was." Joann's words had the ring of confession. "I never told a soul, though I think my mama knows." She glanced at Clarice out on the porch swing, still evidently entertained by her imaginary visitor. "I just didn't think that it would be good for his career at first…then, after he died. Well. I didn't think it would be good for us."

"Did *he* know?" JD asked.

"Jamey?" For the first time Joann allowed herself a small, truly amused smile. "Oh no. Jamey was…he was wonderful. Kind. Very, very kind. And, he was good to us. But, we were both so young. He was so young. Just getting started really. I don't know what he might have done. I knew for a fact that it would not have been a good thing for him publicly to have a Black child. We were in love though. Just so very young. It wasn't Jamey that I didn't trust as much as it was the world back then. It was a different world…" Joann seemed to be looking for forgiveness. She stroked the album in her lap. "I don't know if I would do things differently now. I like to think so." JD could think of nothing to say.

"James?" Joann finally spoke Jimmy's name.

"JD," he said. "Or, Jimmy. No one calls me James." She nodded.

"JD," she said with extraordinary kindness. She hesitated before asking, fearing that she had no right. "Will you come back to meet your uncles? Please?" He hesitated too. He had his own reasons and they were not dissimilar. And then he nodded slowly.

"Yeah," he said. "I will. Just tell me when." Tears welled up in Joann's eyes again. "They will want to meet you as soon as possible. Will you do that? Will you come back soon?" JD rose from his seat and pulled Joann from her's. She embraced him as no one had since Susie Deane's death. His whole body shuddered.

"Just tell me when," he said holding Joann firmly. "Just say when." Joann clung tightly to the child of her child until a deep laughing voice out on the porch made them both turn around. JD peered through the lace at the window. He could just barely see a strong black arm twirling Clarice as if she were a girl. She was laughing in delight. James Dean was gone. With a deep pang, Jimmy knew somehow immediately that this time it was for good. Joann pulled Jimmy's hand and he followed her out onto the porch.

“JD,” Joann said. “This is your Uncle Robert.” For the first time her smile was not clouded by other emotion. Her joy in the moment seemed pure.

Robert Pierce squinted at JD and rocked back on his heels. He let his own confused smile grow slowly into a huge happy grin. Very deliberately he put his grandmother’s hand into his mother’s waiting grasp. Joann watched her son shake his head in wonder. He first stepped back for a long look at his student before the two men collapsed into each other’s arms, laughing and touching their foreheads together like two old friends who had been separated a long, long time. Joann was a little startled but she only pulled her mother onto the swing next to her and simply waited. The sight of her own two beautiful strong young black men, their lovely dreadlocks bouncing merrily as they embraced and parted, embraced and parted, sent a shiver of pleasure through her that she had never once in her life felt before.

It was a day of miracles and this was only one more. She could wait all day for them to explain.

Chapter 59

The insistent knocking on the Troubador's locked front door went on for ten long minutes. The guy was either stupid or he knew somehow that Deetch and Chris were holed up inside. On Wednesdays, when the club was closed, Deetch liked to play the week's demo tapes on the big system so he could imagine what the bands would sound like up on stage. It just wasn't the same on the car stereo or even in his apartment in the Marina. Plus, his big bouncer had a real sixth sense about some things; Chris could usually pick out the winners after less than one whole cut. And Chris also preferred to listen to the offerings down at the club. Most of the time on Wednesdays, an eclectic group of musicians, from mostly rock and roll bands, liked to come down to the Troub just to shoot the shit with each other, and be among like musical fellows doing it. But everybody had left early on account of the unexpected late summer storm, and only Chris and Deetch were still around.

Deetch was twenty plus years sober, AA all the way, and Chris was a devout Muslim so they were both drinking green tea. They had gone through all but three of the demo tapes from the week's haul, separating the aspiring bands into stacks of, *Sometime Soon, Maybe Later* and *When Fucking Hell*

Freezes Over when the knocking started up. Deetch checked his watch. Almost one a.m.

"Let the shithead knock," Deetch told Chris. "He'll get tired and go home. Where we should both be already." The music drowned out the knocking, but in between the cuts it got on Chris's nerves.

"Maybe I should just look, Boss?" he said. "It's comin' down pretty good out there." Deetch pointed down.

"Sit," he ordered. "Let him drown." Chris frowned.

"How do we know it's a him? Could be a woman."

"Likewise," Deetch said tiredly. No one had ever accused Deetch Claymore of chivalry, sober or otherwise. "We ain't the rescue mission." Chris punched up the final demo.

"Stop!" Deetch said after four bars. "Spare me!" At nine p.m. the band wouldn't have sounded so bad, but after a couple dozen, everything sounded like shit to Deetch. Timing and order were everything in music, Chris noted. The club was quiet then except for the knocking, which went on and on while Deetch and Chris prepared to leave.

"Geez, the bastard's persistent. I'll give 'em that," Deetch said as he gathered up the piles. Chris was pouting a little.

"Could be a woman in trouble," he huffed.

"No broad is gonna stand in the rain for half an hour knockin' nicely on the door. A broad would a' drove her car through the door by now, she wanted in so bad." That actually had a ring of truth to it. Chris helped his boss put things away and then they both stepped out the back door. The big bouncer locked the door and watched Deetch run for it across the three-space parking lot to his old Corvette. Chris knew that the 'Vette's top leaked and it gave him a moment of pleasure knowing that his boss would be sitting in a puddle of rain water for ten miles or more. Then, he couldn't stop himself. He hunched his shoulders, pulled his collar up, and walked around the block to the front of the club.

It was no broad. Chris was relieved and he almost turned around to go, but the young man at the door turned at the same time to face him then, and the big bouncer got stopped in his tracks. The guy should have been soaked through. He'd kept up a constant *I'm-not-leaving-until-you-open-up* knocking for what Chris figured was over a half an hour. What the fuck? The guy didn't even look wet. Chris's understanding of the Koran forbade such language but under certain unique circumstances he gave himself some latitude.

It happened that a bright streetlight shone down on the front entrance to the Troubador, and Chris could see that the rain was rolling off the young man's red jacket in the manner of ducks and rolling water. He also had a lit cigarette in one hand. A lit cigarette? *What the fuck*? The man started with purpose toward Chris, and the big guy took an involuntary step back.

"Hey, Chris!" the guy called out. Chris tried hard to remember. He raised his hand up over his eyes like a salute and peered through the pouring down rain.

"D' I know you?" he hollered.

"No," the man said smiling. "You know a friend of mine." Up close the man did look familiar, but Chris still couldn't place him. Chris jumped back a little when the man's arm shot out.

"Whoa!" he said, relieved that only a plastic baggie was extended. It was the kind of baggie that Chris had used himself, way before his conversion to Islam, when he had been adept at weighing out nickel bags of pot for wide distribution in his high school.

"Here," the man said and shook the bag.

"Nah…" Chris started to turn down the offer but the man interrupted.

"I hear that your boss is looking for a drummer for Paul Berman's new band."

"So?" Chris said touching the bag gingerly. Inside was a cassette tape. A *dry* cassette tape.

"Do the world a favor, Chris. Give the tape to Mr. Berman." The young man turned away. Chris looked down at the baggie in his hand and peered in through the plastic. When he looked up again, the man had disappeared into the downpour.

"Whoa!" Chris said. He stuffed the tape inside his own jacket and ran for his car around back. Inside he turned on the dome light and fished the cassette box out of the plastic baggie. A tiny slip of paper, one that looked just like the fortune from a Chinese fortune cookie, had been taped to the box. Chris squinted. "*The fortune you seek is closer than you think. Try looking right next door.*"

Appendix

It was generally acknowledged among the local inhabitants of Key West, Florida that it was the kind of place where a middle aged man, or even one slightly older, could wake up on the beach any given morning and claim that he had no memory whatsoever of any previous life. The townies cared not a wit whether such a claim was true or was simply a fabrication devised to forestall too many inquiries of a personal nature. Therefore, a small amalgamation of such men, referred to in not unaffectionate terms as *conches,* had become more or less a stable and yet internally shifting part of the town's populace.

Thus, when Gillis Wainwright washed ashore on the beach, still clinging after twenty-four hours to what appeared to be the seat of a Bell helicopter, an astonishingly few questions were asked. The specific locale of his beaching, directly in front of Flo's Moped Rentals, seemed to be a very special kind of providence. For three straight days Gillis answered every question, once he regained consciousness, by barking a single word. It sounded a lot like, "*Hank!*" And, as it was usually accompanied by the urgency one might expect from someone conflicted about his identity, Flo made the assumption that this was Gillis's rightful name.

Most of the conches were agreeable enough, and over the years Flo had employed more than her fair share in various capacities, (some legal, some not so much) but when it was discovered that Hank! was a goddamn whiz with Mopeds, it seemed righteous that his foreseeable future was a lock at Flo's. At least temporarily, until she tired of him and something, or someone who better suited her fancy, came along.

So, until then, Flo allowed Hank! to clean out the back room for his lodging, and she watched the nightly news every day for a solid week and even read the entire Miami Herald for longer than that in case a devoted loved one was searching for Hank! (She kept him close to the shop in case the police were.) Not altogether certain that this latter scenario was an impossibility, Hank! took advantage of Flo's hospitality, and laid low. In return, he kept her fleet in tip-top shape and tried to be useful in other welcomed ways. It was a plus that Flo's moped shop boasted an excellent stereo and that the receiver pulled in a station from the mainland that played classic rock. Inexplicably, the high volume old time rock and roll comforted Hank! while he spent his days tuning up mopeds and trying with diminishing effort to recall just who the hell he was.

By Thanksgiving, Hank! had regained most of his speech though none of his memory, and Flo decided that his utter lack of historical baggage, plus his uncanny way with moped mechanics, made him pretty much ideal husband-ish material regardless of who he might be or whomever might be looking for him. She moved him into her house, which was handily adjacent to the shop, and thereafter she made a daily habit of exploiting his mechanical abilities during daylight hours, and his other manly skills most evenings, or whenever she felt the itch.

On New Years Eve the couple cracked open a second bottle of Andre pink champagne and at midnight they toasted and watched the ball drop in Time's Square from bed. Minutes later Hank! laid his head on a fragrant pillow and proceeded to succumb to his bubbly. Flo plumped her own pillows at her back, emptied the last bit of champagne into her glass, and turned up the volume on the TV. Dick Clark proudly and effusively introduced the evening's headliners at the party that was being simulcast from out in California where the New Years Eve festivities were just getting started.

"I used to love these guys," Flo said nudging Hank! "Oh my god! Look how short his hair is!" Hank! of course did not remember that Paul Berman had once, even by '80s standards, been in possession of one of history's finest manes of wavy shoulder length hair. Nor, as much as he'd had to drink, did Hank! really care that Paul still had one of the most famous voices in rock and roll. He did however, as he almost always did, exactly as Flo ordered him to, and rose up to give the band a peek over the covers before he quite literally put 1987 to bed and went to sleep. By sheer coincidence in that briefest of instants the camera closed in on the band's new drummer and lingered. The young musician's face was beaming. Ecstatic, one might say.

Hank! lurched upright before he threw back the covers and bolted out of the bed like a shot.

"I KNOW that guy!" he screamed.

"Who? Who do you know?" Flo screamed back, brushing at her spilled champagne.

"The drummer!" Hank! yelled. "That's my JD!"

"Your who?" Flo said sucking on the hem of the top sheet. The camera was panning the dancing crowd, and then maddeningly it moved to Paul's face again and stayed there.

"Come on!" Hank! implored the TV set. He was on his knees at the foot of the bed. "Come on! Go back to the drummer!" As if the cameraman on the sound stage in Los Angeles had heard Hank!'s request the camera swung around for another good long close up of JD's perspiring face and bouncing dreadlocks.

"That's my boy! My JD! Woo! hoo! JD's on the TV!" Gillis Wainwright jumped to his feet again to dance a jig in the small space next to the bed. He pumped his fist into the air. It was not until he saw the pissy look on Flo's face that Gillis Wainwright realized, and knew that Flo knew it first, that his stint in Key West was as good as over.

*****

About the Author

Corie Skolnick was an adjunct faculty member of the Psychology Departments at California State University, Northridge and Moorpark College for twenty years. She was also a licensed marriage and family therapist in private practice in Tarzana, California. She is currently a full time writer living north of Los Angeles County with her husband. All the pets are in heaven now. Her children, both of them grown now, are working successfully in the arts.

A note about fame

It isn't easy being famous. Some do it better than others. I am grateful to all those famous individuals whose names appear within these pages, not the least of these, James Dean. I hope that I have used these names honorably.

While every element of ORFAN is a pure product of imagination, and thus so, absolute fiction, it is nevertheless true that James Byron Dean was the greatest American actor who ever lived.

David Dalton's biography**, James Dean The Mutant King**, and John Howlett's book, **James Dean a biography**, equally provided much needed background information about his life and also inspiration for the construction of his spirit. I am much indebted to their exhaustive research.